Readers love
TA MOORE

Skin and Bone

"…this book checks all my boxes. I could not put it down."

—Love Bytes

"I would totally read the next book in the series given the quality of writing and emotional engagement I had with the first two books in the series."

—Gay Book Reviews

Every Other Weekend

"It is nicely twisty and fun, with lots of excitement and unexpected elements that kept this one very engaging."

—Joyfully Jay

"This is an absolute page-turner for me, and I'm becoming a big fan of TA Moore's work."

—The Novel Approach

Wanted – Bad Boyfriend

"This was a twist on an enemies-to-lovers trope that was quite entertaining."

—Jessie G Books

By TA MOORE

Every Other Weekend
Ghostwriter of Christmas Past
Liar, Liar
Take the Edge Off

BLOOD AND BONE
Dead Man Stalking

DIGGING UP BONES
Bone to Pick
Skin and Bone

ISLAND CLASSIFIEDS
Wanted – Bad Boyfriend

WOLF WINTER
Dog Days
Stone the Crows

Published by DREAMSPINNER PRESS
www.dreamspinnerpress.com

DEAD MAN
STALKING
TA MOORE

Published by

DREAMSPINNER PRESS

5032 Capital Circle SW, Suite 2, PMB# 279, Tallahassee, FL 32305-7886 USA
www.dreamspinnerpress.com

Dead Man Stalking
© 2019 TA Moore

Cover Art
© 2019 Kanaxa
Cover content is for illustrative purposes only and any person depicted on the cover is a model.

Trade Paperback ISBN: 978-1-64405-338-6
Digital ISBN: 978-1-64405-337-9
Library of Congress Control Number: 2019903599
Trade Paperback published September 2019
v. 1.0

Printed in the United States of America
∞
This paper meets the requirements of
ANSI/NISO Z39.48-1992 (Permanence of Paper).

The sons of God came in unto the daughters of men, and they bore biters and reprobates they called Anakim. And mankind turned against the Anakim and would not sustain them. And they began to sin against birds, and beasts, and reptiles, and fish, and to devour one another's flesh, and drink the blood.

The Enochian Bible, the Book of Watchers, Ch 1 V 25

Chapter One

"Do a bit of private work," they said. "Easy money," they said. It turned out "they" were a bunch of liars.

Took went down on one knee in the wet Georgia dirt next to the ranking detective on the case. Deputy Gatlin hadn't been too pleased when the sheriff ordered him to walk a Charleston PI through his missing persons case, but now he cracked a dazed grin up at Took.

"Feel like I got kicked by a horse," he said raggedly. Gatlin tried to take a deep breath and huffed out a shaky laugh when he couldn't. "Can't catch… my breath. Thank fuck for the vest."

"Yeah," Took said as he glanced down at what was left of Gatlin's lower torso. The explosion set off by the trip wire had caught him from the side and blown the meat off him. From foot to knee his legs were untouched, but above that broken, white bone showed through pulped skin and the stiff patches of charred fabric where his uniform had melted against his skin. "Where'd you be without it?"

Gatlin laughed again. His smile wobbled at the corners, and Took could see the awareness in his glazed blue eyes that something more than a hard knock was wrong with him. His brain just didn't think it was time to let him in on what had happened. Took had been there.

A flash of sharp, self-scathing humor twitched the corner of Took's mouth. Admit it, it dared him, most days he was still there.

Took tucked his phone between his ear and his shoulder as he roughly stripped his shirt off and the expensive little buttons popped off into the long grass. The ringtone trilled in time with Gatlin's blood loss as his life spilled out onto the grass. Took swore through his teeth as three rings seemed to take forever.

He'd *told* Gatlin this was a bad goddamned idea. It didn't matter what Willie Daly had been willing to do back when he was meth-head peeper. He was a Goat now. The local district attorney couldn't come up with a deal that would tempt him to snitch. As for whatever passed for a conscience, that wasn't the first thing to go. It didn't last long, though.

But Gatlin had been determined to show the big-shot detective from Charleston that he didn't know everything. So he'd pulled the wire-and-nerves man off the streets and leaned on him until Willie spilled what he knew—or claimed he had. When Willie led them up here by a series of backwoods turns that scraped the suspension against the rutted concrete, Took expected to be led around by the nose until it got dark. Enough time to give Willie's patron a chance to sneak out with the sunset, not for him to walk them into a well-set trap.

Took ripped the shirt in half and tied the strips of fabric as tightly as he could around Gatlin's ruined thighs. It wasn't good first aid, but their resources were limited and he couldn't see that there was anything left below Gatlin's hips to save. He couldn't see that there'd be anything of Gatlin to save, but he had to do something, even if it was pointless.

The call finally connected.

"Appl—"

Took interrupted the irrepressibly cheerful chirp of the operator before she could finish her script. "This is VINE Agent Bennet," he snapped. Not exactly true. His active agent status with the Violent Infections and Nullifications Enforcement department was on hold, but it was an old habit. It would take too long to correct himself, so he let it stand. Besides, it might make things easier. People might yell about breathing rights when VINE cracked down on Hunter activity, but those same people were always the first to call when they had a feral bloodsucker problem. Invoke VINE and people listened, and Gatlin needed them to listen to Took. Despite his makeshift bandages, blood still soaked the ground. "We have an officer down. I'm out at...."

Shit. He didn't know.

Took sat back on his heels and looked around, his hands still pressed down hard against the raw meat of Gatlin's leg. The ripe smell of hot blood and wet earth was thick enough to taste, but he did his best to ignore it. He could hear the soft growl of the road behind him, muted by the shield of trees and the distance the four of them had walked along the narrow dirt road after they left the patrol car. It hadn't been an official road, just a worn-down pull-off on the shoulder. Gatlin knew where it was, but Took had only half listened to the Goat's directions.

He'd been *sure* it was a wild goose chase.

"What happened?" the operator demanded, her voice high and worried. In the background of the call, keys clicked and people asked muffled, worried-sounding questions.

"Bend," Gatlin wheezed out. The mania had faded, and the realization that something was wrong was etched on his solid, heavy face. He picked at Took's arm with sweat-damp, swollen fingers. "Round the bend."

He might have just meant *he* was, but Took didn't have anything better to tell the operator.

"Something about a bend?" he said. "Off the expressway, just past three big billboards for McDonalds."

The operator gave a relieved sigh. "Round the Bend. I know it. It used to be a rehab facility. We're on the way. Agent, can I speak to Gatlin?"

Took looked down. Dry, quick gasps of air whistled between Gatlin's lips, so technically he was still alive. But he wasn't going to give any more information. His eyes were rolled back in his head, just the bloodshot whites and a rim of hazel green to be seen.

"Not right now," he said. "Gatlin's injured. Your Goat led us into a trap."

"What about Deputy Allan?"

Took's fingers tightened against Gatlin's stained bandages and made him groan weakly. Blood welled up between Took's knuckles. He forced himself to let go and lean back.

"Allan was...." *Taken.* That was the phrase they usually used, spat out with easy familiarity and the understanding that they had to expect the worst. But it caught on Took's tongue and he edited it. "Willie grabbed Allan. He used her to lure Gatlin into the trap. What's your ETA?"

The operator made a frustrated sound under her voice. "Ten minutes. Maybe fifteen? We'll be there as quickly as we can. What are Gatlin's injuries?"

"Extensive," Took said.

The shirt had started out white—fresh from the dry cleaner, the creases still in the elbow—but now it was stained a dark, wet red. It obviously wasn't up to the job. If Gatlin made it, it wouldn't be down to anything Took had done.

He closed his eyes for a second and saw Allan's face as she was dragged away, her mouth lax and her eyes too surprised to be afraid. Yet. A long graze on the side of her face—received when Willie shoved her into a tree—had dribbled blood down onto her starched buff collar.

"Follow the dirt path from the car," Took said as he scrambled to his feet. He reached back and pulled his gun from the holster at the small of his back. It was heavy and solid in his hands, the weight of it familiar as he checked the chamber, and if it didn't feel as familiar as his usual weaponry, it would just have to do. "You can't miss him. I'm going to go after Allan."

The operator tried to argue with him. Took just dropped the phone next to Gatlin to keep him company and broke into a jog as he followed the path—and Willie—farther into the woods.

It was supposed to be a milk run. No one was meant to get hurt.

"Arrogance," his old instructor had told them at training. "Never take a hunt for granted. Never think you know them. Arrogance kills more agents than vampires ever will. Remember that."

OLD SCARS itched as the sun got to them—pinprick nerve twitches that crawled around under his skin and even scratched their way up under the sleeves of his T-shirt. Took knew it would only make it worse if he scratched, but he paused to dig his finger into a particularly irritated comma-shaped scar over his collarbone. It didn't help. The itch just spread down the bone into the nearby tissue.

Took gave one last scrape and let it go. It would fade eventually.

The dirt road had evolved into a cracked concrete path. Muddy footprints—department-issue boots and patched-up sneakers—scuffed over the gray stone and then dried up and faded away. It didn't matter. They could only be heading to the big old house that stood derelict at the end of the drive.

Years of exposure had bleached the redbrick walls down to pink and yellow. Kudzu had made inroads on the foundations, a green crust that had anchored itself in the mortar. The windows were still intact, but the glass was scabbed with dust on the outside and mold on the inside.

Took paused at the gate. A white sign bolted to the gate announced it was the Ron Bern Life Center, the first step on the road to a life free from addiction. From where he stood, Took could see rows of bottles neatly lined up along the weathered porch that wrapped around the house. Tall and small, the distinctive brown beer bottles tucked in among the clear spirits. Someone hadn't taken the place's motto to heart.

He pulled up the hem of his T-shirt and wiped the sweat and a splash of Gatlin's blood he hadn't realized was there from his face. His hands were steadier than he expected. After two years on suspension, he'd started to believe they were right—his nerve was gone, and he wasn't fit for field duty anymore. Instead the punch of adrenaline had left his mind clean and sharp. He felt steadier with a gun in his hand and blood under his nails than he did in his therapist's office as they traded lies about how well he was doing.

It might feel a little too good, but he wasn't going to tell the therapist that.

Took pulled his shirt back down, wrapped both hands around his gun, and gave the gate a nudge with his boot. It had dropped on its hinges and one corner was buried in a well-run rut, but it moved when Took put his weight against it. The scrape and groan of rusted metal might have given him away, but he doubted it mattered. Willie had hung around to gloat over Gatlin's corpse, and he'd seen Took scramble back to his feet in the aftershock of the blast.

The Goat knew that Took was on his heels. Speed was going to work better than stealth here.

The grounds had been landscaped once. Roses grew scrubby and wild among the weeds that overran the flower beds, all thorny canes and small white flowers. The long expanse of the lawn still had a mostly sharp square shape, even though the grass was yellow and spongy under Took's feet as he loped toward the house.

Old habits creaked rustily back into play. Even though he was on his own—VINE two states away, local backup ten minutes out and more concerned with their injured man—his brain broke radio silence anyhow.

Attempting entry through the front door, it chattered to no one as he jumped onto the porch and put his shoulder against the doorjamb. *Unsub is armed and has a hostage. Hold fire.*

Took tried the door. It was locked. *Good.* He left it closed and cautiously made his way to one of the dirt-crusted windows. Filthy curtains, whatever pattern they'd originally had hidden under a spiderweb of frilly mold, were pinched tightly closed in front of them. It was hard to tell through the grimy glass, but Took would bet they'd been sewn.

He punched the glass with the butt of his gun. It shattered—always a louder sound than he expected—and he used his gun to clear the leftover pieces from the crumbled putty.

Front window right, his brain supplied as he grabbed a handful of the slimy curtains and wrenched them down. *Cleared.* The curtain pole snapped and hit the cracked linoleum with a rattle, followed by the crumpled pile of old fabric.

Fresh blood—Gatlin's blood—smelled like pennies and salt. Old blood smelled like rotten meat and sweat, thick and slimy enough to coat your nose and slide down your throat. The inside of the derelict building smelled like old blood—a lot of it.

"Fuck," Took muttered as he spat to clear the taste from his mouth.

That wasn't a two-corpse stink. It wasn't a sane-vampire stink either. Most of the undead didn't want to live in their own filth any more than the people they'd been before the bite would have. Unbalanced and a monster—that was always messy.

Took crawled through the window, bits of glass he'd missed in the frame sharp as they scratched against his arms, and into the dusty, blood-sour room. It had been an office once, based on the broken desk in the middle of the room and the dented filing cabinets on the wall, but now it looked like a squat. There was a pile of sleeping bags in the corner. The shiny blue fabric was blotched with bleached-out patches and wear.

More bottles were lined up along the wall, but instead of spirits they held the dregs of clotted, black liquid. Maggots squirmed in the bottom of them, lively and bloated.

Took grimaced and walked over to the sleeping bags. He poked them with his foot and flies rose in a lazy haze and buzzed resentfully away. There was something wrapped in the old blankets and sleeping bags, but not something that moved.

It was pointless to hold his breath—everything stank—but Took did anyhow as he crouched down and gingerly peeled the folds back. The man had been dead for a while, although he looked like he'd died badly. The pock mocks on his collarbones and gnawed into the bend of his elbow were sunken into rotted wells, and his skin was pulled tight over his bones. His collarbones jutted through his skin like knives, and his hair was dry and patchy.

Someone had tried to turn him, tried quite hard, but it hadn't taken. Some people, all it took was a bite and a lick of spit. Others, though, could have their blood replaced pint by pint with ichor, and all it would make them was dead.

"It might not have seemed it," Took said as he pulled a tattered corner of blanket over the gray, withered face. "You're one of the lucky ones."

Even if he had turned, gone cold, and grown fangs, he wouldn't have been much of a person anymore. The Anakim.... The code-switch to the politically correct term in this situation—you couldn't exactly call your colleagues vampires to their face—was so automatic that it almost amused Took for a second… until he remembered there was no one to offend or to back him up. Vampires cosseted the about-to-be-turned like wagyu beef, inoculated them to the curse with each Kiss they gave until something like them sat back up. Turned like this, the curse spat into him from a dozen different hungry mouths, all that would get up was a body that would hunger and do what it was told. Back in Europe they called it a ghoul, and old families had whole packs of the empty retainers.

Took pressed his gun to the covered head and pulled the trigger. The recoil punched back against the heel of his hand, all the way to his shoulder, and what was left of the man's brains splattered out over the floor.

In the US they called it a mongrel and they put it down.

He glanced at the ichor-stained bottles and swallowed the sour tang of acid on the back of his throat. Before he had to decide what to do with the fat, squirming maggots, he heard a stifled shriek from somewhere in the house.

Allan.

Took swore under his breath and loped to the door. He shouldered it open and stepped out into the hallway. It still stank.

"Deputy," he yelled, his voice calm and steady. "Are you okay?"

"Agent—" the shrill, panicked voice blurted in answer to him. It cut through the musty silence of the house and then cut off abruptly with a yelp.

The single word had been enough to give Took something to work with. He turned slightly and headed toward the back of the house. His feet scuffed over the battered tiles as he lifted his gun and nudged the door open.

Did it smell worse back here, he wondered, or was that just his imagination?

"Willie," he said. "You want to let the deputy go."

A laugh creaked out of the dark. "What?" Willie asked, his voice rasp-rough and arrogant. "They'll go easy on me if I've only killed one deputy? You'll put a good word in for me? Fuck off, Special Agent Man. I don't need help from the likes of you. He's promised he'll see me right."

Took paused to let his eyes adjust to the dim light in the hall. Photos were hung in a regimented row at eye height against the damp-bulged wallpaper. Women with eyes that looked like bruised fruit and men who hadn't unclenched their jaw in years smiled out tightly with rows of identical white veneers. Or they used to be identical. Someone had gone along with a sharpie and assiduously defaced them with blackened gaps and carefully straight braces.

The small show of bleak humor unexpectedly amused Took. He let the feeling wash away as he pushed two doors open and peered into the small, cell-like rooms that hid behind them. Both looked as though they'd been in use recently, with stained sheets tangled on the bed and the smell of old sex thick in the air.

Every time some delusional fangbanger with bite tats and fear-pheromone perfume tried to play vampires off as romantic monsters, Took wanted to take them on a tour of a trap house. It had as much class as a frat house after a homicide.

He let the doors creak shut and walked toward the last door. It had a Staff Only sign fastened to it at eye level. Kitchen or infirmary, Took supposed. Over his head he heard something scrape over the floor. He paused midstep to look up, his eyes on the lumpy plaster as he tried to imagine the layout upstairs.

"What are you waiting for?" Willie interrupted him. "An invitation?"

He laughed at his own joke. Took took his eyes off the ceiling and pushed the last door open. He'd been right, it was a kitchen. Pots hung from racks on the ceiling and a clock shaped like a coffee cup was stopped exactly at 10:00 a.m. forever.

Willie stood on the other side of the stove with his arm crooked around Allan's throat. The point of the knife dug into the tender skin behind her ear, deeply enough that more blood dribbled onto her no-longer-stiff collar.

"Help's on the way, Deputy," Took said as he met her gaze. "Stay calm."

She rolled her deep brown eyes toward the corner of the room. "We aren't alone."

Willie jabbed the knife deeper and twisted it. "Shut up," he hissed. "Stupid cow."

"I see him," Took said.

The pale, naked—he'd never met a vampire that slept in pajamas—figure dangled in the periphery of his vision. Someone had hung him from a meat hook for the day, the point of it jammed into his back and threaded up under his shoulder blade. Lines of black ichor stained the white skin and dripped down into pans laid out under his feet. His eyes were open, but it was a reptile sort of alertness, slow and cold. He'd gorged—his stomach was distended with too much blood, and he needed to digest before what passed for a person could come back.

He wouldn't react unless someone got too close to him.

"Let Allan go," Took repeated calmly as he lifted the gun. "All I want is to get her out of here. Then you and your master can try and get away before they burn this place."

Willie's laugh showed rotted teeth and a white coating of pus on his tongue. Pride glittered in his eyes, which were still unexpectedly pretty despite the drugs and the ichor. He pulled himself up straight.

"Him?" He spat in the direction of the hung vampire. "I don't work for him. Not anymore. He works for me now."

Allan dug her fingers into his arm. "You're going straight to hell for this, Daly," she spat out. "The sheriff will track you down and gut you if you touch me, and for what?"

"I damned myself years ago," Willie said flatly. He licked the blood off Allan's neck, and she grimaced in disgust, but the knife at her throat kept her still. Willie lifted his head, spit and blood smeared around his mouth, and smiled widely. "Might as well enjoy the ride. And once I prove myself, I'll get to enjoy it for a long, fucking time, maybe even longer than the sheriff is around. He's an old man. Things happen to old men, and young ones take over."

Behind Took, on the other side of the door, the stairs creaked.

Time was up. Took swung the gun away from Willie and fired two shots straight into the vampire's bloated stomach. It burst in a welter of clotted blood and a tangle of wet intestine that squirmed and dripped bile into the blood bowls. The vampire screamed itself out of his torpor and thrashed blindly on the hooks as they tore through muscle and meat. As it ripped itself free, Took tossed his gun into the sink.

Allan yelped and tried to bolt, but Willie dragged her back. He tightened his grip on her arm as he backed away from the vampire.

"It was him," Willie yelled, his voice pitched to cut through the eerie, off-timbre screech that vibrated out of the vampire's throat. He pulled the knife away from Allan's throat and jabbed the bloodied point toward Took. "He did it. He shot you, Matthew!"

The vampire dropped to the ground with a thud. Its bare feet slapped against the tiles as it lunged at Willie—the only one in the room with a weapon. It slapped Allan out of the way with an almost dismissive backhand that sent her flying.

"You hurt meee," Matthew mangled out through two sets of fully extended fangs as it grabbed Willie's wrist. The bone snapped with a matchstick-brittle sound as Matthew tightened his fingers and lifted him off the ground. "Little liar."

"No!" Willie writhed like a fish on the hook. He dropped the knife from bruise-purpled fingers and caught it in his other hand. "Not me. You know me! Goddammit, not me! It was him!"

Matthew didn't listen. It latched onto Willie's neck with dagger-sharp teeth and tore it out. The gush of blood splashed over Matthew's face and throat, and it gulped it out of the air like water from a fountain. Pain wrung a cry out of Willie, but the one advantage of being a Goat was resilience. He punched his knife up through Matthew's chin with a quick, brutal stroke and twisted the blade.

With a shriek of garbled offense, tongue pinned to the roof of his mouth, Matthew flung Willie away from him.

"Come on," Took hissed as he grabbed Allan's collar and pulled her up. "We need to go."

She scrambled unsteadily to her feet. Her eyes were unfocused and her lips split.

"I... I.... This wasn't supposed to happen like this." Allan shook her head and blinked hard. Her gaze shifted over Took's shoulder and widened in dismay. "Look out!"

Took ducked and a pretty blonde girl missed his throat by half a foot. Matted hair flapped in filthy elflocks as she flew past. She tried to twist in midair, enough to give Took a glimpse of her pale, half-made-up face, but didn't quite pull it off. She hit the ground and tumbled head over heels into the wall.

"Go," Took snapped at Allan as he shoved her toward the door. "Think later."

He dragged her with him down the vandalized hall of past clients. Three photos down and Allan pulled herself together, the stumble gone from her steps as she pulled even with Took.

"There's others," she said. "They're in the garage. Willie told them to wait until he got Ma… the vampire. We have to stop them."

Took laughed at her. "I dropped my gun. You've lost yours," he said. "What are we going to do, order pizza and breathe garlic at them? Just move."

She looked reluctant but did as she was told. They burst through the doorway into the hall, and the pale gray man in the pale gray suit swung a crowbar in a short, brutal arc at Took's head. There was no time or space to duck.

Took caught the crowbar. The metal hook jarred against his palm and stopped. Slow, dull surprise crossed the gray man's face. Took bared his fangs and growled as he wrenched the crowbar out of the Goat's suddenly slack grip. He jabbed it into the man's stomach, buried the shaft inches deep in soft flesh, and doubled him over in a spray of vomit.

"You're one of them," Allan spluttered. Her voice was threaded with desperate, raw panic as she tried to pull away from him. "What is this, a game? A trick?"

Took reeled her in and shoved her at the door. "Yes," he said—still, two years in, sorta lisped—as he stepped over the groaning gray man. "We're pranking you. Just get outside. I called the sheriff. He should be here soon."

It didn't work to calm Allan down. It had been one shock too many, and she was caught up in her fear. She stumbled forward at his prod, but the muttered round of accusation and plea continued under her breath.

"I don't want to be a vampire. Mary, Mother of God, be with me now. Kill me. Kill me, don't damn me. It should have been… not Gatlin. It was meant to be—"

Took fumbled the door open and both of them fell out into the evening sunlight. He lost his grip on Allan and she lurched away from him, her feet tangling as she staggered down the stairs. He swore and went after her.

It felt like a punch at his back. Took didn't realize what had happened at first. It was only when he crashed into Allan, both of them blown off their feet and his back hot and itchy from fire and splinters, that he registered the crackle of fire behind him.

Allan sprawled under him on the ground, unmoving but still breathing. After a shaken second, Took rolled onto his raw back. Chunks of bricks and glass slid off him as he moved, and he stared at the old house as it went up in flames. Curtains flared with the eagerness of polyester blends, and the closed-off windows darkened and cracked.

Someone screamed. It would be Matthew, Took knew. Vampires were hard to kill, but he couldn't work up the energy past his ringing ears to care. He stared at the fire for a few moments longer and then let the blow to his head drag him down into oblivion.

Chapter Two

APPLETON WORE the tragedy of the last twenty-four hours with the self-satisfied anger of someone who'd wanted an excuse for a while. Handwritten signs were tacked up in shop windows to announce "living only" and "no heartbeat, no service." The schools were closed, and pickup trucks, packed like clown cars with sullen, armed men, drove in slow circuits around the streets.

"Small-town hospitality," Madoc drawled as he watched through the heavily tinted window of the Jeep as one of the pickups drove past. It would be so easy to just reach out and grab one of them and drag them in through the window so he could open their throat. He felt the dull itch in the back of his fangs, but he resisted the urge. It wouldn't make his job any easier, and the car would smell like takeout for the rest of the trip. "That's one thing that never changes."

On the seat next to him, Lawrence looked up from her tablet, over the smudged lenses of her glasses, and sneered at the tail end of the pickup. "Idiots. What good do they think that will do against *us*?"

She'd only had her first bite—the scar was still livid on her throat over the scooped collar of her new shirt—and there was no sign that it had taken yet. It didn't matter. Lawrence was VINE born and bred. Her father had died in the line of duty during the Humans Only terror attack in Savannah, her first taste of blood had been as she nursed at her freshly turned mother's breast as Director Lawrence gave a press conference condemning the violence, and she'd just married into one of the oldest vampire families in Philadelphia.

It would be "us" even if she never grew fangs.

She was a good agent, but that wasn't why Madoc had requested her as his partner. Sometimes he needed a reminder that not every human reached for the pitchforks at the first opportunity. There were many reasons to remember other things about them.

"Why has this incident been such a flashpoint for the community?" he asked.

Lawrence pursed her lips at him. They both knew he was well aware of the answer, but he leaned back against the leather seats and waited.

"Peanuts," Lawrence said, with a flash of sharp humor. "This used to be a dry county, officially human only, but then the local peanut farm went belly-up. There was a mining company interested in opening a pit here, but that fell under the Sojourner rule."

Madoc nodded as the Jeep pulled up outside the sheriff's office. "If you don't want to associate with vampires, don't associate with vampires," he said. "So the town ceded their dry status?"

"Technically," Lawrence said. She unbuckled herself from the seat belt and scooted forward as she reached for the door handle. "It's still a predominantly breathing area, the only blood bank is in the hospital, and even before the recent increase in Hunter activity in this area, the neighborhood's been good recruiting territory for the Hunters for years."

As she opened the door, the muffled sound of voices outside resolved into the thundered cadence of fire-and-brimstone prayer. The group of faithful were clustered on the small patch of green outside the sheriff's office, small candles and photocopies of the not-quite-dead deputy's staff photo clutched in their hands.

Madoc tilted his head as he tried to identify the scripture the preacher had picked apart so he could shove his own anger between the words.

"They walk among so, sit with us, sup with us," the preacher ranted. "But they have the fangs of a wolf, not the teeth of a sheep, and their meat is carved from the flank of a child, a teacher, a—"

Proverbs, then. A bit on the nose for Madoc's taste, but he'd grown up with the compass and fury of the Welsh Methodist church at its most impassioned. It was a lot to expect for Appleberg's resident rabble-rouser to live up to that.

Lawrence reached up to her throat. "Should I—"

"No need," Madoc said as he pulled his sunglasses out of his breast pocket and slid them on. He could have done without it. The purple-toned dusk light was low enough that even *his* eyes could tolerate it, but why not give them a show. That was what they were here for. He gave Lawrence a sly, sharp smile. "They'll have other things on their minds."

He didn't bother to look at the prayer group as he got out of the car and stalked toward the main doors of the sheriff's office. There was no need. The silence that fell over the prayer group, the rote amens strangled in people's throats told him his appearance had the expected impact. People rarely mistook Madoc for human in his civilian clothes. In the midnight black of his VINE tactical uniform, stark against his pallid coloring, it was obvious what he was.

To anyone with the slightest interest in vampire politics, it was obvious *who* he was as well. There still weren't that many dhampirs in the US, and even fewer of Madoc's... vintage. His peers had died out decades ago—frequently at his hands—and most of the next generation had barely cut their fangs. He was memorable.

A low, shocked whisper came from the crowd. "Biter." Someone laughed, a nervous titter of sound, and then fell quiet again. When VINE's elite response team had first hit the papers—in Boston, Madoc thought, ninety years ago—they had been the Bloodcrimes Tactical Response. BTR. Some Hunter-friendly local affiliate out West had coined "Biters" as a mockery for the then all-vampire team.

Madoc had taken it as their own. Legends needed a name, not an acronym. These days no one found the old joke funny for long.

The priest, a short bull of a man with close-cropped, cotton-white hair and small, mean eyes, stepped in front of Madoc.

"God bless you," the priest said as he marked the cross over his breast with heavy, scar-knuckled hands. His lips were wet with the expectation of God's intercession. "And keep you from bringing harm to the innocent."

Madoc could feel the tension in the air as twenty people bated their breath to see what happened next. He reached up to his collar and hooked the medal from under his shirt, the silver faintly warm from his skin when he pressed his lips to it. It stung. It always did. He accepted that.

"From your lips to His ears, Father," he said as he let the chain slide through his fingers. It hung bright against his chest, the bas-relief of Michael worn down nearly smooth after years of being worried at. "Now get out of my way, or do you want to see if you're innocent enough to warrant God's protection?"

For a second, the priest held his ground. Then he stepped back out of Madoc's path. The sound of released breath from the prayer group sounded a lot like a disappointed sigh. The priest stole a quick, nervous glance over his shoulder and then puffed himself up with bluster.

"A God-fearing man doesn't test God," he said, his voice pitched to carry. "God tests him."

Madoc smirked and walked away. As he approached, the heavy glass doors of the sheriff's office were pushed open by a nervous young deputy, his throat flushed raw with razor burn.

"Cardinal Madoc," the young man said, his voice half-strangled in his throat. "We didn't realize that VINE would send—"

"Agent," Madoc corrected him. "Or SES Madoc. Either is appropriate."

The deputy's brain caught up with his mouth, and he blanched. He looked like he wanted to swallow his own tongue and reel the words back in.

"Agent. Of course. That's what I—"

Madoc left him to babble and stepped to the side to let Lawrence in through the door. The deputy glanced at her with a flash of obvious relief at her blood-pinked skin and lack of history.

"Ma'am." He bobbed his head at her.

"Agent," Lawrence corrected him with a hint of tart disapproval. The man's face fell as he nodded.

"Of course. Ma'am," he said. "Sorry. Ah, I'm afraid that Sheriff Anderson is still at the hospital. We weren't expecting you to make such good time."

"The dead ride fast," Madoc said.

The deputy nodded sagely like the old quote explained anything beyond Madoc's fondness for the ballads of his youth. That made things easier. It had taken the privilege of rank to fast-track clearance and a flight plan for the VINE jet, and a very old favor cashed in to make people turn a blind eye to a section chief's inappropriate involvement. Madoc didn't want to justify that to himself, never mind a jug-eared deputy who looked as though his balls hadn't dropped yet.

"We've booked rooms for you in Old Pelican Farm," the deputy said. He turned and scrambled over to his desk. A quick search among the scattered sheets of paper and dog-eared folders came up with a glossy trifold leaflet that he thrust toward Madoc. "It's a B and B. If you want to drop your bags off, I can call you when the sheriff gets back."

Madoc ignored the leaflet. "What I want," he said, "is to see my agent."

The deputy blinked twice and nervously folded the Pelican Farm leaflet between his fingers. "I think the sheriff would rather you wait until—"

Madoc plucked his sunglasses off, folded the legs, and tucked them back into his pocket. His smile was cold. The deputy's eyes flicked from Madoc's pale eyes to his mouth and then flinched away and down to one well-tailored shoulder.

"I understand that disappointment has never killed anyone," Madoc told him. "My agent. Now."

The deputy folded as easily as the bit of paper he'd just mangled.

"Yes, sir," he said. "Right away."

WITH THICK walls and oversized, reinforced windows to flood the small, square space with the sun, the cell had been designed to hold vampires. It was implemented cruelty, but Madoc couldn't help the flash of appreciation as he saw Took sprawled out on the narrow cot. The sun picked out threads of gold in the cropped, sandy hair and gilded the sprawl of lean muscle with the memory of a golden tan.

At least it did between the scars.

There was something about Took Bennett that even now, after two years as a vampire, belonged to the daytime. Madoc didn't know if he should resent that or be glad that he wasn't the only one who'd tried and failed to claim the man.

An off note of guilt was added to the familiar tincture of hunger and frustration that Madoc associated with Took. It was a dark thought, even for Madoc, to imagine himself in lustful harness with the monster who'd nearly killed his old partner.

Not unprecedented—Madoc had never been able to boast about the purity of his thoughts—but still dark.

"Bennett," he said.

Took lifted his elbow and squinted out from under it. There was a scabbed burn on his cheekbone and the faded remnants of a bruise around one of his pale gray eyes. When he saw Madoc, something shifted behind his face, quick and sharp, but it was locked back before Madoc could pin down what it was.

"Get me out of here," Took told him.

Irritation flicked at the back of Madoc's throat, salty as blood. Took had always been too familiar—not disrespectful but not impressed either. But that had been before, when he had Madoc's back and still called himself Luke, not when it had been a year since they'd seen each other—more than that, some embarrassing tally-keeper fragment of Madoc's brain reminded him, since they'd actually spoken—and Madoc had traveled through the day to get Took's ass out of the fire.

"I don't know if that's such a good idea," Madoc said. He rapped his knuckle against one of the bars. It rang solid and he could feel the faint itch of the silver core against his skin. "At least if you're in here, it will be easy to keep track of you. I thought you weren't fit for active duty, Bennett, so you can imagine my surprise when I was notified one of my agents had stormed a trap house on his own."

Took dropped his elbow so his eyes were hidden again. The corner of his mouth twisted up in a bitter smile as he added a dry postscript to Madoc's statement. "Unsuccessfully."

"Maybe you've lost your edge," Madoc said. The snort of disagreement he expected from Took didn't come. "The sheriff thinks you were involved, Bennett. Were you?"

There was a pause, and then Took finally moved his arm. He rolled off the bed in one loose, easy movement. The sheets under him were stained black with blood, and Madoc felt something in his chest crack as though he'd taken a blow. Took stalked over to the bars and glared at him.

"Do you really need me to answer that?" Took asked. The tension in his voice was drawn tight between the old, affronted anger and a new, brittle fear that maybe people did need to ask.

"For the record, yes," Madoc said with cold precision. Then he let the edge soften on his voice. "Personally? I know you better than that."

A bitter smile curved Took's mouth, and he braced his hands against the bars. Muscle bunched and tightened under his pale skin, the faded scatter of freckles pale as nutmeg. "No," he said. "Not anymore, you don't. Look, I'll tell you what happened. Just get me out of here first, okay?"

The urge to be cruel was familiar, almost as instinctive as the need to blink. Madoc didn't want to fight it. The reduction of their relationship to tit-for-tat favors offended him, and he wanted to return that weight and measure.

Before he could let out the aged poison under his tongue, Took closed his eyes. He rasped one word through clenched teeth. "Please."

It was unexpected enough to put Madoc back on his heels. He stared at Took's tight, set face for a moment, and the memory rose up through his mind as though he'd hooked it on a line.

Hope had died six months before. What was left was anger.

Madoc slammed one of the Goats, feral and ruined by blood addiction, against the wall. The man bared yellow, chisel-edged teeth and swung the broken edge of a butcher's knife at Madoc's face. It skimmed over Madoc's jaw—a cold kiss with a hot lick at the end of it. The Goat's eyes caught hungrily on the bead of blood, and in the moment of distraction, Madoc unceremoniously snapped his neck.

The chatter in his earpiece rose and fell in ragged cadence as the rest of the team cleared the house—Lawrence and Pally's clipped professionalism, Kit's ragged, off-kilter humor, and the silence that should have been a body at Madoc's back. It nearly drowned out the sound of a door as it slammed upstairs. Not quite, though. Madoc tossed the dead Goat aside and took the stairs two at a time. He shouldered open the door at the top of the stairs and hit a wall of stench that was almost solid. It stung his eyes and stuck greasily to his tongue—rancid meat and something sour underneath it.

In the corner of the room, a tall, half-turned woman, her throat one ragged scab from overlapped bites, tried to drag something out of a splintered wooden box as a little gray cat, grubby and leggy, swore at her as it chewed on her leg.

"Get off. Get out," she screamed as she struggled with whatever was in the crate. "He'll come back for you. If I have you—"

Madoc pulled his gun and blew her head off. Her face splattered over the window, and her body pitched gracelessly to the floor. The cat screeched as it leaped free and shot across the room and under the neatly made white bed. There was a man in the box, filthy and raw. He stared at Madoc with pale, lost eyes and then cracked a surprisingly familiar smile.

"W... was just about to do that," he said in a rusty, disused voice. "Always... always gotta hog the glory."

There were cuffs on his wrists and a collar around his throat— heavy links of iron coated with silver. Someone had worked magic into the metal as well. It was sticky and painful as hot tar against Madoc's hands as he snapped the locks. His fingertips blistered and peeled, the raw meat underneath turned dry where the curse touched it until he could see bone as he worked.

Took—not that anyone called him that yet—clung to Madoc. He was all wasted arms and sour breath—broken and ruined. Then he laughed, a crazy sound in that horrible room, and swore that he knew Madoc would come for him.

That was the moment that Madoc realized two things—that he would slowly kill whoever had done this and that Madoc had been in love with the man in his arms for a while.

Three days later Took turned Madoc away from the hospital and refused to see him or even talk to him.

That day was still vivid and raw for Madoc, but Took probably remembered it as the best day in a year's worth of raw-meat memories. Seen from the wrong side of the bars, the narrow little cell was just a better-ventilated box.

"Half an hour," Madoc said. He reached through the bars and cupped his hand around the back of Took's neck. The long straps of muscle were set like stone under his fingers, too cold to the touch. It would be too much to expect, he supposed, for the sheriff to fetch his prisoner lunch from the blood bank. "I'll get you out. Can you hang on?"

Took coughed out a ragged laugh and leaned forward to rest his forehead against the bars. The skin pinked where the silver irritated it, but Took ignored it.

"What are you going to do if I say no?" Took asked. He slid his arms through the bars and let them dangle, as though the fact that part of him was on the right side of freedom would make it easier. "Rip the door off the hinges?"

They both knew he could. Madoc knew that he would. Maybe one day he'd tell Took that, but not while all that was left of their friendship was reluctant civility.

"Yell at them faster," he said instead as he drew his hand back. "Hang in there, Bennett."

He turned to leave. As he banged the door to get the deputy to let him out, Took called after him. "You know, I don't work for you anymore, Madoc. You could just use my name."

Madoc didn't look around. The door rattled and creaked as the deputy unlocked it. "It's not your name," he said. "It's what was done to you."

SHERIFF ANDERSON looked like a strip of rawhide dressed up like a man. His weathered, darkly tanned skin was pulled tight over wiry muscles and long bones. The backs of his hands were flecked with liver spots, and his knuckles jutted up through his skin like tombstones.

"Ain't never had any problems with your lot here," Anderson said bluntly as he unbuttoned his cuffs and rolled his sleeves back. Black, blunt crosses were inked onto the backs of his forearms. The ink didn't injure Madoc—it wasn't so easy to package divinity; even a pure heart and a real threat weren't enough sometimes—but it was an open insult to flash it at Madoc. That was telling. "Then people start disappearing, your friend turns up with all the answers and some patter about being VINE, and now I got two deputies in jail and that hotshot human consultant? Well, it turns out he's a wetmouth with no official reason to be here."

The slur dropped ripe and casual into the room. It wasn't clear if Anderson knew it wasn't something to say in polite company or if he just didn't give a damn. Madoc chose to ignore it. He'd been called worse.

"No official reason that you need to know about," Madoc said coldly. "I want my agent out of that cell."

Anderson picked something out of his teeth with his thumbnail. As his thumb pushed his lip up, he flashed a black hollow where his incisor should be. It made Madoc's skin crawl, and he licked his tongue over the back of his own teeth, the edges of his fangs still sharp enough to draw a drop of blood. The crosses on Anderson's arms weren't just superstition, then. There was real piety behind them. Even most of the Hunter cells balked at yanking their own eyeteeth out, if only because the Embrace would bestow fangs on a mewling infant or gummy elder if anyone was ill-advised enough to turn them. Only a few of the more extreme Pentecostal sects—the Levites, the Proverbials—still unfanged their children with regularity.

"Your agent," Anderson said. He rolled the word around his mouth as he said that. "Yeah, Gunnar said you looked real... close... down in the cells. Real cozy. Tell me, VINE going to approve of you pulling rank to get your—"

Madoc's temper slipped. He reached over the desk and grabbed Anderson's arm. He smiled wide enough to flash fang and dug his fingers down into the inked skin until Anderson blanched. The gray smoke of anger wriggled in his throat and swam across the back of his eyes. There was a faint sweetness to it, like an applewood bonfire.

Experience told Madoc there was much he could do from inside the smoke, when he let the part of him that had never been human out to play unfettered, and he wouldn't *really* regret it. He might say he did, mouth the right words and make the right face, but he'd never feel it. He could rip Anderson's fucking, cross-scrawled arm off, see if God cared as he beat the man to death with it, and never care about the screams.

He choked it back, for the moment, and kept the smile on his face.

"Mind your tongue," he said pleasantly. "Or I'll take it with me to Philadelphia, slice it up thin, and let every member of VINE have a taste so they know why your poison flicked my temper."

Anderson writhed in his chair, and pain pinched the high color out of his face, but it hadn't touched his arrogance yet. The scent of him, hot and bitter as adrenaline sweated out of his pores, was sharp and aggressive.

"You can't touch me," Anderson spat through clenched teeth. "This isn't the old country. You can't just do what you want. You can't *take* what you want."

Madoc leaned in, his weight braced on Anderson's arm, and murmured the correction in his ear. "Shouldn't, Sheriff Anderson. I shouldn't do those things. For four hundred years, I served the Haza directly. There is very little I *cannot* do. Remember that."

Madoc let go and stepped back in one smooth, slightly too-fast movement. Anderson sucked in a startled breath as his hand spasmed uncomfortably where the blood rushed back into it. His fingers stuttered against the use-scarred wood until he clenched them into a fist.

"You think you can threaten me into cutting your agent loose?" he asked as he rubbed roughly at the red mark that oozed out from under his ink. "Maybe I can't put you on your heels, but your Haza will if you cross the line. If they don't administer the Accord, even the vampires in the Senate will have to call for censure."

That was true. The cry today was usually that the Accord gave VINE, or *Skazanie* as they'd previously been known, too long a leash. What they didn't understand was that before the Accord—that unprecedented constitutional agreement between the Living and the DEAD—there hadn't even been a collar. Like trusted dogs, the Haza had let them range free over their blood-parishes... which then had run from the East Coast and around the mud-thick Mississippi until it faltered at the Rocky Mountains.

Now there were checks and balances to VINE's remit—oversight and external authority. But Anderson's problem wasn't his understanding of constitutional law. It was the idea that Madoc would care about the consequences if Anderson's hateful mouth caught his temper again.

"You mistake me," he said. Anderson looked smug as he thought he saw Madoc backpedal his threat. "I expect you to let my agent go because you have no evidence he was involved, other than his fangs. If you continue to hold him, I will pursue every legal avenue to extract satisfaction, even if I have to move here."

Anderson scowled as he realized that, not only had he not won, but that Madoc had a threat up his sleeve that couldn't be countered with the Accord. Pettiness, for an immortal, could be an art form. Some vampires had methodically ruined whole families over decades, generations even. Anderson absently rubbed his arm as he considered Madoc's point. It was hard to tell if it was the bruise that preoccupied him or the tattoo.

"Fine," Anderson said finally. "Agent Bennett is still a person of interest, but I'll release him to your recognizance... on the proviso that he stays in town but doesn't interfere in my case. Last thing I need is some interested bystander in the way of my deputies, especially after he put two of them in the hospital."

"He'll stay in the state," Madoc countered. The last time he'd checked—obsessively and protectively—Took had still been resident in Charleston. It was only an hour on the freeway.

Anderson accepted that with a shrug. "As long as I can reel him back in if any evidence turns up," he said. "In that case, he's all yours. Do what you like to him."

Madoc waited while Anderson signed the forms and made the call to the cell. He picked at a burr in his mirror-polish-manicured thumbnail as Anderson growled instructions to the deputy.

"See?" Anderson said with mock solicitousness. "You get more flies with honey than vinegar, Agent Madoc."

Madoc looked up from his nail and gave a humorless smile. "I never said I wouldn't kill you, Sheriff Anderson," he said, "just that I didn't need to, to get Bennett out of jail. If you want to know what will inspire me to rip your tongue out at the root, flap it some more."

Anderson lifted his chin, a muscle tight under his jaw, and curled his lip into a sneer. "I don't like your kind, Agent Madoc. I'm a fair man, so that won't influence my investigation, but I want to make sure we're clear. I don't like you, and if your agent was involved in this or you get in my way, I'll put you both down like you were rabid dogs."

"There we go," Madoc said pleasantly as he opened the office door. "On the same page at last."

Chapter Three

THE DEPUTIES hadn't been particularly careful when they tossed Took's room at the B and B. His bed had been roughly stripped, the mattress tipped off the bed, and his clothes dumped out of his overnight case in the corner of the room. Nothing had been destroyed, just turned inside out and tossed aside.

Took had done it often enough himself—latex gloves dry against his knuckles as he stripped a Goat's bed and checked in the mattress for syringes of hidden blood—so turnabout was fair play, he supposed. He still wanted to gather up everything they'd pawed over and torch it. It felt like hands on his skin, not on his old jeans.

"Did they take anything?" Madoc asked as he looked over Took's shoulder. "Laptop? The rest of your clothes?"

Took waited for a second. It was the sort of question that usually left him off balance, unsure how to justify his pared-down life without any real explanation. Old habits kicked in with Madoc and he snorted instead. "We don't all travel with an eighteenth-century dandy's wardrobe."

"To be fair," Madoc drawled. "I was an eighteenth-century dandy, and I own a plane, so I do what I like."

Took laughed and stepped into the ruined room. "I didn't plan to stay this long," he said. "All I wanted to do was look over the files, see if I was right about the links to my case."

"Uh-huh," Madoc drawled. "We still need to talk about that."

A white plastic pill bottle lay on the floor at the end of the bed. Took tapped it with one booted toe. It was empty. He hoped whatever cop pocketed them had taken down the brand name. Otherwise the poor bastard would have a bad day.

They had not found anything else. There was nothing to find. Took hadn't set up the ambush at the trap house, so there was nothing to incriminate him. As for embarrassing… well, anyone who wanted to know anything about his life—his pay scale, his scars, the size of his fucking fangs—just had to look it up online. If one of the reputable papers hadn't posted it, then you could bet a gossip rag had. They had his pills until he could get the script refilled, and they had his collar size.

He hoped Anderson thought the man hours were worth it.

"I walked into a trap house and spent the day in that hot box," Took said to Madoc over his shoulder. "What I need is a shower and a change of clothes. I can smell myself."

"But you can't look at me?" Madoc asked.

Took scrubbed his hand through his hair, blood sticky as gel under his fingers, and turned around. He looked at the lean, dark sprawl of man, muscle, and bone wrapped in Kevlar-reinforced leather and buckles propped against his rented doorframe. He'd cropped his hair short, gone from shoulder-length to a shaved-up-at-the-sides undercut that drew attention to the gray at his temples. His shoulders were solid and wide with heavy muscle that he'd worked for at some time. There were few other signs of age—his gray eyes were unlined, his jawline still tight and closely shaved—but it was enough to set him apart. Most dhampirs were turned in their late teens or early twenties, before years and sun darkened their hair and thickened their skin from rice-paper pallor. Madoc had been a grown man when his blood finally caught up with him. Humans thought him pale and elegant, but among his own, he was a crow of a man.

"I fucked up," Took admitted, his voice harsh in his throat as he tried to make it sound like his professional pride was all that was on the line. "I got sloppy. I didn't watch Gatlin's back, and I probably got him killed. We both know it."

Madoc didn't look like he was fooled. It wasn't a lie either, so he let it go.

"We do," he agreed with Took instead. "What I want to know is why."

"Ten minutes," Took bargained.

Madoc thought about it for a moment and then shrugged his surrender. "Ten minutes," he said as he strolled into the room. There was only one chair. Madoc put it back on its feet and folded his body into it.

"I can wait," he said.

Took considered a protest, but he was done. He shrugged instead and headed into the bathroom. A shove closed the door behind him, and he took in the mess the deputies had made of his toiletries. Every bottle and tube had been opened, emptied, and tossed into the sink. His soap had been roughly quartered with a knife. He suspected if he rearranged the uneven chunks he'd find they carved a cross into it.

He stripped, grabbed a chunk of soap, and climbed into the shower. A flick of his hand turned the tap on and the water battered down against his scalp and his shoulder. He lathered the soap and briskly scrubbed himself down. His hands were impersonal by habit until he curled his fingers around his cock and lingered on the jut of the half-erect shaft.

The scrape of lust had caught him by surprise earlier in the jail cell. It had been hot and tight and... familiar. Ever since he woke up with fangs, Took's old map of his desires and hungers wasn't dependable anymore. His go-to fantasies, the hard-wired type he always went for, were cordoned off and his wants detoured to darker places... deeper places. Lust came quicker, affection slower.

Maybe it was normal—Took had a shit couple of years under his belt; that had to have an impact—but it scared him that it might not be. Worst-case scenario, it might just be the start of... something.

But he'd never been comfortable with the way he wanted Madoc, and he still wasn't. It had been hard enough to work with vampires, to walk out of a trap house with black blood on his boots and horrors in his head and crack a joke with a monster who wore a badge. That wasn't something he'd learned at his father's knee. And he'd never quite wrapped his head around the fact that he wanted to crawl all over one of the undead.

It had put him on edge then, and it put him on edge now. That was almost reassuring... but not enough for Took to be comfortable with jerking off in the shower while Madoc listened. He flicked the water to cold. It didn't have quite the same impact as when his blood had been above room temperature, but it still shocked his cock out of its high hopes.

Took leaned forward and braced his hands against the wet white tiles. He let the water chill his shoulders and run down over his ass while he counted off Madoc's patience.

A fist thumped the door. "You don't even sweat anymore," Madoc growled his complaint. "How long does it take to get clean?"

The water swirled thick rivulets of gray ichor around Took's feet until it was sucked down the drain. Madoc had made it to nearly two minutes. He'd learned patience while Took was... taken. Took licked the water off his lips and pushed himself upright.

"I thought the need for constant entertainment was something my generation came up with?" he shot back as he turned off the shower. "Read a book or something."

Madoc laughed with a low, throaty roll of humor that gave Took's cock a boost of enthusiasm. "You think the Borgias were big fans of delayed gratification? That the Drakul squirreled brides away for a rainy day?"

"I think they could wait ten minutes."

"You sorely underestimate them."

Took turned his back to the mirror and looked over his shoulder. The explosion had lain his back open. It was a stripe of raw meat with blistered edges that ran from one shoulder to the other. In the hours since, the edges had barely scabbed, never mind stitched back together. He twisted his arm behind him and poked carefully at the wound. It had hurt earlier, but it seemed like that had worn off. Some vampires would have healed already, but he'd take not being in pain as the next best thing.

"Yeah," Took said quietly as he grabbed the shirt. The cotton smelled of latex and cigarettes from some deputy's fingers. He grimaced and shrugged it on anyhow. "Sometimes I do that."

THE NICKEL and Dimer had the aggressively kitschy charm of somewhere that might cover its overhead with local business but needed tourist bucks to make a profit. Last time Took had been with Gatlin and the place had been packed with families having breakfast. They'd had coffee at the counter—it didn't do much for Took anymore, but he couldn't quite give up the ritual of addiction—poured by a waitress with big hair and a bigger smile who'd upsold the PumperNickel pie and called them both sweetie.

That was twenty-four hours ago. Things had changed.

"Sign in the window," the chef, a big, bearded man with a stained apron who probably intimidated most people, said as he glared at Took. "You read it? No heartbeat, no service. You can just fuck on back to your coffin, pal."

Took picked up his menu and unfolded it. He looked over the top of it at Madoc.

"It was your idea to come here," he pointed out.

Madoc pulled a badge out of the pocket of his uniform. The silver stake and stylized fangs glittered against the gold shield. The chef scowled as he took it in.

"Your sign's illegal," Madoc said as he tucked the badge back out of sight. "So if I were you, I'd take our order and then go take it down before a passing VINE agent runs you in."

The chef hesitated. He rubbed the back of his neck, and his eyes cut nervously from Madoc to the cluster of rough, grim-faced locals at the end of the bar. Mud was dried on their jeans, and most of them had silver-shod stakes tucked in their boots and belts.

"Tell them to fuck off, Nick," one of the men called over. The only distinguishing feature of his heavy, doughy face was the mean around his mouth and bloodshot eyes. He laughed like he'd said something funny and slapped the man next to him on the shoulder. "We like our meat well done round here."

His companion slouched from under the heavy hand and drank his beer. Took checked him out briefly—the jeans were battered Levis with work-worn cuffs, but they were clean and there was no wear on the knees or pockets. Unlike the others, he didn't wear a stake at his hip or ankle, but he carried himself like he was armed. Took's money was on a ceramic spike up his sleeve.

Hunter gear but not illegal.

Nick took a deep breath and let it out through tight lips. He rubbed the back of his neck again, his palm slick with sweat, and dropped his voice.

"I don't want any trouble," he said. "But this is a small town. I'm still going to be here when you leave. You guys don't even eat. Just go. Okay?"

Madoc shrugged and reached over to snag the menu from Took. He glanced briefly at it and tossed it back onto the table.

"We'll have coffee," he said. "Green tea and a slice of pie for my partner. She's on her way."

Partner. It startled Took how much it stung to hear someone else called that. He hadn't even wanted to work with Madoc's Biters when he was first assigned to them. Like the name suggested, they were mostly vampires. But Madoc had wanted a "daylight perspective," and even though cardinal was a defunct honor, he still pretty much got what he wanted. Back then he'd resented being designated Madoc's pet. Now he resented that Lawrence had the title.

He swallowed it. His field skills might have gotten rusty over the last year, but he'd only gotten better at not thinking about things.

"Run your mouth on the way back to the counter," he told Nick. "We've heard worse. They'll appreciate the show."

Nick looked trapped.

"What…." He tugged absently at his beard. "What sort of pie."

Madoc shrugged. "Surprise us," he said. "And get on with it. I don't feel this conversation needs an audience."

There was something in Madoc's voice, an edge that itched just above the upper range of Took's hearing. It wasn't exactly audible, but it vibrated in his sinuses. He worked his jaw from side to side as he tried to pop the airlock.

"What—"

"Fine!" Nick snatched the menu off the table. His fingers left wet smears on the laminated fabric. "I'll get your goddamn pie. I'll put my dick in it too. Tell VINE I've got some for them too."

The locals laughed, slapped each other roughly on the back, and urged him on. "Go on, Nick. Let them have it. Think we're just going to sit back and let them kill our kids?"

The quiet man was the only one who didn't join in.

"Lawrence," Took said as he dragged his attention back to Madoc. "I don't remember her. Anything to do with the Director—"

"What are you here for, Bennett?" Madoc interrupted flatly. "And why are two deputies dead?"

"Do you really give a damn?" Took asked. He could have meant either question.

"Yes," Madoc said. He could have too.

Fair enough, Took supposed. He leaned forward and braced his elbows on the sharp edge of the table.

"I'm still the best preternatural behaviorist on the books," he said. "So sometimes people ask me to… look into things."

Madoc raised one heavy, dark eyebrow and smirked. "I always said you were a dick."

"Not exactly," Took said. "Usually I don't need to find people, just mistakes—misinterpreted signatures, behavioral patterns that weren't identified, the occasional Death Valley prisoner interview they want me to interpret. Most of the cases are dusty, no harm no foul."

"If you wanted to keep your hand in," Madoc said, "we'd have paid."

"They pay," Took said.

"So do we."

"VINE doesn't pay consultant fees to their own employees. I had some... expenses... to cover."

Took shifted. He didn't want to talk about how broken he was, about the way vampirism had stitched his body back together—untidy as it was—but left his brain fractured like a dropped glass. So far, Madoc only seemed to have noticed the surface stuff, and Took didn't want to dredge the rest of it out. He couldn't sleep behind a locked door, even in a hotel, and he sleepwalked through most days because he refused to adapt to a nocturnal schedule. He didn't want Madoc to look at him the way everyone else did, like the best they could ever expect of Took again was fucking *functional*. "You have your phone?"

Madoc raised his eyebrows. "Didn't you make your one call in jail?"

He had. They hadn't picked up. Took couldn't blame West for that, but... he did a bit. That—him and West, their first kiss to the never-quite-ended relationship—had always been off-limits for Madoc. It just hadn't felt... fair. Took didn't plan to break that rule now.

"Phone or not?"

Madoc leaned back and unfastened his jacket so he could reach inside and pull out a thin rectangle of glass and plastic. Tech had never been Took's passion, so he didn't recognize it, but he assumed it was expensive. Madoc held it out over the table and then twitched it away as Took reached for it.

"I've changed my passcode," he warned with a hint of his old sly smile.

Took rolled his eyes and grabbed the phone. He wasn't *that* rusty. This was an old game, and he hadn't lost a round since Madoc had cheated and used face recognition. The thing Madoc could never quite believe was that the code didn't matter, it was the person who input it that didn't change.

If Took could work out why Killer Vampire A only bit people who'd bought a Klondike bar from the corner of Main and James Street, then he could figure out the sequence of numbers Madoc thought he'd remember. For reasons both professional and personal, Took had spent a lot more time in the study of Cardinal Madoc than he had of Case File 92.

Every three months Madoc changed his passcode. So he'd changed it, at most, twelve times since Took had last guessed it. Maybe less, he might have slacked off during the investigation into Took's kidnapping.

Occupied in the puzzle, Took let that thought skate over the surface of his brain. It almost didn't sting, and it reminded him of something.

"Got it," he said after a minute. The screen cleared from black to the minimalist apps and empty background that Madoc favored. TOOK35. The anniversary of his kidnapping had been three years ago in May, last month. "Try five. Asshole."

Madoc rubbed his thumb over his lower lip. "Maybe," he said. "Or maybe I just wanted you to know it hasn't been forgotten. I'm still looking for him."

Him.

Although, of course, it could have been her. Or both. More. A random stranger. A vampire with a grudge. Took, with his brain full of blank spaces, certainly couldn't tell you.

Took stared at the phone in his hands and the faint, distorted reflection that slid in and out of the glass. Or it could have been the vampire sitting opposite him—his partner, his friend, and one of the few people who knew where Took had been headed that day.

The suspicion tasted like old blood and ingratitude in the back of Took's throat, but he couldn't quite dismiss it either. Madoc was used to getting what he wanted, and he'd wanted Took… back then.

He connected to the internet and backdoored into his server to pull down a file.

There was no evidence, but there was no exoneration either. Took just had to live with the possibility.

"Storm Warning," he said, his voice rough and uneasy in his throat as he pushed the phone back over the table. At least, that's what he'd called himself online, as he gave the Breathing Rights movement an appealing face. A young man with fair hair and a strawberry birthmark around his eye stared out of the screen with a tentative smile. Madoc knew the face. "Although his legal name is Dominic Waring. His parents think VINE got it wrong. That you got it wrong."

Chapter Four

IN TOOK'S picture, Dominic Waring was seventeen years old, played football because his father expected it, and dated a girl called Mikaila Blake who didn't expect to be treated very well. He had 20,000 followers on his streaming channel and clowned to demand. The year before he'd run away from home to hitch to LA, although he'd been picked up a week later just outside of Michigan, and in roughly four months he would run away again.

This photo was the one his parents used for the missing-person appeal, teary-eyed on TV screens and social media. For a while it had been everywhere, until another photo supplanted it in the public consciousness. In it, Dominic had been thin and fevered, with a shaved head and blood all over his shirt from the family he'd murdered.

"His parents think he's innocent?" he asked as he flicked the photo off-screen. The underlying folder structure spread out over the screen of his phone—a chaos of unnamed files, random stacks of photos, and a dozen identical shortcuts. Took's filing system had always been enough to make a cat wince, and despite the old wives' tales about vampiric OCD, it obviously hadn't changed. "He was caught red-handed. Literally."

"They think VINE framed him."

Madoc sat back and raised his eyebrows. "You know better than that," he said. "So why take the case?"

The arrival of the coffee meant that Madoc had to wait for his answer. He watched Took as Nick slammed the coffee down on the table in front of them and brown liquid splashed over the white Formica. For a second, it had been his old partner slouched across from him, ice-pick mind at work behind that pretty, surfer-boy face. Then it was gone, and the brittle, glassy shell had clicked back into place.

Maybe Madoc should have just opened his phone himself, but he didn't think it was that.

"Choke on it," Nick said loudly for his audience of yokels. His hands shook as shoved a wedge of pie and sloppily applied whipped cream across the table. "I hope your bit—"

"Don't push your luck," Madoc told him. He plucked a napkin out of the chrome dispenser on the table and fastidiously sopped up the spilled coffee. When he was done, he tucked the sodden paper into the pocket of Nick's apron. "And take that sign down. If I have to do it, I'll make you swallow it."

Nick blanched behind his beard and backed away from the table. This time the jeers from the wannabe Hunters were at him, the solidarity of breath forgotten in the joy of humiliation. An old ember of contempt flickered in the back of Madoc's mind. If it hadn't been so easy to convince humans to turn the pitchforks on each other, the Empires of the Undead might have remained nothing but a boyar's fiefdom.

"There was a glutted vampire in the trap house," Took said conversationally. "Fat as a tick and didn't even know his own name."

The reminder quenched the flare of superiority before it could take root. Most vampires sustained themselves with a Kiss—a sip of blood from a lover's ripe vein. Some couldn't stop or didn't want to and drained their lovers to dry veins as they chased the sweet-rot tang of death even as it rotted them out like hollow logs, flesh and fang preserved but whatever made them people instead of beasts sloughed off.

Human or vampire, both had members they wouldn't hold up as the best of their species.

"So I shouldn't look down on them," Madoc acknowledged.

"No, you should understand why they're angry," Took corrected him. "And afraid, which is worse."

"Good point," Madoc allowed. He pulled a hip flask out of his jacket, unscrewed the cap, and poured whiskey-thinned blood into his coffee. The blood had more kick, for him, than the whiskey, but the mossy smoke taste was something he could still savor. He raised his eyebrows at Took and tipped the flask in his direction. "Do you want a shot?"

Took swallowed and swiped his tongue over his lower lip. The hunger in his eyes was for blood, but hunger wasn't so far from lust for vampires. His eyes would dilate the same way if Madoc kissed him, and the points of his fangs dimpled the lush curve of his lower lip. Or not. Madoc roughly pinned the fantasy down and shoved it back into its place. He'd allow them in his sheets, with a warm body under him or his own cold hand on his cock, but that was all. The first time Madoc offered more than that, he'd been rejected. Took had picked chaste friendship and a breathing lover instead, and the last time he'd lost even the friendship.

That old sluggish pain sank its fangs into Madoc, but it was a welcome distraction from the heavy tug of his balls. Love, as he'd found out before, was no excuse to be a fool.

"I doubt you'll find another willing offer in this town," Madoc said as he withdrew the flask and recapped it. "But suit yourself. So go on. Why take the case?"

He took a drink. The coffee was hot enough to burn his tongue and scald his throat with a brief sting before the aftertaste of blood laved it away.

Took wrapped his hands around his mug and looked past Madoc's shoulder, toward the front of the diner. "I might as well explain to you and your new partner."

The bell over the door rattled as someone shoved it open. Madoc didn't need to look around to know it was Lawrence. There could well be other women in town who wore Chanel perfume, but he doubted that any of them would carry the faint, sickly sweet smell of ichor on their breath. That was easy. He was more interested in how Took knew, as far as he was aware, that they hadn't set eyes on each other in the station.

"Are you sure it's her?" he asked.

Took absently reached up and rubbed his throat. The scar was still raised and pink from exposure to the sun—almost raw. It should have healed by now. Not just from the sun's blisters, but the scars themselves should have faded. Vampires scarred, but even holy water would heal eventually. It just took blood and time.

"There are a few vampires who work in town," Took said. His eyes stayed focused over Madoc's shoulder as he talked, faster as the click of Lawrence's heels got closer. "But they keep a low profile. Anyone they bite on the regular? They keep a lower one."

Madoc glanced around as Lawrence reached the table. True to his advice, she still wore the low-scooped top that flashed her bite. Like any sleight of hand, it was less impressive once you knew how it was done.

"She also flashed Nick her badge," Took added as he lifted his coffee to inhale the bitter steam. "That cinched it."

Madoc slid to the side to give Lawrence room in the booth. She hesitated for a moment, her attention distracted by the men at the bar, and then made the same assessment that Madoc had. The local militia would drink themselves stupid before they worked up to direct action. At least they would tonight. Lawrence sat down on the edge of the bench, careful to leave room for the Holy Spirit between his thigh and hers, and nodded stiffly across the table.

"You must be Agent Bennett," she said as she pulled the plate toward her. "I've heard a lot about you."

"Agent Bennett is just about to explain how he ended up in Appleton," Madoc said. He took another drink of his coffee and licked his lips, just to see if Took's gaze would flicker down. It did. "Go on. Tell us Dom Waring is innocent."

Lawrence paused, her fork sunk tine-deep in cream, and spluttered an indignant "What?"

"She was a member of the task force that took Dom down," Madoc said. "So was I."

"I'm aware of that. I did read the files on the case," Took pointed out with a flicker of irritation, but he controlled it. He reached over, picked up the salt, and unscrewed the top of it with a gritty sound. "Don't put words in my mouth. I said that the family thinks he's innocent, that VINE framed Dominic, not that I agreed with them."

He added a heavy dose of salt to his coffee. "I just think that it's possible you missed something."

Lawrence put her fork down with a distinct click. "Dominic Waring murdered five families, breathing and not. Some of the bodies still haven't been found, will probably never be found to be laid to rest or raised again." She tucked her hair back behind her ear with an impatient swipe of her fingers. Her voice was clipped and sharp with resentment as she pushed on. "Do you really think we didn't check everything, look in every dirty corner that we could find? We had forensic evidence, eyewitness sightings… we even got the Nations to agree to let a manhunt cross the borders onto their territory because the evidence against Waring was overwhelming. Or did you somehow miss all that?"

It was a good question. Until today, Madoc had assumed that Took had quarantined himself away from anything to do with VINE or kidnapping. Otherwise it was hard to imagine how a man whose life had been his work had managed to stay on the sidelines for so long.

Except, of course, he apparently hadn't.

"You made a compelling case," Took agreed with her. He took a drink of salt-seasoned coffee and grimaced as he choked it down. "It doesn't mean you didn't miss anything."

Lawrence sniffed and sat back. "Something you'd have caught, I suppose?"

"Maybe," Took said. "I mean, it's something I did catch. So…."

They glared at each other.

"What?" Madoc asked.

"Sir," Lawrence protested sharply. "We didn't miss anything. It was a win when we put Waring under salt. I know you and Bennett worked together, but he's not on VINE's side right now. Don't give him anything he can hang this ridiculous theory off."

Took scowled at her. "VINE is there to catch bad guys, Agent Lawrence," he said, "not cover your ass. You're telling me that if you put the wrong man away, you'd rather let the real killer go than admit you fucked it up?"

"We didn't," Lawrence insisted. "Waring did it. Look, I know you're a basket case these days—"

"That's enough," Madoc cut her off sharply. The smoke in his voice curled thickly enough to layer compulsion over what he'd meant to just be an order. She clenched her fists on the table and closed her mouth so hard it made her teeth click. Madoc winced guiltily at the slip, although he doubted she'd realize what he'd done. To even the score, he turned his glare on Took. If he was going to jockey for position like a junior agent, he could get dressed down like one. "What did we miss, Agent Bennett? Or is this just a fishing trip?"

Took didn't look reprimanded. He paused as he took another drink of coffee and turned to the side, out the window at the brightly lit streets of Appleton. Despite the glare, few of the locals had risked the night. The diner was the only shop on Main Street still open.

"Appleton, the cider capital of South Carolina," Took said. "Twelve thousand residents and, based on the census, all of them are breathing. Have you ever been here before?"

The compulsion made Lawrence hold her tongue, but she snorted her impatience.

"It's on VINE's radar," Madoc said. He glanced over his shoulder at the local militia, who superstitiously avoided his eyes. "But no. Why?"

Took drained his coffee and wiped his mouth on his sleeve

"Dominic Waring was here," he said. "You missed that. Now if you'll excuse me, I don't intend to spend another night in Appleton, and it's a long drive home."

He tossed a ten on the table for his drink, got up, and left. Madoc could have stopped him. Common wisdom said that "if you love them, let them go", but so far, it hadn't gotten Madoc anywhere.

"MAYBE WE should have gone after him," Lawrence said. She stood at the window of the police station, her arms crossed, and frowned at the prayer group as it reformed on the grass. "People in town still think he's to blame for those two deputies ending up in the hospital. There could be trouble."

Madoc looked away from the computer to study Lawrence. Her hair was clipped neatly at the back of her neck, so he had a good view of her reflection in the dark glass. Her lips were set in a tight line.

"Bennett can take care of himself," he said. "What's really bothering you, Lawrence?"

Her shoulders stiffened. "I don't know what you mean," she said dismissively. "There's nothing wr—"

"Enough," Madoc said. He hit Mute on the video call with Philadelphia. It had been on hold for five minutes while the agent on duty ran down Madoc's request, but he didn't want anyone to walk back in at an inopportune moment. "Either spit it out, Lawrence, or get over it. Your choice."

She turned around and stared at him for a moment as she chewed her lower lip. Then she shrugged.

"Like I said, it's nothing," she said. Madoc waited. It didn't take long for Lawrence to fold her arms defensively and blurt out, "I just don't understand. Our—VINE's—investigation in the Waring case was above reproach. There's no question of his guilt. You know that. Bennett, well, he might have been a good agent once, but he's obviously off the rails now. So why did you hear him out?"

The edge of suspicion in her voice was familiar. No one, so far, had been confident enough to voice it aloud, but the doubt curled through mission briefings and lurked under filed reports. People thought that Madoc's decisions where Took was concerned were based on emotion instead of logic. After Took vanished, he'd pushed the search too hard and held on to hope they'd find him long after everyone else had given up.

It was true, but that didn't mean that Madoc wasn't annoyed by the veiled insinuations. He might make his decisions with his heart instead of his head, but they were still the right decisions.

"We missed something," he said.

"Because *he* said so?" Lawrence asked skeptically. "Is he really that good?"

"He's the best," Madoc said bluntly.

"Better than me?" Lawrence asked. She flushed slightly as she caught the need in her voice, and she raised her eyebrows as she redirected the question. "Better than *you*?"

Madoc snorted. He spread his hand out in front of him. The brand of that old rank, of Cardinal Madoc and all his sins, on the back of it had faded years ago, but he could still feel it in his bones. When the six Haza still held court here, the cardinals had been more executioner than investigator. The boyars over the sea hadn't cared so much for guilt, as long as those they blamed bled.

"Violence has always served me well enough," he said. "I never had a subtle turn of mind."

"So just me?" she cracked. Then she sighed in annoyance. "I sound like a jealous girlfriend, don't I? It's just… was Bennett *really* that good? People talk about him like he was basically a sorcerer."

In the corner of his eye, Madoc saw Agent Rory Quick flop back into the chair and peer quizzically at the screen. He held up a finger to buy himself a second as he tried to think how to answer Lawrence's question. Took had the mind of a con man or a cult leader, unsentimental and observant as a snake, and a moral compass someone had managed to wedge in late in the day. Lawrence might be a better VINE agent one day—anywhere but the Biters, she probably already was—but Madoc didn't know if determination and hard work could give her the edge on the cold turn that came naturally to Took.

"He's that good," Madoc admitted. "I don't think it ever made him that happy."

Lawrence looked at him as though he'd missed something, but she just pointed at the laptop with her chin. "I guess we need to find out what we missed, then."

Definitely a good agent. Madoc turned back around and unmuted with a tap of his finger. He caught the tail end of Quick's absently tuneless hum before the man swallowed the rest of the melody.

"Sir," he said as he straightened up. With one finger he pushed the glasses he hadn't really needed for half a century up the bridge of his nose. "Did Bennett really blow up a trap house?"

The preliminary report from the county fire chief had understated the cause as "misadventure." One of the Goats apparently had a fondness for jury-rigged booby traps and homemade explosives. In addition to a perimeter of trip wire IEDs that matched the one that took out Gatlin, there had been a stash of homemade explosives in the garage. The theory was that the fight Took started in the kitchen had caused a gas leak, caught a spark, and then everything went up.

That was the theory. Madoc would wait for VINE's CSU techs to have a look before he called it fact.

Those were just the details, though. Quick wanted the story. He hadn't liked Took much at first, or at least he hadn't liked the fact Took was his superior despite that five-decade head start. In the end he'd come around. People always did. Now he wanted to take this and roll it out for the rest of the Biters. Proof that Took could still make any situation more dramatic, that he hadn't changed.

"Looks like it," Madoc said dryly. "What's that make it. Four?"

"Are we counting cars too?" Quick asked with a chuckle. He sobered quickly as he glanced over Madoc's shoulder at Lawrence. "You think this has something to do with the Waring case."

"There might be a connection," Madoc said.

At the same time, Lawrence said, "Bennett thinks so."

Quick hesitated for a moment but then accepted both answers. He absently ran his hand over his cropped, salt-and-sand curls as he looked down at a notebook.

"Well, our system throws up a few red flags where Appleton is concerned, but mostly to do with pockets of support for Hunter extremists in the area," he said. "There's nothing to do with Waring. I just checked in with Lopez and Tsosie, who had the case before it fell under Biter jurisdiction, and it hadn't crossed their radar either. They weren't even sure where it was. Did Bennett have any timeline for when this place was relevant?"

"Not that he was willing to share," Madoc said.

Quick rolled his eyes. "Some things never change, eh? So, do you need me to file a flight plan back, or…."

Everyone in the room knew it would be *or*, so Madoc ignored the question. "Send me everything—everything—we have on the Waring case. Get me an update on the parents as well and check how Waring has fared since we put him under The Salt."

At the bottom of the screen, Quick's hands were just visible as he quickly typed the instructions. He poked his tongue between his teeth in concentration, and then it disappeared back into his mouth.

"Will I get the Charleston office to send over an Eclipse sedan?" Quick asked absently.

"If we're going to poke our nose in," Lawrence pointed out, "we should run it past the local VINE SSA, make sure we don't step on any toes."

Madoc curled his mouth in a thin, sour smile. His presence had already stepped on the relevant toes. He doubted a belated effort to pretend he gave a flying fuck what SSA Crane thought of Madoc's presence in his territory would smooth anything over.

It was the effort that mattered, though—the acknowledgment that they all served new masters now and none of them thought wistfully of the old days of Empire. It would also mean that Madoc could make the drive to Charleston in relative comfort. He had served his time in car trunks and, before that, the scratchy beds of carts as he breathed in hay and chicken.

"You can liaise with Crane," he told Lawrence. "Find out what he knows about Bennett being on this case while you're at it. Quick—"

"It'll take me a bit to chase down everything on the parents, but I'm on it," Quick said. "The Waring file and all the associated forensic evidence is in the cloud."

He glanced up briefly with a flash of pale amber eyes over a smirk. "Do you need me to help you get into it? Again?"

Madoc snorted and disconnected the call. He might be old, but he hadn't started the slow calcification that took some of the elders. They weren't senile as the living experienced it—more reluctant to knit new memories into long-term recall—but it was close enough for Quick to think his jokes were funny.

"It doesn't make sense," Lawrence said. "Appleton doesn't fit as one of Waring's hunting grounds. It would be like hunting trout in a parking lot. It might not be a dry town anymore, but no vampire is going to move here with their family, not when they have other choices."

She wasn't wrong. Of course a hunter didn't just need a hunting ground. They needed a bolt-hole too.

"Get in touch with West, smooth his feathers about our involvement," Madoc said. He stood up. The leather of his uniform had been shaped to his body by years of blood and sweat, until it was too supple to creak or pinch, but he still felt the weight of it sometimes. "I need to go and talk to the sheriff and see what story Bennett fed him."

THE BRUISE on Anderson's arm looked stark against tanned, weathered skin as the sheriff wearily stripped off his jacket and hung it up on the back of the door. He looked tired, with purple stains thumbed in under his eyes and deep grooves etched into the skin around his mouth. If the slurs from earlier hadn't been fresh in Madoc's mind, he'd have felt sorry for the man.

"Gatlin died an hour ago," Anderson said grimly as he went to the metal cabinet on the other side of the room. He pulled the top door open and lifted out a half-drunk bottle of unlabeled booze. "I had to go to his house, wake his wife up, and tell her that she'd need to bury him. So don't get me wrong, but right now I don't give a fuck about your agent. Maybe he walked Gatlin into that trip wire, maybe not, but none of this would have happened if he'd stayed out of our town. Hell, if we stayed dry, then there would be a helluva lot of our people up and walking. At least, that's the way I see it."

Madoc perched on the edge of the sheriff's desk and watched as Anderson took a swig straight from the bottle. The liquor stank of smoke and oak, a nauseating tang in the back of Madoc's throat as he inhaled.

"My condolences," he said formally. "If you need someone to put his heart to rest—"

"It's done," Anderson said flatly. He wiped his mouth on the back of his hand and screwed the cap back on the bottle. Once it was tucked back into the file drawer, he gave Madoc a dour look and gave in. "Annabelle Franklin, that's what brought your boy to town. He rolled up a couple of days ago, flashed his badge, and said she had a connection to one of his cases. It pissed off Gatlin—he'd been the lead on the case—but I figured why not let the hotshot VINE agent take a look. Maybe he'd see something we hadn't, find something for the Franklin family to put in the ground."

"Who was she?"

"Nobody," Anderson said. The taste of the word made him grimace, but he stuck to it. "Sounds harsh, but that's who she was—not the smartest, not the prettiest, not the most trouble, just nobody much. When she disappeared, nobody even worried at first. She'd run away the year before—some cockeyed notion she got in her head from the internet—and eventually came back with her tail between her legs. By the time her parents got worried and called us in… trail was cold. Never found hide nor hair of her."

"And Gatlin had a theory?"

Anderson shrugged and leaned against the filing cabinet. "Call it a theory. Call it experience. She wasn't the first girl to disappear since the county wet its head, and she won't be the last. We clean out the trap houses when the stink attracts complaints, but there's always another derelict place for them to move into. This time it was the clinic. A year ago some wetmouth turned old Mattie Sharpe, a God-fearing widow, and she cut the throats of field hands for him. There's always somewhere for a kid who doesn't see any future in growing up."

It was a sad story, all the sadder for being a common one. Madoc had seen it play out more times than even Anderson had, although when he was a cardinal, it had too often been his duty to turn a blind eye. What it lacked was the connection that had drawn Took down here. Vampires weren't enough. Ninety percent of the Biters' cases dealt with the undead.

"She ran away before," Madoc said. "Why?"

Anderson coughed out a sour laugh. "Some boy catfished her on the internet, talked her into some cross-country hitchhike, and then stood her up. If she'd been smart, she would have realized she was lucky."

There it was. Madoc wasn't a subtle thinker, but he had learned to follow the tracks of those who were.

"This boy," he said. "Was she supposed to meet him in LA?"

Anderson scowled at him and reached up to toy with the cross that dangled from his neck. "But the magicians did the same by their secret arts," he quoted in a mutter as he pinched the sliver of metal between thumb and forefinger. "A man's heart should be known only by God. Keep your fingers out of my thoughts, sorcerer."

After so many years, there were few accusations that Madoc could straight-faced claim his innocence against. That he had paid the price for true magic, though, he could deny. He had always been too indulgent to deny himself anything significant enough to buy power.

Still, Anderson's suspicion was answer enough.

LA. Where Dominic Waring, back when he'd still been the innocent boy in Took's phone, had been headed. His family had pulled out the stops to get him back, but Madoc had the feeling Annabelle's parents didn't have the same clout.

"Tell you what, Sheriff," Madoc said as he stood up. "Get me all the files on the Franklin girl, anything else Bennett looked at, and I'll have no call to carve the answers out of your gray matter."

Not that he could; he could overwhelm but not vivisect the mortal will. Only the true Risen, those who'd gone into the dark and found their way back, enjoyed that gift. Even then, it was rare and a trial as much as a gift. But Madoc found a silver tongue and straight-faced lie just as useful.

Anderson gave him a dour grimace of a smile, a flash of gum between his square, white teeth. "At least you make no pretense about being a monster," he said. "I thought Bennett was a man until we saw him bleed."

"A better man than you, Sheriff," Madoc said coldly. "I leave in a few hours. Get me what I want by then, or I take it."

Chapter Five

THE CAT and Mrs. Waring were at Took's front door to greet him when he pulled into his drive. Neither should have been there. The cat was supposed to be behind the state-of-the-art security system that was meant to make Took feel safe inside the narrow, sea-green house. As for Mrs. Waring, she was on the right side of the security, but she shouldn't have known where to find Took.

Not many people did.

Paranoia tapped a nervous drumbeat against the back of Took's eye as he watched Mrs. Waring get up off the rickety plastic lawn chair and brush the wrinkles out of her trousers with nervous hands. She looked like her son, even down to something in the weakness of her jaw that suggested she was younger than she really was.

None of Waring's alleged victims had put up much of a fight. Mostly that made sense. Not all vampires were created equal—a Risen trumped a still breathing dhampir, a dhampir outclassed a ghoul—and a blitz attack could put some down and keep them down. But some of them had been old and trained and should have held their own. Others had security systems that never went off, alarms that were never hit.

Had they, Took wondered, found a nervous, stoop-shouldered redhead, young enough that he still got carded at liquor stores, on their porch and thought he was harmless? Maybe he learned the trick from his mother.

Fear was a habit. The black hole in his brain wanted to be filled, and until he found out what happened the night he was kidnapped—the how and the who—it tried to make any other nightmare fit.

Took dragged his mind out of that familiar sinkhole, the mire of it wet and reluctant to let go, and got out of the car.

"Agent Bennett," Mrs. Waring said as she stepped to the edge of the narrow porch. In all the old pictures Took had of Heather Waring from before her life took a left turn into hell, she'd always been elegant and fashionable, with tailored designer dresses and perfectly manicured nails—the perfect wife for an aspiring judge. The mask was still there, an on-trend mauve dress buckled tightly around her body, and her bag matched to her heels, but her nails were chewed down to the scabbed quicks and her makeup didn't quite cover her grief. "We got a letter from The Salt. They're going to execute my son, on his birthday. Please. Tell me you've found something."

"You shouldn't be here," Took said. "How did you get my address, Mrs. Waring?"

Fresh tears welled in her eyes. She dashed them away with a furious swipe of her hand and glared at him.

"I tell you that you're going to kill my son, that they're going to cut his heart out and bury his body where we'll never find it—" Her voice cracked harshly, and she stopped for a second to take a ragged, damp breath. "Never find him. And you want to know how I got your address? Does it really matter?"

Took shoved his keys into the pocket of his trousers. He could have made it home last night. It was only two hours from Appleton to Charleston. Even with the midnight rush hour, he could have made it back in time to sleep in his own bed. Instead he'd crashed in a McDonald's parking lot, slouched in the front seat of his car as he watched the dull-eyed employees yawn and trade milkshakes for joints under the neon glare of the Golden Arches.

"I guess not," he admitted as he took the steps to the front door. The house hadn't felt safe when no one knew he lived there. It wouldn't change anything that now people did. He bent down to scoop the cat up from the doormat. It hissed in disgruntlement at being handled—a flash of white fangs and the pink curl of its tongue—and scrambled up his arm, claws hooked in his shirt, to perch on his shoulder. "You might as well come in. If someone sees you on my porch, everyone will know where I live."

Heather exhaled sharply between her teeth. "You do remember that you work for us," she said.

"Billable hours, Mrs. Waring," Took said as he keyed in the security code and pushed the heavy, steel-core door open with one foot. "Until the clock starts on this dawn consultation, you're just another solicitor who's ignored the sign."

She gave him a dirty look but held her tongue as she stalked over his threshold. "You shouldn't let your cat outside," she said as she passed him. "White cats can't take the sun."

"Snack does what he wants," Took said. To prove the point, Snack used his shoulder as a launch pad to leap over to the carved ball that decorated the banister. He didn't look like a white cat, he looked like a talented child's drawing of a cat, with milk-pale fur and crayon blue eyes and nose. Took could swear the kitten had been darker, his fur gray and his eyes green, when someone tossed him into Took's box. Maybe he'd just been dirty. Snack stretched and dug his claws into the polished wood, his tail crooked up in a question mark as he gave a pointed, rusty mew. "And he can take care of himself. My office is down the hall."

Snack didn't bother to follow them. The cat sitter would have left his food out. He just liked to make a reproachful point when Took was away for longer than a couple of days.

It was optimistic to call the small room in the back of the house an office. There was a computer and a filing cabinet, but Took had barely used either. His therapist had suggested he try to write a book, to distract himself from the emptiness of his day-to-day with the memory of adrenaline. Took hadn't gotten very far. He'd never had the patience for stories and, right now, thoughts of the past just reminded him on the stuff he *couldn't* remember.

There were chairs and a desk… currently covered with glossy, bloody pictures of Dom Waring's crime scenes. Took cursed under his breath and ducked around the desk to sweep the photos off and into a drawer. Red and white, shattered bones, and wet meat.

"I've seen them all," Heather said in a tight, precise voice as she sat down. "The ones we didn't see in court the press were happy to show us."

"Still," Took said as he shoved the drawer shut and slid into the leather swivel chair. The still-raw skin on his back, open under his shirt, ached dully with something like pain. It wasn't exactly welcome, but in a weird way, it reassured Took. When the sun was up, he felt close to human, enough to remember what it was like. He tried to hang on to that. The thought that he might forget one day scared him. "Not what you need before breakfast."

Heather sat back and raised her chin with brittle defiance. "They're just ugly photos," she said steadily, "of ugly things. It's sad and it's horrible, but it's nothing to do with me. Because my son didn't do that to people. He's just who they blamed for it. And who they're going to kill for it."

She broke up and covered her mouth with her hand. Her knuckles pressed down hard against her lips as she blinked back a fresh spill of tears. Her grief made Took look away uncomfortably and wonder what to do if the dam broke. It wasn't easy to comfort someone when you didn't entirely trust yourself that close to their throats or the crook of their arms.

That admission made Took's humanity feel a lot further away. He pushed his tongue against his teeth. They were sharp enough to cut, and his own blood was like burnt molasses as he swallowed it, but they were still where they belonged.

"Do you have the letter from The Salt?" he asked. "The latest one."

It was a distraction that worked for them both. Heather sniffed, wiped her eyes on the back of her wrist, and pulled the bag into her lap. She had to wipe her eyes again, pinch tears away between her finger and thumb, before she could dig into the dark interior.

"Here," she said as she finally pulled out the creased, ripped-open envelope. Her hands trembled slightly as she looked at it, frozen for a second, then thrust it toward Took. "It arrived yesterday, by special courier. He said... he said that nothing I have to say would be heard."

The familiar seal of The Salt was stamped in blue ink on the envelope and embossed in raised threads of silk on the heavy sheet of paper inside. Took unfolded it on his desk and looked it over quickly. He'd seen execution notifications before. A copy of this one would have been sent to Madoc and the director of VINE so they could attend if they wanted.

The date of execution had always been a grim sort of tick mark for his personal files. Job done. Monsters gone. It had never been a functional deadline before.

"Tell me you can stop this," Heather said.

Took hesitated. He knew—it was an itch down deep in the fold of his brain—that VINE had missed something. That didn't mean Dom Waring was innocent, not innocent enough to sway The Salt, anyhow.

"I can try."

She choked out a rough bark of laughter. There was no real humor to it, just a desperation that didn't know where else to go.

"You know, you could lie," she said. "I won't mind."

"Trust me," Took said. "You would. Eventually. People always do."

She closed her eyes and pulled her mouth into a blind, ragged smile. "Right now," she said bitterly, "I can hardly face tomorrow, never mind 'eventually.'"

Took averted his eyes from her pain for a second time. He folded the heavy notification letter back into the ruler-straight creases to give her a moment to compose herself.

"As I said before, it would help if I could talk to your son," he said when he finally looked up.

"If Dom would speak to *anyone*, it would help us all," Heather said bitterly.

"I don't need him to talk. Just listen."

Heather shrugged. "My husband said he's working on it. I'll get him to email you if there's any progress."

The Waring parents made statements to the press hand in hand, in lockstep on their son's innocence and the stable home they'd given him. Since they'd hired Took to consult on the case, he'd only seen them together once. The space between them was so full of blame, guilt, and resentment that they could hardly look at each other. He had practically been able to hear the unspoken accusations. *Heather coddled him.... Liam pushed him too hard.... He/she/we should have seen something.*

"Thank you." Took held up the neat rectangle of the letter. "Can I keep this? I can make a copy and get this back to you."

Heather gave the ivory paper a disgusted look and waved her hand in a brusque, dismissive gesture. "Keep it," she said as she fumbled her bag closed. "I'll remember what it says. Until my dying day."

She hooked the bag over her shoulder and stood up. Then she stopped, as though there was something else she needed to do before she left.

"Mrs. Waring?" Took prompted as he stood up.

She blinked and cleared her throat. "I remember when I was Dom's age," she said. "I thought I was so grown up, an adult who wasn't going to mess up like all the other adults in her life. Now I look back, and I was just a kid. I didn't really know anything."

Her hand worked around the strap of her bag as she talked, the leather twisted and folded between her fingers. She paused for a second to take a quick breath between words.

"Liam thinks that it was all nothing, that VINE framed Dom because of Liam's political ambitions, because he's a breathing man's politician. I know that's not true," she said, the words like stones she had to spit out. Maybe it was the first time she'd admitted it to herself. Took was sure it was the first time she'd admitted it to herself. "I know Dom did something. I'm his mother and, like you said, I don't need him to tell me, I can see it in his eyes. He did something, but not—" She jabbed a shaky finger at the drawer where Took had shoved the pictures. Out of sight obviously wasn't out of mind. "Not that."

Took wished he could reassure her, or at least part of him did. It had been easy to pick apart the Biters' case against Waring with the detachment of nearly two years. Since Madoc pulled his fat out of the fire and reminded him what it was like to be part of the team, despite the unignorable suspicion that Madoc had betrayed him first, it felt disloyal to hope they'd fucked it up.

Took left the letter on the desk as he stood up. He settled on "If I can prove that, I will."

She looked grateful. Took felt the weight of it against his shoulders as he showed her out. He wasn't sure he was a good bet to be anyone's best hope these days. The cat waited until Heather was gone and then mewed rustily for his breakfast.

That, Took thought as he headed toward the kitchen, felt more his speed.

He made a mental note to call the dispensary and get an emergency refill on his… medication.

"DID YOU give her my address?" Took asked.

He stood at the window in VINE's Charleston offices, close enough that he could feel the heat of the setting sun through the glass, and looked out over a skyline of narrow gray towers and brassy mosaics that glittered sourly in the sun. Most depicted Tepes in some form, his distinct crown—some rendered the pearls on his crown in ivory and others in glass, but all placed seven for the souls of the Solomonary—more faithfully recreated than the sketch of his stern face. Charleston had been one of the first footholds the Haza had in the New World, and the boyars had wanted to show their loyalties hadn't faded as they crossed the salt sea. They were all under The Salt now, but their stamp lingered on the city.

Took had lived there for over a year. Before that he'd spent a decade in Philadelphia, where they'd purged the mosaics but embraced the harsh, defensive lines of crenellated parapets and arrow-slit windows. He should be used to it by now, but sometimes he missed the low, easy sprawl of the towns out west, where he'd grown up... where the buildings didn't need to stake the sky.

"She wanted to speak to you," SSA West Crane said. The dim ghost of his reflection in the long, dark windows signed something and sat back in the big leather chair. "I didn't expect her to turn up at dawn."

"I think she turned up at midnight," Took said. "I'm not used to being nocturnal yet."

"Does it matter?" West asked in *that* voice, the one that was carefully uninflected to give the impression the question was free of weight when it wasn't at all. Took knew the voice. He used to be the one to use it. Now people used it on him. "So someone knows your address. What's wrong with that? Do you think she might tell someone else? That someone will find you that you don't want to find you?"

Yes.

Of course he did, Took thought bitterly. He bounced from hotel room to randomly chosen parking lot because he was afraid that the vampire who'd snatched him would track him down again. Sometimes he woke up, curled into the perimeter of that fucking box, and he was too scared to straighten himself out in case his feet hit cold metal and he breathed in the stench of his own body as it rotted.

In case his escape had been a dream. Or a trick.

"It sounds stupid when you say it," Took drawled as he turned around. He shrugged under West's curious stare. "I guess secrecy gets to be a habit, and after everything that happened after I... got back, it's been nice to leave the house without having to wade through the press."

West chuckled and took his glasses off. Without the heavy, square frames, the SSA's face looked younger, his eyes a ridiculous shade of blue. West was more pleasantly nondescript than handsome, but he had beautiful eyes. There had been a time when Took spent a fair amount of time appreciating those eyes.

"I doubt that will be a problem," West joked with a crooked smile. "No offense, Took, but you're old news."

Took tried to pin down the flicker of nostalgic attraction that fluttered in his gut, hold on to it, but it faded like a ghost. Once upon a time, he'd been pretty sure he could fall in love with West, or close enough to make him the better choice. Now he didn't know. They'd tried after Took got back, but…. Well, nobody wanted something that broken. Took couldn't hold that against West.

"Maybe not once people find out I'm working for the Waring parents," he said. "A VINE agent who wants to overturn one of VINE's big profile cases? That's newsworthy."

West surrendered to that point. "I won't give anyone else your address, then." He pointed at the chair opposite with the leg of his glasses. "Sit. What have you found out about the Waring case?"

"Nothing solid." Took walked over to the chair, but he leaned on the back of it instead of sitting down. "Nothing you can take to The Salt, just some dropped threads and gaps."

The spark of satisfaction made West's pretty eyes look mean for a second. "Things the original investigation missed?"

"Just because they didn't follow up on it, doesn't mean they should have," Took pointed out. "Maybe what they missed wasn't relevant. I don't know yet."

He did, but it was gut instinct, an itch he knew he was about to scratch, and that wasn't something you could present to The Salt.

West hissed in disappointment. "If you can prove the Biters didn't do due diligence on this," he said, "it would be very useful for me. Liam Waring still has influence. If he throws his weight behind me, certain obstacles could be removed."

"Like?"

West grimaced and sat back. He slid his glasses back on and the man Took had sort of thought he could love vanished behind the plastic-and-glass mask. "You know how hard it is for a breathing man to rise beyond where I am in VINE. The old guard… well, immortality causes a certain stratification of hierarchy. Sometimes it needs to be shaken up, and if the Waring case was a clusterfuck, well, there's plenty of senior agents who bet their career on the Biters' reputations. It wouldn't hurt to have the redeemed, relieved father speak out in my favor for one of those spots."

It was just politics, Took reminded himself, nothing personal. That didn't make him feel any better about it.

"I'm a Biter," he pointed out.

"You're the token human," West shot the old jibe on autopilot. His gaze cut down to Took's mouth and then away quickly as he corrected himself. "Or you were the token human."

There was a bitter edge to that acknowledgment. Took understood that. He could taste the old sour resentment in the back of his throat over the idea that he hadn't been a Biter. It might be hypocritical, since he hadn't *wanted* to join the division, but he had still earned his place.

Like it or not, they'd been the closest thing he had to a family.

But that was an old fight. It tracked from one side of their relationship to the other, worn deep from repetition, and Took didn't particularly want to have it again. He pushed himself up off the chair and straightened his shoulders.

"There's no sign of any wrongdoing or corruption," he said. "If something was missed, then it was by mistake, not from malice. I'm not interested in pinning blame on anyone."

"I don't need blame," West said. He smiled and spread his hands out in front of him. "Just an opportunity. If this isn't it, there'll be another. I'd never expect you to manufacture any evidence, Took. You know that. If there's anyone here on your side, it's me. Still."

The reminder made Took bite the inside of his cheek. He owed West, and not just because he'd been a piss-poor boyfriend before they broke up. It was West who'd sorted him out sanctuary here when the press attention in Philly had nearly driven him to distraction, and without his influence behind the scenes to counteract the psych reports, VINE would have dismissed Took months ago.

Gratitude was the least Took owed him. It wasn't West's fault that obligation felt like a stranglehold to Took. His family had wielded it like a weapon, and the echoes of it were still sharp as they battered against his brain.

"Be grateful for the roof over your head."

"You should appreciate the food we put in your stomach."

"If I was you, I'd be thankful that only broke your wrist."

"Just do as you're told, boy. You owe us that."

Took slammed the lid down on that—fuck the past—and clenched his jaw on the urge to be ungrateful. Not everyone was like his family. People really did deserve his thanks and didn't just expect them.

"I've just got threads," Took said. "Until I pull them, I don't know what's on the end… but I don't think any of this had to do with the Hunters."

For a heartbeat West looked surprised, then satisfied. "If you're right, Took," he said, "that's all the opportunity I'll need."

He got up from behind the desk and limped over to the door. The halt to his step caught Took off guard. Anything that changed while he was… gone… still did, as though his brain couldn't quite believe he'd missed so much.

"Keep me updated," West said as he pulled the door open and braced it. "Anything, no matter how small it seems. I might be able to use it to help Liam delay the execution. And Took. Where you live is already common knowledge in VINE. So if someone wanted to find out where you were?"

Tension caught at the back of Took's neck like a wire hooked into his spine. He clenched his jaw against the extension of his fangs in response to what his brain saw as a threat.

"He already does," West said. "And he's already here."

Of course he was. Took supposed it would be disingenuous to pretend he was surprised. He'd tossed a mystery and a challenge into Madoc's lap.

"And?"

"He wants to talk to you," West said. "I've put him off for now, to give you a chance to prepare yourself, but technically he's still your SSA. Unless you want to make that transfer request."

A year ago Took had needed that buffer. It wasn't entirely fair to West that it pissed him off now. Of course, Took thought dryly, when had he ever been entirely fair to West?

"He's a dhampir, not Medusa. I won't turn to stone just from looking at him."

"Are you having doubts?" West asked as he let the door close and sealed the room again. He sounded almost hopeful. It was hard to blame him. If Took was right, then being on his side was dangerous. "I know you think Madoc had reason to kidnap you—and I can't argue that he'd have liked to fuck you, he didn't bother to hide that—but just because he was one of the people that knew your schedule doesn't mean he did it. He knows he's not a cardinal anymore. He can't just take what he wants."

The hole in the center of Took's memory tried to spackle itself over with that theory. It wanted to accept it, to set the imagined events in stone as a memory. Took didn't know why he balked at it. This was his theory, his gut-check hunch. He'd accepted the Waring case because of that itch in his brain. Why couldn't he commit to Madoc's guilt?

He tried—again—to remember the woozy, blood-dehydrated days in the hospital after his rescue. Something had convinced him that Madoc could be his monster, but the line of thought was lost in a tangle of delusion and denial. He'd thought he was still alive, that it had been days—at a push, weeks—since he'd been taken. Exactly what triggered his suspicion of Madoc was lost in that jumble. All he could pinpoint was the moment when he'd opened his eyes and stared at the cracked old ceiling of his hospital room with an entire, logical case against Madoc nested in his brain.

It had made sense then. He supposed, on some level, it still did— not enough to convince him, but enough to make it hard to dismiss.

"Madoc always hated the word *can't*," he said dryly. "But like you said, he's still my SSA. If he wants to see me, I don't have a choice. Tell him he knows where to find me."

"Does he?" West asked, an edge to his voice.

Took reached past West to pull the door open. "I don't know," he said. "If he doesn't, I guess you could always give him my address."

Chapter Six

SIX GENERATIONS of Warings were buried in the Charleston dirt. On the worn gray headstones, fenced into their own plot, the ashes of their hearts were displayed in sealed lead urns sunk in under the names of the dead. The same slogan was carved into all the stones, just visible under the family name.

Life for the Living

"We already knew they were a family of bigots," Lawrence said. She squinted as though the moonlight bothered her eyes. It was the Kiss at work, the last defense of her soul as it lost the fight to keep her human. "What new information are we going to find here?"

"Nothing," Madoc said. He crouched down in front of the graves, his weight balanced on the balls of his feet. "It's just courtesy to visit the family first, isn't it?"

Lawrence snorted as though he'd said something odd, and stepped back. She stuck her hands in the pockets of her trousers and turned to survey the graveyard while she waited for him.

The stubs of two older stones on Debbie Waring's grave had been ground down level with the dirt. When she'd been put in the dirt, Life for the Living had been a posthumously defiant statement of support for breathing rights in a city where the rule of the undead had seemed immutable. She had, based on the history the Warings boasted, campaigned for the right of humans to take public office and had offered up her family home as a way station for Hunters.

Until recently that last had been mostly dismissed as family folklore, a statement of support for Hunters that was safely defanged by time… until Dominic's arrest. Seven slaughtered families in a staggered path that led from Charleston to San Antonio and a family legacy that tied to the Hunters made a tidy story.

Too tidy maybe?

"It would have been convenient if you'd not been so fervent about death, ma'am," Madoc murmured to the dead woman as he straightened back up. "Some answers would be useful around now."

Lawrence watched him out of the corner of her eye. Curiosity and a reluctance to actually ask warred on her face.

"Did you think there was a chance she might answer," she half joked, half asked as Madoc turned away and headed down the overgrown alleys between less well-tended graves. Spanish moss dangled from the upraised arms of an angel like a spooled-out soul, gray and unnerving in the moonlight. Lawrence fell in next to him. "That would be handy, if the dead could talk."

He glanced at her and raised an eyebrow. It took her a second to snort dismissively as she caught the mistake.

"Not like you," she said. "You know what I mean. The real, still dead."

Madoc reached absently for his medal, the silver cold under his fingers. He twisted it on the chain.

He'd been born dead—blue instead of white and cold despite the coat of blood. His mother had bruised air into him and chafed him warm with handfuls of bloody straw, desperate for something to survive the byre she'd hidden in. She'd been a surgeon's daughter, and she'd cleaned up enough pints of blood from the floor to know when too much had been lost. The job had been only half-done when she died.

Death had been his twin, his ally, and a loyal companion who never explained why they jilted him at that last smoky altar. It seemed odd that Debbie Waring's death was more "real" than his.

"If I wanted to talk to the dead, I wouldn't do it at their graveside," he said. "That would be like trying to interrogate someone by yelling at an empty suit."

Lawrence hesitated and nearly tripped over the step she hadn't quite finished. "But you could?" she asked. Her voice was suspicious. Took had always taken Madoc at his word, but Lawrence wasn't so sure of him. "Why don't we do it, then? If we can interrogate the dead, the spirit of the victim, that would make our jobs a lot easier."

Madoc tucked his medal back under his collar. It felt colder than it should, but that was just imagination. "Only once in history has magic lived up to its promise," he said. "The consultation of spirits has never led to a murderer's arrest, Lawrence, and it's more likely to generate a tragedy. Don't trust the dead."

It was her turn to expectantly raise her eyebrow at him as she waited.

"Present company excepted," she suggested eventually. The dull, background drone of mosquitoes picked up as they walked along the long, narrow moat that symbolically guarded the church from the undead. Lawrence swatted one off her neck, cursed, and slapped her arm to smear one against her skin. They didn't bother Madoc. Ichor didn't smell like food to them.

He flicked one of the bugs off her shoulder. "Never trust a predator when you're prey," he said. "Hunger erodes good intentions."

Lawrence scratched her shoulder with blunt, nude-pink nails. "I won't be prey much longer. Can I trust you then?"

For a moment Madoc considered the truth. Lawrence would always be prey to someone, because no matter how long she lived or how dangerous she was, there'd always be someone older and meaner. Even Madoc, old and mean enough to get by, bent the neck to the Salted Boyars. If Tepes ever found his way across the wide, barren sea, then Madoc would bend the knee. Again.

"Of course," he lied instead. The last thing he wanted to see when he looked at Lawrence was reality. He wanted to see the reflection of the better world she believed in. That idealism was part of why he'd picked her for the team, and he wanted her to keep it, as much of it as was safe. He abruptly changed the subject back to the case. "I want you to get in touch with Pally and dig into the Warings' background. Between the family legacy and Liam Waring's politics, we assumed extremist connections somewhere. However, once we caught Dom red-handed—and everything else—the court decided we didn't need to chase it down and muddy the waters. Focus on the weeks after Annabelle's disappearance. If she and Dom were somehow contacted, then maybe what happened to her was the hook someone used to bait him."

There was already a welt on Lawrence's shoulder. She scratched it again as she frowned. "That's just motive," she said. "It doesn't change what he did. All those people, Madoc, he still killed them."

"Maybe not alone."

"Where are you going?"

Madoc turned slightly and gestured toward the east at the surrounding streets. "The Aron family lived three blocks from here. They were murdered in the middle of dinner, their throats cut as they ate a chicken Kiev, and left there until Mr. Aron's law firm came to see what had happened to him."

Lawrence narrowed her eyes as she sifted through the files in her head. "It wasn't one of the cases VINE liked Waring for?"

"It was considered," he said. "But the Arons were breathing, until they weren't. All of Warings' other victims included at least one vampire. But… if we're looking for connections VINE might have missed, that's the one that stands out locally."

"So you *do* believe Took?" Lawrence asked. "You think we made a mistake?"

Her version of the question lacked the smug edge that West Crane had given it. It still made Madoc want to show fang, just from the reminder. He'd never liked West, but he'd always assumed it was because West had what Madoc wanted. Now neither of them did, and West was still a smug little bastard.

"We'll see," Madoc said. "Take the car. I'll make my own way."

Lawrence hesitated briefly as she rocked back on her heels. "I'd like to see him work sometime," she said stiffly. "Took. If he's that good, maybe I could learn something."

"Next time," Madoc promised… when he trusted himself not to moon over Took like a lovestruck, lustful idiot, or snap at him like a jilted never-quite-lover. It would be—was always—a coin toss. "For now, track down any communication between Waring's family and the Hunters, even sympathy expressed on a message board."

She looked disappointed but accepted his decision. "Any chance I could get Kit's viewpoint?" she asked.

Madoc resisted the frown that tried to settle onto his face. It wasn't that it was a bad idea—Kit Maguire was VINE's expert on the different Hunter factions—but the price of leadership was that some worries you ate so your team didn't have to be distracted. Kit's too-long stint undercover—for the last month with only brusque sporadic check-ins that he was alive—was one of those.

"He's still in Casper," he said. "We can't risk his cover with unnecessary contact. It's dangerous enough."

There was a flicker of more-than-professional disappointment in Lawrence's eyes at the decision. Madoc made a quiet note of it. If she thought her dalliance with Kit had been anything other than a bad idea or a one-night stand—or a secret—that could come back to bite the team later.

And look at that, he thought dryly to himself, now he could disapprove of inter-team relationships without being a hypocrite. At least until Took realized that whatever had happened to him hadn't changed the fact that he was made for VINE.

"Pally it is," she said. "I guess I do the talking with anyone connected to Hunters."

"Probably wise," Madoc said mildly. For some reason, of all of them, humans could always see the predator in the old vampire. Not that Pally ever made more than a token effort to hide it. They reached the gates that walled the dead away from the rest of the world. The Eclipse was parked at the curb, the hemlock-treated windows only lightly tinted in reaction to the moonlight. He tossed Lawrence the keys.

He waited until Lawrence was in the car—an old, sometimes bad, habit of chivalry—before he crossed the road. It was nearly midnight, the zenith of darkness, and Madoc could feel the sun's lock on his soul loosen, but not fully. The night wasn't freedom from the warden's locks—he was just around the corner—but he'd looked away for a second.

The uneasy union of America—the dead and the breathing, the blow-ins and the ones whose roots were buried deep—was balanced on the compromise of twilight. Diurnal and nocturnal met in the middle, where none of them were exactly happy with it. Usually by midnight, Madoc was buried in paperwork or strategy meetings. It felt good to taste the hot night air on his tongue as he walked.

He could taste the warm bodies behind the walls—the aroma of blood mixed with the spice of sweat or sex, a nightmare tang of fear adrenaline behind one window and the cured edge of insomnia a few doors down, the heady pulse of blood and endorphins that leaked, along with music and laughter, from the neon-lit clubs along the main street. Some vampires spent their nights mourning the varied tastes of mortal cuisine, but Madoc had grown to savor the subtle varieties that spiced blood.

Although he had to admit he still dreamed of rarebit sometimes—the click of his gran's best knife on the carving board as she carved the sharp cheese, the dense, brown bread toasted over the fire, and the heat of it in his mouth as he chewed. There hadn't been much kindness to his grandmother, certainly not for her wayward daughter's bastard, but what there was, she doled out morsel by morsel in that kitchen.

Not, he thought dourly as he padded from shadow to shadow farther into the city, that there was any psychological reason to dwell on people who didn't love him tonight.

THE ARON house was tall and narrow, old enough to have been squeezed carelessly into a plot between two larger houses. The clapboard siding had been blue in the crime-scene pictures, but it had been repainted with a fresh, bright coat of sage—probably by whomever had inherited the property. It was hard enough to sell a house where a murder had been committed, never mind one that still looked identical to the old pictures. The lights were on, and bright gleams peeked through the narrow windows.

Madoc climbed the narrow steps to the cracked-open door. He stood for a second and listened to the house. The markers of Took that he'd gotten used to were gone—no heartbeat, no soft murmur of blood in his veins—but he still muttered to himself as he worked. It was a stop-go commentary that narrated, dismissed, and edited whatever theory his brain had put together.

"Hide-and-seek is for children," Madoc said as he entered the open-plan shell of the house. Then, since he'd been put out today, he added, "Or lovers."

Took looked up from the folder he held in one hand and tucked his thumb into the papers to mark his place. For a second, it was like he'd never been gone. How many times had Madoc walked into a crime scene and found Took already there, in a tailored gray suit paired with polished black combat boots and hair that looked as though he hadn't brushed it since he left school.

"It didn't take you long," he said.

"You know monsters," Madoc said as he nudged the door shut behind him. "I know you."

He hadn't meant it as a jab, but it still made Took grimace and run his tongue over his lips behind his teeth.

"Kind of the same thing these days," he said. His gaze flicked over to Madoc. "No offense."

"Some taken," Madoc drawled sardonically.

It made Took flash a short-lived grin, just a glimpse of recessed fangs behind full lips before the humor faded. Took was in his thirties—Madoc was pretty sure of that, although he usually only kept track of decades—and he'd lived some of them hard enough to leave marks. Lines were grooved into his forehead and deeper ones creased around his eyes when he smiled. Despite that, he still looked almost boyish, all taut jawline and clear, guilelessly blue eyes.

The coin flip in his head landed. Lovestruck and lustful it was, Madoc supposed.

"So what did you want to talk to me about?" Took asked as he closed the folder, thumb still in place to mark that one page. He couldn't hold his blankly curious look under Madoc's narrow-eyed glare, and he let that faded, oddly sweet smile flicker over his face again as he gave in. "You talked to Sheriff Anderson about the missing girl?"

"Annabelle Franklin," Madoc said.

Took paused for a second and then gave Madoc a quick nod of acknowledgment. Sometimes he forgot the person behind the puzzle.

"Annabelle," Took repeated aloud. "She disappeared a month before the Aron family were murdered. Right there."

He pointed to a patch of empty floor. Madoc's mind helpfully layered the crime scene pictures over the space and filled the empty room with the ghosts of the Arons' furniture. Took was out by a foot. The dining table had been angled into the corner of the room. It was glass and the blood had spilled off it onto the floor in sheets. Madoc hadn't been here when the scene was fresh, but he'd swung by during the Waring investigation. The dead had been taken away and blood sopped up, but the stains had still been on the floor and the white walls. He still smelled the death on the air.

"And she probably knew Waring," Madoc said. He smirked at Took's sidelong glance. "VINE did exist before you came along, Agent. I *do* know how to do this. So what is your theory? That Waring made his bones by killing humans before he graduated to murdering vampires? I don't think that's what his parents had in mind when they asked your oversight on the case."

Took scratched his cheekbone. "I told them when they asked me to do this, I won't manufacture evidence. If what I find doesn't suit them, that's their problem. Besides, I haven't said that's what happened. It would make sense. His first kill is impulsive—someone he knows but who isn't going to be missed. Second time is closer to what works for him, but not quite as difficult a target. Most killers don't have their brand down with the first few victims, but Waring seemed to know exactly what to do from the start. Unless VINE missed some of his early kills. But look at this first."

He gestured for Madoc to follow him as he headed around the waist-high island—trekked his boots right through Madoc's imagined puddle of blood—and into the glossy kitchen. It had been refitted. The parents had died at the table—peas and slices of ham in a broth of blood on placemats in front of them—but the children had fled into the kitchen. The bodies were still missing, but they'd found rope and cracked tiles and one pastel-painted little-girl nail dug into the *inside* of a cupboard.

"The scene was cleaned a year ago," Madoc pointed out. "It looks like the kitchen was ripped out and refitted. I doubt there's anything to see in here."

"Some things haven't changed," Took said. He stopped in front of the sink and laid the folder, opened to his kept page, on the draining board. A glossy, blown-up photo was clipped to the paper, screen-grabbed from some social media account, based on the caption that shorthanded across the bottom. *This is one of the photos from Annabelle Franklin's phone. She took it just before the first time she ran away from home.*

"That's a lot of teenager's selfies to look at."

"She didn't take many," Took said. "Dom was only all the time. He made vlogs, short films—"

"We saw them," Madoc said. "They didn't help his case."

The glossy, overlit videos, mostly filmed in the Waring kitchen or his mother's cafe, were a call to action shy of Hunter recruitment, but only just. Waring hid his intent behind "what if," but he'd already been on VINE's radar before he disappeared.

"That was homegrown bigotry," Took said, "not Hunter-led rhetoric."

"Our analysts disagreed," Madoc said. They hadn't, not all of them. The majority thought there was no evidence that the Hunters hadn't recruited Waring, and with Waring sitting in a cell with the blood of a dead family still set on his clothes, that had been enough to convince them. "Is that relevant, or are you just showing off?"

Took ducked his chin and scratched the back of his neck. Tufts of blond hair stuck out between his knuckles.

"Bit of both," he admitted sheepishly. "Look."

He tapped his finger against the page. Madoc leaned in closely to study it over Took's shoulder. A pretty girl with brown hair and big brown eyes grinned into the camera, her arm slung around a skinny girl with dishwater hair and the hunched shoulders of someone who didn't want to take up space. Annabelle Franklin must have been the one who'd taken the picture. It had been on her phone. She looked like she was sorry to have wandered into the shot, but her smile was pretty, even with her lips folded over her braces. Behind her a window was open into a small, sunlit garden, where an ostentatious magnolia in full bloom blocked any other details.

"In the big city with my BFFs!" Madoc read out.

"It was tagged Charleston," Took told him. He stepped away from Madoc and took two long steps over to the wall where he flicked the lights off. The high wattage took a moment to fade as the dull glow of the filament died reluctantly, and then Madoc stared out into the garden. Moonlit instead of sunlit, but the magnolia still blocked the view of the street behind.

"Are you sure you aren't a sorcerer?" he asked. Took snorted a laugh, but Madoc could taste suspicion in the back of his throat. He glanced from the photo to the window and wondered how much money the Waring family could scrape out of the political coffers. Who could they buy? It worked its way into his voice, a scratch of accusation that was blunt in the sterile, dressed kitchen. "This is beyond luck. Nobody else made this connection, Bennett. Not one fucking member of VINE even heard of Appleton. What made you go there? Who made you go there?"

There was a pause. Then Took abruptly flicked the lights back on, and the actinic glare was enough to make Madoc blink as his eyes tried to adjust.

"Go to hell," Took said.

Madoc knuckled the water out of his eyes and turned to look at Took. "That's not an answer," he said. "I know you wouldn't… stage… the investigation, but if someone else did?"

"And I just followed along, like a dog on a leash? Might be an issue with Agent Lawrence, but I know what I am doing."

"So does she," Madoc defended his new agent sharply. "I'm still your SSA, Bennett, and I did not approve this investigation—"

"It was approved, though."

"I don't care. How did you find Annabelle Franklin?" His temper had slipped enough that it crawled into his voice, and there was an edge of command to the words. It was somewhere past the amygdala jerk of a drill sergeant's bark, but not within the rungs of a boyar's silky, "this is your idea" compulsion.

It should have worked—not as well as when Took was human and Madoc's voice had been the goad that got a dazed agent back on his feet after a car crash, but enough to drag an answer out of him, enough to leave Madoc's gut sour with regret that he'd jerked strings as though Took were his puppet and not his friend. Instead Took just worked his jaw to the side as though his eardrums had popped on a flight and rubbed the side of his head. Madoc wasn't sure if he was relieved or not. Guilt might be the price he'd pay for a good answer.

"I investigated," Took said. "You should try it."

He grabbed the folder from the counter and stalked out of the kitchen, toward the front door. Madoc glared at the span of gray cotton over broad shoulders and refused to chase after Took like some abject suitor. He reached inside instead, through the crack in his soul, to where the smoke and shadows lived.

The world went cold around him, the colors stripped down to tones of gray, and slow. His bloodline dragged at him, a net that wanted to wash him away to drown in the sterile salt sea before it ever got him home, and it took effort to move against the current.

All he'd wanted was the cold shadow, but the effort of it let the smoke slip away from him. It was hot and dry, the cloy of burned apples strong in his throat, but it made it easier to push against the pull of his blood. The walls faded out as he stepped through them and stalked around the house.

Things moved out in the dark. He could hear the click and growl of them, the massive, bony outline of something's skull against the sky as it turned. A star flared and died in the dry pit of an eye socket, and even Madoc's mind, armored and set by years and blood, creaked under the weight of the brief illumination.

In the Old Country there were haunts and dark, strange creatures in the shadows of the world, but they knew to skirt the heels of vampires. The gods and spirits native to American soil saw no reason for that. It was one reason that the Anakim had been forced into the Accord. Under the shadow of Tepes's wing, the living would never have massed enough influence to force a compromise. They certainly never had back home.

The great thing caught sight of him and raised a thin, stringy arm with too many joints. Madoc stepped out of the shadows as it pointed a claw in what might have been a greeting or a threat. He preferred not to think about which.

The weight of his bones settled back under his skin, the warmth of the night air sticky on his skin, as he turned solid on the front porch. Took yanked the front door open. Surprise flashed over his face as he saw Madoc already there. He opened his mouth to say something, but Madoc grabbed the collar of his shirt and shoved him back into the house.

He kicked the door shut behind him.

"You want to hand in your badge and play private eye? Do it," he rasped out as he let go of Took's shirt. "You want to be a VINE agent, then you better be willing to justify this. It doesn't look good that you picked some ghost connection that none of us knew about."

Took stepped back and impatiently yanked his shirt straight. "Apples," he said shortly.

For a second, Madoc thought Took had caught the smell of the smoke on the air. He licked the taste of ashes from his fangs. "What?"

"I'm not going to just take poisoned bait," Took said. He crossed his arms and leaned back against the staircase. The folder dangled from his fingers. "Appleton isn't any of the leads the Warings served up for him. It was apples. Have you ever heard of Apple and Pear Teas?"

Madoc clenched his jaw. He hadn't missed this part, the walk-through of how smart Took had been with his puzzle. Okay, that was a lie. He'd missed nearly all of Took, but it wasn't as though he'd ever had the patience to sit through the "Look How Clever I Am" show. He'd understood Took's need to establish himself when everyone else was a vampire, but never enjoyed it. "I don't need a lesson in profiling, Bennett. Just give a good reason that you, and only you, found this link. You're good, but you're not magic."

"No, I'm not," Took said. He slid down the banister and sat on the stairs, long legs stretched out in front of him. "But VINE did a good job on the investigation. There weren't that many angles you hadn't already nailed down, so that made it easier. I just chased the ragged ends… and the apples. There was a vlog—"

Glass shattered and a heavy brown bottle rolled over the expensively laid floor. A trickle of liquid spilled over the waxed surface, and the sweet-bitter smell of accelerant and juniper filled the air. It hung for a moment—long enough for Took to lurch to his feet and Madoc to tackle him back down onto the stairs—and then it ignited with a deceptively soft *whoof*.

Fire spun toward the ceiling, and licks of soot marked over the blistered paint and spilled out over the floor. The heat of it scorched Madoc's side, leather and metal tight around his ribs, and stung against the exposed skin of his throat and jaw. He tucked his arm around Took's head and swore into the hollow of his throat.

More projectiles smashed and splashed against the outside of the house. The heat banked and pitched, the sudden alarmed squall of a siren somewhere in the house a too-late warning of fire.

"Get off," Took growled as he shoved Madoc's shoulders and hitched his hips to roll him away. He flinched as sparks hit him and left shriveled pocks on his shirt and pinprick blisters across his cheekbones. "I don't need to be protected. What the hell?"

Madoc laughed with a strangled sound that scraped at his throat. "Apples," he said. Old—very old—rage clawed at the back of his mind and tried to get out. It was the smoke, even though it tasted like paint and gas instead of lantern oil and the charred boughs of the orchard. He scrambled to his feet and grabbed Took's sleeve to drag him up. "I guess it meant something to someone other than you. Move."

He gave Took a shove to get him to take that first step.

"We could go out the back," Took said. He pulled his gun and held it down against his thigh as he took the stairs two at a time. "Fire rises."

"I know what fire does," Madoc said roughly. Inside, the flames had started to crawl up the walls and the floor was already pitted and bowed as the heat steamed it, and outside, the fire flickered and flashed as it caught on the wooden slats. It sounded hungry as it bit into the house with a hushed, crackly grumble like a demon's stomach. "They came armed with holy oil and fire. They'll have a plan of attack. The back will be covered."

It shouldn't have been enough. Madoc could side-step the fire, into the cold shadow and smoke world that lay alongside it, and slip away, like a dead fish against the blood-tide. Even if the bone and star-stuff creature had lingered—and it could have been centuries to it, or a heartbeat—he could slip those stripped raw fingers. He had before. The boyars had been forced to a compromise, not a defeat, when they signed the Accord.

He would be alone, though. Even the eldest among them couldn't take a passenger into otherworld, where the gods, Gods, and demons lived. Attempts to do so had been fatal for the passenger, disfiguring for the guide. Madoc wouldn't—couldn't—lose Took like that.

Was that love, he wondered, or just old, singed guilt?

"Nobody knew I would be at the Aron house," Took said. He looked back over his shoulder as he reached the top of the stairs. "You?"

Madoc hesitated for a moment and then admitted, "Lawrence." It felt like a betrayal, even as he added, "She can be trusted."

"Me, myself, and I can be trusted," Took said. He paused to cough and looked surprised at the bark of it. "I thought one advantage of death would be no more coughing."

"You don't *need* to breathe," Madoc said. He could feel the tickle of it in the back of his throat—the prickled heat in his chest—but his body mended before any of that became a cough. "But you still do, and smoke irritates, especially when the holy oil has filled the air with juniper and myrrh."

He opened a door with his elbow. It was the master bedroom. This part of the house hadn't been part of the murder downstairs, so none of the violence had made it up here, and the room had just been stripped instead of redecorated. The carpet on the floor was lightly worn, and the ghosts of old furniture were marked out in dust on the walls.

Madoc stuck to the wall of the room as he made his way to the window. The last thing he wanted was to give anyone a clear shot. Smoke hung overhead in a dour gray pall. He pushed the heavy brocade curtain back with one finger and peered through the crack down into the garden.

The magnolia wouldn't betray anyone's location again. The fragile white flowers were withered, and fire crawled up the trunk and turned the spindly branches to kindling. Two men in black, faces masked, sprayed the back of the house with accelerant from tanks strapped to their thighs.

"Hunters," he said.

"Waring wasn't a Hunter recruit," Took insisted.

"Not the point," Madoc countered. "We've had a lot of chatter about an uptick in Hunter activity down the coast over the last few years. They've been more aggressive than they used to be."

"When I'm investigating this case? It's the point," Took said. He ducked through the door and made his way around the room to the other side of the window. His voice sounded odd, slightly strangled. Madoc supposed it had been a while since he'd been in the field. "They shut the water off."

Madoc hissed under his breath. He fished his phone from his pocket and called Lawrence.

"Fire strike at the Aron house," he said. A quick hand sign told Took to stay in place while Madoc went out into the hall and opened a door into a front-facing bedroom. Smoke hung lazily in the air and glazed the window with grime. He peered onto the street outside, at a row of firmly closed curtains and a man in black with a machine gun cradled lazily in his arms. It would be enough to kill a young vampire, and even a boyar would be slowed down if they got cut in half by high-velocity customized bullets. "Four hunters. Fire and silver. They've cut the water, so make sure the fire department is prepared—"

"Sir?" Lawrence spluttered. He heard tires screech in the background and horns blare for a second. Then she flicked the siren on to drown them out. "What happened?"

"Get here in time to take one alive, and we'll know," Madoc said. He stared at the man outside as he tried to pick out identifying details in the featureless black. Something happened down the road—a man's voice raised in worry—and the man turned to fire off a quick burst of bullets. Someone screamed and doors slammed. "We have injured. I—"

Glass smashed in one of the other rooms. Madoc turned toward the noise, and out of the corner of his eye, he saw the man outside do the same. The gun was hitched up onto his hip, ready to fire.

"Wait for backup," he clipped out to Lawrence. "I don't need a dead agent."

Or not another one, he thought grimly as he headed back to Took, because you only got lucky enough to have them come back once.

Chapter Seven

VAMPIRES' FIRST suspects were always Hunters, just as the first word in a Hunter's mouth when they raised the hue and cry was "Vampire." When you needed someone to blame, why not someone you hated? It was easy. Sometimes it was right.

Not this time.

Took leaned his shoulder against the wall and took aim through the window. He pulled the trigger, and one of the men below staggered as it hit his shoulder. He tripped over his own foot and went down in the dirt with a grunt. His hand flew up to his shoulder, groped at the heavy black fabric, and he laughed when he pulled it away clean.

"Stupid fucking wetmouth," he yelled as he scrambled to his feet. The mask over his mouth muffled his voice. "Didn't have Kevlar in your day, eh?"

He hitched the wand of the tanker up and aimed accelerant in a wild arc up the side of the house. It splashed over the windowsill and flicked droplets onto Took's jacket. The fire scuttled up the side of the house after the spray of fuel. A spark caught on Took's cuff, singed, and died.

"Fucker," the other man yelled as he backed away. He swiped at his mask with a gloved hand. "Keep it low, you moron."

The moron didn't listen.

Took aimed again, took a breath, and held it. He probably didn't need to anymore, he supposed, but being a good shot was muscle memory—habit, training, anger. His finger tightened and the bullet hit the slim metal tanker strapped to the man's thigh, exposed by the tight line of the strained hose. Accelerant spilled out in a wet gush down the man's leg, like he'd pissed himself with gas.

"Son of a bitch," the man spluttered as he landed on his ass in the grass again. The spray of fuel trickled down the wand onto him. "Stupid undead thing. Don't even know when to lie down and burn."

His friend stepped away from him in disgust. He kept his stream of gas aimed into the hot, wild heart of the fire. "Would you just—"

Took stripped his jacket off and tied it roughly around his gun.

"What are you doing?" Madoc snapped as he came back into the room.

"Improvising." Took stuck his jacket into the flames that flickered along the windowsill. The fabric lit quickly as the drops of gasoline flared and wicked the fire through the tightly woven fabric. One more suit down, Took thought dryly, as he turned the bundle to light the other side.

"Bennett, don't," Madoc snapped.

The words pushed at the inside of Took's head, a pressure against his eardrums that needed equalizing. He shook his head as much to dislodge that ache as to disagree with Madoc.

"Hunters know about backsplash," he told Madoc and pitched the flaming ball of metal and silk-woven linen out the window. It hit the man in the chest as he struggled to his knees and he went up like a firework. Took's tongue flicked against the edges of his adrenaline-extended fangs and he tasted the thick, treacle-sweet of ichor. "And this vampire knows Kevlar is no good against fire."

The man screamed and rolled on the grass as he batted frantically at his arms and crotch. It only spread the fire around like a halo. His companion took a step toward him, and a damp spot of fluid on his boot sparked and spluttered over the sole. He jumped back and stamped his foot on the grass. The black rubber melted in long, tangled strings.

"You could have waited for backup," Madoc said as he dragged Took away from the window. "Now we just have more fire to deal with, no water, and you just threw your gun into the garden."

Took crouched down and unclipped his holdout from the ankle holster. Paranoia could have its uses. After Heather Waring turned up on his doorstep, he needed the extra security. There was a narrow stake holstered in his other boot, but he couldn't tell Madoc about that... just in case.

He shoved the sick tangle of suspicion and guilt out of his way as he stood back up, flashed the gun at Madoc, and tried to ignore the raw, blistered meat of his fingers. They would heal like everything else, eventually. "One problem solved," he said. "Your turn."

Something exploded outside with a hollow bang that rattled the windows. Took stepped back and looked out. The man still lay in the burned starburst, his leg and side a charred mess. He was still alive, but barely.

Took's brain caught on that. It was important. There was no time to work out how yet, so Took tucked it away in the back of his head. *Later.* The other man was at the back of the garden as he yanked and hammered his fist on the gate. He kicked it with a heavy, half-melted boot as he looked back over his shoulder at the house.

"Madoc," Took said. "They locked their men in. Why—"

"Life for the living," Madoc muttered. Beneath their feet the fire glowed through the floor, the heat hot enough to crack the plaster. "How much influence do the Hunters have in Charleston?"

"There's no Hunter cells in Charleston," Took said. He ignored Madoc's snort of disagreement. The move to Charleston had been done when he was still… off his game… but he'd done his due diligence on the city. He knew how to sniff out Hunters and their haunts, nearly as well as he could vampires. In the end they weren't that different, although both sides would slit his throat for saying so. "Hunter money, sure, but people like Waring are the face of the anti-Accord movement in Charleston. They don't like you—"

"Us."

Took swallowed the reminder with a mouthful of hot air and acrid smoke. The seasoning might have made it more palatable than usual.

"They don't like *us*," he corrected himself as they skirted the fire-weakened spots on the floor and got out into the hall. The staircase was gone, and the banister poked out into the smoke like a stained, broken bone. Heat soaked into his skin, but it didn't feel like living warmth, more like a fever that would cook him from inside. He suddenly missed sweat. "But the focus is on politics and policies, not stakes and garlic. There's some violence, but mostly they stick to rhetoric, not Molotov cocktails."

Madoc absorbed that as he opened a door with his shoulder. A wall of heat and smoke shoved out with almost physical force. It had been a child's room. The furniture was gone, but it was still painted sky blue and interrupted with multicolored balloons stickered over the walls. Smoke had grimed the blue down to a cloudy day, and the balloons peeled off the sweaty paint as though they were about to deflate.

Sometimes the tragedy of a case caught Took by surprise. He licked his lips and looked away from the ruin of someone's dream bedroom.

"Can we get out?" he asked.

"We have armed men out the front," Madoc said. "You sure they aren't Hunters?"

Took peered down into the street. He could feel the heat off the glass like an oven, and his skin was tight and painful as he reddened. The butt of the gun was tucked into the man's armpit, and he held the weight of it with casual confidence. Other than the bandana pulled up over his mouth and nose, his gear could pass for streetwear at first glance. Under the tight leather jacket, Took would bet he had on a nondescript cotton shirt or a worn T-shirt with a funny slogan. That was popular too. People rarely suspected a man in a funny shirt of being dangerous.

"Him, maybe," he admitted.

Madoc looked smug for a second. He wiped it away on the sleeve of his shirt as the smoke got dense and hot enough to drag a wet cough out of his throat. His skin was flushed, more red than pink, and cracked painfully around his mouth and nose. Fat, wet blisters ran in stripes up his throat and splattered along the side of his face.

It would heal. Took had seen him hurt worse. It still made him care more than was probably safe... or fair.

"Okay," Took said. "What are they going to do? Why lock their own men in the garden? It won't burn."

Madoc frowned and the long blisters pulled tight against his skin, but the screech of an approaching siren cut through whatever he was about to say. Took ducked his head to peer up the road and saw the sleek black police cars fishtail onto the narrow road just ahead of the fire engine.

"Backup is here," Took said with relief. "We might get a ladder down."

"No," Madoc said abruptly. "We get out now. That's why they cut the water. Get down. Get out of the line of fire. Let me deal with the Hunter."

"Fuck off," Took said. He hesitated as he struggled to swallow with no moisture in his throat. "Remember Michigan?"

Madoc did. He hesitated for a moment. "You're not Kit," he said.

"No," Took agreed. "You can tell, because I don't want to die."

He never had. That was one of the solid threads he *could* remember. Even at the worst, he hadn't been able to let go of the hope for tomorrow. It hadn't felt like a strength then.

"Good," Madoc said. "Because if you do, I'll find you again and drag you back by the scruff of your neck."

Tension plucked the air between them. Last time Madoc had said something like that, Took had banned him from the hospital. The time before that, he'd asked West to move in with him.

This time Madoc didn't give Took a chance to ruin it. He reached up to his collar—a good faith tap of his fingers to St. Michael—and smashed out the window with his elbow. The hot glass exploded out with a pop, a starburst of fragments with the fire reflected in each of them, and he went out through the charred frame. Flames licked around him as he dropped to the ground, charred lines etched into his sleeves and over his thighs.

Hesitation caught Took for a second. He didn't have his Biter's uniform. All he had was an expensive ruined suit and good boots. It wouldn't be enough to protect him from the fire. The scars under his shirt flared with the dull, hot memory of pain. Sunlight made them burn, but this would be worse.

Contempt stung more. He'd live. Or not die anymore. His place had always been on Madoc's heels, and then he'd only been human. If he couldn't do it now, with all the undying advantages of the undead, maybe he was as broken as West thought.

He tightened his grip on the gun—not that he thought his scorched tendons could let go right now—and vaulted out the window.

The fire hurt about as much as he expected. Took had found out early on that death shut off the brain's gateway control. There was no switch to cut off the feedback from blistered skin, and the nerves gamely regenerated, like it or not.

Took's hit the ground, tucked, and... for a second his brain went blank. What way had Kit gone when he hit the ground in Michigan? Left or right. Fuck, if he picked wrong, he'd end up under Madoc's feet and screw them both.

He went left. No one tripped over him.

There were ashes in his eyes, hot and gritty under his lids, and his ears rang with chatter from scorched eardrums. As he got his feet back under him, Took scrubbed his fist over his eyes enough to give him a scratch-blurred field of vision.

His ears were fine, he realized. The pulsed chatter that echoed in the bones of his head came from the Hunter's assault rifle as he trained it on Madoc. Despite the protection of reinforced leather over Madoc's vital organs, the bullets chipped bone and shredded flesh. Madoc had his arms up to protect his head from a kill shot, but he couldn't fight the percussion of impact that drove him, reluctant step by step, back into the fire.

Even through the mask, Took could make out the sneer that curdled the Hunter's face and the hot glitter in his eyes. The satisfaction of the sadist—it made them stupid.

"If they'd told me I'd get to kill the likes of you," the man laughed over the rattle of gunfire, "I'd have done this for free."

Took took aim at his head first. The curve of skull made a good target under the streetlights, but the hood would be armored. A bullet wouldn't kill him. It would just rattle his brain and put anyone else in the street at risk from a stray shot. Took dropped his arm to below the knee and fired.

The bullet ripped through the Hunter's boot and punched out the other side. Blood and scraps of leather sprayed over the pavement. The Hunter screamed in pain and fumbled his gun as his leg went from under him. One bullet went wild and blew out the windscreen of a parked Porsche. The persistent drone of a car alarm joined the cacophony.

Took staggered to his feet and braced his gun with both hands. This time he aimed at the head.

"Drop the gun," he rasped out. His voice sounded like someone else's. It was rough and cracked, raw from the smoke. "Or I drop you. Tell whoever's in the car to get out."

The Hunter choked out a ragged laugh as he painfully straightened up and balanced precariously on one foot. Blood dripped from his shredded boot and puddled on the pavement.

"Better than handing myself in to VINE," he said with jagged bravado. "At least death is clean. I won't end up infected with your disease."

He clumsily tried to lift the muzzle from where it threatened the pavement. Took curled his finger around the trigger of his gun, ready to take the shot if he needed to.

"There are rules against turning the unwilling," Madoc interrupted as he straightened up and limped forward. He spat onto the ground, a splatter of black lost on the charred concrete, and bared his fangs at the man. "But a corpse has no rights. You might Rise, you might not. We'll still have our way with you."

The Hunter spluttered out a curse and waved the rifle in a wild arc. He stumbled back toward the car, his ruined foot barely able to touch the ground. His eyes, white rimmed in the letterbox view of his balaclava, cut down the road as a black Eclipse screeched up.

"We're done here anyhow," he said. "Fuck you, Dead Man."

He lurched backward toward the open door of the car. Took spat a curse through clenched teeth and took the shot. The bullet hit the Hunter in the ribs and threw him sideways off his precarious balance. He grabbed the door, arm hooked through the open window, and the car peeled away with him half-in and half-out. The bloody ruin of his foot bounced and dragged along the tarmac as the loose door battered and jarred the dangled man. He managed to pull himself in as they reached the end of the road, and the door slammed shut as the driver swung sharply around the corner.

Took swore in frustration. "They'll find him dead tomorrow," he predicted sourly. "Idiot."

"If he were smart, he'd have gotten into a different line of work," Madoc said. He dropped to his knees on the cracked pavement and doubled over, his hand pressed to the tender scars that pocked his lean stomach and chest. "I forgot how much this hurts."

Took shoved the gun into his waistband and limped over to him. He put his hand on Madoc's shoulder and tried not to lean on him. Worry picked at him with cold fingers.

"Don't do it again, then," he said. Despite his best intentions, he slid his hand around to cup the back of Madoc's neck. He could feel the delicate ridge of Madoc's spine and the heavy clench of muscle under soft, fire-warm skin. "Do you need someone to call Pally?"

Madoc retched and spat up a sour goo of black bile and shredded tissue. It splattered over his knees and the ground. A stray bullet that had gotten caught somehow, instead of punched straight through his body like the rest, hit the ground with a dull chink. It glittered in the vomit, silver-alloy bright as the ichor clotted and scabbed around it.

"If I *can* answer that question," he said as he straightened up, fists braced on his slimed knees. "You don't need to ask it."

Lawrence scrambled out of the Eclipse, gun in hand and VINE-issue body armor half fastened around her torso. The ID sprayed across the front—a stenciled white BTR-27—had been Took's the last time he looked. It was just the code for human, so the other Biter agents could factor that info into tactical decisions, but it still flicked Took's ego on the raw. He looked away from her as she paused in the middle of the road, her eyes focused toward the end of the road as she barked orders into a radio.

"Bennett," Madoc said as he grabbed Took's wrist. He broke off as he gagged and had to spit again, with a choked curse mixed in the bile. His fingers tightened hard enough to hurt as he cleared his throat of obstruction. "Luke! Stop the tanker before they hook it up."

The use of his real name caught Took off guard. It had been years since that had felt like *him*, but apparently some habits were ingrained deeper than identity. The urgency in Madoc's order pushed Took into motion. He loped down the street toward the fire truck, hand raised to flag down the tall, soft-faced woman in the chief's jacket.

"VINE!" At least this time he had some sort of actual authority behind him. "Don't hook the tanker up."

The chief pushed the visor of her helmet up and glared at him. She had a soft, round face, but her eyes were hard and impatient. "Water's off," she said. One gloved finger jabbed toward the still-flaming house. "Without the tanker, we gotta spit the fire out. So get out of my way and let me do my job."

There was a reason Madoc was in command. Took could follow a twisted mind down whatever broken path it took, but strategy and tactics weren't his strength. He'd only *just* put the pieces together.

"Tanker's compromised," he spat out between his fangs. "You want to use it? Tap it first."

She frowned dubiously at him. "I don't know your face," she said. "I know the local VINE boys."

"You know me?" Madoc asked from behind Took. He braced his elbow on Took's shoulder and put his weight on it. His body still felt hot, almost alive, and the sour-sweet tang of ichor on his clothes made Took's throat ache. The flash of surprise on the chief's face was enough of an answer. "Tap the tanker."

It took a moment, but she finally grimaced and gave in. "Fine," she grumbled. "But any extra property damage? That's on VINE."

She turned around and broke into a jog as she barked orders at the crew by the tanker. Whatever doubts *she* had about their request, she didn't appreciate being questioned in turn. She cut short the frustrated queries from the other firefighters and scrambled up the welded-on ladder to crack the seal on the tanker herself.

The liquid that she dipped out in the palm of her hand looked like water. From the sudden blankness that settled over the chief's face, she didn't agree. She lifted wet fingers to her nose and grimaced at whatever she smelled.

"Back it up!" She scrambled a few steps down the ladder and jumped the rest of her way to the ground. The other firefighters hesitated as she stripped her gloves off. Her hands were latticed with old scars, pink against her dark skin, and she spun her finger in a "get a move on" gesture. "Get it the fuck off this street. Right now!"

"What is it?" Madoc asked as he finally took his weight off Took's shoulder.

The chief shot him a black, angry look. It probably wasn't aimed at them, but Took didn't envy whoever she was angry at. She wiped her hands on her pants and checked her sleeves.

"Contaminated," she said. "Ethanol. We sprayed that on the fire, we'd have all been dead. Just like whatever shithead did this when I find him."

She gave her crew a bleak, furious once-over and then stalked away. "Move your asses! Get this goddamn thing out of here. Tap the sewers. Better that shit than this shit." She smacked her hand against the side of the tanker to underline her point as it started to roll. "Move it!"

As the crew scrambled to get the tanker moved and the neighbors started to spill out onto the street now the gunman was gone, Took sagged and sat down on the curb. His hands were still raw and blistered, but they'd start to heal soon enough.

Lawrence jogged over to join them. The thin leather soles of her brogues were deformed from the heat, and chunks of tar stuck to the sides where the tarmac had gone soft.

"What happened here?" she demanded. "Who was in that car, and why did they want to burn this street?"

An hour ago Took would have been confident he could give her at least an outline of an answer. Now he ignored her.

"I missed something," he said. Unsaid, pinched between the teeth that he still couldn't push back down, was that he wouldn't have before. He waited for Madoc to realize it, to finally see that Took was just the taped-together bits of who he'd been, able to function for a while, but then the sharp edges would start to cut through the tape that held him in.

"Good," Madoc said. "Now we're even."

The strung-wire tension in Took's spine loosened at the dry jibe. They'd never been *nice* to each either. Once Madoc was kind to him, Took would know he'd seen the shabby joins. Not yet, apparently.

"They set fire to a house," Lawrence said. "We all missed something. Obviously."

Took wasn't sure if he appreciated the fact that she could see that too, or resented the *we* from someone wearing his tag on her vest. It was stupid to be jealous that she'd taken his place, someone would have had to, but it didn't stop him. The fire truck finally got the pumps to work, and the crew sprayed the Aron house with water that stank of shit and old grease.

"Come on," Madoc said. He grabbed Took's wrist and pulled him to his feet. "Let's get this over with. Then I can get you home and you can show me this evidence we missed."

Took supposed that answered the question of whether Madoc knew where he lived. He'd worry about that later.

Chapter Eight

THE STAKE was a thing of murderous intent and well-crafted beauty—blood-cured cherry wood carved and smoothed in a tapered spear the length of his forearm, shod with steel at one end and a barbed electrum tip at the other. Tally lines were burned into the side, a charred baker's dozen of deaths someone had doled out with this.

Madoc picked it up as he waited for Took to finish his shower, and turned it between his fingers. He'd grabbed a spare uniform from the back of Lawrence's car before she left last night. It was just cotton and Kevlar instead of his preferred tailored, reinforced leather, but at least it didn't stink of his own shredded guts. There was a pair of gloves tucked into the belt, but he ignored them and ran his bare fingers along the wood. It made his fingertips itch with a sharp sting that worked its way down into the meat, so it had been soaked in holy oil at some point.

It was the sort of thing passed down in Hunter families like an heirloom or purchased by breathing politicians to mount behind glass—a mute reminder of what the alternative to their reasonable bigotry was. Took used it as a letter weight in his kitchen.

The stairs creaked.

"A trophy?" Madoc asked as he carefully set it back down on a letter from VINE's human resources department.

"A gift," Took said as he padded down the stairs. The rasp of the fire was still etched into his throat. "From my mother."

"That would have gone over well in the office," Madoc said dryly. "Sometimes I forget you're from Cali, land of sun, salt, and stakes."

That wasn't entirely true. Sometimes he wondered if all that old prickly wariness toward the Anakim was still there, and that Took had just gotten better at his mask.

He brushed his hands together to shed the itch of cherry poison and the cobwebby question he didn't have an answer to as he turned around to give Took a quick once-over. His eyes wanted to linger on damp, shower-dark curls and the way the threadbare academy T-shirt clung to broad shoulders and lean waist. It was tight enough that Madoc could pick out the web of old scars through it, but he focused on the fresh injuries. The smoke-cracked skin around Took's mouth had softened and pinched back together into thin scars, and the raw blisters on his hands had dried up and faded down to pink. "Did you feed?"

"You didn't need to stay," Took said as he slung a damp towel around his neck and leaned back against the door jamb. "I can still put myself to bed."

Madoc had tried, but there was only so far good intentions could take you. He let dark heat slide into his voice as he looked Took over.

"If I'd put you to bed—" His scorched throat had healed hours ago, the rough note in his voice was for something else entirely. "—we'd still be there."

Took looked away uncomfortably. He rubbed the back of his neck and cleared his throat, a faded flush pink around his temples.

"Don't, ah," he said awkwardly. Madoc cursed himself and tried to lock the old, cold shell back into place. It had never stopped any injury to his heart, but no one else got to see they'd drawn blood. Took glanced up at him and twitched the corner of his mouth up in a short-lived smile. "Don't write checks that your, um, ass can't cash."

Madoc blinked. If a judge had sworn him in right then, he couldn't have testified to what the expression on his face was. Whatever it was made Took laugh harshly, from more than a scalded throat and push himself off the door. His cat slunk in from behind him, rubbed against his ankles, and then jumped up onto the counter in one smooth leap. It sat down on the stove and stared at Madoc with watery blue eyes while it licked its paws.

"Sorry," Took said as he went to the sink and flicked the tap on. Water spat out. That was apparently what the cat wanted. It abandoned the oven to stick its freshly cleaned paw into the stream and then lick the droplets off its toes—all the while with those watery, pink-blue eyes trained on Madoc. Took rubbed his finger along its head in a brief pet that made it twitch its pointed ears in irritation. "I guess I'm rusty. It's been a while."

The hot ache of temptation settled in Madoc's cock, heavy as a stone. He was tired of this careful dance. In the beginning he just wanted to press the newcomer, to test whether he'd brought more from the West

Coast than a tan. He'd baited a trap—flirt and retreat, be sexual without any sex, provoke with no promises—and then fallen into it himself.

He wanted to bend Took over the counter, bury his fingers in those damp-dark curls, and give him a refresher course on fucking. Except there was two years' worth of silence behind them, and maybe—*maybe*—that moment of absolute confidence last night when he'd known Took had his back was all Madoc would ever get.

It wasn't everything he wanted—because he wanted everything—but it would be enough.

His cock disagreed with a spiteful throb that clenched back to his ass, but it didn't appreciate anything but broad shoulders and nice thighs. Madoc knew it was harder to find a good friend than a good fuck. Maybe one day he'd risk it and see if Took would be both, but not yet.

"You rusty on debriefings as well?" he asked. "How did you connect Waring to Annabelle Franklin, and Annabelle Franklin to the Aron house?"

There'd always been something guarded about Took. Years with the Biters had worn down his suspicion of the unbreathing, but unlike Lawrence, he never forgot that his friends and coworkers were predators. Even with Madoc, in those moments when Madoc could have sworn that Took had been about to give in to the tension between them, there'd always been something held back. A year spent being imprisoned and tortured hadn't made him any easier to read. There were hints of that old, unguarded charm that lit his handsome face and Madoc treasured, but only sometimes, and it faded quickly.

So the flicker of emotion that passed over Took's face like a shadow could have been relief or disappointment. Even if Madoc had wanted to take the chance that it was the latter, it was gone before he had a chance.

He left the water to run and gestured for Madoc to follow him through the house.

"THE MODERN fascination with the lives of witty nobodies will prove the first grains of grave dirt on my head," Madoc grumbled as Took slouched at his desk and flicked through a dozen thumbnails of Waring's face. "It is senseless."

Took absently combed his wet hair back from his face with one hand. Water trickled down his neck and into his collar, and Madoc licked the imagined taste off his lips and looked away.

"Says the man with a dog-eared first copy of *The Letters of Pliny the Younger* in his office," Took said.

"He was hardly a nobody," Madoc countered. "Nor did he clown for paramilitaries in a search for fame."

Took clicked his tongue behind his teeth but didn't argue. He pulled up two videos and nested them on the screen next to each other.

"Look," he said as pointed to one and sketched an area just behind Waring's shoulder. It showed a stack of cardboard boxes with bright green lettering over the front. "Those are from Appleton."

Madoc reached over Took's shoulder and enlarged the image with a flick of finger and thumb. Habit and a little worm of malice made him settle his weight on Took's shoulder as he studied the screen. If he had to ache, then he saw no reason to make it too easy on Took.

"Apple and Pear Aphr...." Madoc paused and raised his eyebrow skeptically. "*Aphrodisiac* tea?"

"Alchemy has experienced a recent revival," Took said in the learned-by-rote cadence that meant it was a quote from some journal or website. "Particularly in areas of rural deprivation, which Appleton qualifies for by a number of markers." He paused, and his voice dropped into a drawl as he flicked the video off the screen. "For most of these people, the only magic they ever see are fangs in the night and dead children on the news."

Madoc grimaced at the turn of phrase, but he couldn't argue. The Anakim had laws and morals, laid out in the Book of Enoch and evolved in the thousands of years since. Outside of war, most would never tap an unwilling throat or pitch a weighted corpse into the shallows so as not to alarm the rest of the herd. But, like any group, they had their outliers—the mad, the bad, and the lonely—and for a rogue, the easiest prey were the weakest in society.

"They claim that God is on their side," he pointed out. "Isn't that enough?"

"Divine intervention tends to be assumed, not witnessed," Took pointed out. "When someone does survive within the event radius, they rarely say what people want to hear. The sort of people we're talking about most likely have set ideas about divinity, based on the teachings of their denomination. It doesn't satisfy to hear that the human mind, however pious, tends to get the god stuff wrong 80 percent of the time. So they turn to 'breathing' magic, like alchemy and astrology—disciplines that don't need to invoke the 'other,' that belong to them."

"And how is it connected to your case?"

"Apples and Appleton," Took said. "See the connection?"

"That's a reach."

Took snorted and leaned back in the seat as he hit Play on the other video. "Not really. The orchards are the town's major agricultural export. Around here, if it has apples on it or in it, then it probably has something to do with Appleton. Like the company that makes these teas, a start-up cottage industry run out of Bernice Franklin's kitchen."

That was a lead solid enough for Madoc to tug. "Annabelle's mother?"

"Aunt," Took admitted. The lead finally settled into something solid enough for Madoc to catch with his fingertips. "But the fact that alchemy and anti-Anakim feelings tend to share a slice of the Venn diagram caught my attention. Then I found her."

He hit Play on the screen. The still image of Waring turned fluid and alive as his mouth tilted into a smile around a just-finished sentence. Bony, teenage-boy hands finished a gesture, dropped to the table, and cupped a mug of tea.

"I don't think tea is going to help me with football," he said as he toasted the camera. "But it tastes good. Thanks, Worm!"

Took hit Pause.

"Her?"

"Worm."

"Nice."

"Worm_in_the_Apple," Took said as he scrolled down to the comments. "She only follows Waring, and she's based in Appleton. Her aunt makes that tea she sent Waring."

"Annabelle," Madoc said.

"I checked her out to see if her family have Hunter connections," Took said as he pushed back from the desk. "They don't, but they go to a Proverbial church, so they've probably tithed for the cause."

"I'd bet the sheriff has too," Madoc said.

Took acknowledged that with a shrug as he closed the laptop. With the need to look over Took's shoulder removed, Madoc made himself step away.

"And how did you get from there to the Arons?"

The flash of doubt on Took's face surprised Madoc. Until then, Took had seemed confident that he had the answers.

"I… a hunch?" Took admitted reluctantly. He scratched absently at the still-raised scars on the back of his hands. "They could never find any connection between Waring and the Arons, and once I found out that Annabelle had gone missing, it seemed possible that she had been involved somewhere along the line."

"You were right."

"Yeah, but I don't know why," Took pointed out with a scowl. "If it isn't reasoned, then it isn't analysis. It's just a lucky guess. *Kit* does lucky guesses. I work out what the evidence means."

Madoc snorted. "And I don't care as long as I get a result," he said. "We know that Annabelle visited the Arons. Do you have a guess as to why?"

Took shot him a sour look but dug into a drawer to unearth a repurposed folder, the original title scored out and written over in Sharpie. Madoc didn't need to open it. The word *MISSION* in Took's neat block capitals was enough to jog his memory.

"They were Proverbials too," he said. "Two years before they were murdered, they sent a missionary group to Europe, lost half their faithful to Russian fangs."

It was centuries on since Madoc had followed his old master across the sea, but it was different in Europe. Or rather, still the same. The blood cardinals were still cardinals there, and while they paid lip service to international law, any dissent the missionaries fomented among the breathing there with their preaching was put down swiftly. Bloodily. The Proverbial faithful knew that and accepted it, embraced it even. A mission that came back without at least a quarter of their party lost was considered a failure.

"Annabelle was with them?"

"Her brother," Took said. There was a dry edge to his voice, that old bitter note that crawled up sometimes when he talked about religion. Madoc had always assumed a break with his faith was what had convinced Took to leave California, where he got to hunt vampires, and come to Philly where he had to work with them. "They were very proud. He was their first-born, to be sacrificed to their faith. Annabelle was the one they expected to excel in his memory."

Or maybe he was wrong, Madoc thought with a slice of dark amusement, and there were no personal feelings there at all.

"So the fact that the Arons oversaw their oldest child's death wouldn't have been a reason for the Franklins to keep their daughter away from them?"

"Quite the opposite," Took said. He held his hand out for the file and, when Madoc handed it over, flipped through until he found a police-tagged copy of a sun-faded photo on a bloody fridge. It showed Benedict Aron, gray hair pulled back from his face in a ponytail, surrounded by preteen kids in front of—based on their T-shirts—Lake Santa Ana. Took tapped a finger against one small, wan face in the sea of tanned grins. "It's an incentive to send her to their bible camp, so she can find out what a hero her brother was and prepare her to make the next generation of martyrs."

"What were you?" Madoc asked.

Took paused for a second and then shrugged. "Too gay to make more martyrs," he said, but the edge was gone from his voice, so it was a lie... or a truth that didn't matter. "What I don't know is why Waring decided to take out the Arons. If VINE's profile was right and he had ties to the Hunters, there's no reason for him to decide to kill a good Proverbial family."

"Unless they weren't so good," Madoc said thoughtfully. "Unless whatever they were doing was something the Hunters wanted wiped from the face of the earth. Abuse?"

The corner of Took's mouth tilted in a rueful grimace. "No. That would just be... leverage, even if they touched up a Hunter kid. They would have drained them dry of anything useful and gotten rid of them quietly."

The door creaked open and the cat slunk in, all carefully placed paws and belly low to the ground. It gave Madoc a distrustful side-eye on the way past and then scaled one of the bookshelves so it could tuck itself into a loaf and watch them from a height.

It should have been bled out and gotten rid of in a sack. One way that Vine tracked rogue nests was through reports on missing pets. A handful of kittens were even easier prey than the frail or the weak and good enough for a just-Kissed vampire not ready the Hunt. Instead, here it was, alive and well.

"Sometimes things don't go to plan," Madoc pointed out slowly as he worked his way through his sudden inspiration. "Maybe you're right—*maybe*—and Waring didn't work for the Hunters, not when he started, anyhow. So whatever they had planned for the Arons was interrupted by their murder. And Annabelle's body was never found."

The flash of delight on Took's face was one of the few things that had made his smart mouth tolerable, even before Madoc wanted to drown himself in it. As much of a showboat as Took could be about his wits, it delighted him when someone beat him to the end of a puzzle.

"Maybe she's not dead," Took filled in for Madoc. He got up from his desk and paced around the room as he hunted through the filing cabinet and between books for something. "Damn it, where'd I put the—"

The cat jumped down from the bookshelf in a smooth, long ripple of motion, like poured milk with eyes, and landed on soft paws. It padded across the room and shoulder checked the trash can. It fell over and Madoc saw the buff folder impatiently shoved in there.

"You threw it out," he said. The itch of irritation at the back of his throat surprised him a little. He did his job because he was good at it and because, a long time ago, he'd been told to do it. It had never occurred to him that he might take pride in it, perhaps because no one he cared about had ever insulted it before. "Are you sure you still work for VINE?"

Took looked as though he would flush if he had the blood for it. He padded across the room and retrieved the file from the bin.

"I was just frustrated," he muttered as he brushed it off. "And Lawrence pissed me off."

"Why?"

Took straightened the dog-eared corner of the file. "She's not bad," he admitted stiffly, the requisite faint praise before damnation. "But just because she still has a heartbeat doesn't mean she understands Hunters. It doesn't mean she understands people. She grew up with VINE bodyguards, had family with fangs. End of the day, she's more Anakim than me."

The irritation took root in tight bands around the inside of his throat. "Maybe that was in her favor," Madoc said coldly.

"Yeah, well, it shouldn't be," Took fired back. "She missed stuff. Right from the start, no one could understand why people would answer the door to Waring. Lawrence dismissed it, said that the Anakim just saw a distressed young man and anyone would answer the door. We both know that's not what you'd see."

The fact he was right—no Anakim, not even ones with only a decade fanged under their belt, would see a stranger unannounced at their door as anything but a threat—didn't settle Madoc's hackles at all. Took was the one who'd left, who'd walled himself off behind red tape and a refusal to speak to anyone on the team. He didn't get to sneer at Lawrence, who never wanted to be anywhere else.

"And you?" Madoc asked. "What would you see?"

Took's laugh was harsh and as full of mockery as a guard dog's bark. "Monsters," he said as he pulled a piece of paper out of the folder and slapped it against Madoc's chest. "What else is there that knocks on your door at night. If you're right about Annabelle, though, you better prepare your protege for worse criticism than a file in the garbage."

"Why"

"Because *she's* not the only body they never found," Took said. "If she's still alive, then the missing children could be too. The minute the Haza realize that, the case is open again, and she'll be first in line to be gutted by the press."

By the end of the statement, some of the sharp glee had gone from Took's voice. They had all been on the end of bad press from one side or another over the years. The satisfaction remained. This was what, after all, he'd wanted. The case reopened, of course, but mostly the satisfaction that Took had been right and everyone else had been wrong.

"Waring is still guilty in this theory of yours," Madoc said grimly. "At the end, when the children turn up dead or in pieces, he'll still be executed. All this does is give people a handful of false hope, solve your puzzle, and maybe ruin Lawrence's career."

The flash of guilt over Took's face was enough to confirm he had no real hope that his investigation would exonerate Waring. It was just enough to paper a good cause over his obsession with the puzzle and soothe his conscience.

And the worst of it was that Madoc's frustrated anger made no difference to the sweet ache in his heart when he looked at Took. He'd always known that Took could be a self-interested, self-righteous fool, that he'd pull everything down for his own satisfaction. That just didn't matter as much as his loyalty and ready humor and the easy charm that lit his face when he smiled.

"It looks like your flirting isn't the only thing that got rusty," Madoc said. He glanced at the sheet of paper that Took had handed him. The names of the missing children marched down the page, from Anatoly to Yvette. He knew that Took was right. The smallest chance to bring these children—alive, undead, or just at rest—home to their families, and Madoc had to take it. "Your morals need freshening up too. But at least if VINE reopens this case, we won't need any help from an independent contractor."

That last point caught Took on the raw where the morals jab had only made him wince. He scowled. "I'm better than Lawrence," he said. "We both know it."

Madoc grabbed Took by the T-shirt, hand twisted in the worn cotton, and yanked him close enough that he could smell the fresh-scrubbed skin and the lemon of his soap.

"You understand monsters," he said through fully extended fangs. The pulse of blood in his ears made the smoke curl hot and dry in the cavity of his heart and hang heavy in the air. He'd put upstart boyars on their knees with his power before, made them show throat so he could shred his master's tithe from their veins. Part of him knew he would regret this later, when the anger faded and the edges of that broken trust cut deep. The scars on Took's skin drew the eye, but Madoc had lived long enough to know that the deepest scars were the ones you didn't see. Regrettably, his temper had never cared for foresight, and his voice snarled out of his throat. "That doesn't make you better than her. It makes you broken."

Took barked out a harsh laugh. "Do you think I don't know that?"

Despite the bluster, his gaze flickered nervously across Madoc's face, to his eyes and then nervously down again. Madoc waited with a quietly grim satisfaction for Took to backtrack.

Instead Took kissed him.

Madoc wasn't sure which of them was more surprised. It was rough and eager, with Took's hand cupped at the back of Madoc's neck and his compact body pressed against Madoc's.

He *should* pull away. It was too sudden and too caught up in the ever-more-divisive Waring case to be anything but ill-considered. If he didn't, there would be no way to back down from it, no more patience with Took's slow recovery or sly reserve. If they did this and Took withdrew again—turned Madoc away at the door like an unwanted bastard with a hungry belly—there would be no kindness left in Madoc for either of them.

So he should close his mouth, step back, and push Took's lean, soap-fresh body away. The excuse would ring flat—Madoc already knew that—but they'd live with it. They had before. All you needed to do was emphasize the *unexpected* in "that was unexpected" or downplay the hot awkwardness of a kiss in New Orleans on drinks, blood, and relief that a bad case had wrapped up. It just took commitment.

Instead Madoc growled into the sweetness of the kiss and dragged Took closer. He had been good. He'd played by the rules he'd set himself and tried to keep his distance. And it had gotten him nothing but frustration and lonely nights, an ache in his balls, a hole in his heart, and everyone's careful, well-meaning advice about how "fragile" Took was.

It was enough. He either wanted Took back or he wanted to let this thing between them burn out completely. No matter who it took with them.

As one last sop to his conscience as he leaned back, his throat parched with hunger for one more breath of Took, he asked, "Are you sure you want this?"

He supposed that, technically, Took's snort as he pulled him back into a kiss wasn't an answer. But it would have to do.

Chapter Nine

TWICE. IN the months—years now, he supposed—since he crawled out of that box, he'd gotten this far with someone twice. Eager mouths and rough hands over clothes, shoulder blades pressed against a wall and fingers twisted in his hair.

Then he'd find his mouth on their neck, taste the bloom of hot blood under the skin as he worried at the tender flesh, and he'd recoil. his hand on the back of their neck, thumb against the base of their spine, and right there at the front of his brain, the dark, poisoned knowledge of how easy those delicate, human bones would be to *snap*.

That was usually enough to throw cold water over the evening, as whatever was left of him that was human shriveled at the slide toward monster. He hadn't been celibate this long since he was fifteen and decided he didn't give a damn what his family thought of him.

Madoc's lips were cool under Took's mouth, his breath still flavored with smoke where the ruin of the Aron house lingered in his mouth. Took could be gentle and graze his fingers along the sharp bones of his jaw, the slow growth of stubble just long enough to prickle against his fingertips, or he could push Madoc back against the wall hard enough to rattle the bookcase next to them and not worry that he'd kill him.

He chose both and buried his hands in Madoc's hair, the clipped nap of it like velvet under his touch as they stumbled into the wall. He worked his knee between Madoc's legs, the heavy jut of a cock hard against his thigh, and his tongue between the sharp, ivory sickles of Madoc's extended fangs. He didn't even feel the sharp edges cut his lips until a second later, when the familiar taste of his own black blood filled his mouth.

Fangs had taken him a while to get used to, more or less.

He hesitated for a second, his bloody tongue curled behind his own teeth, as he foggily tried to work out what the etiquette was. The mechanics of sex between humans and vampires was something he'd spent, maybe, a little more time on that he could really explain away as just work. What exactly two vampires did today had never seemed relevant, personally or professionally.

Did their blood taste good....

Madoc growled into his mouth. The sound vibrated through the bones of Took's skull and didn't read as human at all. A misfire of whatever atavistic impulse should have made Took pull back but instead shivered hot, electric delight down his spine and into his balls. Madoc gripped the back of Took's neck, fingers cupped around the curve of his skull, and chased the taste of Took between his lips and over his tongue.

That answered that question. Maybe he should write a paper on it for the Academy—the normal courting behavior of the undead? That serial killer in Montana who'd turned out to be Anakim, some of his patterns could have—

Madoc bit Took's lip neatly, a sharp nip with blunt teeth that folded the soft flesh. The little jolt of pain focused Took's mind back in the ache of the present. "No." He licked the last drops of blood from the razor-thin cuts on Took's lips and pulled back slightly. "No thoughts. No plans. Just be here."

Took licked his lips and wondered if it tasted the same—like bitter honey—to Madoc. Or what Madoc's blood would feel like on his tongue.

"Make me."

Heat flashed through Madoc's dark eyes. It was as much anger as lust, but Took didn't care. He wanted to feel safe. Nothing could erase the scars that kept him up during the day and restless and unmoored at night because of his fear of what was in the dark. But maybe Madoc could convince him, for a few hours, that there was no monster in the dark inside Took. Or at least if there was, that it wasn't one Madoc had to be afraid of.

Even if Madoc is the monster?

Took wasn't sure if that was a jab at his frustration or his lust. He didn't have time to decide. A foot hooked around his ankle and tugged and both of them toppled to the floor in a tangle of heat, denim, and tangled limbs. The question was lost in a blur of lust and rough, careless kisses that slanted across mouths and down to the jaw. Half foreplay and half tussle, one minute a kiss pressed wet and openmouthed against Took's collarbone made him groan, and the next he rolled his hip to flip Madoc under him.

It didn't work, but then it never did. He'd sparred with Madoc to get better, not to win, and that had been without the distraction of sharp-fanged kisses and hands eager for his ass and his thighs.

Not as much of a distraction anyhow.

Either way, it always ended the same—with Took pinned to the ground, although Madoc usually went with his forearm across Took's throat instead of pinning his wrists to the floor.

"If you paid attention to right now and not the inside of your head," Madoc said as he straddled Took's hips, "maybe you wouldn't end up here."

Took grinned at him. "Maybe I wanted to."

Madoc leaned down and teased a featherlight kiss over Took's mouth. "You could have been here a lot sooner."

It was nearly dawn, but the dusky grays were close enough to press in against the windows. Took could feel the pressure of everything he should have considered before he kissed Madoc push in against his ears.

"Who isn't here now?" he asked.

Madoc rewarded him for that with a kiss that pressed Took's head back against the floor. He slid his tongue neatly between Took's extended fangs. The twinge of that in his jaw felt different with Madoc's weight on him, not the usual dry socket burn but an almost pleasant ache that throbbed to the need in his balls.

"I want you to fuck me in your bed," Madoc rasped as he finally raised his head. He tightened his grip on Took's wrists, and the pressure of his fingers was enough to make the bones ache as Took reflexively tried to move. The image in his head—the long, hard sprawl of Madoc's body, the clench of his shoulders, and the sheath of him around Took's cock—made Took absently lick his fangs. The heady, sweet drip of ichor down his throat made him squirm with wanting more… although exactly what he wanted wasn't clear. Madoc kissed him hungrily and shuddered as he caught the taste. "I want to bend you over that desk and fuck you."

Took's groan was a low, raw noise in his throat. His cock rubbed against the rough denim of his zipper as he helplessly lifted his hips off the ground.

"What do you want?" Madoc asked. He shifted his weight back so his ass pressed firmly against Took's groin, the pressure of lean, firm muscle enough to drag another groan out of Took. "What do you want, Took?"

"You," Took admitted. "Any way I can get you."

Madoc flinched back for a second, a flutter of pain briefly, sharply, visible on his face. A cold little bit of Took filed that reaction away for later, for analysis. He hated that part sometimes, useful as it could be, but he lost track of the thought as Madoc let go of his arms and sat back.

"Then you get to fuck me." He dragged the borrowed T-shirt up over his head and tossed it away. His mouth curled in a sly, almost shy, smile as he looked down at Took. "See if you can do a better job than you did trying to pin me."

His stomach was still laced with faded pink scars from earlier, but the almost-evisceration had already smoothed down to not much more than a tint of red and a seed of scar tissue. The bullets had shredded the smoky ink that Madoc had worked into his ribs. The skeletal dragon was splintered, and the smoky lines scattered across white flesh. When he had time, Madoc would get it excised and re-inked. He always did, no matter how many times he denied he was a cardinal anymore. Still, for now, the ruined ink almost felt like Madoc was off-duty, a once-a-decade dose of freedom.

Took ran his fingers over the exposed skin. He traced the web of scar tissue over Madoc's lean stomach and up across his ribs. Between the faintly rough stripes of pink, Madoc's skin was warmer than Took expected, a little over room temperature, and smooth as silk.

"What if I'd wanted to be fucked?" Took asked.

Madoc hooked his fingers in the neck of Took's old T-shirt and pulled him into a quick, hard kiss.

"Next time," he murmured as he nibbled the curve of Took's mouth. "Now, are you going to take me to bed or not?"

"We could stay here," Took said. "No one will see."

Madoc rolled to his feet in one easy motion and held his hand out. After a second, Took grabbed it and let himself be dragged to his feet. Madoc promptly reeled him back in until they were pressed together again.

"I am old enough that fucking on the floor isn't a novelty," he rasped into Took's ear. "And I want to leave my smell on your sheets, in the air. Whatever you do tomorrow, Luke, you won't forget that I was here, that you asked me in, that you begged me to stay."

Took sucked in a ragged breath. He didn't need the oxygen, but somehow he still needed the pressure of air in his lungs as he tried not to get flustered. The rough words could have been a promise or a threat, and Took didn't care. Heat pulled heavily in his groin, like hot sand, and he turned his face into Madoc's throat. A kiss turned into an almost-bite as he scraped his teeth down over tendons and the soft spot where Madoc's pulse used to live. The blunt pressure made Madoc shudder and clench his jaw.

"Told. I told you to stay," Took said. "And I have never forgotten a single thing about you, Madoc."

"Always the profiler," Madoc said, almost affectionately.

Took didn't correct him. It would take too long and be too real. Instead he hooked his hand in the waistband of Madoc's trousers and dragged him toward the stairs.

SNACK HISSED like a kettle and shot out from under the bed as Madoc landed on it. Most of the time Snack's ownership of the room, of the whole top floor, went unchallenged. He swatted Took's leg on the way past, hard enough to sting even through denim, and disappeared out into the hall.

"I don't think that cat likes me," Madoc said as he stretched out on the sheets, his weight braced on his elbow.

His skin was nearly as pale as the linen, the darkness of his hair and scattered tattoo stark against all that pallor. The idea that the long sprawl of dangerous muscle, the hard bulge of his cock under the zip of his trousers, was there for Took, seemed like as much of a trap as a cat's exposed fluffy belly… and was just as worth it to stick your hand into.

"I don't think she's the one who needs to," Took pointed out. "So I can do anything I like to you?"

Madoc laughed and tilted his head back, his dark hair loose and his throat bared in one lean, tempting line.

"One tip I will give you on the vampiric life," he said. "Never say yes to a question like that. Exactly what did you have in mind?"

It was the moment to ask what Madoc expected. Took didn't. As far as VINE was concerned, his ability to patch things together into a believable behavioral whole was all he had left going for him.

"I thought you hated spoilers?"

Madoc raised an eyebrow. "Big kinky talk and nothing to back it up, huh?"

It shouldn't be possible for a vampire to flush, but Took could feel the heat at the top of his ears. He scrubbed his hand through his hair and realized it was still damp at the back.

"Bite me," he muttered.

Madoc smiled at him widely enough to show all his teeth. The tips of his fangs dimpled the lush curve of his lower lip, and his dark eyes were hot. "That I can do."

The thought made Took's scars burn. He might have locked away most of the memories of what happened that year, but his nerves remembered the slice of fangs and the acid of the curse as it worked into his bones.

The memory flicked like a lightbulb, sharp-edged and hungry. He wasn't sure when it was—sometime when Madoc had still wanted to tease a rise out of the rigid new boy from California—but he knew where. It was the loft in Philadelphia that provided a waypoint between the office and wherever the various Biters called home. Madoc had stumbled in that nearly-morning with his latest lover, a pretty boy with sleepy amber eyes, stories about his job as a docent, and no boundaries.

Madoc's hand was pale against the black-leather-covered thigh, a trickle of spilled blood vivid against his pale jaw. His tongue flicked out to lave the boy's throat in a slow, wet swipe that dragged a raw sound of surrender from his lover and made Took shift with discomfort. The distaste he expected—the sneer he caught behind his teeth bitter as cigarette smoke—but the quick rise of lust caught him off guard.

"So much better," Madoc purred against the pale, flawless column of throat, "tapped fresh."

Madoc's jaw tightened, his lover moaned in abandon, and as they tangled around each other, Took realized they'd forgotten all about the undeclared game of chicken.

He ceded the win anyhow as he looked away.

"If you're good," he said.

Madoc's eyes were unreadable as he ran his hand down his chest to the broad black belt cinched around his lean waist. "Goodness isn't something associated with my name," he said as he tugged the leather strap loose. "Would you accept wicked?"

"Like I said," Took admitted raggedly as lust jolted through him. "Anything."

Took grabbed the hem of his T-shirt to haul it over his head and then hesitated with it hitched halfway up his stomach. The scars were the least of his problems usually. They'd fade eventually, and sometimes, when the world demanded he buck up, it was oddly reassuring to have the journal of everything bad etched into his skin. This was the first time they'd made him feel self-conscious with the sharp wish that he'd done this before he was broken.

Even if it *had* been even more of a bad idea when he had something to lose.

"I've seen the scars," Madoc said. "I saw you before the scars. If they bothered me, do you think I'd be here?"

"Pity?" Took joked bitterly as he dragged off his T-shirt. Scars stitched across his torso and arms. They were worse where he had let the sun get to them—thick knots of white tissue that ringed his neck, and tight, divoted skin on his forearms—and had faded to shiny welts across his shoulders and the hard plane of his stomach.

"Maybe you aren't such a good profiler after all," Madoc said. He hitched his hips up off the bed and pushed his thick, black cotton trousers down over heavy thighs. His cock jutted up eagerly from his groin, the skin drawn tight over the thick, curved shaft of it and the head dark and shiny with come. He wrapped his fingers around it and dragged his fist from base to head in one slow movement. "Get over here and fuck me. Or did you decide you just wanted to watch and feel sorry for yourself?"

Took laughed with a harsh bark of real humor that caught him off guard.

"I have reason," he pointed out as he scrambled out of his jeans. Whatever legendary grace the Anakim were meant to embody escaped him as he tripped over his own clothes. His cock bobbed awkwardly as he caught his balance. It was so hard and ready that the warm, still air on it made him ache. There were scars on Took's thighs too, but the clots of keloid in the back of his knee and the crease of his groin had been the first to fade.

"Who doesn't?" Madoc said as he kicked his trousers all the way off. "Ask any priest and they'll tell you we were put here to suffer. You, on the other hand, get to fuck me, and not everyone can say that."

"So I should just cheer up?"

Madoc shrugged and sprawled back on the bed. "That's up to you," he said. His fingers tightened roughly around his cock, and he hissed in air between his teeth. The muscles in his thighs clenched, and it took him a moment to drag words back over his tongue. "You don't have to cheer up to get it up. On the other hand, you have a limited time to get up me."

"I didn't realize we were on a deadline," Took said dryly as he crawled onto the bed. He ran his hands up Madoc's thighs, from his knees to his lean hips. The skin was soft under his thumbs as he explored the taut skin. Between the vee of his wrists, Madoc lazily stroked his cock. "Is it a soft or a hard one?"

Madoc's laugh trembled against Took's palms.

"You are definitely rusty," he said as he let go of his cock. Pale and heavy, it tilted up toward his flat stomach as Madoc reached up to cup his fingers around the back of Took's neck. The smell of sex was ripe on his skin. "Come here."

He pulled Took down on top of him and into a sharp, hungry kiss. Took groaned helplessly into Madoc's mouth at the nip of fangs and the rough rub of Madoc's thigh against his balls.

Pleasure hitched ragged along his nerves, rerouted around the congestion spots where scar tissue was thick, and Took ground his cock against Madoc's hip. He pulled away from the kiss and explored Madoc's body with his mouth and hands. The long planes of it were familiar enough from his old fantasies, the breadth of his shoulders and the tight curve of ass estimated from his leathers and the brief, rough clinches when they sparred.

This close, this naked, there was more to find. His nipples were pale but flushed under Took's lips and between his fingers into tight pink buds that made Madoc groan and dig his fingers into Took's hair. There was a scatter of silver in his chest hair, bright and distinct against the dark scruff, and it curled and matted under Took's tongue. When Took slid his hand down to Madoc's cock, it was heavy and thick around, and Took's thumb rubbed roughly over the base made Madoc swear between clenched teeth and buck his hips up off the mattress.

His navel was pierced too, with a slim iron ingot laced vertically through the dimpled skin.

Took traced a circle around it with his fingertips. "I didn't think piercings worked on… us."

He touched the bar with his fingertip and hissed in surprise at the unexpected sting of it. Madoc caught his hand and pulled it up to his lips to kiss the small hurt away and then scrape his teeth over the pads.

"They don't," Madoc said. "It's different. A gift from the old, dead bastard that fathered me."

Madoc was a dhampir with no acknowledged kin, a cardinal whose recorded life began the day he swore to the Haza. Took knew he should ask, draw out the nodule of information while Madoc was in the mood to talk. Instead he shivered as Madoc sucked on his fingers and then pushed Took over on his back so he could return the favor. He kissed his way down to Took's stomach, his tongue and lips attentive to every old knot of scar tissue as though he wanted to map them—until he reached Took's cock.

"Now I know your parents were religious," he said as he pressed a kiss to the wet head. The flick of his tongue made Took squirm, and Madoc pushed his hips down to hold him in place. "Does it really decrease sensation?"

Took was used to the question. Even on the West Coast, circumcision wasn't common. It was practiced by Jews, Muslim, and a very few of the more passionate Christian sects. If your cock was docked, it meant your parents really thought it mattered to the divine. From what Took understood, his Dad had just wanted to sell it to a witch, but he tended to let people believe the religious angle.

He swallowed hard as Madoc worked his tongue under the glans and flicked it over the tight thread of skin there. Pleasure knotted in Took's balls and pushed at his muscles, and the need to move twitched under his skin.

"Not that I've noticed," Took rasped out. "But maybe you should try a bit harder. Just in case."

Madoc chuckled—a breath against Took's cock—and wrapped his mouth around Took's cock. The cool blades of his fangs grazed the tender skin as he worked his tongue over the underside of the shaft.

Took wanted to groan. The sound was caught roughly in his throat, but he'd forgotten how to breathe as Madoc's mouth took in the length of him. It was wet and slick, it was Madoc, and the twisted threads of pleasure, pain, and stale fear twisted in his gut until it felt almost sweet. The sharp tip of Madoc's fang caught the base of his cock with a scratch that flicked a weird, dark pleasure up his spine and finally knocked the ragged moan of need from his throat.

With his tongue, Madoc traced the small injury as though he needed to memorize it, dark hair soft against Took's thighs, and Took could barely remember his name....

"Sit up," Madoc told him finally as he lifted his head. He licked a smear of dark blood from his lower lip as he leaned back on one arm, his elbow braced against the mattress, and waited. "On your knees."

Took had the notion that just because he got to fuck Madoc, that didn't mean he was the one in charge. He would have complained, but the clip of order in Madoc's voice latched on to that dark pleasure that still lodged in his spine....

He swallowed hard and did as he was told. The mattress gave under his knees as he sat up, and his cock protested the sudden lack of attention. It was smeared with black blood, slick and shiny against tight skin, and Took felt....

A faded revulsion that poked at the back of his brain, and a hot tremble of raw hunger that made him ignore it. He could worry about what that all meant later.

Madoc crawled into Took's lap and straddled him. His cock pressed hard against Took's as he leaned in for a kiss, one hand cupped around the nape of Took's neck. His mouth slashed down on Took's in a kiss that bruised lips and scraped teeth. The care he'd taken earlier was gone, and he laid his tongue open against Took's fangs.

Instinct made Took recoil. "I'm sorry, I didn't—"

Madoc's hand tightened on the back of his neck. "Don't be." This time the kiss was slow and wet, a spill of blood into Took's mouth that was sweet and sharp as honey whiskey. It coated his tongue and slid down his throat, the back-of-the-throat parch that he'd gotten used to suddenly quenched.

He groaned in the back of his throat and gripped Madoc's ass in both hands to pull him closer. The need to be in Madoc made him ache, the muscles in his jaw and thighs clenched and ready. He couldn't resist the pale, taut line of Madoc's throat, and from Madoc's jaw to his collarbone, he chewed bruised kisses that faded even as he bit. It frustrated something in the pit of his soul that *wanted* to leave a mark. What was the point of fangs, it wanted to know, if he didn't bite down, pierce the film of skin, and drink it dry. The need was a thick, heady compulsion—

lust with an edge of violence—and it would have scared him if Madoc had left any room for it. Instead he mouthed encouragement between kisses, his voice more smoke than silk as lust roughed his words, and ground himself hard against Took's stomach.

Pleasure twisted in on itself until it was almost an ache, and the need caught at his balls and the back of his tongue like hooks.

"God, please," Took whimpered as he dragged his mouth away from Madoc's spit-slick neck, the hunger for *more* of him—all of him— held back by wire and will. "I can't…."

Madoc laughed, low and smug and satisfied, as he reached down between their bodies to grab Took's cock. He dragged his fist down from head to root in a slow, tight stroke.

"Really, I think you can," he rasped. "Now fuck me before I change my mind and bend you over the desk."

Took shuddered as the temptation of that clenched from his balls back along his taint to his ass. It was hardly a bad alternative, but Madoc was already in his lap, and if Took wasn't going to bite him, he needed to be inside somehow.

Took gripped Madoc's lean hips and hitched him up off his thighs. The thought of protection or lube flicked briefly through his head, but Madoc had already shifted his grip on Took's cock. The quick squeeze of his fingers around the base scattered everything in Took's head. Madoc grazed a kiss over the corner of Took's mouth and down his jaw.

"I'm going to bite you," he said reasonably as he lowered himself onto Took's cock. Pressure ached down the length of his cock as the head nudged against Madoc's asshole, blood slick and slippery against the tight entrance. The throb in Took's balls as his cock pushed past the tight seal drowned out the quick, sour rush of panic that filled his skull. Nearly. His hand flexed nervously against Madoc's hip, and a clot of words caught on his tongue, although he didn't know if they were consent or not. Madoc slid his hands down Took's back in a slow caress that ended at his ass. "Do you trust me?"

That was the question, wasn't it? *No. Yes. Sometimes.*

But the confusion of answers in his brain didn't slow down the quick "Yeah," that tripped off his tongue.

"Good."

The teeth pinched at first, so sharp it took Took's nerves a second to catch up and scream pain back down the relay to his brain. He hitched his breath in, ready to protest, but Madoc pushed his ass down against Took's cock at the same time. The tight grip of it sent cramps of pleasure down the length of the shaft to clench tight as a knot in his balls.

By the time his brain remembered the teeth, the sharp pain had peaked and spilled over into something like pleasure. Instead of the battery-acid sting he expected, that he *remembered*, the curse spilled into him like poison-laced wine. It felt like warmth in his cold veins and spread a slow, sweet pleasure under his skin.

Took flexed his fingers around Madoc's hips and felt the appreciative purr against—*under*—his skin. He pulled Madoc down onto his cock and the tight grip of muscle flexed around him as he slid deeper. Pleasure pulsed and tightened in his balls as Madoc's ass pressed flat against his hips.

He held him there for a second and then let Madoc lift himself up. The air of the room felt hot against his cock as it slid out of Madoc. Cool fingers clenched around Took's ass, dug down into the muscle as Madoc thrust down again and Took rolled his hips up to meet him. The slow build of pressure banked low in Took's stomach, a heaviness in his balls and weariness in his tight thighs as Madoc moved on top of him. The cool grip of his ass as Took buried himself in it pushed against the hot pressure of fangs as Madoc worried himself deeper.

Had it felt this good when whoever turned him ripped the veins in his throat or his arms? If it was, he shuddered away from the idea. He didn't want to know.

Despite the flicker of doubt, he couldn't help the whine of disappointment as Madoc finally unlatched from his throat. It felt… unfinished, like something had been left blue-balled and undone.

Blue-fanged, he supposed.

Madoc sat back, his ass against Took's thighs and Took's cock buried in his ass, and braced his hands against Took's shoulders. He flexed his fingers around the heavy slope of muscle and shoved Took back down onto the bed. Took sprawled backward, sticky with blood and come, and kicked his legs awkwardly out from under him.

Madoc leaned over him, shoulders tight as he put his weight on his arms and studied Took thoughtfully. "Next time, it's your turn," he said. "Fair's fair."

Fang or fuck, Took wondered. Or did it matter?

Madoc dipped down for a quick, rough slant of a kiss, the taste of mingled blood odd and salty on his tongue. It pinned Took's mind in the here and now, in the taste of Madoc's mouth and the roll of his hips as he drove himself down onto Took's cock with quick, rough thrusts. Took grazed his hands up lean thighs, the muscles under that pale skin hard as bone, to the rigid jut of his cock. Before he could do anything Madoc caught his hands and pulled them away.

"Later," he said through clenched teeth. "I want to pay attention."

He rocked faster against Took, and Took obligingly bucked his hips up into each stroke. The undead, even dhampir, didn't sweat, but they did groan and bite their lower lip hard enough to draw blood when a cock bumped their prostate.

Took wanted to touch him, but Madoc just smirked and tightened his grip when he tried to pull away.

"Wait," he said as he thrust down.

"I don't want…." Took pressed his head back into the mattress and clenched his hands into fists, his nails digging down into his palm. "I can't…."

Madoc pulled him up by the arms and pressed a hard kiss against his still-bloody neck. "Then don't," he said, as he rasped his tongue over the bloody wound. "I want to see what I did for you."

It was enough. The hot flash of pain from his worried neck was pleasure by the time it hit his spine and spilled out. He groaned as he thrust up off the bed, his cock settled a little deeper inside Madoc, and his balls untwisted with a wet spill of come. He leaned against Madoc's shoulder, a soft, openmouthed kiss pressed to the crease where shoulder met neck.

For a second, he was tempted to bite down, but he lost his nerve at the last second.

Madoc pulled them both down onto the bed, legs tangled together and stickiness smeared over their thighs. His cock was still rigid, and he guided Took's hand over to it. Took easily cuffed the shaft and idly rubbed his thumb along the thick vein on the base of it. It made Madoc clench his jaw and move his thighs apart. He reached over and tucked a finger under Took's chin as Madoc turned his head toward him.

"I want to see your face when I come for you," he said. The corner of his mouth tilted with amusement. "I like your face."

Took stroked his hand, fingers tight as the skin creased around it, from base to tip. It was slick with precome and blood, fine skin pulled tight over the thick shaft. Madoc hissed softly between his teeth and arched up into Took's fist. He pumped again and twisted his fist around Madoc's shaft on the way down. Took could feel the wire-taut tension under Madoc's skin, and Madoc's balls were clenched up tight between his legs. Madoc came after a few more strokes, with a rough sound in his throat and a spurt of pale liquid that dripped between Took's fingers and over his knuckles.

They both sprawled out against the sheets. After a second, Took made a halfhearted attempt to roll away but was pulled back. He let himself settle against Madoc's side, one arm slung over lean hips and his chin propped on one broad shoulder.

"Should I be self-conscious my fangs are smaller than yours?" he asked.

"Yes," Madoc said without missing a beat. He waited through Took's chuckle and then brushed his finger over Took's lower lip. "I have missed you."

"Me too," Took admitted. The truth slipped out before he could catch it back. He let it be for a second and then made himself ask, or try too. "That night. Do you remember—"

Madoc stiffened under the sprawl of Took's body and scowled. "Not today," he said as he stroked a finger down Took's back. "I don't want to think of that here. Tonight."

Neither did Took, but it was hard not to when he was curled around the man who probably did it. Or it should have been hard. Instead he let it slip and relaxed into Madoc's body.

When he woke up that evening, Madoc was gone.

Chapter Ten

LAWRENCE STOOD with her hands braced on the wrought iron railing of the balcony and stared out through the glassy, gothic skyscrapers, toward the skyline. Her jaw was set, and she didn't look around at Madoc once as he outlined what was going to happen next for her.

"I doubt we'll get any of the children back alive," he admitted as he leaned back against the wall. The moon hung fat and yellow overhead. Drakul keeping an eye on them went the old superstition. Madoc had met the man—or whatever you would call what Tepes had made of the raw material of his birth—once, but he had no idea if the great old vampire really could see through celestial bodies. He wouldn't put it past him. "But when we find their remains, or find nothing at all, that will be laid at our door too."

Lawrence sighed and leaned forward, her weight braced on her arms. Her gaze finally dropped from the skyline to the street below. Madoc didn't move from his sprawl, but he was ready to grab her if she suddenly pitched forward. She was a good agent, and he would call her a friend if someone asked, but he'd never had to see her take bad news before—not this bad, at least.

"When you say 'our door,' what you mean is at my feet," Lawrence said acerbically. "I'm not a child, and I don't need the facts of life spoon-fed to me. Took caught something I didn't, and now I have to take the consequences. That's fair enough."

Madoc relaxed slightly. He'd had men about to kill themselves vent their spleen on him before, but not with a declaration of responsibility.

"Everyone missed this," he said.

"Took didn't."

Divided loyalties stung when they caught you unexpectedly. Madoc hesitated on the edge between support for his agent and loyalty to his... whatever that worked out as. *If* it worked out. That pessimism should have made it an easy choice, but it didn't.

"He's the best. After the incident, the Academy in California invited him back as an instructor," Madoc said. "And even *he* only saw this because he was bored and followed a shadow on the file further than anyone would think made sense. If you'd come to me with the same lead, Lawrence, I'd have told you that it was a waste of your time."

She leaned back against the rail and crossed her arms. The smile on her pale mouth was wry. "But what would you have told him?"

It was a good point, and they both knew it. Madoc acknowledged that with a lack of acknowledgment as he changed the subject back to the present rather than answer her about the past.

"It's not a sanction, Lawrence. It's a heads-up," he told her. "When the boyars get this new information, they'll reopen the case, and that won't be easy for any of us. We'll get questioned about our protocols, they'll probably want to do audit on this case, and the press will rip us to shreds."

Lawrence's shoulders slumped under the weight of his words. She licked her lips.

"Will I get fired?"

"Don't act stupid," Madoc told her, not unkindly. "You're the director's daughter. No one will ever fire you. They'll just promote you to a dark room in a far-off state and avoid your calls. Except I won't let that happen. You're a Biter, and you'll stay as long as I say I want you to stay. Got it?"

The medicine tasted sour, but Lawrence swallowed it anyhow. She never traded on her mother's influence, not that Madoc had seen, but it would take a more naive soul than Lawrence not to know it was there. She rubbed her neck and pressed her fingers down on the neat scar just above her collarbone.

"And this? Will the schedule for my Kiss go ahead as planned?"

Probably not. Maybe never. The Anakim could pass the Kiss like a contagion if they wished, spread it through a city until the only prey left was each other and their fragile society collapsed into cannibalism and legend. They weren't meant to offer the Kiss too often, and what rose from the human shell wasn't always *right*, but they could.

Their own children, though? Dhampirs were rare even in Europe and—except in unfortunate cases like Madoc's—treasured and cosseted throughout their fragile childhoods by any vampire they came across. If people discovered there had been a chance to save these lost children, one that VINE had squandered, there would be an uproar. After that, there was no way VINE could be seen to reward the human who'd caused it all, no matter how high her connections ran.

"Not until the case is closed," he hedged around the harsh truth. "If nothing else, they won't want you out of commission until this case is over."

She pressed her hand protectively over the scar and nodded tightly. "So what now?"

Madoc pushed himself up off the wall and brushed a fastidious hand down the borrowed uniform he had on. He could smell the sex on it, still on his skin under the cotton.

"I am going to get changed," he said. "You're going to brief our host about last night's events. Then we get ahead of this story. By the time this filters down to the press, we'll have answers to most of their questions."

"Will Took work with us?" Lawrence asked.

Madoc hesitated as he pulled open the heavy door. Where did last night leave them? Rough sex and tender afterthoughts meant nothing on their own. Madoc had lived long enough to know that. It had been more lust than love, whatever Madoc's feelings, and the morning after was where regret lived.

"If we need him," he said as he gestured for Lawrence to go through the door ahead of him. "I don't know if anyone told you, but we used to solve crime at VINE before Agent Luke Bennett flew out from LA."

Lawrence looked thoughtful as she stepped through the door. "I just wonder what he'd do next? If he were here."

"The same thing you're going to do," Madoc told her as he gave her a nudge down the corridor. "Brief SSA Crane. Then meet me down at the car."

YELLOW-AND-BLACK TAPE cordoned off the street at both ends. A few reporters lingered at the curbs as they filled the air with morning-after updates on the fire. The houses either side of the burned-out husk stood empty, doors left open in the neighbors' haste to get out.

Madoc couldn't blame them. The fire had left the house a skeleton of charred timbers, full of smoky ghosts and a replenished stock of bad memories, some of them his. Madoc absently scratched his jaw. The skin had healed already—the trickle of ichor he'd tapped from Took's throat was more potent than a draft from a human—but he could remember the hot, bubbled scorch of pain. It hadn't changed.

When humans came to kill him, they always brought fire to do the job. It hadn't worked yet, but sometimes Madoc wondered if the fire had scorched something that he couldn't heal, that one day what walked out wouldn't be him anymore.

Not this time, but one day. That would end well for no one.

Back at the tape, fingers pointed as Madoc crossed the road and the cameramen swung around to grab some quick, static-blurred images of him. He ignored them as he headed to the tent the fire department had set up as a makeshift on-site office.

Chief Kendall pinned her glove under her armpit to pull her hand free and offered it to Madoc as he joined her outside the house. Her palm was hot and sweat-damp as he gripped it.

"I just wanted to thank you for last night," Kendall said gruffly. "If you hadn't realized someone had adulterated our tanker, the whole damn street would have burned down. There were other fires set around the city. We wouldn't have been able to get back up here until it was… far too late."

Madoc smiled at her. He'd always appreciated courtesy, the more so when it was grudging. Gratitude was easy if it didn't bother you. It had more impact from someone who'd rather withhold.

"I was here too," he pointed out. "There was some self-interest involved in that warning."

Kendall chuckled roughly and ran her fingers over the buzz-cut fuzz of curls that clung to her skull. "Fair enough," she said. "You want to walk through the scene?"

"Want isn't quite the word," Madoc said. "But yes. Hopefully, if there was something other than me in there that the Hunters wanted to destroy, we managed to stop them in time to find it."

Kendall turned and gave the ruin of the house a dubious look. "I don't know about that," she said. "It's pretty gutted. You'd probably have more luck with the man they grabbed from the backyard. The survivor."

"Another agent is already talking to him," Madoc said. "I like to have the answers *before* I ask the questions."

Kendall shrugged and gestured for him to follow her. She pulled the glove back on as they walked around the house. Burned grass crunched underfoot, and the sour smell of old shit rose from the puddles that pocked the charred ground. Madoc filled his lungs in case he needed to say something and then stopped breathing.

"The fire investigators have been and gone," Kendall said as she led the way around to the back of the house. Metal scaffolding had been laced across the building, struts burrowed into the walls to keep the slouched architecture on its foundations.

"Did they work out what caused the fire?" Madoc asked sardonically.

She snorted but shrugged it off. "Protocol. I told the detectives on the case they couldn't go in until we'd finished securing the building. There's some risk of collapse still. I doubt health and safety is much of a worry for you, though."

Madoc used some air to chuckle along with her, even though she was wrong. The thought of being buried under burned timbers, the charred smell worked into his clothes and his lungs filled with splinters and smoke, picked at his brain to release stale, aged adrenaline.

He remembered what the apples smelled like when they burned. The weight on his back. How long he screamed for.

No. Not useful. Madoc pushed the memories down, dragged the scented taint of smoke back from his brain like a recalcitrant dog, and headed into the kitchen.

Smoke eddied up from stubborn spots of char on the ground, embers still dull red despite the drip-drip of water that ran down the walls and soaked into the floor. Linoleum curled up in black, withered scabs on the floor that cracked under Madoc's boots.

Desecration smelled like burned apples and piss. Madoc was barefoot, his soles gouged by charred splinters as he staggered through the remains of the first home he'd ever had. Where his first love—

Madoc shoved the old memories away with a flash of frustrated anger, wedged them back into the overflowing cupboards of his mind. One benefit of a long life should surely be the ability to forget, or at least take the edge off, old injury.

He thought of Took instead—the sharp brain hidden under that golden scruff, the taste of his skin, the tickle of an unexpected laugh against his throat, the secrets and unexplained silences. The jag of lust and frustration was enough to drag him back into the here and now as he headed into the other room.

The echoes of the Arons' murder were gone, wiped out by this fresh violence. The plaster walls were cracked and the wooden floor burned down to concrete in a wide, black ring where the Molotov cocktail had landed. He scuffed the edge of his boot over the blackened rim and the wood crumbled into cinders under the weight. He wondered if the owner—an aunt, he thought, in Detroit—would be glad to see it go. Or would it sting to see the loss of the last thing her family had left behind?

Madoc shrugged off that thought—it was perilously close to brooding about his past—and started a cursory search of the space. Cracked walls, ruined floors, a house that—historical significance aside—would likely have to be taken down to the foundations and built up again. There were some signs of a termite infestation in the cavities of the cracked open walls, but that didn't seem like such a worry anymore.

It certainly didn't seem like a reason for Hunters to want to burn it to the ground, especially not when their overkill approach would have taken out a whole street of the breathing, mortal citizens they claimed to protect.

Madoc paused on the way to the stairs. He claimed that he wanted to find the children, so maybe he should start in the place where he knew one had been?

He backtracked into the kitchen and crouched down in front of the counter. The doors were blistered and melted into place. Madoc dug his nails into the warped seam of the door and pulled. It cracked and groaned as he forced it open.

The revealed cupboard was smoke-stained and still a pathetically small space to imagine an eight-year-old wedged into as she tried to hide. Fire had buckled the sides and cracked the back of it, and there were burn marks on the Formica where the counter above had burned. The base of the unit had fallen through completely, and something metal glittered in the torn linoleum underneath.

Madoc reached in and brushed the ashes and debris out of the way. He peeled back the stiff, brittle flooring in cracked shards until he could see a long, metal lid sunk into the floor. It was, he supposed, big enough for a child to hide in. Or to think they could.

VINE hadn't missed this—it hadn't been their case—but someone on the local police had. He wondered bleakly, after the fire truck last night, if it had been deliberate.

"You okay?" Kendall yelled from outside.

"Fine," Madoc gritted out. A cursory examination of the box didn't reveal any obvious way to get into it. He supposed that he should wait for CSU to cordon off and deconstruct the area, record each step as they removed the box. However long that took.

Or....

Madoc stood up and wrenched the countertop off the wall. He tossed it aside—the heavy length of pressed board cracked as it hit the wall—and went to work on the cupboards. Screws screeched as he wrenched them out of the concrete floor and revealed the four-foot-long metal box that had to have been installed as a feature of the kitchen.

"Hey!" Kendall snapped as she pushed through the door, hard hat on and gloves tugged over her hands. "You want this place to come down on your head? Keep doing that."

"I intend to," Madoc said. He kicked a metal pipe out of his way and straddled the box. "Get out."

"This is my—"

"Get out," he repeated coldly as he bent down and dug his fingers into the concrete. "Or stay. It's up to you."

It cracked under the pressure he put on it, splinters of it dug into his fingertips and under his nails, and gave way in divots. After a moment Kendall took the path of least resistance and retreated. Her voice rose angrily outside as she radioed in for backup. Madoc ignored it. There was only half a house left as it was. If it came down, it wouldn't kill him. Maybe it would even be for the best. There had been enough horrors associated with this address, and Madoc suspected he was about to add another. Better to rip it down and salt it clean.

He clenched his jaw and wrenched at the box. The concrete groaned audibly under the strain and then cracked in deep, jagged fissures that fractured out under the ruined linoleum. One hit the wall and spiderwebbed up through the plaster and the few tiles left on the wall popped loose. Heat spread across Madoc's shoulders as he dragged the box one reluctant inch after another out of its grave. It finally came free with a brittle crack as the bolts sunk into the floor snapped off at the roots.

There wasn't much weight to it once it was free of the concrete. Madoc could have tucked it under his arm to carry it out. Instead he cradled it carefully to his chest as he carried it outside to lay it down on the ground.

"Fuck. Me," Kendall muttered succinctly. She walked forward to peer at the box. "What the hell is that? Some sort of safe?"

Madoc ran his fingers along the edge of the box. There was an electronic combination lock on the top, or there had been. Even if the fire hadn't gotten to it and the plastic screen and black rubber buttons weren't a clotted mess, he didn't have the patience to play Took with passcodes. Luckily he didn't need to.

He broke the hinges on the box and lifted the lid off.

The little girl curled up inside looked like she was made of cobwebs and ash. Pale hair tangled around her face, and she was curled up in a tight ball with her withered arms wrapped around her legs. The heat from the metal during the fire had singed her elbows and the heels of her feet dark as charcoal. Her bed was a handful of curled papers and booklets.

"Oh damn," Kendall sighed with the weary compassion of someone who'd seen too many small bodies carried from too many burned buildings. "Poor little thing. How did she—"

Madoc lowered the lid back into place.

"She's in VINE custody," he said. "This whole building is quarantined until VINE has completed a sweep and decontamination. I'm sorry, Chief Kendall, but you need to get off the property."

"What?" Kendall spluttered. "This is *my* scene, Agent. You can't just—"

"People keep making that mistake," Madoc said flatly. "Trust me. I can and I am. I don't want any city employees on this property until I've given the all clear. Or are you completely confident you've cleansed the corruption from your house after yesterday?"

He waited. She set her jaw, angry color high on dark cheeks, and glared at him.

"We'll see what SSA Crane has to say about this," she said brusquely. "Until then, the scene belongs to you, Agent."

She stalked away out of the garden. Madoc looked back at the little metal coffin and rested his hand on the lid. He flipped his saint's medal out of his collar and kissed Michael's image as he mouthed a prayer over the girl.

That done, he got up and called Pally.

"I need you in Charleston," he said the instant the line connected. "And I need a deep dive on the Aron family. I want to know everything about them. Crack juvenile records, break into the Proverbial's files on them, scrape out their secrets. I want it all."

The pause conveyed Pally's doubt. He was the only Biter who'd also been a cardinal, the only one who was older than Madoc. He didn't need to ask if Madoc was sure. He knew Madoc wouldn't have said it if he didn't.

"It will take a while to convince the Senate to crack open Mission records," he said in his quiet, ruined voice. "The Proverbials have a lot of support among Senate breathers, and the boyars respect religion still."

He didn't. The contempt in his voice betrayed that.

"Off the books, then," he said. "Do what you need to do."

Pally exhaled softly and, for once, wasted the words to state the obvious. "If this backfires, even you might not weather it intact."

Down the street, a flash went off in a window. Some homeowner had let a photojournalist install a telephoto lens in one of their upstairs rooms. Madoc scowled and let the smoke out of his heart. Even if no one ever took another photo of him, his face was well-known and his nature too indisputable to ever pass unnoticed. The child was a different matter.

He looked down at the sad little coffin and sighed.

"I want to find out why the Arons had a dead dhampir buried under their kitchen," he said. Pally forgot himself enough to swear with a guttural rasp of Old Country coarseness that would usually make him wince. "If anyone, breathing or boyar, has a problem with that, they can address me directly. Get it down, then get down here."

"Before you wake next," Pally promised. It was an old promise and less impressive than it had been in the days before planes, but still worth something. "Keep the child safe."

"She's past that," Madoc said bluntly. He hung up on Pally's resigned sigh, so the older vampire didn't hear him. "But I will."

Chapter Eleven

TOOK SCRATCHED his shoulder as he poked through the depleted stash of suits in his wardrobe. They were all nice—no more and no less. The neatly folded shirts stacked on the shelf were better quality because he liked the expensive cotton against his skin, but you could get away with that. It was hard to price a shirt without actually touching it, but an expensive suit spoke for itself. That wasn't the impression Took wanted to give.

He picked out a dark gray, fitted suit and the band-collared shirt that was a shade darker. Usually he didn't wear them together. They were too matched and slick for a trustworthy agent. Today he wanted to look more like a successful professional, someone people with money would listen to—lawyer, accountant, security consultant—someone who'd cost enough that you valued them.

Took shrugged the shirt on and then peeled the suit off the hanger. He dressed quickly, the truth of him, and his scars, buttoned down under the well-tailored silk mix.

People tended to see style as self-expression. It was intrinsic and immutable. You either had it or you didn't. Most never consciously realized that appearance was the first metric when you profiled someone on the street, how what they wore indicated class and interests, that the woman with the Cath Kidston baby bag was someone to hold a door for and the boy with the shiny tracksuit bottoms and white sneakers was someone to avoid.

Took had learned that long before the Academy. Pull on a collared shirt and shine your Sunday shoes and people never pulled you up to ask what you were doing. A lot different than if you scuffed up in boots and a work-stained T-shirt and they recognized you as "that boy" from "that family."

His dad had always said, "There's the clothes you wear *to* work, and the clothes you wear *for* work."

So when Took went to the Academy, he presented himself, day one, as who he wanted them to think he was. The only one who ever saw through it was Madoc, and even then, not all the way down to the bone.

The thought of Madoc made Took falter halfway up the shirtfront as he glanced at his reflection. His collar would cover the bite on his throat, the pierced skin and bruise still dark after two days, but he'd know it was there.

What the fuck, he thought bleakly as he finished up his shirt, had he thought he was doing? He'd spent two years twisted like an overtightened spring with the morbid suspicion that Madoc was the one who had taken him. Who'd *broken* him. How many sleepless nights had he spent on a hundred fruitless polished theories about why Madoc did it?

Even when West picked holes in his theories, he'd never been able to let the notion go. It stuck to his heels like a bad smell, because who else could it have been? All that, and yet, first opportunity he got, he still fucked Madoc.

Took absently touched the raw bite with his fingertips, Hell, he'd let Madoc do whatever he wanted. The punctures felt raw still, the itchy pang of a fresh injury, but when he pressed down, his nerves rerouted the ache into a slow wash of pleasure. He swallowed, throat dry, and pulled his hand away. How he wanted was apparently not the only thing that had changed—he didn't know *what* he wanted anymore either.

Something blunt and harsh in the back of his mind called him a liar. He ignored the brief stab at honesty as he fastened the collar and put last night away with all the other scars. Dressed down to his socks, Took padded downstairs and looked for his pills.

It took a while. They were gone from the drawer where he usually kept them and not on the table or the counters. In the end he found them on the floor. Snack had batted the little round bottle under the fridge with the detritus left by the last person who lived there and did anything with their stomach.

Took fished them out and scrambled back to his feet with a muttered curse for his cat to dodge. He popped the pack open and shook them into his hand. The last prescription had nearly run its course. There were only six left.

Dehydrated. Powdered. Packed into gelatin caps.

Took stared at the oblong pill in the palm of his hand. It wasn't even red. The capsule was colored a crisp blue and white that made it look medical. The whole effect was innocuous enough that it could have been a vitamin or a painkiller. They sold it as a "diet supplement," the vegetarian alternative to vampirism.

For two years Took had taken one of them every morning and two in the evening. They tasted of chalk, he washed them down with tepid water, and he never really thought about it… until today, when he ached from sex and the headiness of the Kiss and wondered if it would be so bad to just accept it.

Took had to come to terms with the sun-raw skin, the fangs, and the creepy silence that used to be filled with the soft rush of blood in his ears. He'd even adopted the name that online assholes had laid at his door, because he could call himself Luke all he wanted, but he'd never really be him again. Why not just let the rest of it go too? He was Anakim now—bloodsucker, vampire, monster, no matter how politely someone mouthed the right words—so did it really matter how it happened?

The idea tempted him. No more questions about who betrayed him, about what had been done to him when he was gone. No more hours spent in church as he bargained with the silent Divine, with drymouthed immortality on his side of the table and redemption on theirs. Maybe. Theoretically. In some denominations.

And he could have Madoc, cold and deadly and oddly sweet, without any guilt or suspicion. If it turned out it had been Madoc who did this to Took, maybe Took would even think it was a favor. People had fed him that line before, that at least he'd come out of that missed year with fangs. As though that was a fair enough trade for his scars and his mind held together with platitudes and staples of blank time.

Took wanted to agree with them. If he could grab that version of himself, the one who could cope with this new life, he would. Like a nettle.

Except he couldn't even suck blood from a bag without a popped staple and a spill of pus-sour half-memories that were just fear and no useful details, never mind from someone's throat. And he'd never been able to let a lie go. Even as a kid, he gnawed on them until he worked out the truth.

He closed his eyes for a second and let himself remember Madoc's body under his, the fingers that tangled in his hair, and the rough scrape of Madoc's voice as he promised things in a language Took didn't know. His tongue curled around the memory of a drop of Madoc's blood, heady as coffee and honey, and then he banished it with the hard, dry caplets that rolled down his throat like stones.

It didn't matter if he wanted it. That wasn't someone he could be. Whenever Madoc was around, Took could forget every creeping, dark thought that had ever scabbed over his brain. He could even sleep easy in his own bed, but he couldn't stay at Madoc's side all the time. Lawrence was his second-in-command, the one who had his back these days. Once Madoc was gone, the doubts came back, whispered in his ear in the dark. Took couldn't live with that.

But right now wasn't the time to come to terms. Took needed to talk to Liam Waring. Took needed to speak to Liam's son before the boyars reopened Dom Waring's case.

Once the Anakim got the idea that their lost children might still be alive, Dom's situation would get a lot more precarious. There was no way the Senate let anyone they didn't trust approach the man. Took might have fangs now, but he had always been too good at killing the undead for any of them to call him trustworthy.

He fed Snack and scratched her ears before he headed to the door and yanked his boots on. Right now his job was the one thing he could do well, and he was going to.

If he lost out on… something… because of it, so be it.

IT WAS obvious from Liam Waring's fogged eyes that the man didn't stay up this late very often. For a man with his political affiliations, being an early bird was an ideological stance that his weathered tan and his heavy coffee use for forced midnight meetings testified to.

"So this girl," Liam said. "This Worm—"

"Annabelle," Took corrected him, because he thought that Madoc would have. He replaced the book he'd plucked from the shelf. It was new. Lawrence was, Took had to reluctantly admit, good enough that she wouldn't have missed a copy of Stoker's *Secret History of the Dragon*, otherwise known as the Hunters Bible. It could indicate that the Warings were more involved with the Hunter cause—either all along or since their son's arrest—than Took had believed. He still thought it was just set-dressing for the role that Liam was ready to play. If the man had real faith, the book wouldn't be dusty. Took brushed his fingers against his leg. "Annabelle Franklin."

Liam ignored the interruption as he topped up his coffee from the carafe. He took it black, unadulterated by coffee or sugar, with a shot of garlic syrup from a small bottle. The smell hung in the air. Took was allergic to it now, but he didn't think he'd ever have enjoyed the stench of it mixed with burned coffee.

"Whatever. She murdered all these people, and my poor son had nothing to do with it? Maybe she even framed him, or the Biters did?" Liam tested the theories out loud as he weighed which one would serve him best. He sat down behind his modest but nicely made desk and pointed at the papers stacked on it. "I speak for a lot of people who demand to be heard, people who don't usually have a voice. The boyars want to silence us all so their words are the only ones that matter in the halls of power, even if they have to have to attack me through my son."

He waved a hand at the narrow chair on the rug opposite his desk. "Sit," he instructed.

Took dubiously eyed the neatly positioned chair. The complicated death traps and psychological games that Hunters played with the Anakim were—mostly—the preserve of movie makers. In Took's experience, most Hunters depended on sneak attacks and overwhelming violence. Still, the chair made the back of his neck itch like he *knew*, unlikely or not, that there was a trapdoor and a pit of gators under it.

He kept his post. "I'd rather stand."

Liam scowled briefly and then composed himself as he got back to the new narrative he'd crafted. It had already gone from theory to fact inside his head.

"So when will the boyars admit that they made a mistake?" he asked. "How soon can we get Dom out of that hellish jail they've put him in? The Salt is for monsters, not a young boy."

"I think they'd argue your son is a monster," Took said. He saw the disagreement brew on Liam's face and didn't give him time to voice it. "Your son was still found bloody-handed at the crime scene. He's never defended himself, and the murders stopped when he was arrested."

Liam snorted. "Murder," he muttered through a sneer.

It was an old argument. Took could feel the edges of both sides on his tongue—"it's not murder to stab a corpse" lined up against "it's murder to stab someone who begs for their life."

He swallowed it. Even if he wanted to have that argument again—and he didn't—he had a reason to be there that didn't require Liam to agree with him on Anakim rights.

"Either way, the evidence against your son is still compelling. This doesn't guarantee him a stay of execution or even a retrial if the boyars don't think it's necessary."

Hard, flinty anger glittered in Liam's eyes.

"I will make them see that it *is* necessary," he said. "Once people know that VINE framed my son—"

"They didn't," Took cut in harshly. "And the boyars know that. Never try and bluff a vampire, Mr. Waring. They can tell."

"I thought you didn't like that name."

The aftertaste of the word was bitter on Took's tongue. It was the unvarnished, unsweetened truth of what he was, and something he didn't want to always have to confront. But then, it was old, unvarnished advice from some*one* he'd never wanted to confront.

"But you do," Took said, the deflection sharp enough to make Liam draw back with a sour look. "So think the worst of the boyars, Mr. Waring, because if you embarrass them, your son's stay of execution will be a short one."

For a second, fear showed on Liam's face. It wasn't often he let the mask of ambition slip and the man beneath exhale a real emotion. Then he plastered contempt over the crack as he curled his lip at Took.

"When I hired you, I assumed that even if you bled black, you'd know better than to trust just any goddamn wetmouth," he said. "Crane said I could trust you, that we could trust you to take the humans' side over the monsters. I should never have believed him. Never trust a Goat should be the motto of my family. Once some fucker like you takes the fang—"

It wasn't like Took had never been angry before, just not like this. The usual cold, almost logical itch of it had turned into an icy blast that slivered through him on cold, splintered fingers and toes and dragged him along with it for a fast, vicious slide. When he slipped off the ride, he found his hand around Liam's throat and the man bent so far backward in his chair that it was about to slip from underneath him. Took's fingers were dug so deeply into his neck that the darkly tanned skin was blanched white. Liam's breath smelled of garlic and coffee. It made Took's eyes sting but nothing else.

Irritation still scraped at Took like grit in an oyster, but the pearl of anger it generated had already crumbled away to nothing. It left Took with a dry mouth, a dull ache behind his fangs, and no idea of what to say. The blank fear in Liam's eyes and the acrid smell of adrenaline that rose from him suggested Took hadn't looked like he planned to say anything.

"You don't pay me enough to insult me," Took said as he scrabbled for the right words. He hauled Liam back upright and let go of his throat. Liam coughed, spluttered, and scrambled away to the other end of the desk so the long length of wood was between them. He rubbed nervously at his neck with anxious fingers while Took stepped back and fastidiously straightened his jacket. "And whatever SSA Crane might have told you, I don't care about sides. I just want to know the truth. If your son killed those families, I have no interest in getting him from under The Salt. And I'd have said that when I had a pulse. If that's not good enough for you, Mr. Waring, pay the balance of your bill and we'll call it a day."

Took drew back to the chair he'd originally rejected and sat down. A pool of sharks didn't open under him, but the hard-backed seat wasn't particularly comfortable either. Not a death trap, but the small meanness was still meant as a trap. His chest felt hollow and empty, the fizz of his panicked brain lonely without the company of a heart to pound. Last night there had been so much going on, and the overlay of pain as a distraction, that he hadn't noticed it.

A draft of coffee, cup held in a shaky hand, didn't do whatever Liam thought he needed. He choked out a rough curse, fumbled in the drawers for a moment, and dragged out a bottle of whiskey.

"You think you can scare me?" Liam said with a rough laugh. He twisted the cap off the whiskey and took a swig. It made him wince as the liquor ran down his raw throat. "What scares me is that my son is in a hell hole with monsters. What scares me is that I'll never get him back. So fuck you for giving me hope and then acting like I'm the dick for wanting it. Dom's just a little boy. Under that stare he gives people, all he wants is to come home."

"I can't promise you that," Took said. "All I can give you is the assurance that if he stays in The Salt, you'll have a good reason as to why."

Liam took another long, sweaty gulp of booze. A twitch of thirst caught at Took's throat, and he rubbed his tongue over the roof of his mouth after the memory of taste. He'd tried to get drunk since he died, but it didn't have the same tang and it didn't take.

The tumbler cracked against the table as Liam smacked it down.

"I was told to drop it," he said. Blue eyes flicked to Took and then back down to the mouthful of whiskey left in his glass. "That I shouldn't worry about my son when I was the one in trouble."

Took leaned forward. "By whom?"

He didn't really expect an answer, which was good since all Liam gave him was a brisk, tight-lipped head shake.

"How?"

It took a second, but Liam finally tossed back the last of the whiskey. He wiped his mouth on his sleeve and leaned down to pull out the bottom drawer. When he sat back up, he pushed a handful of letters across the desk. The one on top was an official visiting order to The Salt. The other three were folded, stained scraps of paper with blunt, block-lettered threats scrawled onto them.

"A martyred son gets you votes. A grave will get none." It was signed with a scrawled wolf's head, which effectively answered Took's question about who'd sent it. Took frowned and folded the note over. "How did you get in touch with the Hounds of Gabriel, Mr. Waring?"

Liam choked out a cracked laugh. "Never. Not once," he swore. "What good is it to jump from the vampire's fangs into a wolf's mouth? They're all monsters."

He seemed to have forgotten to count Took among them.

The Hounds weren't all real werewolves, of course, despite what they implied. The Anakim had helped to nearly eliminate the curse. It turned out the cure was quite simple—a silver knife to the heart of the newly bitten to end the spread. Technically, sufferers had more rights today. The Nations had insisted on protections for their shifting types, and the lycanthropes, even if not quite the same, had been bundled in with them, but there were a lot of nurses and cops who still thought the silver stroke more merciful than life cursed.

The wolves who survived the purge disagreed, and the Hunters had made an uneasy peace with their new allies. They might be monsters, but they hated the Anakim more than humans did.

"When did you get them?"

"After I got the letter," Liam said. He braced his elbows on the table and pressed his knuckles to his lips. The words filtered out between his fingers. "I pulled every string I could reach, burned all my bridges, called in every favor I was owed or will ever be owed. It finally paid off. Someone finally came through, a week ago. The next day someone gave the first note to my… to a friend… and the next was tucked into my mother's door. I found the last one in my bed."

"They wanted to scare you."

A grim smile twisted over Liam's face. "They succeeded. When you came in tonight, I thought that maybe I wouldn't need to defy them. Instead I had to decide who was more important, me or my son. I think it might be the first time I've ever picked him. You've got what you want, Bennett. Help my son."

"If I can."

Took tapped the letters together and tucked them into his pocket. He left Liam to finish the bottle of whiskey.

MORGUES DIDN'T smell any better to the undead than they did the living. Even when Took held his breath, he could taste the corruption, coffee, and cheap bleach on his tongue. He could practically feel it in his nose and throat, ready to slip down the next time he took a breath.

The corpse of last night's competent killer lay on the stainless steel slab. Stripped of combat gear and weaponry, he looked like a dead man with a weak chin and not much left in the way of a foot. His throat had been cut, and his associates had finished the job with a bullet to the forehead. The black hole was punched just above his eyebrows, like a powder-rimmed period to the problem caused by a disposable thug in need of medical attention.

"Alan Beam," Dr. Forrester said as he pushed his glasses up his forehead to squint at his paperwork. "He's a two-time felon with previous for arson and sexual assault. That was ten years ago. It looks like he didn't get religion when he was inside, just this."

He pointed with his pen at Beam's naked, pallid chest—not that he needed to. The tattoo was clumsily drawn, all blown lines and rough scars, but the ink had been worked deep under the skin. It was stark black, and each letter was a foot long.

DNR.

It stood for Do Not Rise—not that it was an issue for Beam. The bullet in his head wouldn't stop him rising to the Kiss, but what came back wouldn't be much use to itself or VINE, and it was a popular slogan for antivampire paramilitaries of a nonreligious bent. After all, what religious schism could be bitter enough to prevent common cause against the undead? For the likes of Beam, though, it was because Hunters who carved crosses into their arms and had the Word of God in their mouths expected a certain standard of behavior from their recruits. Murder and torture they could turn a blind eye to, but rape was the sort of thing that made it hard to keep up the pretense that you were the good guys.

"How did you get his ID so quickly?" Took asked. He lifted Beam's arm off the slab and turned it over. As expected, Beam's fingertips had been scoured clean years ago. There was just a pad of smooth white scar tissue where his prints should be. "Even VINE would have taken a while to run his DNA through the system."

Forrester used a pen to pull his glasses back down onto his nose as he looked up at Took.

"Luckily enough, he's a local boy," Forrester said. "Charleston born, bred, and with an old warrant for burglary hung on his sheet. So he popped up quickly enough, especially since Special Agent Madoc made this a top-priority case."

Forrester was, by all accounts, a good pathologist, professional enough not to *ew* over corpses or flush at the mention of a handsome man. Took could still… feel… the suddenly quickened blood under night-job-wan skin, smell the cocktail of hormones and spunk on the air.

The scrape of hunger in the back of his throat wasn't unexpected. His regime of dry little pills was guaranteed to satisfy his dietary requirements, but that didn't mean they *satisfied*. Like a thirsty alcoholic with a glass of milk, it did the job but left the craving. But Took didn't expect the flash of razor-sharp, wholly hypocritical possessiveness that dug its claws into his spine.

Madoc wasn't his, would never be his. Even if Took wanted more than last night's satisfyingly bad idea, which he didn't, he'd just be an itch for Madoc to scratch. Even if they were together a decade—ten times longer than Took's longest relationship to date—he'd still be nothing more than a brief digression to the immortal.

Although, he supposed, he was immortal now too.

For a moment, with an indrawn breath of realization, he almost understood the people who acted like he'd come out of that box ahead.

Then the taste of death hit his stomach and shriveled his cock—blood soured quickly in the body—and he remembered they were full of shit.

He dragged his attention back to the corpse.

"Any known associates?" he asked.

"Plenty, most of whom wouldn't have a good word for him," Forrester said. The flush faded from his cheeks as his mind drifted away from Madoc. "Mr. Beam had a good habit of turning snitch when he needed and a way about him that got the wrong people to talk. 'All hat and no cattle,' one of the officers said. SSA Madoc has the file."

The corner of Took's mouth twitched in a dry smile. Until today, West's more-or-less unofficial approval had been enough for Took to forge a fair relationship with the local cops. At least in the morgue, that was apparently now on hold. Forrester wasn't going to go against the Biters.

God knew, Took couldn't judge. He'd done the same thing, way back when. It had made sense at the time.

"Thanks for your help," he said.

Forrester had the grace to look abashed but didn't back down. He started to turn away, but he hesitated as he frowned at something he'd written down on his pad.

"There was one other thing," he said. "He has another tattoo in his armpit. It could just be art. I ran it through VINE's database, but I couldn't find anything like it listed as having significance. But it's a painful place to get inked and not one that's seen a lot."

"What is it?"

Forrester tucked his clipboard under his arm and leaned over the table. He grabbed Beam's bony elbow and lifted his arm. Flaccid underarm skin, whatever muscle tone Beam had gone flabby with death, peeled away from his ribs with a dry, sticky sound. Under the gingery stubble of coarse hair in Beam's armpit, a spindly ink nightshade bloomed.

Only an idiot, after all, would use the publicly known sigil of their organization as the secret sign of membership. The Hounds were a lot of things, but none of them were idiots. Instead the werewolves and their groupies took the thing that could kill them and made it their own. Literally, since normal ink would bleed out of a werewolf's skin within days.

"People do stupid things when they're drunk," Took said. "If it isn't in the database, I don't imagine it means anything. The VINE database is quite exhaustive."

Forrester looked dubious as he stared at the blob of ink as though it might turn into words if he squinted the right way. When it didn't, he dropped Beam's arm back onto the table with a meaty thump and scribbled something on his clipboard.

"If anyone would know, you would," he said. The look Took gave him made him pause. "You were Agent Bennett, right? He was the one who did the latest compilation on the database. I attended his training course on how to use it effectively. That's why the tattoo stood out."

Took should have appreciated it. He had spent two years as Took, because the person he'd been before that box in that room had gone forever. The Endorian view on the undead—that they were shells puppeted by a curse that thought it was alive, the soul long gone—should have been a welcome acknowledgment. Instead he felt disoriented at the relegation of his whole life to the past tense, thrown off balance when his balance was already shaken.

"Glad you paid attention," he said stiffly. His brain scrambled for something to change the subject, and he grabbed at the sudden memory of Forrester's early, absentminded comment. "You said that Agent Madoc had made this case top priority?"

It hadn't been top priority last night. It was important because of the children involved, even if they were dead, but not enough to slide it into the category usually used for active, ongoing Hunter attacks. The last time something had been shoved that unceremoniously to the top of the list was when they closed down the compound in Utah.

The expression on Forrester's face said that Took had missed something. That always put Took's back up, and frankly, right then, the little pathologist wasn't on his good side.

"What?"

"I… it's VINE business," Forrester said.

"I'm an agent."

"Bennett was an agent," Forrester countered. "If you were, then you'd already know what happened."

The cold storm of anger stirred in Took's brain for the second time. He could feel it crackle in his marrow, but that was all. Everything warm huddled down inside until it passed.

Forrester stepped back. His hip bumped the edge of the slab and he jumped, dropped the clipboard, and blurted out a nervous laugh. It steamed in front of his lips. "Sorry. I think someone dropped the temp in here again."

"I—"

A hand scruffed the back of his neck and squeezed down. "Agent," Madoc said, his voice sharp with anger. "I need to talk to you. *Now.*"

The familiar command in that word cut through the anger, right down to the ten-year-old boy whose immediate response was "I didn't do it!" By the time that protest got to his tongue, it had turned into the more respectable "Sir?"

It wasn't enough to get rid of the anger, but it shrunk back down into Took's bones. Away from the hot tug of lust that ached in his thighs at the clipped command in Madoc's voice. He wanted to ignore it, to shove Madoc against a wall and remind him that Took didn't work for him anymore. He wanted to go down on his knees and do anything Madoc told him in that clipped, controlled voice.

Maybe that would stop Forrester's cow-eyed admiration of Madoc over Took's shoulder. As though Madoc could feel the dark chill himself, his fingers tightened on Took's neck.

"Agent Bennett remains a VINE operative, Doctor," he said. "His clearance level hasn't changed."

Took wondered bleakly if that was real, or if it was because Madoc had taken Took apart and fingered all the bits before he put him back together? He didn't know. At this point he didn't know if he even really suspected. Sometimes it just felt like an old, sour habit that he chewed over, like tofu with no seasoning. But he'd trusted that bit of his brain that stitched together motivation his whole life. He couldn't stop now.

"What the hell did you think you were doing?" Madoc snapped as he hauled Took down the corridor and into another empty room. The walls were lined with filing cabinets, and the only thing on the desk that was pushed back against the wall was Madoc's heavy leather combat jacket. He'd stripped down to a thin silk T-shirt and fitted jeans, and maybe that had been for Forrester. It was the last resentful jibe from the cold under Took's bones. "Do you think you can just kill someone in the middle of the police station and no one will do anything?"

"Don't be ridiculous," Took snapped. "I wasn't going to kill him, just—"

He trailed off. It was obvious he hadn't been about to kill a police pathologist, right? But put on the spot, he couldn't map out what exactly he had been about to do. That was the beauty of the cold, after all—he didn't have to.

"Did you find your talent?" Madoc asked abruptly as he grabbed Took's chin to yank his head down. His eyes narrowed as he looked for the reflection of something in Took's. "It comes to most with the final kiss, but your situation then could have repressed it."

Took pulled away. "I don't have any," he said. He sounded bitter, which made no sense. It wasn't that he wanted powers, he just didn't want to be what he was. At the same time, he didn't want to have to pretend he was something better. "I'm not someone's surrogate child. I'm not your precious Lawrence to be coaxed along by a Kiss. I'm the mongrel dog the whole fucking town gathered to kick. At least a dozen different bite marks on me, Madoc. That I have enough of me left to button my trousers—"

He choked on the ugly words that filled his throat when Madoc kissed him. His lips were warmer than they'd been last night, his mouth faintly flavored with salt. It should have made Took recoil, but instead he leaned in. He skimmed his hands over Madoc's sides, the silk cool and slippery over hard slabs of muscle, and it made him ache to pull back.

But he still did.

"You can't pretend—"

"I didn't bite Lawrence," Madoc said, as though that flash of jealousy were the problem. "She's my colleague, she's my partner until I get you to get off your ass, and she's a good agent. That's all. I don't love *her*, Took."

Took knew what that meant. Even Lawrence—and he *knew* he was being unfair—could tell what Madoc was ready to confess. It would be easy to draw it out, to turn a suggestion into a statement. Took just wasn't ready to deal with a world where Madoc was maybe a breath away from saying who he did love.

"What was it that Dr. Forrester couldn't tell me, then?" he changed the topic abruptly. "What did you find out?"

Chapter Twelve

MADOC WAS too old to be a fool, but he could play one if he wanted. There was no one on this side of the world, not even the boyar he still served, who had the authority to bar him from that. He could ignore Took's silent rejection of his declaration, the sticky taste of old fear that clung to his mouth from Took's, and even resist the realization that his love for Took had done neither of them any favors.

Should he, though?

The only reason he'd let Took withdraw so totally, even handed over supervisory duties to West, was because he wanted to preserve something of that delicate not-quite-a-thing between them. Anyone else he'd have dragged out of their hermitage and done the due diligence that a man owed those beneath him.

His father's morality. It made some old, still-petty part of Madoc cringe to realize that he hadn't lived up to the low bar his father had set.

"We will talk about this." He caught Took's hand and lifted it to his mouth. His lips brushed over fight-scarred knuckles in a gesture that was half courtly and half courtship. "Later."

There was a hint of bitterness in the corner of Took's mouth as he tilted it in a smile. "Later is always convenient," he said. Then he grimaced as though he'd accidentally caught himself on the jab. "After this is over, then we talk."

Madoc wasn't sure what to make of the grimness in Took's voice. He wished there were time, but every discovery in this supposedly dead case pressed the accelerator on the investigation.

"Right now," he said. "I'm putting you back on active duty."

Took flinched and pulled his hand away. "You can't do that."

"You know that's not true."

Panic flashed through Took's eyes as he shook his head. "I'm *broken*, Madoc. What if I have a panic attack if I'm trapped somewhere? Or lose control in an armed situation. I can't be trusted in the field."

They were the same bullet-point excuses that Madoc received every time he queried when he'd get his agent back. He had lost patience with them a year ago, but he throttled back on his frustration the best he could—not particularly well, but it wasn't something he'd ever cared to practice.

"Then stay out of the field," he said flatly. "It isn't as if I can't replace you with any of the other Biters there. I have for the last two years."

The flash of resentment that crossed Took's face for a second was simultaneously hypocritical and reassuring. Whatever he might say about his unwillingness to get back in the field, he obviously didn't expect anyone to agree.

"Then why bother?" Took asked.

Madoc reached up and tapped his fingertip against Took's forehead, right between his eyes. "What's in here," he said. "I can find a dozen capable Anakim to throw on a Biter's uniform, hold a gun, and pull the trigger. What's in your gray matter is harder to train, and the boyars won't let you near this case if you aren't a paid-up agent."

"I made a commitment to the Warings."

"You need a payday that bad, I'll give you a bonus," Madoc snapped as his patience finally frayed. "You want to play Judas for the bigots? If you can live with it, go right ahead. Pretend they think you're still a bleeder under the skin. I don't care. All I care about is that I need your brain, or whatever is left of it after two years spent feeling sorry for yourself."

That time Took didn't bother to hide the glare. Anger made him look brutish as the open surfer-boy features tightened and piercing blue flashed from under heavy brows. It was probably a symptom of lovesickness that Madoc found that attractive.

"I thought Lawrence was your go-to expert now," he said sullenly.

Madoc snorted. "Now you want me to pet your ego?" he asked as he stepped into Took's space. He watched Took's eyes flit over his face and then drop to his mouth, pupils dilated as a flush of hunger edged out the lust. "Fine, even with half a brain and twice as needy, you're still a better profiler than Lawrence, but she'll be your boss one day."

That made Took's eyes flick back up, and he snorted. "Like I'll be in VINE by then. I have one more assessment to go, and then, temporary return to duty or not, I'm out." He stepped back and tugged absently at his collar to pop the small ivory buttons. The hint of a bruise, a curve of ripe purple stain against tanned skin, made it Madoc's turn to be distracted by the lust that flared to life in his balls. "If I do this, we treat the Waring family fairly. Nothing brushed under the rug, no evidence that gets buried because it would be embarrassing to overturn a verdict."

"That's not your call to make."

The corner of Took's mouth twitched into something that wasn't quite a smile. "I'm still making it."

They stared at each other for a second. There wasn't any aggression in Took's face. It was a blunt statement of the facts as he saw them.

"You know I don't work like that," he said.

"I know. The boyars do, and once it gets out that VINE thinks there's a chance the dhampir kids are still alive? They'll do whatever it takes to get them back *and* come out of this scented with roses. Whatever Dom Waring *did*, he can pay for, but not for anyone else's sins."

That helped. It had caught Madoc a little on the raw that Took thought it needed to be said. His tender heart preferred the explanation that it was the boyars Took didn't trust.

"You know I can't make promises for the boyars' behavior," he said, "but I won't bend the neck if they play the villain."

Finally Took nodded, and his shoulders relaxed as some tension that Madoc hadn't even noticed let go of its hold on him. He flicked another button on his shirt. Madoc glanced away from the bruised temptation of his lean throat.

"I take it I can borrow a uniform?"

"Ask Lawrence."

Took gave him an annoyed look, but nodded. "So why?" he asked. "If I'm officially back on duty, what's the big secret?"

"I found the youngest of the Aron children," he said. It wasn't often he surprised Took—a kiss, a rescue, this—so Madoc savored the moment. "She never left the house. So, don't kill Dr. Forrester. We might need him."

"THERE AND back by candlelight," Madoc said as he greeted Pally at the Sword Gate entrance to the police station. "Good as your word."

Pally slung his go bag onto his shoulder with an ease that belied the arsenal of weaponry that Madoc knew was in there—guns mostly. He'd have a few knives, but Pally didn't trust himself with edged weapons.

They got you too close to the blood, and his control was… not what he might wish. He glanced up at the slice of moon that hung on the black velvet of the sky.

"Not quite," he said in his low, ruined voice. "I tried, though."

"It's appreciated," Madoc said. "The Aron files?"

"I tried," Pally repeated with a faint grimace at the admission. "Quick is at the local chapter of the Proverbial Church to get into the records on their missionaries. He said I needed to let him off the leash if we wanted access to their records without the stamp of a boyar. I don't exactly know what he meant, but I gave him permission anyhow."

"It was the right call," Madoc said, "and my responsibility."

Pally shrugged. "Let the boyars rage if they want," he said. His pale, amber-yellow eyes always had a disconcerting effect. They were a beast's eyes in a human face, but the flash of anger that lit them from behind drained the humanity out of them. "If the Proverbials had anything to do with the loss of this little one, there won't be enough of them left to raise a hue and cry on our methods."

The hot edge to his voice made Madoc scowl. On most days he trusted Pally. They'd been enemies once. The reasons for that were all sealed under The Salt, but Madoc remembered times he'd ridden into a settlement and found it gone, wiped away root and branch by Pally.

Or Paladin, as he was called back then. No one had wanted to be intimate enough with him for nicknames.

Of course all the cardinals had done terrible things. Pally had just done them with confidence in the justness of the cause. The same steel-shod self-righteousness that made him strap on his country's cause, back in the day, had seen him visit atrocities on those who endangered his new faith in his boyar.

In Madoc's experience, a man with a cause was the worst enemy— or ally. A wicked man might, at least, hesitate to add something new to their tally of sins, but someone who believed they acted for the Greater Good could commit any sin and still sleep at night.

"We don't know who's involved yet," he said as he gestured for Pally to follow him up the blanched white steps to the heavy doors. "Waring could still be the sole actor. The fact that Nora Aron was a dhampir puts the family within his victim group, or this could be some new brutality from the Hunters. Even if the Proverbials are involved, we don't want to sow disputes within the Accord if we do not have to."

The old motto of the Empire of Blood was still carved over the door, scarred and chipped in places where public opinion had run against it. There was something dourly appropriate about the grim old words—*If you would be our enemy, we do not bend, and you will break.*

Pally paused in the doorway under them. He had the sort of looks Tepes favored in his court—dark, pretty, and dead-eyed. "If they murdered our children," Pally said coldly, "the Accord is worthless, and it's war that we'll court."

It was the sort of sentiment that Madoc should stamp down on and then send a report up through the hierarchy to whatever politician oversaw VINE. But for all the things Madoc had lost in his long life, and he would unsentimentally note that his losses had been many, he'd never lost a child.

To rebuke Pally now would be as pointless as when they'd told Madoc to stop looking for Took.

"It won't come to that," he said.

Pally tilted his chin in acknowledgment. "We can hope for a better outcome," he said, "but be prepared, Madoc. If we find more dead children, then I will fuck over every last, toothless bastard between here and California. And I will not be alone."

"MAY I?" Pally asked as he extended his hand, his fingers poised just above Nora's bone-white brow. Death had made him pallid a long time ago, but his fingers still looked darker than the child's skin.

On the other side of the table, Forrester looked uncomfortable as he fidgeted with his glasses, but he nodded.

"Yes," he said. "I've already collected all the trace evidence that was on her… um… on her clothes and skin. Not that there was a lot."

Pally settled his fingers on the girl's skull and closed his eyes.

"It seems as though the winter tree has withered." He murmured the Enochian prayer in a soft, reverent voice.

Madoc grimaced but crossed his arms and waited. Enochian piety had never come easy to him. He'd been raised as a weed in the local church garden, an example to point to when they preached original sin and a cautionary tale for young girls with an eye for the boyar's guard, but it was still the faith he fell back on when he was in need. Madoc absently reached up to tap the worn medal under layers of leather and silk.

Like his father's old gift, the silver stung, but he'd grown used to the itch.

"So?" Took interrupted as he pushed open the door to the morgue. "Are we sure this is Nora Aron?"

Madoc turned to gesture at him to shut up, but his brain tripped up on itself as he saw Took back in full uniform. In *Madoc's* livery, essentially, since he'd been the heart and the head of the Biters since they were conceived. Took had always looked good in black, pared down so you could enjoy the broad shoulders and the harsh taper down to lean hips, the lack of any design element or color to distract from the earnest, corn-fed good looks and salt-blond curls. He looked even better now that Madoc had touched and kissed everything that lay under that fitted cotton and kevlar.

The ache caught at Madoc's heart and his balls at the same moment, but he couldn't decide which was stronger, his satisfaction to see Took back in uniform and back at work or the desire to take the uniform right off him again.

Before he had to decide, Pally tossed a black, dangerous glare toward the interruption, but it turned to an expression of delight as he saw Took.

"Bennett," he said with a slow, sweet smile. It was a rare expression to see on Pally's face, and Took looked surprised. They had always worked effectively together, but they had never been friends. "You've come back to us."

"I was—"

Pally walked briskly across the room and pulled Took into a rough, affectionate embrace. He kissed him on the cheek.

"For every one lost to sleep, we raise another," Pally said. "Are you well, brother?"

Took stood awkwardly, arms at somewhere between "I surrender" and "awkward aunt hug." He gave Madoc a confused, slightly terrified look over Pally's shoulder.

"I'm… better than before," Took said. He sounded nearly as surprised by that answer as he had the hug. "Not well, yet, but getting there, I guess."

Pally nodded and stepped back. Then he slapped Took on the shoulder and gripped it in slim, elegant hands that could punch through brick.

"The first decade is hardest," he said.

Madoc bit the inside of his cheek and held his tongue. What Pally had just said was a lie, and they both knew it. The first *decades* were the hardest—whether you were born or turned—as your mortal friends and family aged and died and the world changed around you as though it were made of quicksilver and ideas.

Eventually you either got used to it or you let it end you, mired down in some dark hole or strung up by a mob wielding pitchforks.

No one ever told that to a newly fanged Anakim. They still imagined the passage of time as mortals, and a hundred years of slow misery seemed like a lot.

"It's better than the alternatives," Took said with a flash of humor, but it faded as he glanced toward the slab, and then his eyes narrowed as he registered the details of the body. "That's not Nora Aron."

Forrester, secluded firmly on the other side of the table, away from the fangs and the hugging, cleared his throat.

"Actually," he said in an uncomfortably tight voice. "According to dental and hospital records, she is. Nora Elizabeth Aron, six years old at the time of her death and unvaccinated on religious grounds. Based on a cursory external examination, she died of either blood loss from a penetrating stab wound to her stomach or asphyxiation once she entered the… ah… lockbox?"

Took ducked from under Pally's grip and stalked over to the slab. He studied the girl briefly and then gestured briskly for Forrester to pull the sheet back. Pally made an offended noise under his breath, but Madoc silenced him with a hand on his arm.

"That looks relatively shallow," Took said as he studied the livid red slit that cut a crooked line across Nora's flat, almost translucent stomach. "It might have nicked her stomach or—" He paused to angle an imaginary knife over Nora's stomach to map out where the point would end. "—possibly her intestines or liver?"

"Well, yes," Forrester said with a touch of pique at his role being usurped. "The main problem here was blood loss, not damage to the organs. It looks like it was inflicted from behind, possibly during a struggle, since I found blood on her that didn't seem to come from her injuries. At that point she managed to get away, fled, and somehow accessed the lockbox. Without treatment the blood loss would probably have killed her on its own. However, there are also signs of asphyxiation on the body as well as—"

Forrester gripped the girl by shoulder and hip and lifted her up. There were dark, smoldered singe marks on her back, spread across her shoulder blades like wings and cupped around her hips like hands.

He went to lower her back down, but Madoc stopped him with a quick gesture. He joined Took at the slab and bent down to study the marks. The blistered cracks on her elbows and raw meat on her knees and the heels of her feet where they had pressed against the hot metal of the box. The long vanes on her back looked like something else, the edges curled by heat but worked down under her skin.

When Madoc traced along her shoulders, he felt no damage to the skin.

"Does that look like a burn pattern?" he asked.

Forrester frowned and adjusted his glasses again. "Well, no," he admitted, "not a common one, but nothing about this is common. The body—"

"Child," Pally corrected.

Forrester cleared his throat and started the sentence again. "The child has, theoretically, been entombed in this box for nearly five years. Sans any of the usual complications, she should have...." He stumbled over what he wanted to say as he looked over at Pally, but there was only one word for it. "Decomposed. There's no evidence of that whatsoever. Based on the body, she could have died yesterday in that fire. If it isn't a burn pattern, I should be able to tell you more once I have permission to get started on the autopsy."

"Don't expect that," Madoc told him.

Pally stepped forward and produced a black silk winding cloth from his pocket and shook it out. There was enough of it to swaddle a full-grown Biter in his gear. They had no Enochian priests on the team, but Pally's devotion was close enough for most, and the child fit easily within the folds.

"We take care of our own," Madoc told him as Pally lifted the body as though it weighed nothing.

Forrester gawped for a second and then gathered up his indignation as he cut across the room. He barred Pally's way out with spread arms and a glare. "The Aron case belonged to Charleston. Whatever VINE's interest in this child is, you can't just cut us out of the investigation completely. Dhampir or breathing child, she's in our jurisdiction and it is our responsibility to find out what happened to her."

"I admire your dedication," Pally said harshly. "But you will not change my mind. Now move or be moved."

Forrester looked around the room. Usually it would have been Took he looked to for backup, an assumption more than a few people had made and regretted. Now he just found another Anakim face in a room where one more dead person wouldn't be noticed for a while—not that Madoc intended to kill the man, but vivid imaginations had spawned more defeats than anything else.

"I am going to report this," he warned stiffly as he moved away from the door. "And if this case is challenged because you broke chain of custody...."

Pally just snorted and walked out the door. It swung shut behind him and Madoc caught it in one hand. "Took?"

"Just a second."

Madoc leaned against the door and waited as Took grabbed a notebook from the table and scrawled something in it.

"Any trace you find," he said, "run against this name."

Forrester glared at the scrap of paper. "I don't work for VINE," he said. "And even if I did think it was a good lead, why the hell should I tell you anything about it?"

"Because dhampir or breathing, she was just a little girl," Took said. "So were the others. We're better equipped than anyone to find whoever did it."

MADOC'S PHONE was full of agitated texts and insistent voice messages. NBC wanted a quote about the Aron house, the boyars wanted to speak to him immediately, and the Charleston sheriff wanted a reckoning.

"Are you going to answer them?" Lawrence asked as Madoc flicked his phone off. She was perched on the edge of one the armchairs.

He tucked it into his pocket. "I'm an old man," he said dryly. "Modern technology confuses me. Maybe I got upset and threw it out a window."

She rolled her eyes at him and then looked around the small living room. They had decamped to the nearest VINE safe house, which was Took's current residence. Madoc had braced himself for a fight over it, but Took just shrugged and told them not to bother the cat.

The cat bothered Madoc. Reminded of its existence, he turned around and, after a quick search, found it crouched on the top of the door—a loaf of white fluff with malicious eyes.

"It's not what I imagined his house was like," Lawrence said, and Madoc glanced back at her. "He was one of the best profilers VINE ever had, and after what happened to him… I mean, you wonder what happens afterward."

"And you'd decided?"

She shrugged. "More Miss Havisham—books and texts and files of old cases," she said. "Less… renter on a short lease."

Madoc tried to see the space with her eyes. He liked it, but then he'd spent a night here tangled around Took. Satiation improved a man's opinion of a space. There were no mementos, no knickknacks—unless you counted the stake in the kitchen, and Madoc doubted Lawrence would approve—and the layout of the place had the disinterested appeal of the generic.

It looked much like Took's old apartment had, just like the small office-library, the only space he'd bothered to claim as off-limits, looked like his desk at VINE. It had never occurred to Madoc, who'd lived in luxury but owned nothing as a cardinal, that it was odd.

"He's not a sentimental man," he said as he walked over to the door. The cat gave him a pink-rimmed glare and leaped down. It darted off down the hall, probably to go glare at Pally, and Madoc closed the door. "What did the Hunter they caught at the scene tell you?"

Lawrence wrinkled her nose. "Not much. Took was right. He's not a real Hunter. He's just some blowhard wannabe who got together with his friends to vandalize Anakim homes and harass Anakim women. He's a bottom-feeder. Only a few nights ago, the real deal in the morgue came to him with an offer he didn't want to resist."

"Did they know each other?"

Lawrence shrugged. "They used to run in the same circles, but our friend is a dead end for anything that happened between the last time Alan Beam got arrested and what happened after they went to the bar. He did say… well, boasted, that Beam had gotten in tight with some big name."

"Who?"

Annoyance soured the corners of Lawrence's mouth as she shrugged. "He wouldn't tell us unless we offered him some sort of deal. The discussions on that are ongoing with the Charleston DA."

That did complicate things. VINE didn't have to negotiate or keep their word if they decided someone didn't deserve the second chance they had on offer. But while the boyars debated whether to reopen the case, they had to abide by the local rules. At least they did until decided not to.

It was one thing to wrest the body of a dhampir child from the morgue. To invade the local watchhouse and seize a human who was affiliated, however loosely, with the Hunters? That was a different kettle of sharks entirely, and too redolent of the bad, old days when the only law was what Madoc said.

Well, some people called them bad.

"Did you believe him?"

Lawrence tilted her head to the side as she considered. "Yes," she said finally. "He's not bright enough to make something up, and he's confident his information is good enough to seal him soft time in daylight. Who, though? None of the major Hunter cells have their fingers in Charleston. The Templars?"

Madoc glanced upstairs to where he could hear the soft creak of Pally's feet on the floorboards. "If there were, Pally would know. Waiting for them to step out of line so he can come down like the hammer of God is the first hobby he's ever indulged. I'll get Quick to run through the chatter, see if anyone has made inroads that we weren't aware of. You? Stay in touch with the DA's office. The minute your bottom-feeder spits out a name, I want to know."

She nodded and stood up. "Can I stay to see what Quick found out about the Proverbial involvement?" She paused for a second and then punctiliously corrected herself. "If any."

Madoc raised an eyebrow at her. "You're a Biter, Lawrence. I'm not going to dismiss your service because Took is back."

"Is he?" she asked. "For good?"

That was the question and, if Madoc was honest with himself, the answer was probably no. Took had rejected every clean bill of health VINE's psychs had offered him. He clung to his PTSD like a "get out of jail free" card. Even after the other night, Took still had the date of his last psych eval pigeonholed as his fully pensioned release.

Madoc resented it. He bridled at the idea that he was bundled in with VINE as a bad memory to be left behind, but he couldn't entirely blame Took for it either. He suffered because of VINE.

But probably wasn't definitely.

"If he is," he said, "it's not as your replacement."

"No," Lawrence said as she pulled the door open. "I was his. There's one hole in the team to fill, and he called dibs."

Madoc laughed with a low, dark growl of sensual amusement as he thought of the other night. The sound made Lawrence go pink around the ears, a flash of awareness that Madoc was wryly pleased to see. His tastes had always run to men, but it was mildly reassuring to see he could still charm a woman if necessary.

"It doesn't work that way," he told her. "You have qualities he lacks."

"Like?"

"Never ask that question. The next person might not have an answer," Madoc told her. "You are better with victims, your political instincts are impeccable, and frankly, you're a better tactician."

Lawrence snorted. "He took out two Hunters and helped you escape a burning house."

"Counterpoint—he set himself on fire, caused a major explosion in a residential neighborhood, and shot a suspect in the foot. It *worked*, but if we'd planned that, I like to think one of us would have pointed out the flaws."

"I can hear you," Took said dryly from the other room.

Lawrence cackled despite herself and then sobered as they walked in and found Took at the dinner table with the charred box from the Aron house in front of him. She gagged, one hand pressed against her mouth.

"What the hell are you doing?" Madoc growled.

Chapter Thirteen

"PETER ARON'S father bought that house nearly fifty years ago," Took said as he tossed his tablet across the room to Madoc. "Fifteen years ago he died and Peter inherited the property. Six months later, one of the neighbors made a noise complaint. It turned out that Peter had decided that he needed to put in a new kitchen for his wife and him."

Madoc glanced at the tablet, handed it off to Lawrence, and raised his eyebrows.

"Your point?"

Before Took could say anything, Lawrence answered the question without raising her eyes from the tablet.

"It wasn't just some weird feature of the house," she said. "At the least, they knew it was there. More likely they installed it along with their new counters. The question is what for?"

Took resisted the quick, petty urge to sneer "obviously." It caught in his throat to see Lawrence at Madoc's shoulder, but that wasn't her fault. He needed to remind himself of that.

"Exactly," he said stiffly. "There was some paperwork in there with Nora, but between the fire and her blood, it was too damaged to read easily. It looks like the family passports and some medical records, but until the lab gets through with them, we can't be sure."

Madoc, jaw still set in a tight line, walked around to the far side of the dining table and leaned on the waxed, golden wood. He reluctantly ran his eyes over the coffin, his attention caught on the dry scraps of burned flesh in the corners.

"No one builds a box this size for some papers," he said. "They just put them in the safe or under a floorboard if there's something that needs to be concealed."

"Contraband?" Lawrence suggested without much conviction. "We've had cases before where people smuggled sacred items out of the Nation. The Nations' reprisals are usually tidier, though, and I've never known them to target children. And what's the connection with the Warings?"

Took had wondered that too. He didn't have an answer, so he pushed it back at her.

"It seems like that would have come up in the original investigation," he said. Lawrence flushed, two quick stripes of angry color over her cheekbones, as though it were a jibe. It wasn't, not entirely, at least. "Did you ever find any connection between his victims? Or work out how he picked them?"

"Took," Madoc said softly, a warning under his smooth voice.

"It's fine," Lawrence said. She glared at Took and her voice was scathing when she answered him. "And no, we didn't. All we had to go on was his confession and that we caught him red-handed at a murder scene."

"He never confessed," Took corrected her.

"He didn't *deny* it either," Lawrence pointed out. "If you hadn't killed someone and you were accused of something, wouldn't you say something? React? Respond?"

Took shrugged. "Probably, but what does that prove? Other than being white and male, I haven't got much in common with Dom Waring." It was McCallan's influence, Took thought dourly as Lawrence glared at him. For the last two decades, McCallan had taught preternatural behavioral science at Quantico and convinced too many of VINE's best and brightest trainees that empathy was the key to a killer's motivation. It worked for him, but the rigid old vampire had given his students an unreasonable faith in the idea that they could put themselves in a killer's shoes. "Did you look for a connection anyhow?"

"Of course," Lawrence said as she folded her arms over the tablet. She tapped out a brisk tattoo against the metal back. "We knew… we thought he'd done it, but you can't predict how a jury is going to react. Especially once Liam Waring rolled his political game into full gear. So we tried to belt and suspenders it, but the only connection was that they were mixed families with dhampir kids."

"If we assume you didn't miss anything—"

"She didn't," Madoc interrupted, a flat note of reproof in his voice as he looked up from the box.

"I might have," Lawrence said. "I missed Annabelle Franklin."

Guilt pinched at the back of Took's brain, a vinegar sting in the back of his throat. The lash of self-flagellation in Lawrence's voice was too familiar to ignore. He'd always been a piss-poor teacher, but he could hardly sneer at her for McCallaning stuff up if he didn't give her an alternative.

"Always assume you missed something, because you probably did. It's human nature to edit out stuff we don't think is important. This—" He tapped his knuckle against the box. "—has to be what links all the others. Somehow. And everyone missed Annabelle Franklin, or rather no one did. She was made to pass unnoticed."

That fired a neuron in the back of his mind—a flash-fire burst of satisfaction as he realized that he had the key to stitch all the pieces together. But it turned flat as the inspiration flashed by too quickly for him to catch. It was something, but… what?

"Do you think the Arons had smuggled things out of the Nations?" Madoc asked. Something clouded and cold flickered through his eyes. "The local gods have been restless of late. Maybe something has moved through. From your research it looked like the Arons were interested in magic."

"Human magic—distillations and concoctions, formulas, vials, and control subjects," Took said. He felt the twinge of "got it" again but ignored it for the moment. He'd have time to worry at that later, pick the neurons apart to reverse engineer the idea. "Besides, even if they were willing to… contract out… the divine to a god they didn't worship, the Nations' gods wouldn't answer. Not their worshippers; not their circus. They didn't build this to hide something."

Madoc pulled himself away from the table. It was habit to register his discomfort, the way he didn't take a breath to speak until he was as far away from the box as possible in the dining room. Took remembered Madoc's weight on him in the Aron house as the first Molotov went off, the protective hand on the back of his head.

Fire. Madoc had never liked fire.

"Then what was it for?" Madoc asked.

Took rubbed his fingers along the edge of the box. It was thinner than the rest of the metal, shiny where someone had taken a grinder to it.

"Have you ever seen people in an evacuation?" he asked. "Hardly anyone takes the designated escape route. They run along routes they know, the rat runs that they think no one else will find."

When they were done with him, someone usually dragged him back to the Box. Tonight someone else was screaming. Some old habit made him pick apart the vowels and weigh the consonants, but he couldn't find the part of his brain that knew how to make sense of that.

Ruined. Broken.

The words were in his head, but it wasn't his voice. It was a liar as well. He was ruined, he knew that, but they hadn't broken him—not yet. He didn't know why not, exactly, but he knew.

"It's not *my* fault," *the woman screamed.* "I didn't tell her anything. She never found out from me."

The woman's voice cut off raggedly, like someone had clamped a hand over her mouth. Someone else spoke up....

The memory fritzed out into static and a dark, cold rage that hung on to something Took couldn't see.

Clipped orders echoed up the stairs, and cars revved outside on the street. There was a plan. Took curled up in a ball on the floor and thought about if he could make it downstairs, outside, away.

A door slammed and he heard THE VOICE snap orders. He shuddered and crawled, his bones ground together like salt under his skin, back into the Box.

They hurt him to put him in the Box and sometimes they took him out of the Box and hurt him. No one ever hurt him in *the Box. It was, right then and right there, the closest thing to safety he could imagine.*

"Well?" Madoc asked. "What's your point, Bennett?"

His voice was sharp and expectant, the SSA Madoc who expected you to do your job and have the answers. The hand on the back of Took's neck was the Madoc who'd taken him to bed, patient in his own way.

For a second he felt like an idiot as he realized that Madoc would never hurt him. Then the dark sneak of doubt crawled back in, because he'd thought the Box was safe as well, hadn't he? Took shuddered and pushed himself away from the table as though he could shed the dread like a coat.

"When someone came to her house and killed her family, Nora didn't run to her room or try to get out. She went to the Box. It was somewhere she thought was safe, her harbor," Took said, his voice rough as he stalked out of the room. He didn't really have anywhere to go, but he couldn't stay in the room with that metal coffin anymore, not least because he had the obscure compulsion to crawl into it. "You want to know what they kept in the box? It was her."

IT WAS light out. All the good little vampires in the world, or the half of it the sun shone on, were tucked up in their coffins. Or at least decamped back to hotel rooms and VINE offices. The only ones left in the house were Took, Pally, and the little girl.

Took stood in the silent kitchen, tipped two pills into his palm, and washed them down with whiskey. It tasted like nothing much. The back of his throat caught the burn of it, but none of the wood and rye flavor. He'd never been that much of a drinker—honesty floated to the top of a drunk's bottle—but he missed the taste now he couldn't indulge.

Not as much as fried chicken, though.

His mom had made terrible fried chicken. He still remembered it now—two legs of chicken charred to the color of rust and served with last night's fries and half a can of beans, the paper plate soaked with grease and thin, orange ketchup. It had been tough as wood to chew and tasted like… hot grease, mostly.

She'd never been a good cook. Her skills lay elsewhere. In service to the Hounds.

Took tossed the rest of the whiskey back in one. Even if he couldn't taste it, muscle memory gave him enough dutch courage to pick up his cell phone. He dialed the number from memory. Over a decade since he'd last punched that number into a phone, and his thumbs still remembered the order of numbers with no help from his conscious mind.

It rang out the first time. The second as well. Took hesitated as he got ready to press Redial, his thumb pressed against the small, rubber button. It didn't feel right. He glanced upstairs and wondered if Pally could hear the other end of a phone conversation through the floorboards.

Took couldn't, but he'd been spat up as much as made. There were probably plenty of things he couldn't do that other Anakim could.

Anakim. Took wondered when he'd started to think of himself like that, even sporadically. Was it a good sign that he had started to come to terms with his situation, or was it some evidence of the corruption of the soul that the priests warned about?

Call it what you like, and God knew his mother would, but Took supposed it didn't make any difference.

From the kitchen counter, he grabbed the stake she'd sent him—the wax-smooth wood blistered his fingertips on contact—and let himself outside. It was muggy out, and love bugs flitted aimlessly across the handkerchief-sized square of courtyard garden. At some point someone had tried their best with it, but the plants had died long ago and the pots had cracked in the weather.

It was the sort of day his mother loved. She'd strip down to shorts and a cutoff top, arms and legs tanned like teak, and drink flasks of cold tea while she gardened. Sometimes she'd even sing—the long, blessed days of summer she called it, although the tunes she sporadically visited on any listeners were always from the charts.

Took retreated to the first scrap of shadow he could find, under the overgrown bush of wisteria that hung over the fence. The sickly sweet smell of mulched flowers was heavy in the air.

He pressed Redial. It rang until he thought it was about to cut off again and he'd have to start from scratch. Just before the last ring—halfway through it, in fact—she picked it up.

"What?" she said, her voice cold with suspicion over the delay. "Who's this."

Took leaned back against the fence, eyes trained on the top windows of the house for any movement. He relaxed his hold on his vowels and let the northeast Cali drawl slide back into his voice.

"Hey, Mom," he said. "It's… Luke."

That felt strange. He hadn't introduced himself as that in years, not said his old name at all for months. It didn't feel right on his tongue anymore.

Silence on the other end of the phone. Took imagined her—a lean woman with short, bobbed blonde hair and bare feet. It would only be getting light on the West Coast, but she'd have been up for hours. There'd be something on the stove in that old, copper pot she lugged from house to house, and the crossword would be done. For a sentimental moment, Took almost missed her.

"Have you called to say goodbye?" she asked.

Took tapped the point of the stake against his thigh. He could feel the point of it sharp through the worn-thin denim.

"No."

"Then call back when you're ready to do the right thing," she said briskly. "If you do it yourself, Luke, we'll bring you home."

The point of the stake dug deeper into his leg. He tightened his grip on it and kept up the drumbeat rhythm against his thigh. It ached as a bruise formed, tried halfheartedly and half-fed to heal, and then bruised again.

"I need to speak to Gabriel."

"He doesn't want to speak to you."

"Have you asked him?"

"Don't need to."

Jab. Jab. Jab.

"It's important."

"To the vampires. To you. Not to us."

Took was vaguely surprised that she hadn't resorted to a direct slur to get her point across. Not that she needed to. He understood exactly how she wanted to make him feel.

The point of the stake hit his thigh hard, and he felt the denim give way under the metal point. It gouged down into the meat—not deep enough to disable, but enough to sting. Blood welled up and wicked away into the denim, a patch of muddy crimson against faded cotton. He grimaced and gingerly pulled it out to wipe on his sleeve.

"Mom—"

"My son died. His corpse will realize it needs to follow suit soon," she said. "Until then—"

"Do you still visit Granddad every Friday in that nursing home?" he asked. He didn't need to put any threat in his voice. Like the unspoken slur she hadn't quite spat out earlier, they both knew where they were. "Still go out of your way to get the lilies Grandma always liked before you go to visit her and your brothers in the graveyard?"

She was silent, so silent that he thought he could hear the blood in her ears shush down the line.

"You'd threaten your own grandfather?" she said skeptically. "My son might just be a bag of skin for you, but I don't believe his soul has rotted out of his head so soon."

"You're right," Took said. "That's why I'm not threatening him, I'm threatening you. There are plenty of people who would cross state lines to get their hands on you, Mom. Last I checked, you still had a double handful of warrants on you in nearby states."

"I'm not scared of the cops."

"Good, because you should probably surrender to them before everyone else you conned, crossed, or condemned turns up for their pound of flesh. Unless you've put on weight, there won't be much left of you once they're done."

A breath hissed between her teeth.

"I can get in contact with Gabriel. That doesn't mean he'll want to talk to you."

"Like I said, this is important, so run the same logic past him," Took said. "I'm the best profiler that VINE has. If I tell them everything I know, how long before someone puts a noose on both of you?"

"It won't do you much good either," she pointed out.

"I might not be quite ready to kill myself, Mom," Took said. "But trust me, I haven't got a whole lot left to lose here. I'm going to be at The Salt in Nevada in two days. Tell Gabriel to meet me there or I tell them everything I know about you both. Got it?"

She grunted her acknowledgment and scuffled about for a paper and pen. Took flexed his hand around the bloody stake as he waited. He finally gave her his number, reminded her that he would ruin them all, and was about to hang up, when she blurted, "Wait."

It wasn't kindness. There was no sentimentality in Took's mom's heart, no inch of her that would waver from her convictions. There came a point in life when you've committed too much to something to ever think you've been wrong. Forty years was a lot of investment to release as a sunk cost.

Yet he still felt that hitch in his throat, a child's pointless faith that this time would be the storybook.

"What?" he asked.

"I appreciate that you don't use my son's name," his mom said. "It's insult enough that you use his body."

She hung up. Took slumped back against the fence and tilted his head up to the sun. It wouldn't kill him, not unless he waited there long enough to grow very old and very weak. The papers had been full of that a few years ago. Archaeologists in Russia had found some ancients asleep under the ice. The photos had shown shadows that had to be ten feet tall caught up a glacier as it crawled down from the mountains, and when they uncovered them, the great bodies had just crumbled to ash in the daylight before they could even get a picture. The public had called the archaeologists murderers, and they'd had to go into hiding.

But who had that amount of free time these days? Everyone had things to do.

Took pushed himself off the fence and stalked back into the house. He needed to arrange a flight to Nevada before Liam Waring got the news that his pet wetmouth had been reinstated as a Biter. Took didn't want to have to talk the man down again.

He remembered the flash of cold, mad rage in the office, and despite the fever sweat of the sun, a chill ran down his back. Liam might not come out of it alive this time.

THE OFFENDED scream of a cat cut through the house like a rusty chainsaw. It sounded like something was being murdered. Took tucked his phone between his ear and his shoulder as he ducked out of the office.

"I'll be at the airport at nine," he said to Madoc's answering machine. "If you don't approve the use of the VINE jet, I'll take a commercial flight."

He hung up abruptly as he reached the stairs and before he could begin to pad his decision with excuses. It had been a long time since he'd given a crap about the consequences of anything he did—a twinge of guilt for others, sure, but nothing for himself. So why did he care if Madoc was angry about his decision?

Maybe he'd lied to his mother after all and he did have something to lose.

It was an awful thought. He shuddered and put it to the back of his head as he followed the offended swears of his cat to the back of the house, to the guest room, as the VINE agent who'd handed over the safe house to him had described the small back room with the narrow bed and solitary chair. This was the first time that anyone had used it. Took didn't knock. He just barged the door open.

"What the fuck are you doing to my cat?" he asked sharply. Then he took in the scene and revised the question. "What is my cat doing to you?"

Blood dripped down Pally's narrow, pretty face in fat, wet ribbons. His eyebrow was laid open, one ear was freshly pierced, and the scratches ran up his face from lip to forehead in ragged stripes. He wiped blood out of his eyes with a lacerated hand.

"Cat?" he said. "It's a demon."

"Same thing," Took said. As though concerned they had forgotten about her, Snack screamed again. She was perched on the bed knob, ears flat and fur bushed out and spiky. Blood stained her paws and muzzle. He reached out, grabbed her under the front legs, and scooped her up. Nine pounds of angry, midsquirm cat dangled from his hand and tried to rabbit kick Pally. "What did you do to piss her off?"

Pally gave him a sharp look of disbelief as he poked his eyebrow back together. "Me? That hellspawn tried to claw my face off."

As though to prove it, Snack twisted her head around and sank her teeth into Took's thumb. Her fangs punched through his nail and into the meat beneath, the sharp pain an electric jab up his nerves into his armpit. He tossed her back onto the bed with a curse, and Pally dropped his hand long enough to bark out a mocking laugh.

"See?"

Snack lashed her tail, hissed at both of them, and slunk up the bed to the dead little girl laid out on the pillows. She pawed at the gossamer fine winding sheet with a bloody paw, her claws extended enough to tug at and pluck the fabric.

"And see," Pally said as he jabbed a finger at the bed. "That's what that hellcat was doing before, and when I tried to stop it, the bastard thing tried to claw my face off. What sort of animal isn't scared of our ilk?"

Took shrugged. It was a good question, but he didn't care. What mattered was that Snack was the only thing that kept something like Luke Bennett alive in that box. Everything else they had picked out of him, gobbets of "him" gone forever, but they couldn't make him kill the scrap of kitten they had tossed in with him.

If Snack, now a slightly bigger scrap, wanted to eat Pally's nose for breakfast, she could have it.

"Maybe you should have asked what she wanted," he said.

Pally snorted. His face was nearly back to pretty again, stitched together seamlessly with only smears of blood to show for his trouble. "Maybe you should have drowned that thing when it would fit in a glass instead of a bucket."

A snarl twitched at Took's mouth before he could throttle it back. He wasn't used to banter from Pally. The old vampire had always interacted with him the same way he now did with Lawrence, quietly competent professionalism. That was respect on his part—most humans rarely rose to his immortal notice. The few who did hadn't ended well.

But their new friendship didn't mean he could threaten Took's cat.

"She doesn't know what this is," Took said. He reached down and pulled the folds of silk away from the child's face. Snack pulled back and sat down, faded blue eyes fixed on the doll-like perfection. "See? Now leave her be, Snack."

Snack tucked her tail around bloody feet and gave a quiet, barely audible mew.

"Strange animal," Pally muttered sourly. He grabbed one of the washcloths that Took had, in a vague burst of hospitality, handed to him and wiped his hands. "Where did you get it?"

"What happened to her?" Took countered. "Blood loss and suffocation isn't enough to kill a dhampir. Not for long. We both know that."

"It didn't," Pally said with a sigh. "She was just down there too long, too young. Like the elders who fossify, a sleep as good as death, she just… gave up and stilled. Dammit, that cat—"

He snatched for the scruff of Snack's neck, but Took grabbed his wrist before his fingers could make contact. On the bed Snack crawled up onto the little girl's chest, put her muzzle on the child's chin, and purred bloodily against white, rosebud lips. Red smeared the dead skin like lip gloss, shone, and slowly sank down under the surface. The pale folds of skin were—maybe—a little less perfectly pallid afterward.

"She's a demon, remember," Took said after a second where nothing else happened. He loosened his grip on Pally's wrist. "Maybe let her work."

Pally pulled his hand away and stepped back. His face was creased into a frown. "What is it doing, Took? What kind of animal is this?"

"A good cat, I guess," Took said to the first. "And I don't know what she's doing, but what harm can it do to leave her to it? Nora Aron spent too many hours in that box. If she's just in some unending sleep, then let her hear a cat purr for a while."

Pally's face softened with an emotion that almost reached pity, but pulled up just short—for the little girl, or that's what Took chose to believe.

"When I was a boy, they said cats stole the breath of babies," he said. "But what need does a dead child have of breath. Very well, as long as the creature does no harm, I will leave it to its business."

"Speaking of which," Took said. "Do you plan to do anything with.... Nora... in the next few days? As long as Madoc lets me use it, I need to use the VINE jet to go over to California."

Pally paused as he glanced toward Took's throat and then away. "I think Madoc would allow you a lot."

For a blank second, Took didn't remember. Then he reached up and rubbed his throat. He'd healed faster than usual from the burns. The tight skin on his hands and the scorch in his throat was already gone, but the bite lingered.

"I don't.... it wasn't exactly planned," he said. "It's not why he asked me back."

Pally slapped him on the shoulder. "When I was young, human resources were what we threw into the grinding machine of a war," he said. "I don't plan to question your life. I'm just glad that whatever made you pull away from us is undone now."

"I don't know that it is," Took admitted. "I just.... Did you ever wonder who took me, Pally?"

He got a sharp side-eye for that. "No," Pally said with a dry bite to his voice. "That never occurred to anyone."

"Jokes now?" Took asked. "Fangs really make me so different?"

Pally tilted his head in acknowledgment but switched back to the previous question. "It was someone in VINE, someone you knew," he said confidently. "Human or not, you were well trained and had a native paranoia that served you well before. It had to be someone you trusted enough to let them get close to you."

"Like a Biter?"

"No," Pally said. "We were questioned, our whereabouts pinned down and dissected. We know you were taken from the parking garage, you flashed your pass when you drove in but never made it upstairs, and none of us could have gotten there and back to our stations in time. None of us could have done this to you, Took."

That didn't make sense. Took rubbed his throat as he swallowed hard, the dull ache of the half-healed bite sharp in his head. West had told him that the Biters had obstructed the case, refused to cooperate, and that they'd focused outside VINE. That it could have happened anywhere, anytime. Took didn't remember the parking garage that day. His life as a linear thing ended the night before and started again with Madoc's arms on him. Everything in between was scattershot and disorganized, like a broken Magic 8 Ball.

"Not even Madoc?" he asked in tight, raw voice. "Where was he?"

A flash of anger tightened Pally's jaw, a touch of contempt sharp as a knife in his eyes.

"That question is unworthy of you both," he said coldly. "Do you really think that Madoc, of all of us, would ever have hurt you?"

No. Yes.

"Sometimes."

Blood had dried to a scab on Pally's lip. He picked it off and flicked it away. "Then I will answer you, so that you don't wound him with this. How could Madoc have done this, when he had left for New York the night before? He was with the Senate when you were taken. Even dhampirs cannot occupy two spaces at once."

New York? Took could feel the blank space in his head, the ache of it where he thought he knew the boundaries.

"That was… *after*… the weekend," he said. "I was taken on Friday? After Kip's party, when I told you all I'd moved in with West?"

The coldness lingered on Pally's face, but the pity was definitely for Took now. He put his hand on Took's shoulder.

"I wasn't there, but I recall. Madoc was dour, but you weren't the first to reject him. He weathered it, went to New York, and before you could change your mind, you were taken."

Took made himself take a breath and let it out. He needed something internal to concentrate on, something he could *count.* West had lied to him. It didn't make sense. Took had told West about his suspicions, and he'd had to fight to convince him to listen when it sounded crazy.

The pressure in his head made it feel like the stitches in his brain were going to rip. Maybe his answers were down there with all the crud he'd forgotten, but he didn't think he could live with them.

A switch flicked. The hot panic in his head that made his body feel heavy and unwieldy wasn't helpful. So he turned it off. All that was left was hard logic and the scratch of that old, cold anger as it whispered, "See." He might not remember why he was angry, or at whom, but the anger didn't care.

"Like I said, I need the jet," Took said as he stepped back from Pally. "If Madoc needs me, he knows where I'll be."

Pally frowned but let Took take his leave.

As the door closed behind him, Snack was still on the bed, purring her bloody breath into the dead child's mouth.

Chapter Fourteen

QUICK WAS slouched on a bench outside the airport, tapping assiduously at his computer when Madoc got there. A game probably. The Anakim all found something to flex their brains as they aged, like Madoc and the Biters. Quick was young, turned just a few decades before, but his sire had been old and senescent, so he feared it more than most.

Madoc jumped out of the Viper before it came to a full stop at the drop-off curb. The VINE driver behind the wheel blurted something that could have been "Good trip" or "Go to hell." The doors slammed behind Madoc before he could catch the end of the sentiment. He stalked across the pavement toward the entrance.

Quick looked up from his game and cracked a grin as Madoc approached him. He pulled the earbuds out of his ear—a zap of weaponry and tinny insults squawked out of them—and opened his mouth to stay something.

He swallowed it as Madoc stalked past him without a break in his stride.

"Shit," Quick muttered.

A minute later he loped up alongside Madoc, laptop tucked under his arm and bag slung over the opposite shoulder.

"Late night?" he asked. "You and Bennett finally get down to brass tacks, huh?"

Madoc stopped abruptly and grabbed Quick by the collar of his shirt to yank him back a step and up onto his toes. "You have something to say?" he asked.

Behind the horn-rimmed glasses he didn't actually need, Quick blinked and then laughed.

"I just meant about the humorless bastard coming back," he said. "But you and he actually got *down* to brass tacks and bare asses, huh? Good for you, boss."

Madoc thinned his lips over his teeth, the prick of his fangs against the tender skin a reminder that he wasn't some callow boy who flashed fang at neck every ten minutes.

"Wind in your tongue," he warned. "I may be more lenient than some, but push me again, and I'll remind you I was the one who made your sire piss himself."

"And it did not go well," Quick said with an agreeable nod. "Point taken. Lip zipped."

He mimed a key-lock gesture in front of pursed lips instead and flicked the imaginary key away. It was the closest to good behavior Madoc would get from him. The attitude, as much as the horn-rimmed glasses and the hoodie that made him look slighter, was the defense he hid behind, much like Took's need to demonstrate he was smarter than everyone else in the room.

"It's not a good time for levity," he warned as he let go of Quick's collar. "Although you're free to try it on Pally if you think it will charm."

Quick had fed last night. Or this morning. Recently enough or well enough that he had enough blood in his system to bleed into his throat and over his cheekbones.

"Is he coming with us?"

"No, and if you can brief me before we reach the runway," Madoc said, "you won't have to either."

Quick straightened his hoodie over his shoulders and preened. He smoothed one hand back over his sandy hair to tuck the collar-length strands behind his ears.

"You make it sound like a reward," he said. "I'll have you know I always planned to go to Cali one day. I mean, I'll enjoy the sun a lot less now… but still."

Madoc snorted and started to walk again. His heavy boots scuffed over the floor as he strode through the security check. He didn't even need to flash his badge. The uniform and his face were enough. It shouldn't be, but Madoc would make his opinion on that known once he was off the ground.

"We aren't going to Cali," Madoc said bluntly. "It's Nevada. We're going under The Salt. You can enjoy the heat there if you still want to come."

The borrowed blood drained from Quick's face, and he pulled his laptop out from under his elbow. He balanced it on his forearm and typed unsteadily away as he briskly worked his way through the annotated summary of what he'd found about the Aron-led missions.

Trips to Europe. Dead children. Squashed sexual-harassment complaints. A rotation of canons and embezzlement complaints.

Madoc would look over the files when he got on the jet, but so far it sounded like what he'd expect in the hacked records of a Proverbial church's evangelical mission to Russia.

"Anything about the Arons personally?" he asked as they stepped outside.

The sun's glare scraped at Madoc's eyes and bleached the world down to flare white and hints of color. He winced and pulled his shades out of his pocket to slide them on. The purple glass cooled the world back down, although his eyes still stung.

In thin sneakers, Quick hotfooted it along a step behind Madoc as he juggled his laptop from one forearm to the other and flicked through windows.

"Not much. They tithed, they led missions, they kept to themselves," Quick said. "There was a complaint from a girl a few years back. Jesus, she was sixteen, but apparently she already had a husband."

"It's legal," Madoc said as he stopped at the stairs up onto the plane. He cocked his foot back to brace the heel against the step as he waited for Quick to get to the point.

"It's gross. Anyhow, she claimed that her husband had managed to get in touch with her and told her he'd found something out—he didn't get a chance to say what—about the Arons and they'd deliberately left him behind. There was a bit of an outcry in the Church, but by the time the canon found him, the boy had been turned, so…."

"So."

Quick bared his teeth in a humorless smile as he shrugged that away like it hadn't caught him on the raw. His parents hadn't been Proverbials, or even particularly religious, but they'd still iced him out the first time he went back to see them. Quick had claimed, with brittle humor, that the whole story was just too sordid for them.

"Anyhow, it went nowhere. I did get the feeling that the canon and the local *session* would have preferred it had. When you read between the lines, they didn't seem to actually like the Arons that much. A few little comments about how they were still 'so kindly disposed to their old church' and a disciplinary that told them that, unlike their old parish, the Charleston

Proverbial church abided by the reform *Book of the Confessionals*, whatever that is. If Took is still talking to you, you should ask him."

"And their old church?"

Quick grinned like the next words out of his mouth would be "I was hoping you'd ask that!" Instead it was simply the answer that Madoc expected. "Appleberg."

Of course it was.

"Anything else?" Madoc asked as he glanced back over his shoulder to gesture "a minute more" at the pilot who hovered at the door.

Quick jabbed a finger down against his keyboard. "If there is, it's all in your cloud. So can I...?" He jerked his thumb back over his shoulder at the airport and raised his eyebrows hopefully.

"Go," Madoc told him. "I'll call you from Nevada if I need anything."

Relief flashed raw over Quick's face as he backed away, but after a few steps, he hesitated.

"If you see... him," he said and then choked on whatever words came next. Even without putting a name to him, the unstable presence of his sire hung over Quick. The agent's expression was a miserable tangle of fear, love, and hatred.

"I won't," Madoc said. "No one does anymore."

Quick nodded. "I guess," he muttered and turned away. He waved a hand blindly behind him as he jogged away over the tarmac. Madoc watched him go for a second and then climbed up into the plane. "Let's go," he told the pilot as he reached the top.

"Sir," the woman nodded.

As she whistled for the ground crew to pull the stairs away, Madoc walked down the narrow aisle. He braced against the seat for balance as the plane started to move. In the back row, Took looked up from his tablet and blinked in surprise as Madoc dropped into the seat opposite him.

"What are you doing here?" he asked suspiciously.

"It *is* my jet," Madoc pointed out. He swallowed hard as the engines grumbled to life, and it took him a second before he could finish. "And my prison."

There was no arguing with that.

A STORM had rolled in. It buffeted the plane unsteadily and turned the air under them lumpen and dark. Madoc breathed in the taste of smoke and looked past the mundane into the gray world. On the other side of reality, a bird made of electricity and smokeless flame hung in the air beside the plane, wings canted as though it could soar forever. The eye it turned on the inhabitants of the metal tube, with the same lazy interest a man considered a can of ham, was the size of a small car. Behind it, through it, shadows with sharp teeth and tiny, screaming eyes dipped and spun as they tore apart blind gulls of white, drifting material that Madoc worried might be souls.

"I don't need my hand held," Took said sharply. "If that's why you're here."

"That's not what you told me," Madoc said as he blinked smoke out of his eyes to focus on the solid world, where they merely roared through empty air in a heavy, metal dart piloted by a mortal woman who could keel over suddenly for any reason. Flight, except by wing if you were lucky enough to have your blood run that way, was clearly unnatural. It also put Madoc on edge enough that he welcomed the opportunity to bicker. "Not ready to come back. That was your stance the other day."

Took pulled a face. "I don't want to get anyone killed," he said. There was a glass of water on the table in front of him. He fiddled absently with it as he talked. "I can still interview a suspect. Just because the shrinks think I'm not ready to have your back doesn't mean my brain's broken. Just my nerve."

The bitterness in his voice was sharp as lime. Madoc paused long enough to shelve the petty desire to jab at him for distraction and studied Took for a moment.

"So what do you think?" he asked. "Are you ready to come back? I can make this permanent if you want."

The last time Madoc had seen such raw hunger in someone's face, he'd had Took's cock in his ass. It was only for a second, and then Took wedged it down out of sight and shrugged as he glanced out the small window.

"It's not up to me."

"If it were?"

Took looked away from the window. "It's not," he said harshly. "I can't sleep during the day, 'cause I don't want Him, whoever he is, to win. I can't sleep at night because I'm scared the fucker knows where I am. You know why I had to take the Waring case? I'm broke. VINE health insurance covered my medical care, got me back on my feet, but most nights I go to a hotel. Sometimes I drive a couple of hours and just stop at a random motel on the road. That eats into your savings pretty damn quick, Madoc. I'm *scared*, and the only thing you call a scared Biter is retired. But you know what? I'd still take your hand off if it was up to me. Sick, scared, and suspicious as I am, I'd be back out there because it's the only thing that feels like me anymore. And then I'd get someone killed or…."

He stopped and clenched his teeth, as if the words would squeeze out, given a chance.

"It's not up to me," he said. "I'll do this, and then… whatever. I don't know. Maybe I'll go back to Cali. It's home. I could go and see my mother. She's probably got another gift for me."

There was a stack of letters in Madoc's desk in Philly, half of them still crumpled from where he retrieved them from the trash and smoothed them back out, that used 90 percent of the same words, maybe even 95. They had just been tweaked and rearranged enough so that they said something very different from Took's reluctant acceptance of someone else's decision.

Madoc swallowed the harsh question, or maybe it was an accusation, in his throat. He needed to ask some other questions first, the ones that he would have already asked and demanded answers for—if he hadn't been so desperate to respect Took's decisions. Instead he just reached over the low table and grabbed Took's hand in a cool clasp.

"I hate flying," he said as Took gave him an odd look.

He knew the statistics. Most flights were safe as long as they stayed overland or skirted close to the coast. It didn't matter. Immortality loaned the Anakim a sense of control. They could die, but they always had some influence over how and when. Not up here.

It was why there were still only a few flights per day, despite how convenient it made long-distance travel.

"No one asked you to come," Took muttered, but he didn't move his hand.

Madoc blinked and peered back into the gray through the window, as a hand constructed of twig bones and strung together with strips of bloody sinew stretched out from somewhere and snatched one of the hungry, darting shadows out of the air. When it squeezed, the shadow exploded, its essence bled out into the sky like ink, and its brethren shot in to pick it apart.

"You took the jet to come get me," Took said. "In Appleberg. I appreciate it."

Madoc looked at him and wondered if he was really that dense. Although he supposed that was a stupid question. For someone who unstitched emotion and motivation for his career, Took had always been blind when it came to how people saw him.

"I would do almost anything for you, Luke," he said.

Took looked stunned for a second and then glanced away to scowl out the window. He scratched his jaw with his free hand and cleared his throat. Madoc was, he thought wryly, in love with someone who had the emotional range of a teenager.

"You could call me Took, to start with."

"It's not a name," Madoc jabbed back.

He expected an argument, but Took just snorted and went back to the files Madoc had shared with him. His hand stayed curled around Madoc's, and it was odd how cold fingers could still make Madoc feel warm.

It was some comfort on a flight that didn't have much else going for it. On most flights Madoc could at least look forward to when they'd land and he would be back on solid ground. Not this time. When they landed, all he had to look forward to was The Salt, where the monsters knew his name.

IT MADE you feel human again, the heat. It was only a few degrees, the temperature announced in red letters over a sign that encouraged staff, human and Anakim both, to hydrate, but it was hungrier. It felt like a punishment, like Madoc was a scrap of meat caught between the hammer blow of heat from the chalk-blue sky above and the hot, white skillet under his feet.

It made him rue the lost ability to sweat. Any trickle of moisture to cool him down would be welcome.

"I feel like a lobster," Took muttered as he flapped the hem of his black, BTR T-shirt in an attempt to generate a breeze. It didn't do much good, but Madoc appreciated the glimpse of lean, scarred stomach. "Couldn't we find a salt mine in Montana to keep them in?"

"It's not meant to be pleasant," Madoc said as he watched an open-topped jeep bounce and judder across the stretch of salt-bleached sand toward them. "Besides, if they ever break out, where will they go?"

Took turned to look around. It was the sort of landscape you would call beautiful in a picture, with long stretches of ragged salt waves that smeared into the horizon and curves of colorful striated rock that curved up out of the sand like a snake's back. A blast furnace in the day and cold enough to find chips of ice at night.

"Would it kill you?" Took asked. When Madoc raised an eyebrow at him, he amended the question. "Them. Anakim… us."

He'd asked people to kill him in the hospital. Berated, the doctors said aggrievedly, which had been so *him* that Madoc hadn't known whether to laugh or weep. If Took still wanted to die, he could have done it himself by now. Madoc still weighed the tone of the question. Hopeful or just curious? In the end, as he watched Took track the horizon, he came down on "uncomfortable." That was appropriate. Madoc wouldn't trust anyone who wasn't uncomfortable around here.

"Maybe," he admitted quietly. "Not how I would choose to go."

The jeep finally pulled up to the fence, and the day warden climbed out. Like everything else laid down in the Accord, The Salt was an unhappy compromise. The Senate liked the idea of an Anakim prison well enough, but not the idea of the Anakim being in sole control of it. On the flip side of the coin, the Anakim definitely didn't trust the living with a prison full of their monsters and their near-gods.

Nobody who wasn't sentenced to be here was willing to stay long.

The latest Senate representative, who governed the prison during the daylight hours and therefore got to cope with the Hunter hit squads and boyar groupies who tried to force an entry, was James Tac. Madoc realized, with a flicker of surprise and jealousy as the other man walked toward them, that it looked like Took knew him.

"Bennett," James said as he stalked up to the gate. He was one of those tall men, who, from a distance, looked short with the amount of muscle they carried. He was handsome enough to make Madoc's jealousy hook deeper, with cool brown skin over elegant bones and cropped hair so black it had blue highlights. "You look like hell. Who are you eating, lepers?"

That startled Madoc into a laugh. Most of the agents who came from the Nations and worked for VINE were leery of the Anakim. From Egypt to Ireland, the Anakim existed in one form or another, although no one knew if they were native to those regions or had just roamed there long enough ago that it was the same difference. Until they had arrived here by boat, there had been none of them in the Americas.

Or in Australia, reportedly, but Madoc had never hated himself enough to venture there. The native gods were unfriendly enough here. There, they made the poisonous fauna look hospitable.

"I blame the heat," Took said. He smiled crookedly through the diamond wire. "I haven't seen you since your last stint at the Academy. I certainly didn't expect to see you out here."

James scowled and rubbed his left shoulder. "I broke my shoulder in an incident up in the mountains," he said. "Since I was off active duty, when the last warden made for the hills, the boss tapped me in."

"What happened?" Madoc asked.

James's eyes were like chips of dark granite, hard and pointedly empty as he glanced away from Took. Whatever tolerance he would give Took obviously didn't extend to Madoc. It was almost reassuring.

"Nations business," he said. "None of the East's."

"Or the West's," Madoc pointed out. He gave James a smile that was as empty as the other man's eyes. "Technically."

"We like them better, though," James said. Then he held up his thumb and forefinger, pinched close enough to touch. "A bit. What brings a red cardinal all the way to The Salt, Agent Madoc? Want to make sure your boyar is still with us?"

Madoc grinned back, enough to flash his eyeteeth, even unextended. "We'd all know if Elizabeth had shucked the Salt," he said. "I'll pay my respects while I'm here, but it's someone else we've come for."

He held his hand out. After a second, Took dropped the letter of invitation into his palm.

"Dominic Waring," Madoc said as he tucked the letter into the crack of the gate and left it. "The Storm Warning of the Hunters."

James plucked the letter free and unfolded it. He read it thoroughly, top to bottom, despite the sweat that beaded his hairline and flushed his throat. When he finished, he grunted and keyed in the code to unlock the door.

"He won't talk to you," he said as he waved them through. "But this letter gives you full authority to talk to him."

"Do you think he's guilty?" Took asked as they walked toward the jeep. The driver, young and lobster pink under his uniform, stared at Madoc with nervous, fever-bright eyes. "Waring?"

James snorted as he swung up into the passenger seat. "I knew who you meant," he said. "I don't know. Boy's done something bad, you can see that in his eyes, but I'm not looking forward to executing him. Some of them, the ones we can kill, that come through here? I can't wait to put them in the ground, get rid of them. Not Waring. Maybe that's just because he's quiet, though. It's easier to like someone who's not howling slurs at you."

"I can sympathize," Madoc said dryly as he scrambled into the hard bench seat in back.

"No," James said as he slapped the dashboard to get the driver to throw the car into reverse. "You can't. I appreciate the effort, though."

That was a lie, but Madoc didn't bother to call him on it as they bumped toward the outpost that stuck up out of the desert like a thumb. If something went wrong down there, they would need the warden onside.

It took five minutes to get to the tower and another sixty to descend the roughly chipped steps that corkscrewed down under the sand. The driver had been left above, so only one of them had to breathe. It pettily annoyed Madoc that James didn't even sound out of breath as they climbed down.

"They say you can take the air whenever you want," James remarked. His voice echoed up the shaft. "After a few climbs, though, you can hardly be bothered. Most months, unless we get a new resident or supplies, we only go topside once or twice. Some of the Anakim lot, not even that often. The biggest problem? Agoraphobia. You'd think it'd be the other way around, but you get used to being down here."

The warmth leached away as they went down, sucked away into the rock until the only source of heat seeped from James. It was hard not to pull closer to him, steal the warmth from his back, and draw it from his throat.

He made a point to keep himself between Took and James. The respect of personal space hadn't been written into the Accord, but people either liked the undead in their personal space or loathed it. Madoc didn't approve of either option when Took was involved.

"Someone got to your driver," Madoc noted as they took the last flight of steps. "He's bloodstruck. You can see it in his eyes.

"I know," James said as they reached the bottom. "That's why he's upstairs and we're down here. It's not far now. I kept Waring close by. It gets creepy farther in."

Madoc could taste the salt in his throat, the scratch of tiny crystals, and feel the weight of the ground above pressing down on him. Salt inhibited the boyars' gifts—and compared to them, Madoc's ability to sidestep the world was a party trick—and being deep underground made them sluggish. It was instinct.

"It's already fairly creepy," Took said. "I read about The Salt, but this is the first time I've been so close."

James smirked as he picked up a heavy torch from the floor and flicked it on. "This is just a hole in the ground. It's no creepier than a rock or a hollowed-out log. Anakim, though? Once they've done here for a while, they forget to pretend they're human. Down in the deep tunnels, you carved out mansions for boyars who sit in the excretion of their own salts for years without moving. Between Waring and them are all sorts of monsters."

He led the way down a side tunnel, the stone walls shod with rusty layers of metal. It wouldn't be enough to stop Madoc if he'd wanted to sneak in, but it would have slowed him down.

A titter of excitement eddied down the tunnel as the light pierced the darkness. In the first cell, a narrow, wrinkled-scarred face appeared and spat thick, greasy sputum at Madoc. A Hunter they'd kept alive to get information from but who'd killed too many to ever walk free. Farther down, a dark arm laced with pink scars stretched out to claw at the air with stubbed fingers, the first joint taken off for a ritual the rapist had never explained and everyone had eventually decided not to care about.

The Biters had filled a lot of these cells.

"Madoc," a voice hissed. "The Bastard Cardinal."

Another cell picked it up and then another. The tunnel echoed with hatred and pleas for clemency. The din of it rocked Madoc back on his heels, the assault on his sensitive ears almost physical.

"Underestimated your popularity," James muttered as he pulled a remote from his pocket. He held it up and roared, "Arms in the goddamned cells!"

Everyone recoiled, the arm was dragged back inside hastily, and James hit a button. Steel doors snapped down in every single doorway and clicked into place as they locked. The only one that didn't was the one they had stopped in front of.

James tucked the remote away again and pulled out a key. "Here you go," he said as he wrestled the heavy tumblers, designed for vampire usage, around in the lock. "Dominic Waring. Alive for now."

There was a single cot in the room, pulled up in front of the small fireplace, and a bookshelf against the far wall. As prisons went, Madoc had seen worse, but misery rarely made for an untroublesome population.

Waring lay on the cot. Framed in stark whites—the walls, his prison smock, the harsh spray of light from the ceiling—Waring looked vivid. He reminded Madoc of a pet fox he'd seen in a Russian Anakim's palace once, the same color and the same wildness in his eyes—not tame, just collared.

"These two are here to talk to you," James said. "You don't get a choice about listening, but you want to piss on the dark one's boots, I'll shed no tears."

Waring didn't laugh at the joke, but a shred of the wire-taut tension loosened in his shoulders. He sat up on the bed and folded his legs under him. Nearly two years under The Salt had made him seem oddly younger. The harsh-featured man, all stark bones and greasy skin, had faded back into the boy with the heavy glasses and a YouTube account where he spouted juvenile bigotry to the world. His Salted pallor made the birthmark over one green eye look crimson.

He stared at them, blank as a doll, as James let them in. The only signs of emotion were the white-knuckled fists he twisted in his smock.

"You've got half an hour," James said. He closed and locked the door. "If he isn't in the same condition when I come back for you... well, I don't have to open this door. Understood?"

He left. Madoc dragged a chair from the corner of the room to the end of Waring's bed and sat down. They stared at each other, and Madoc wondered how hard you'd have to push to break that shell. It could be done—anything could be done—but it would take a concerted effort to drill back down to anything human.

"Nora Aron is alive," Took said. "We found her."

A desperate, reluctant joy bloomed on Waring's face as he stared at Took. Tears swam in his eyes and he dragged his glasses off so he could wipe them away.

"Son of a bitch," Madoc said precisely. There was too much purity in that unguarded moment, an innocence that he'd never have attributed to the boy in the videos, never mind a killer. "He's right. You didn't do this, did you?"

Chapter Fifteen

SOMETIMES ALL it took was one crack to bring the whole facade down. It worked with suspects and witnesses who'd been less isolated than Waring had been these last months. They walled up their secrets and sat there, alone with them, until they were actually desperate to talk. All it needed was one crack in it and they could just let go.

That's why Took had led with Nora, the one child whose fate Waring didn't know. Relieved she'd survived or disappointed, either way, they'd get a reaction. That had worked, but now Waring had tucked in the corners of himself and huddled under it.

Setter-red hair hung over his face as he stared at his bony knees in gray prison leggings. It moved with his breath every time Took edged closer to something that the boy held close. His fingers were twisted in the hem of his smock and his knuckles whitened when he wanted Took to change the subject.

He didn't *need* to talk to tell them what they wanted to know. It would just have been quicker.

"We tracked down Annabelle," Took said. He watched as Waring's fingers tightened, bones sharp under his skin, but the flicker of his eyes up and away was contemptuous. He knew they hadn't, because…. Took didn't know that exactly yet, but Annabelle was significant enough that she'd have changed everything that VINE did. "Or where she was anyhow. Appleberg. Such a small town for such big secrets."

Closer. That was something Waring wasn't so confident about. The taste of fear cut through the salt. How did anyone lie to a vampire? Took didn't know why Madoc didn't just do these interviews. Maybe Took was there to keep the living in the Senate, and the Anakim born or made since the Accord was signed happy that their evidence wasn't based in magic.

"We don't know everything yet," Took admitted. He slid down the wall until he was on the floor, legs folded to mirror Waring's. The honesty seasoned the mix, a touch of comfort amid the panic. "But we think it all started with Annabelle."

Waring looked up. His eyes were almost black, and Took leaned forward as he met them.

"Or maybe with their mission?"

TOOK KNEW time had passed. He was used to the glitch in his brain, the hiccup of missed minutes. He rolled with it as he registered the blood in his mouth—his own from the taste—and the odd ache in his brain. There were slivers of something in there, caught on old mental scars like a cat's fur on barbed wire. He filed it away for later as a hand grabbed his collar and yanked on it.

He snarled and lunged forward into them. His shoulder rammed into a hard gut and they both lurched backward. The narrow cot tangled between their legs and they pitched down onto it. Took threw a punch, and his brain finally caught up with his panic. He recognized Madoc just as it was too late to pull the blow.

Madoc grabbed his wrist before Took's knuckles connected with his jaw. He used the leverage to casually throw Took off the bed like a sheet that had gotten in the way. Took hit the ground with a thud and skidded into the bookshelf. It pitched forward, a rainfall of books showered down over the floor, and it landed on him.

Fuck. He kicked the shelves off and scrambled to his feet. Old, hard-earned instincts wanted to fight, because defiance had been all that kept him together. Instead he made himself back away on stiff legs.

"I don't exactly know what's going on," he said—lisped, rendered ridiculous by shredded lips and extended fangs. Took licked his lips and tried again. "I don't want to fight."

"Could have fooled me," Madoc growled as he prowled to the side. He wiped blood from the side of his face and smeared black liquid into the black fabric of his shirt. The scrapes were as deep and thin as if Snack had been at him. "Who are you?"

"You're the one who can't remember my name," Took pointed out. He tripped over a tangle of naked flesh on the floor and just about caught himself before he landed on it… him. A risky glance down revealed it was Waring, naked and charred. "What the fuck?"

Smoke in the air made him cough and then resolved itself into Madoc, eyes narrowed and fangs exposed as he grabbed a handful of Took's hair and yanked his head back. He leaned in and sucked in a breath of air straight from Took's mouth.

The slivers of… something… in his head convulsed with panic. Took's cock thickened with the conviction it was hot. The dissonance of it made him shudder and suck in air that tasted like salt, blood, and….

"What is that?" he asked as he grimaced around the flavor of something he couldn't define, not even as "like" something else.

"Took?" Madoc said. Then he dragged Took in close and kissed him with rough, almost desperate, possession. One hand stayed twisted painfully tight in Took's hair and the other touched his face like it was precious. After a moment he leaned back and gave Took an exasperated glare. "Next time, you stupid bastard, close your eyes."

It took a moment for Took to remember he didn't need to breathe, so he couldn't be literally breathless. He hitched a breath in raggedly. "What? Why?"

Madoc let him go and bent down to grab the naked Waring by the scruff of the neck. He dragged the limp sprawl of body to its feet and let him dangle. His lip curled with disdain.

"Because now we know how Waring got into his victim's houses," Madoc said. "He was inside them."

That wasn't right. It wasn't wrong either.

Took rubbed his forehead. The stuff in his head felt like… light and cinnamon, alive as it writhed in an effort to get free of him. It ripped away, shred by shred, but he grabbed at it as it went.

A girl with no eyes and tea that made his mind splinter.

Books. Frustration. Surrender.

Skinny scarred arms, the flutter of black wings. All the little pale kids made of matchsticks and fire.

A car. A name. A—

"I didn't do it," Waring rasped as he opened his pale green eyes.

The threads of *something* that Took had fitted together went up like foxfire. He flinched away from the inside of his own head, but it didn't want him just the bits of… *other*. Waring convulsed as the foxfire backlashed into him, his veins lit up from within as it scorched through. His eyes rolled back in his head, and he screamed.

It was only the second noise he'd made in years, and it flecked his lips bloody.

Madoc spat out a curse and wrestled Waring down onto the bed. Bare heels battered against the frame until they split and the fire struck out from his body at Madoc's arms. Took reached for his gun, but other than the comfort of its weight, he wasn't sure what to do with it. Madoc pinned Waring down by the shoulders as the boy flailed and screamed until the energy that burned through him finally flickered out and he went limp.

"Remember when people thought you were a sorcerer?" Madoc said as he finally leaned back. Unlike Took, who the fire had mostly left alone, Madoc's fingers and forearm were striped with burns. "He *is* one."

Took expelled what air he had left in his lungs on a whistle. "That was magic? Real magic?"

"This?" Madoc held up his burned arm and flexed his fingers. "That was magic. The cost of it was his…. No. Not silence, he could have written his denials, then. His voice. The ability to communicate."

A car. A name. A… something….

It wasn't a memory, more like a dream. Someone *else's* dream, sketched in their dream symbols and scribbled lines.

"He hid them," Took said. He rubbed his forehead again as if he could squeeze something else out, but it had all burned up. "Somehow he hid them. That's why he held his tongue for so long, to keep them from being found."

"Why speak now?" Madoc asked as he got up off the bed. He waved one hand at the still, singed boy draped on the thin cot in the uncomfortable sprawl of the profoundly unconscious. "What did it gain him?"

It had been just at Took's fingertips, whatever scrap of memory he'd caught from Waring. He could see the car—the long, sleek Mustang nose that faded back into a sort of car-shaped notion, and the name was Gra… ce? Gra… y? A second longer and he'd have what came next.

Maybe? How could he?

"What happened?" he asked.

Madoc rubbed his thumb down the raw lines that ran from his lower eyelid to the corner of his mouth. "He jumped into you, crawled in through your eyes, and then tried to rip my face off. Luckily he didn't seem able to access any of your training, and he was a piss-poor fighter. Sorry about the—"

He pointed at Took's mouth. Took licked the blood off his lips. It had tasted better before, when he hadn't tasted the heady sweetness of Madoc's blood.

"I'll assume it was necessary," he said. "How did you… dislodge him?"

Madoc shrugged and walked over to hammer against the heavy metal door. "I didn't," he said. "He just didn't seem to be able to keep control of you. Twice you just sort of collapsed, like your strings had been cut, but he managed to hang on to the reins. The third time he just spilled out of you, like old milk from a jug, and collapsed."

"So you hit me again?"

"You came up swinging," Madoc countered coolly. "I didn't know what effect the… possession… might have had on you."

Took wondered what it would be like for someone to find themselves in his brain. It was locked doors, trapdoors hidden under rugs, and basic things that he never thought about—the wine they'd had at the party when he'd been… thought he'd been taken, for example—because it triggered a cascade of bad memories until something split a scar open and the worst memory spilled out.

He could hardly blame Waring for cutting out. If he had the option, he might too.

"I think he left… thoughts, memories… behind," Took explained slowly. He paused while Madoc hammered on the door again. "Bits of magic maybe? I could see them in my brain, fragments of Waring caught in aspic. I think he could see it too as I picked through them. When he broke his silence, I'd just seen a car, half of a name, and… something important. Something he really didn't want me to see."

"Like what?"

Took spread his hands helplessly. "I don't know," he said. "When he spoke, it all went up in flames. Only impressions are left. Guesswork."

"Better for him if you got more," Madoc said dourly. "Once the boyars know he's a sorcerer…? Some of them were too, once. They know how to track the fracture lines. It might take a while, but they'll crack the boy open like a lobster."

The last thing that Took wanted to feel for Waring was sympathy, not when the inside of his mind still ached with the intrusion. On the other hand, he knew what it was like to be used, to be broken open and your insides picked out. He wouldn't wish that on anyone.

"Do you have to tell them?"

Madoc gave a fatalistic shrug and gestured at the salt-crusted walls around them. The flare of magic had spread fractal patterns of green through the medium. "They'll know."

The hatch of the door popped open and James stared in. Gray eyes found Madoc first and then flashed to the sprawled, naked, bruised body on the cot. In the absence of any other context, Took couldn't blame his old instructor for the flash of bleak, terrible anger that crossed his face.

"I will have your badge for this Madoc," James snapped, his face pulled in tight, angular lines framed by the narrow rectangle of the slot. "Then I'll lock you up down here in the deepest hole I can find, down where you'll never even smell fresh air on my clothes again. And what the hell, Bennett, you just let him brutalize that kid?"

Took flinched at the accusation. He'd have hoped that James knew him better than that, but then…. Madoc could say the same. Took *should* have known better than to suspect him, yet he still had.

"The boy's a sorcerer," Madoc snapped as he rapped his knuckles against the door. "He nearly killed us. We're lucky salt blocks pure magic as well as inhibits us, or he would have walked out of here in your skin."

James looked dubious. "I've never seen him do anything like that. Not even light a match or stir a breeze."

"It takes a year to work a spell," Madoc said. "And magic is fickle."

That still wasn't enough to convince James. It was Took's turn to gesture at the walls. "Look at it," he said. "If it wasn't magic, what did we use? Limeade?"

It took James a second to pick out the lightning-bolt spray of green over the walls, half-hidden between the one set of shelves upright and the door to the small, barren bathroom. Once he did, he still had a suspicious cast to his mouth, but he let them out.

"I had no reason to suspect the boy was—"

"No, we all had reason," Madoc said blankly. "We just didn't see him. Do you know the protocols to bind a sorcerer?"

James reluctantly shook his head. He frowned at Waring's still body as though he wanted the unconscious young man to do something to prove Madoc's allegation.

"I never had need," he admitted. "I've seen a dozen so-called magic users, claim they can cast a miracle to summon a dragon or ride the storm. They were all left with their dick in their hands when nothing happened."

"Trust me," Madoc said grimly. "The one time their spell works, you'll be glad to have some recourse. Do you have a graveyard on site?"

James drew back in distaste. He still looked suspicious. "What possible fucking reason do you have to ask that?"

"Because I assume you have no stable," Madoc replied with a grim smile. "I need iron nails, from a horseshoe or a coffin. Whichever is easiest to find."

James rubbed his hand over his head. "Neither is easier," he said. "Would a nail from the store not do as well?"

"No."

"Why not?" Took asked. He felt suddenly exhausted, as though he could just lie down and sleep in the salt. The inside of him felt raw, as though whatever Waring had done had chafed him on the way through. Revulsion curdled in his stomach at the thought—the same sick knot he felt whenever the VINE psychiatrists probed too hard about what he'd forgotten—but he couldn't muster anger. That flash of Waring's motivation was still too sharp in the back of his head. If Took had been that desperate to protect something, maybe he'd have done the same thing. "Iron is iron."

Madoc shrugged. "Or it isn't," he said. "A coffin nail or a horse nail is what's prescribed. Why risk being wrong?"

"I'll send a guard to the nearest ranch," James said. "It will cause fewer questions than if I sent him to defile a graveyard. That will take a few hours, though. We don't encourage people to settle nearby, even if the land were hospitable enough to draw them."

"Take your time. I still need to speak to the boyars, add this wrinkle to the ones we already handed them." Madoc paused as he turned to look at Took. "You should go back to the plane. The boyars wouldn't speak to you anyhow, even if I wanted you to be under their attention. Feed. Rest."

It was masochism that made Took take a sidelong look at James. He already knew what he'd see, the discomfort in gray eyes and distaste in the curl of a lip, because they were what *he* felt... usually felt. After the last few days he had spent too much energy to muster much self-loathing.

A little of course—he was tired, not dead—but it was mixed with a dose of bitter defiance. Maybe it was all the salt. He hoped it lasted.

"If you're sure?" he said.

Part of him squirmed uncomfortably at the idea he'd just leave Madoc to deal with this. He'd gotten used to aggressively pulling his weight as the only human Biter in the field. But he still had a meeting to attend, and it would be easier if he didn't have to sneak from under Madoc's attention to do it.

"Go," Madoc said. He kicked the leg of Waring's cot with his foot. "This doesn't fall under your purview."

Calculation flickered over James's face. It didn't take VINE's best behavioral scientist to follow his train of thought. However uncomfortable he was with the idea of Took's hunger, he judged he'd be a lot more uncomfortable with a tired, pissed-off cardinal in his passenger seat. And no one ever seemed to come away from the boyars without being pissed off.

"I'll drive you," he said. "I have to go into town anyhow, and then Agent Madoc will have the car when he's ready to leave."

"That works," Took said. "Thanks."

Madoc scowled but nodded reluctantly. "That's convenient."

After one last look around the cell, James shook himself and stepped back into the hall. "Give me five minutes to brief my team. This will have roused some of the lighter sleepers. I want everyone prepared and with answers for the ones that still talk."

"I'll come with you," Took said quickly. He guiltily avoided Madoc's eyes as he ducked out the door after James. Maybe he couldn't muster much anger against Waring, but the idea of being shut up with him—

He didn't know why he still fought. It never worked. Maybe it was stubbornness or the fear just short-circuited everything else to hijack his body and make him flail. One of them dealt him a casual blow that made his ears ring, before they threw him into the room. It stank like a trap house, that acrid stench that reached down to what was left of Agent Luke Bennett, and they locked the door behind him. In the dark, he sat up and said... The words were gone, scratched out of his brain. *They wouldn't come back for him for a long time.*

—was something different.

Madoc stepped out after them. Maybe he didn't like the idea of being locked in there either, or the singed, biological smell that clung to the salt.

"Three nails," he told James. "Best to get six, in case you need to do this again."

"He's slated to die soon," James said. "If it takes a year for him to muster a spell—"

"They won't execute him now," Madoc said. "Not even for dead dhampirs. There are *maybe* a hundred sorcerers in the US, all in the Senate's employ, and *maybe* a dozen of them have any real power. Most would spend a year to win an hour's glimpse into the future or give their enemies scabies. He's too valuable to kill if they can break him. And if they can't break him, they can trade him back to the home country. Tepes collects magic users like a child collects baubles."

For the first time, James seemed to register the bitter chill of the prison. He shuddered and rubbed his hands together.

"I'd choose the sword," he said.

"As would I," Madoc said. "But he won't get the choice."

He turned to Took and caught his hand. The brush of his lips over Took's knuckles, the hint of fang behind the soft curve, was sweetly familiar but felt more intimate than a kiss under James's watchful eye. Heat caught at the tips of Took's ears and between his legs as Madoc grazed his tongue along the dip between Took's knuckles.

"Rest," Madoc said in a low, rough voice that was somehow thickly sexual. "You'll need it."

Then Madoc cast a sidelong glance at James, and, in reaction to whatever he saw or didn't see, tugged Took in close for a kiss. Took had been wrong; this was more intimate—the cool, sticky sweetness of blood on Madoc's lips, like salted lemonade on a hot day, and the pressure of his hand against the small of Took's back.

It was a pissing contest and it should have raised Took's hackles, but instead he leaned into the kiss.

New York was too far, even for Madoc, to get back. Whatever reason West had for the lies that now rattled around Took's head like old dice, this was okay. He could have this.

After a long moment, Madoc broke the kiss. He gently brushed the back of his fingers over Took's cheek, and then James cleared his throat uncomfortably. Fair enough, Took thought as he stepped back and tried to compose himself. It wasn't the place, and no matter what he thought in the heat of the kiss, it probably wasn't something he could have, not realistically.

Bu it was, he realized with an ache in his chest, the only thing he could think to want.

Point made to… Took? To James? To the vampires behind their steel doors?…. Madoc stepped away. He smoothed his ruffled hair back from his face with one hand.

"I won't be long," he promised. "Then we can work out what Waring needed to hide."

"Who," Took corrected. He hadn't realized he was certain of that until he spoke, but he saw the matchstick girls that Waring remembered sharply in his mind as he spoke—colorless children against the black of his mind, almost see-through, as though they'd been emptied out, with pipe cleaner arms and legs. "Them."

Madoc briefly raised his eyebrows at the confidence in Took's voice and then nodded. "For his sake," he said, "I hope you're right. Living children might be the only thing to buy him… some sort of life."

James cleared his throat. "Nine nails, then," he said, his voice harsh and unkind as he bounced off the salt. "If I'm to watch the poor bastard rot."

THE NEON letters marched the bar's name crookedly across the front of the building—Gone to the Dogs. Took checked his phone, but there'd been no other messages since the address he'd received just before he left the East Coast.

Took rolled his head from one side to the other and felt the bones in his neck pop. Undead or not, that still felt good. Prepared as he'd get, Took shoved his phone into his pocket and walked up to the front door.

The big old boy slouched in a chair next to the door stuck his leg out into the threshold, cracked motorcycle boot braced against the frame. He thumbed the brim of his cap back and peered at Took from under the shadow of it.

"You got the teeth to drink here, boy?" he drawled.

Took took a twisted satisfaction in peeling his lips back from his fangs in a humorless threat display of a smile. He'd spent too many hours of his life trying to bulk himself up with enough testosterone to earn entry to this bar, every other bar, his mom's house whenever his dad rocked through and felt like stopping. The flash of fear on the bouncer's face was payback for every shove, cuff, and shake he'd weathered.

With his tongue he pushed his fangs back up into their sockets. For once, they didn't pop back down.

"Good enough?" he asked.

The bouncer lurched to his feet, his eyes nervous as he searched the darkness of the parking lot for backup. He hammered the door behind him with a heavy-knuckled hand.

"You picked the wrong bar to slum in, wetmouth," the bouncer growled. He reached around to the small of his back and pulled out an extendable sap. A snap of his wrist extended it. "You ain't gonna have any teeth when we finish with ya."

He swung overhand, and the metal glittered in the moonlight as it descended toward Took's head. Took swayed to the side and easily grabbed the thick muscled wrist. The guy might be one of Gabriel's dogs, but he wasn't a wolf. Took twisted the wrist until the arm cocked awkwardly, and then threw a punch up into the exposed armpit. The shoulder popped audibly out of the socket, and the bouncer foundered at the knees with a shrill whine.

"Stay down," Took told him. He reached into his pocket and pulled out his wallet to flash the VINE ID in front of the man's nose. "Or where you go next, everyone's got bigger teeth than you."

The man tried to snarl through a pain-twisted face. "Gabriel will fuck up your life."

Took gave the man's arm another twist. The dislocated joint made a strange noise as it turned.

"He already tried," Took said as the bouncer writhed on the ground at his feet. "Someone else did it better."

The door to the bar finally opened and Gabriel looked out. He glanced down at the bouncer on the ground and grimaced in disappointment.

"You're a shit guard dog, Harry," he said.

Harry whined and kicked at the ground with his boots, his face red with pain. He didn't seem to care too much about Gabriel's judgment.

"Are we going to talk?" Took asked. "Or should I just rip off his arm and hit you with the bloody end?"

Harry tried to scream his objection, but all that came out was a strangled squeal. It made Gabriel crack that crooked grin of his, a flash of stubbled dimple and white, white teeth.

"It'd be rude not to at least hear you out after you came so far," Gabriel said as he stepped back and waved his hand in exaggerated invitation. For a second, Took wondered if he should just skip to the fight, but he needed answers. He let go of Harry's arm—the big man went limp on the ground in relief, his breathing ragged and the faint smell of piss in the air—and stepped over him. As he crossed the threshold, Gabriel leaned in to growl in his ear. "Then once we're done, I'll put you in the ground where you belong."

Took didn't even flinch. It wasn't the first time his father had threatened to kill him.

Chapter Sixteen

SHE'D BEEN beautiful once—more than beautiful. When her beauty palled on her admirers—like rich food you'd overindulged in—she'd spent her fortune to reclaim their admiration. When it wasn't enough, she sold her soul.

Elizabeth Bathory, one of only two vampires in the USA who didn't trace their stunted family tree back to Tepes himself, the boyar who claimed the lion's share of this new land when they arrived, before the terms of the Accord whittled it down to an advisory role and a throne room carved from salt.

"Countess," Madoc said as he knelt in front of her.

The woman who inspired the Wicked Queen in every human fairy tale was a salt-wrapped husk. Stiff white armor plate creased and folded around her, the salt caked over silks and velvets long since rotted away. She was a shriveled brown thing with dry, white eyes in the heart of it.

Her voice rattled in her throat as stick-like tendons rubbed together like cricket legs to make a sound.

"A sor... cer... er killed the... children?" she murmured. "Put to it... by the... humans?"

Even in that ruin of a voice, Madoc could sense her weigh the idea. She had to decide if she wanted to believe it or not.

"Probably not," he said.

"If I... say... they did," Elizabeth ground out coldly, "they did."

"But you don't have to decide yet," Madoc said. "Reopen the case. Give me Waring. The children who disappeared might still be alive."

She didn't need to speak. He knew that wasn't motivation enough for her. Of all the boyars, she was the only one who hadn't given the Kiss to her own children, who never wanted a dhampir to quick her womb. Daughters grew too beautiful, she always said as she watched them age and sicken, and sons too ambitious.

"Or dead," he admitted. "Either way the Proverbial Church and their missions are implicated somehow. Even if we don't want war—"

He didn't. Peace, however full of compromise, had proved to his taste. And if there had to be war... not yet, not while Took's traumatic rebirth was so fresh in his mind, when his loyalties still leaned toward the breathing.

"—we'll have leverage," he finished.

That made Elizabeth stir herself enough to nod in approval, and her dry ball of a head wobbled on her stalk of a neck inside the cowl of salt. She had no fear of war. Blood delighted her and death aroused her, but politics were her one true love.

"You think this... boy... of yours," she ground out, "can be... trusted?"

Madoc felt his back tighten. He didn't like the thought of Took in Elizabeth's mind, didn't want her to dwell on him.

"He's mine," he said, confidence layered over his words. "I won't let him do anything to endanger us."

A sigh like a man's last breath rattled out of her. "Do as you think best, then," she said. "I will... grease the wheels of the other boyars."

The salt cracked and crumbled. Madoc set his jaw and watched it season the ground. A cured hand on a stick-thin arm, fat rendered down greasy and white, reached out toward him. Jewels still glittered cold on her fingers.

"You owe... a tithe," she said.

Madoc did. He took her hand and let her pull him to his feet. Even in her desiccation, she was stronger than him. No one would call her beautiful now. Her hair had rotted and turned brittle, her face was a skull loosely covered with cheap leather, and her mouth was a slash of vanity red around a snaggle of rot-browned teeth. But her fangs were still sharp and white—sickles jabbed out of receded gums, as though she chewed on the salt to keep them sharp.

He obediently tilted his head to give her his throat and set his teeth to endure it. Her bone-hard fingers twisted his head and yanked it farther down, nails dug down into his scalp. Excitement rattled in her chest as she licked his throat with a dry strap of a tongue. Then she ripped into him. Pain was the point, not pleasure. Her fangs tore his skin and scraped over the bones of his neck like a peasant who sucked the meat off a goose's bones. His blood spilled down her throat and seeped out of her rotted guts, the wet, black stain of it soaked into her thighs. She ripped at the edges of the wound with her fingers to tear it open, fresh gouts of slow, cold blood left to drip over the dried up sacks of her tits.

Madoc gripped the arm of her salt throne until it cracked and crumbled under his fingers. The pain took his legs from under him, and he slumped into her lap, cradled like a child as she tore his throat open from one side to the other.

It would end. He'd always been her favorite, the one servant who didn't lust after her like a dog, and he was still useful. She wouldn't kill him.

As she sucked at his throat, supped him like she'd starved, Madoc slid down into the dark. He didn't *think* she'd kill him.

BACK AT the jet, Madoc slouched in the leather seats with a pint of cold blood curdled in his gut and another mixed into a bottle of whiskey at his elbow. It would do, but there was little pleasure in it.

"Did Took try to call you?" he pressed Lawrence on the other side of the computer screen. "He should have been in touch to update you about Waring."

She hunched over on her desk, her face too close to the screen. "Not yet," she said. "Maybe he stopped to feed."

Jealousy scratched at the inside of Madoc's throat. Or maybe that was just the scars healing. He took a swig of tainted whiskey. It was petty, worse it was selfish. He'd wanted Took there to swear over his injuries and bare his throat for comfort, the cradle of a lover's hand against his torn scalp as Madoc gave pleasure instead of pain.

He shifted as his cock thickened at the idea, his fantasy eager to expand further to Took naked under him and the low, hungry noises he made as Madoc fucked him.

"Maybe," he said. His voice caught and he took another drink to moisten it. "The boyars agreed to release Waring to our custody. The case is ours. So if West obstructs any of you, if he even drags his feet, remind him exactly who he works for."

Lawrence raised her eyebrows. "My mother?"

Madoc tilted his glass toward the screen in acknowledgment. "And those whom she answers to."

"The boyars," Lawrence said. Her voice trembled with something too close to awe for Madoc's liking. "Did you really speak to them?"

"To one," Madoc said. "Elizabeth."

Lawrence sighed and absently brushed a hand over her hair. "Is she still as beautiful as ever? Of them all, she gave up the most when they agreed to confine themselves for the Accord."

Not how Madoc remembered it. Not quite.

He set the whiskey down. It didn't have much effect on him, but most of a bottle was still enough to loosen his tongue more than he should allow, if only from the old habits of company.

"She hasn't changed," he said. It wasn't much of a lie. The withered raisin thing in the shroud of salt had already plumped back up to simply raddled from her feast of Madoc's blood. She could be beautiful again if she wished, and the person under the salt was the same monstrous bitch she'd always been.

Madoc had given her his loyalty, but it had never blinded him.

"Why bring him back?" Lawrence asked. "I thought you were going to just interview him there."

"There were developments," Madoc said. "Is Pally there?"

Lawrence scowled but turned the laptop around to aim it at the other side of the desk. The sight of his face caught on camera made Pally scowl, as if that would make it less pretty. His beauty had never pleased him, not when he was a Knight who viewed his own comely face as an invitation to sin or as a new vampire whose beauty had become a commodity. Behind him Quick looked up from something that flashed on his laptop. He gave Madoc a quick nod.

"What could develop under The Salt?" Pally asked.

Madoc grabbed the tablet and got up. He walked up to the front of the plane, where he'd left Waring cuffed to the steel rings sunk into the structure of the jet.

"Don't look into his eyes," he warned as he turned the tablet around. It was likely that Waring had ruined his spell when he spoke, and it would take a full year to cast another. And unlikely that he could do… that jump… through a computer screen. That wasn't a risk Madoc was willing to take, however, when it would end with Waring in Pally's body. Once upon a time, under another name, Pally had been the closest thing Madoc had to a peer in slaughter. "Our young murderer has more… esoteric talents."

Waring looked more the sorcerer now. Char marks fluttered under his skin where the magic had turned on him, flecks of ash caught in his eyes and inked over his lips. He'd been bridled with a nail, a leather strap twisted around the back of his head to hold it in place, and the other nails were driven through his hands and feet.

Barbaric, but Madoc had done his best to minimize the damage. The nails were laced between the bones, not through them, and by rights, he should have put one of the nails through Waring's tongue.

Despite his situation, Waring looked aggressively placid and had remained silent even when they pierced his hands. Now he just stared blankly to the left of the screen. His eyes only flickered slightly when Pally snarled at him.

"Sorcerer," he spat. "What else can you expect of Hunters? First they lie down with dogs, now they get up with demons."

Madoc could have pointed out that Tepes was a sorcerer himself, or had been before he was bitten. It was Tepes's sorcery that let him bind his boyars to him, seal the blood-hungry greed that always destroyed Anakim alliances, and rise up to rule the Empire. He didn't.

Pally's prejudices might not make any sense, but they were his.

"Took thinks...."

Madoc paused as he considered how to shorthand the possession and eviction and then how to convince Pally and Lawrence that Took's story of those "tufts" of memory caught in his mind wasn't just the rags of old trauma.

"Took managed to get him to talk," he said. It wasn't even a lie. "That's why his magic backfired on him—it had its pound of flesh."

Waring groaned out something like a bitter laugh and leaned his head back against the headrest. It mustn't have counted as communication by magic's rules, for his skin didn't darken any further.

"And learned what?"

"That some of the kidnapped children are still alive," he said. "Somewhere. And that he doesn't trust VINE to be the good guys."

"We did imprison him," Lawrence pointed out in the background, guilt in her voice. "Brutalize him, just by sending him to The Salt. I can't blame him for holding a grudge."

Madoc took a second to make a note to deal with that. It was good for Lawrence to acknowledge her mistakes—God knew, it wasn't something Madoc could model for her—but not to wallow in regret. If this was enough to wipe the stain from her file and she was turned, she'd live too long and have too many mistakes on her ledger to dwell on every one.

If not, well, Madoc still expected her to be a functional agent and trust her own judgment.

Lawrence's self-worth could wait, as harsh as that sounded. The case couldn't. They didn't have to worry about Waring's death anymore, but the fate of the dhampir children was a deadline that Madoc actually cared about.

"No," Madoc told her as he studied Waring's face. The magic might have bridled Waring's tongue, but it didn't seem interested in a block on simple understanding. "Waring sold his tongue for this secret, stayed in The Salt for two years rather than let someone down. This isn't about him. He doesn't trust VINE for the same reason I don't."

In the background he heard Lawrence splutter, but he ignored her. She hadn't been there when Took disappeared, she hadn't been part of the investigation. Madoc leaned over and braced his hands on the armrests as he stared into Waring's scared eyes. It was a risk, but even witch-hobbled as he was, Madoc thought it was worth it.

"Someone at VINE, or connected to them, hurt someone he loves," Madoc said. "Didn't they?"

It was the slightest nod, but it still filled the recycled air of the plane with the smell of charred meat. Waring twitched in the chair and clenched his jaw against the pain, but it wasn't as violent as before. The attack left him shaken, and smoke exhaled around the nail that muzzled him, but he was still conscious.

Madoc made a disgusted sound and pushed himself back from the seat.

"So now we have a witness who won't talk," he groused, "and even if they change their mind, can't talk. "

"I don't think so," Quick corrected him.

Madoc glanced down at the tablet and into the old vampire's narrowed eyes. "What?"

"I don't think it's silence," Quick said but then corrected himself. "I don't think so, anyhow. It's like computer code. You have to be precise. He can't excuse himself, he can't say, gesture, or I don't know, tap out in code anything that would justify what he did. It probably seemed a good deal when he made it, but now he can't even ask to go to the toilet. Since the minute he speaks, people start to ask why he won't talk about something else. Right?"

Madoc turned to look at Waring, who stared back through tangled, singe-ended hair. The only expression on his face was desperation and maybe frustration.

"He couldn't risk it when the spell, whatever it was, still protected... whoever he's protected," Madoc said. He flipped his hand to dismiss the details for later. "Especially not when he didn't trust anyone."

That was a familiar feeling.

"Not even the people he should," Pally muttered. He looked sour when Madoc glanced at him. "I... need to tell you something. When you get back."

It wasn't a question that Pally had secrets. He'd been a cardinal too. All of them held close some of their boyar's secrets, bloody tinged and weighted. Then they had their own, the only things they could really claim as their own possessions during their long service.

That he wanted to spend one on Madoc was the unusual element.

"Now," Madoc corrected him sharply.

Pally reluctantly tightened his mouth. "Privately," he bargained down.

"Hold on," Lawrence said as she grabbed her laptop back again. "If this is about who we should trust, we should all hear it. What happened to Biters don't have secrets?"

"That's a lie," Quick told her. "We all have secrets, like you sending reports to your mother."

Shock made Lawrence gape, and she tried to stammer out what couldn't decide whether to be a confession or a denial. As she tried to navigate her way through a bit of both, Quick grabbed her arm and pulled her up and away.

Madoc waited until the door slammed. Then he flicked his attention back to Pally.

"If you have done something dire," he said. "I've done worse."

Pally rubbed his hand over his face. "I would rather do this face to face," he told his palm. "When Took... when Luke was kidnapped—"

The low, scraped noise caught in Madoc's ears a second after he realized it had come out of his throat. He could taste smoke on the back of his tongue, and he nearly choked as he swallowed it back down.

"Or perhaps not," Pally said warily. He held up both hands. "Not that. There's not much I can deny I *would* do—my history always makes a liar—but that, I *didn't* do."

"Talk." Madoc walked away from Waring. Anger could make him cruel, and he needed Waring to trust them enough for the gauntlet of speech at some point. He made himself inhale, his lungs ached as they expanded, and let it out again. "Quickly, Solomon."

Maybe Pally had forgotten that Madoc was one of the few who still remembered that name. He flinched as though it had stung him and clenched his jaw. They glared at each other as they remembered who they had both been, once.

It was Pally who backed down first, or at least, unclenched his jaw.

"Took thought you were the one who kidnapped him," he spat out. If it was revenge for Madoc's use of that raw, old name, it worked well. Something hollow opened inside Madoc and sucked everything into it— anger and smoke and any words that could have cut Pally back. Was this what heartbreak felt like, he wondered idly. Every other time he'd lost someone he had anger to feed the pain into, something to stoke and let consume him.

This just felt empty.

"You lie," he tried out on his tongue.

For a second, Pally looked thickly delighted with his cruelty. Then he scrubbed Solomon away with a pass of his hand and plastered on regret. Madoc wondered with a flicker of malice, before he was sucked down into the emptiness, if Pally knew which emotion was the real one.

"I don't think he *believed* it," Pally said carefully. "Even 'thought it' was just my cruelty, but he feared it. How could he not, Madoc? When you fear betrayal, you don't care if it was a stranger."

"My first love *feared* I was a monster," Madoc rasped out. "Everyone knew what I was, but when people in our town sickened and died, it was Gwynn who whispered to people about how I went out late at night. He told the priest how I'd seduced him. He told them where to find me."

It seemed only fair, after all, to give Pally a secret for a secret. Although he looked as though he'd rather not hear this one.

"Madoc, I—"

"Don't be sorry. He paid the price," Madoc spat. "After they'd done with me, they burned my poor stupid love alive, just in case. A lot more people died after that."

It turned out that Madoc had been wrong. The anger was still there. It just needed a moment to regroup. He welcomed the taste of burned apples in the back of his throat and thought about all the times he'd imagined what he'd have done to Gwynn if the mob hadn't turned on him next.

In the back of his mind, he remembered how often he'd thought he'd have forgiven the stupid bastard anything if he'd just been there.

"There's a difference," Pally said quietly.

"Really?" Madoc sneered. "What? That Luke at least knows how to end me properly."

Pally looked at him as though he were an idiot. "That someone he knew sold Luke to a monster that tortured him for a year. That he can't even use his own name anymore, because that's who it happened to. He can't even trust his own memories, never mind anyone else. Yet he was still brave enough to even think he could trust you? Trust *any* fucker? When you still chew over a centuries-old betrayal as if some inbred Welsh farm boy had any idea what he'd cost you both with his fear? You weak bastard."

That wasn't the gentle justification that Madoc expected. He spluttered at Pally for a second.

"He was the baker's son," he said stiffly.

"All the fucking difference, then," Pally said with a sneer. It was disconcerting to hear him swear so casually. He usually chose his words carefully, a mannered facade between him and the coarse-tongued Solomon. "Do what you want, Madoc. Remind everyone that no one can stop you from being a fucking bastard. Prove to Took that he was goddamn right not to trust you. There will be plenty of people willing to pick up his pieces."

"Like you?" Madoc asked harshly. "You were never his type."

The sharp, hard-edged grin was all Solomon. "I can be fucking convincing when I put my mind to it, Madoc. He might be worth the effort."

He slapped the lid of the laptop down before Madoc could snarl a reply. Madoc was left with the scratch of the idea that Pally might have a point, and a ball of rage in his chest that he couldn't unleash on anyone with a clean conscience. Sometimes he missed being Elizabeth's collared bastard. There had never been any end of people to work his anger out on.

How many of them had deserved it, a quiet voice in the back of his head asked.

The answer was "not many." Madoc already knew that, but it didn't help quell the sick heat in the pit of his stomach.

"Fuck you too, Paladin," Madoc snarled in frustration as he threw his phone at the ground. It shattered against the carpet-sheathed metal, bits of glass and plastic ricocheted across the floor and embedded in the soft leather of the seats. It was too petty of a tantrum to actually spend any of the dark, sullen energy that settled in his muscles, but it would have to do.

He locked his hands behind his head to thwart the urge to break anything and flexed his fingers against the back of his neck until he felt the ache of tender skin where Elizabeth's fangs had dug deep. When had Paladin… had *Solomon*, of all people… grown a fucking heart?

"Damn it," he breathed out. Then he pulled a face at the shape of the words on his tongue. "Damn me, then. Fair enough."

He kicked the broken phone with his foot, cracked glass splintered under his sole, and he stalked back down the plane. As he passed Waring, the boy leaned warily away from him. Madoc stopped and looked down at him.

"When you tried to get into Took's head, he saw your secrets," Madoc said. He kicked Waring's foot to make sure the young man paid attention. "Did you see his?"

The shadow of a haunted expression crossed Waring's lean, on its way to handsome, face. It would have to be answer enough.

"You can trust him," Madoc told him. It wasn't a question, and it didn't need an answer. "If you tell him where to find your friends, or whatever they are to you, we'll do our best to help you. Hold your tongue, and whatever happens is on you. I think that will hurt you more, in the long run, than whatever the magic does to you."

He left Waring to think about that under the VINE pilot's watchful eye, while he went to find Took. There had been a time he'd hunt Elizabeth's enemies from one end of the territory to the other. If he couldn't find one awkward vampire in the middle of a Nevada town, he would take himself under The Salt to rot.

And when he found him? Madoc weighed that question as he loped across the pocked runway to the flimsy wire fence. No answer immediately occurred to him.

Chapter Seventeen

GABRIEL TOOK the phone and looked at the photo of the dead man on the screen as he took a sip of straight scotch from a grubby tumbler. It wasn't, Took supposed dourly as he sat back and tried to ignore the itch of eyes on the back of his neck, as if the Hound had to worry about germs.

The lore said it was easy to pick out a werewolf. They were bestial in appearance and behavior, stank of raw meat, and could barely control their appetites, whether it was lust or gluttony. Of course the lore came from VINE and had been written by vampires. Gabriel's palms weren't hairy, his eyebrows didn't meet in the middle, and if his eyes shaded too much toward yellow, it wasn't beyond human norms. The outward betrayal that Gabriel was anything but human was the glimmer of eyeshine as he looked up, the bar's fluorescent lights reflected green from his pupils. As a kid, Took had just thought he was a human with a quick temper, less volatile than a lot his friends' parents who just drank away the full moon.

Took wondered what it was that gave him away as a vampire—other than the fact he'd bared fang in a dick-measuring contest outside.

"Don't get cocky," Gabriel said as he looked back down at the phone screen. "Harry out there isn't a Hound, he's barely a Hunter."

There were plenty of Hunters who'd argue with the order that Gabriel put that in. Took let it stand as he picked up the beer he'd ordered. The narrow neck was cold against his fingers as he lifted it to his lips.

"I worked that out when his arm came out of the socket like an overcooked chicken wing." Took took a swig of beer. At least he knew no one had spat in it, since watering it down could only have improved the taste. "Do you know him or not?"

Gabriel put the phone down and pushed it back across the table. The Hunter from Charleston stared blankly out of it, black hole in his forehead like a third eye. "What's it to you?"

"He tried to kill me."

"He's a Hunter," Gabriel said. "The only thing wrong with that sentence is that he only tried, not succeeded."

It shouldn't have stung. Took expected nothing else, yet some adolescent part of him still wanted to dance for Gabriel's approval. Family knew you too well. It made it easy for them to find the quick and dig in. Of course, the opposite was true too.

"Well, send a Hound to do a Hunter's job," Took drawled as leaned back. "And what can you expect but for him to piss on the carpet?"

Gabriel glanced at him and then at the photo. "If I'd sent a Hound after you, Luke, you wouldn't be here to ask questions."

"He had the ink."

That made Gabriel scowl. Hunters might be happy to have a werewolf to send into a firefight, but few wanted to drink or train with one. The werewolves had made a virtue of exclusion and stuck with their own and their wannabes, if the dead man had been a Hound, then Gabriel would have known.

"You sure?" Gabriel asked with a small tilt of his chin.

"In his armpit," Took said. "I couldn't tell you how old it was off the top of my head, but it wasn't raw. He'd had it on him at least a few months. He wasn't a wolf."

That was something Took hadn't been sure of until now. He'd never smelled a werewolf before, not as a vampire. His childhood memory of what Gabriel smelled like was of whiskey, blood, and clean sweat, but now he could smell the sour, wet-fur stink of the curse on him. He'd have noticed that in the morgue.

Gabriel scowled. "And he wasn't one of my Hounds. I don't know him," he said. "Some groupie who thought our mark would get him jobs, let him coast on my reputation. Does it matter? It doesn't look like he'll do it again."

"I shot him in the foot," Took said as he reclaimed his phone. "His associates finished him off. If he got that so he could tell them he was a Hound, then they don't have much respect for you."

They stared at each other for a second, and then Gabriel sat back. He slung his arm over the back of his chair. The glass of scotch tapped against the wood. It wasn't that he didn't see the trap Took had set, he just admired the setup.

"What if they knew he wasn't?"

"And they let him get away with it?" Took said. He shook his head. "That shows even less respect."

"I'm not sure that quite tracks," Gabriel said. "But not a bad effort. I tell you what. If you give me a truth, then I'll give you one."

"Flip it," Took said.

"A lie for a lie?"

Took shook his head. "You first."

Gabriel pursed his lips in a shrug and waved his glass at Took in agreement. "Ask."

"This guy wasn't the sort who'd come up with something like this. He wasn't smart enough to come up with it on his own, or stupid enough to think the Hounds would let him get away with it. So who did he work for?"

It took a moment and a slow sip of scotch before Gabriel decided to answer.

"I don't know." He raised one finger from the glass to quiet Took before he could say anything. "If I *knew*, I'd put a stop to it. If I had a strong hunch, I'd throw a few punches and see what shook out. As it is, all I have are stories about people who call themselves the Hounds of God, not Gabriel, and use my mark. Whoever they are, they back it up enough they aren't questioned, but aren't any dog I've collared."

"Who?"

"Your turn."

Took exhaled. He suspected he wouldn't enjoy this game.

"Ask."

"VINE?"

Gabriel had never been one to use a lot of words when one would do. It wasn't just a tendency to the laconic, but because people tell you more if they make up the question themselves.

Why VINE when he'd been raised to be a Hunter? Why the Biters when he could never be bitten? Lycanthropy wasn't inherited—although the offspring of a wolf was more likely to turn than die if infected—but whatever original sin a child inherited from their wolf parent inoculated them against vampirism. Or, Took poked at the sharp end of a tooth absently, that was how it was meant to work.

"I'm not cut out to be a plumber," Took said. "And I'm not pretty enough to marry for money."

Reluctant humor slanted one of Gabriel's rare, crooked smiles. It looked weary. His smiles always did, as though they'd already seen the pratfall.

"I don't know," he said. "There's someone for everyone, or so I fear. Word on the street is that you've slummed it with the cardinal."

"Nice try," Took said. "You've heard stories about these new Hounds. Like what?"

"They're better, faster, stronger, and they're house-trained," Gabriel said. He finished his whiskey and set it down on the table. "Not like us. They do the job and lick the boot of whoever loosed their chain. They haven't quite worked up the balls to come West yet. Unlike you. The local Hunters going on about them, about how they might not need me anymore, pissed me off enough that I tracked some of them down a few years ago—"

"You came back East?"

"Is it against the law?"

"Kind of."

Gabriel shrugged. "I grabbed one of them after they led a raid on some sucker and her bloodbag down in Gainesville. Put a few pointed questions to him but didn't get anything. He just mouthed fucking scripture at me, like any god is going to take time out of their day to intervene for some Southern idiot. He wasn't a wolf, though, I could smell that. I lost my temper in the end and figured if he wanted to be a Hound, he should get some teeth." He shrugged and glanced over Took's shoulder to give a slight nod to someone. "After that, suddenly they were a lot more careful."

"What happened to him?"

"My turn," Gabriel pointed out, almost gently. "But since you asked so nicely, it didn't take. Sometimes it doesn't, although he died worse than most. I was tempted to give him the silver stroke myself just to shut him up, but you know my rule—survive and all is forgiven."

Took could feel the puzzle in his head. It was almost there, all the pieces lined up in order. He just needed to poke the right one into place and it would all fit together. He was so close it made his fangs ache.

"Stronger, faster, better," he said. "Was he?"

"Than me? No," Gabriel said. "Than he should have been, a lot."

"And he definitely wasn't a wolf?"

Gabriel paused and frowned as he took a drink. A man—or wolf—of few words needed to find the right ones. "Couple of my people who've crossed paths with them—the Hounds, not the dogs—say that they are. Or might be. They've got the smell, but they don't have the eyeshine. Like someone bit them and they never turned. This one, though, he wasn't. Not a vampire either. I would have figured him for a Goat, but the only bite on him was mine. Didn't stink like one either. So I figure, who's more likely to be right? Everyone else or me? It's me and they aren't wolves."

Except he'd made it a point to say that some of them might be, that people who should know thought they were. That meant Gabriel wasn't going to claim this as his problem, but if someone else wanted to clean it up, he'd point it out to them.

Wolves that weren't exactly wolves. Lost dhampir children. A sorcerer who'd bound his own tongue.

It was right there. Took knew the answer was right in front of him, but he couldn't quite reach it. And time was up.

"My turn," Gabriel said. "When are you going to learn not to always take point?"

There it was.

Gabriel meant it as a threat. Took's grin caught him off guard, but that was the—well, *part* of the—answer Took was after. Now he had the who and the where. All he needed was the rest of the why… besides the obvious.

"When are you going to learn to duck?" Took asked. He swung the bottle around in a fast, hard arc. The heavy base connected with the side of Gabriel's head. It dented the fine bones of his temple in and then shattered. Gabriel's eyebrow split in a welter of blood that dripped down his cheek to his jaw, and he slumped backward as his brain rattled around his skull.

Took didn't expect it would last. He kicked the chair out from under him and spun around to punch the broken bottle up into the face of a bearded, blond werewolf who grabbed at him with long, muscle-heavy arms. The shards of glass dug deep into the soft meat of his cheek, and then Took twisted his wrist hard.

The blond howled as Took shredded his face—most of the left side hung loose in long strips of ragged, raw steak—and staggered backward. It would heal, but not cleanly. Took grabbed the guy by his bloody shirt and threw his weight against him, the burly square of body a serviceable shield as Took charged the door.

A wiry girl, her blonde hair teased up like a wolf's ruff, lunged at him from the side. She swung two knives in a practiced, crisscrossing pattern that flicked out to nick at his forearms and face. Actual training meant Took couldn't just bull his way through. He had to alter his plan instead. He grabbed one of the knives in his hand as the girl slashed at him. The blade caught on his palm and slotted between his middle and index fingers.

The pain throbbed up his arm and into his throat, but he ignored it as he smashed what was left of the bottle against her head. The dregs of beer matted into her hair, and Took used his grip on the knife to yank her close enough to headbutt. Her nose popped like a crumpled plastic mug and blood sprayed over Took. He gagged in surprise. Her blood tasted acrid and had a bitter, herbal bite to it.

He pulled his gun while she lurched backward, eyes glazed as she shook her head. A hard blink was enough to focus her, and she tensed as she shifted her grip on the knives for another attack. Took shot her in the throat. She shrieked—or tried to around the open flap of her throat—and stumbled backward as she tried to plait the shreds of her throat together with her fingers.

Rule number one for fighting things that healed faster than you— messy and upsetting was sometimes a better choice than what would be a kill shot on a human.

Bones crunched behind him and flesh ripped as the body underneath it decided to be something else. Five minutes. That was how long it took for a werewolf to finish the change. Less for Gabriel.

A big man, head shaved down to an elf-locked mohawk and the sides tattooed like torn flesh, tackled Took from the side. They crashed into a table, and it collapsed under them in a welter of splintered wood and broken glass.

Someone laughed—a cackle of sound more like a hyena than a wolf—as Took went down. A clumsy roundhouse punch caught Took a glancing blow on the head. He squinted through the static blur that rattled his brain and drove his knee up between the man's legs.

Bone cracked and a small, horrified sound squeezed out of the man's throat. Something wet soaked Took's leg—blood or piss. Some of them were human, Took remembered, but he didn't have the luxury to discriminate.

He got his elbow under the writhing man's shoulder and shoved him off, just in time to catch a foot to his ribs. The impact lifted him off the ground, and his ribs popped with that weird starburst pulse of pain and pressure. It felt like a safe assumption that whoever was on the other end of that foot wasn't human. Took managed to hang on to his gun with numb fingers, but his arm wouldn't cooperate when he tried to raise it.

The woman put her boot to his shoulder and leaned down to sneer at him. "Not so tough when you're up against someone as strong—"

Took spat blood into her face. The dark liquid spackled over her eyes and dripped into her mouth as she recoiled in shock. His gun hand was still numb, but the other worked as he groped through the glass and wood for a chunk of something heavy. He came up with a chair leg, splintered where it had snapped off the seat.

"Never was," he said as he rammed it underhanded up into the meat of her leg. It wouldn't slow her down as much as it would a vampire, who wouldn't heal around wood, but the raw, wet wound gouged into her muscle would hinder her for a while. "Tough doesn't win. Mean does."

She yelped in pain and lurched backward. The splintered stick of wood ripped the hole in her thigh wider as it pulled free. Took rolled over and scrambled to his feet, shook the buzz out of his ears, and broke for the door.

The wolf with her throat half stitched back together lunged at him. He spun and shot her in the head this time. It wouldn't kill her. Biters got silver as standard issue, but Took had grabbed his stand-in gear from VINE. The impact did knock her back on her ass and she sprawled there, out of commission until her brain rerouted around the pulped gray matter.

He shouldered through two thugs who fumbled a grab at him. To his left he caught a glimpse of a vaguely familiar face in the crowd, a silver streak in dark hair longer than Gabriel would usually leave on his Hounds.

Took put the pieces together a second too late to dodge as Grey, Gabriel's best friend, whipping boy, and second-in-command, braced his ever-present sawed-off shotgun against his hip and fired. The spray of silver-mixed buckshot caught a few of the Hounds on the way through and human squeals of pain mixed with the whine of silver-touched wolves.

The silver pellets caught Took as he twisted away from it. They ripped into his back in a rash of pain that spread and cramped through his muscles and caught his thigh. A couple punched through his throat, the scrape of poisoned pain like the world's worst laryngitis, and peppered his side and stomach.

He coughed up blood, clots of it sour as they burst on his tongue, and he felt the ping of metal shot against the back of his teeth. His knees cracked against the ground a second before his brain realized he was on the way down.

"Wet-mouthed bastard," Grey jeered. "This ain't your hunting ground."

Two shells in a shotgun, Took reminded himself. He threw himself the rest of the way to the ground and felt the force of the blast cut through the air over his shoulders. If he hadn't moved, that would have taken his head off.

Not that it mattered.

Gabriel used Took's vest like a handle as he hauled him up off the dirty floorboards. Without much effort at all, he tossed him across the bar. Took's back cracked against the door and he slid down onto the floor.

"Tell me, Luke," Gabriel growled as he stalked forward on bent-backward legs. No one would say he didn't look like a werewolf now, seven and a half foot of slimy black fur and a bony, heavy head with high-set ears and a muzzle with too many teeth. Muscle bulged around his jaw, heavy enough to show the ridges through his skin, and anything human had bleached from his eyes to leave them as gold as coins. "How did you think this would end?"

Like this? Maybe, Took supposed, if he was honest. Six months ago this would have been the perfect result, an out he could deny responsibility for. He hadn't *wanted* to die, but he basically already had, so why not.

Things had changed—not enough to fix everything, but the easy intimacy of a kiss across his knuckles was something—and yet he'd still walked in here.

Took laughed wetly and spat out blood and chips of metal. He got his feet under him and pushed himself up the door. "Fuck if I know," he admitted. "You?"

A wolf's face wasn't meant to look rueful, but Gabriel still tried.

"Like this," he said as he padded forward on bare paws, his boots ragged leather strips around his ankles. His huge hand snapped out and closed around Took's head, cupped around the side of his skull like it was *almost* affectionate. Sharp claws pressed in against Took's neck, and Gabriel's thumb dug in the soft skin under his jaw to force his mouth shut. It pushed his fangs back up into their sockets, which hurt like fuck. "Always like this, kid."

He started to squeeze.

It wasn't the pain that disoriented Took—although it pulsed black and static between his ears—so much as the sound of his skull as it creaked. He slid his free hand around behind his back and groped for the sheath on the back of his belt.

Took's knife, the one he supposed was either on Lawrence's belt now or back in Philly, had spent his career clipped just under his spine. He'd used it to open plastic seals or jimmy locks. The only blood it had ever drawn was his own the time he tried to pry up a floorboard with it and slipped. He still made sure it was recoated with colloidal silver gel every time he went back to work.

Hopefully whoever had dropped this kit off had been just as exacting.

He slid the blade free, the weighted hilt tucked into his palm, and swung in a wide, vicious arc that cut across the underside of Gabriel's arm. A spray of skunk-sour blood flicked across the wide, thick-haired chest and then across the underside of his muzzle. The end of the blade scraped over his jaw and flicked under the corner of his lips. It sliced the black flews up to his cheek and up toward his eye.

Gabriel jerked his head back in time to avoid a patch. He snarled as the silver suspension worked its way down into his blood, the edges of the injury pale as the silver tried to undo the curse. It wasn't enough to kill him, but he'd have that mark for a while.

Blood and slabber splattered as Gabriel shook his head to dislodge the pain. His hand tightened and Took gagged as the claw under his chin pierced up into his mouth. He curled his tongue away from the scrape of it.

"Was there a point to that?" Gabriel rasped as he plucked the knife out of Took's suddenly nerveless hand. "Did you think this would kill me?"

He flicked the knife away. Took gargled out a laugh around the talon.

"If I could give up," he said, "life'd be easier. Death would have been easier."

Gabriel snorted. "It'd have been over anyhow. I guess I get to fix that now," he said. His fist tightened. "Goodbye."

The edges of Took's vision squeezed into a black blur that faded until all he could see was Gabriel's face. But he could still hear. The low growl of a heavy engine cut through the scrape of his bones as it approached.

Took always took point, even if it made no sense, and Madoc saved the day. A flash of will pushed back the black rim of pressure in his skull.

The matte-black bike, Harley engine under a road-bike paintwork, smashed through the window of the bar.

"Son of a bitch," someone yelped as the Hounds and their groupies staggered back from the broken glass and the dangerous spin of the bike's tires as it skidded toward them.

Madoc stepped off the bike as it fell, composed as though he'd just come through the front door, black on black, silver bright against his collar and across his chest. He smiled at Gabriel, no humor in the flash of sharp white fangs and bloody tongue.

"Hounds. Last I heard you were in Montana," he yelled across the bar. "That's where I've had people looking."

Gabriel flexed his fingers around Took's head. It would have been easy enough to end it there or make a good try at it, but instead he let go. Took had a half-formed plan on how to help Madoc, but good intentions weren't enough to keep him on his feet.

"Maybe he's not so good at hide-and-seek, then," Gabriel growled. "You didn't seem to have any trouble."

One of the shifted wolves—built along the same lines as Gabriel but blond furred and not much taller than normal—swung a clawed paw at Madoc's head. He swayed back and caught the wolf's wrist before the blow connected. His fingers were pale against dark skin and tawny fur as he used the force the wolf had put into the punch to slam him down into the ground. The already scarred planks that floored the bar splintered further under impact. Madoc braced his boot in the wolf's armpit and torqued the thick, shifted arm off at the shoulder.

The shriek that came out of the wolf was high-pitched and shocked, the death squeal of a farm animal that had just realized it was food. Sudden, unexpected fear rippled out through the crowd as they watched the curse try to stitch the wolf's body back together. It didn't get a chance as Madoc pulled his personal 410-bore shotgun pistol out of the holster. His equipment came from the BITER quartermaster, and the saltpeter and silver shot punched the wolf's skull into the floor.

"I just followed the stench," Madoc said as he dropped the arm. "Tell me, wolf, are you going to fight me or tuck tail and run away?"

Gabriel chuckled. "Not my—"

Before he could finish, Grey shoved to the front of the crowd. His face was only half-changed, bones sharp as they twisted under his skin and made him twitch, but his hands were still steady enough to jerk the shotgun up to his shoulder.

"Think you scare us?" Grey sneered, as his fangs carved new homes in his gums. "Fancy coat, fancy title. You're just another fucking wetmouth to us."

"It's silver!" Took forced the warning out through his raw throat as Grey cocked his finger back.

The blast cut through where Madoc stood, just as his body came apart like tattered smoke. Someone in the crowd was stupid enough to cheer. It was strangled to death in his throat as the smoke dragged itself back together, and Madoc stepped out of the dark wherever he went in front of Grey. He grabbed the end of the shotgun in one hand and punched it back into Grey's face.

"Fight it is," Madoc purred.

He spun and fired a shot into the gut of one of the human Hounds as the man lunged at him, stake clenched in one hand. The blast tumbled the man back in midair and threw him into the crowd behind him. By the time they recovered, Madoc had stepped away again.

"Not what you had planned?" Took asked Gabriel as the big wolf snarled in frustration and watched Madoc take the bar apart.

Sharp yellow eyes cut down and narrowed with a flash of mixed rage and humor. With Gabriel, everything was mixed with rage.

"See?" Gabriel chewed the word between his fangs as he bent down to grab Took's foot. His claws punched through the heel of Took's boot as he dragged him away from the door. "You always thought you were so bright, boy, but you forget other people are too. This—give or take a few dead whelps—is exactly what I had planned. Or did you think I couldn't smell that killer's stink on you?"

He winked a yellow eye as he dropped Took by the door. "And eat something, boy. You look like hell."

Chapter Eighteen

THEY HADN'T made Madoc a cardinal because of his pretty face or let him live after the Accord was signed because they had a choice. He was dangerous, well trained, and he liked to kill. Death had been with him all his life, and he'd gotten good at introducing it to others. And once he let the smoke out of his cage, he *was* death—or the closest thing anyone who didn't sidestep the world to see what lived in the dark would get to it.

Blood dripped from his hands as he let the smoke drag him through the shadows. On the other side, in the gray lands, it had gotten crowded. Birds strung together of bones, with tattered rags of wings, hopped and croaked as they mobbed him. He batted them aside easily enough, but they drew blood with their sharp beaks and dirty talons. Even Madoc could smell how sweet his blood stank here, like black perfume on the still air. It would draw worse than the scavengers.

There were always worse things to draw here.

Madoc snatched one of the creatures off his back and crushed it in his fist. His blood caught at him like hooks, bruised dark and tender under the skin like rot, and he had to lean in to stop it from pulling him away. It was always like walking into the wind here, but now it felt like a hurricane. Madoc dropped the bird to the ground. It squawked at him in offense, started to peck its bones back into shape, and then headed over to the silver-and-gray wolf that snarled over the barrel of a reloaded shotgun. Drool hung in thick strings from his lips, the black flews caught half-wrinkled as they peeled back.

He had surprisingly pretty blue eyes—a shame he wouldn't for much longer. Madoc pressed his gun against the creased patch of skin between those pretty eyes and let himself snap back to the solid world. His bones ached under his skin, the shadows worked down into the marrow, but it was done.

The wolf's eyes filled with shock, but before Madoc could pull the trigger, a big, heavy, furred hand closed around his wrist and yanked.

Werewolves were fast, but not that fast, Madoc registered. He tucked the question away for later as he drew the heavy dagger on his thigh and laid the edge to the big wolf's neck. They stared at each other, caught in a moment of mutual hurt, if not destruction.

"I'll be harder to kill than you think," the wolf said. He sounded almost human, the words crisp as he wrapped the flat ribbon of its tongue around them. "And you ain't here for me anyhow, right?"

Madoc didn't look at Took. He'd finally muzzled the injured rage at the discovery that Took thought he would ever have hurt him. It was still there, caught in his chest like rocks, but he'd netted the damn thing until… later, when he could be angry without ruin. Then he tracked Took here, the heady smell of his blood mixed in with the skunk and meat stench of the werewolves. Madoc didn't know if he wanted to rage at the idiot, kiss him better, or some combination of the two. Whatever he decided, he didn't intend for it to have an audience.

"I'm not the dog warden," Madoc said. "But mangy curs who attack a VINE agent need to be put down. That's just for the public good."

The big wolf snarled at the insult but controlled itself. That was more impressive than the speech.

"You aren't my business either," the wolf said. "So tell you what… we both just walk out of here? No hard feelings. No broken bones."

The silver-and-black wolf snarled as it stepped forward, the shotgun raised to butt against Madoc's temple.

"He killed our fucking people, Gabe," he snarled. "Put him down now, while we have the chance. We'll be fucking legends."

Gabe. Gabriel. The hand on the collar of his Hounds. That explained a lot—not everything, but a lot. This wasn't just some werewolves who'd gotten cocky because vampires either avoided The Salt or were locked under it. Madoc smiled thinly.

"Gabriel and his Hounds," he said. "I know someone who's been looking for you."

It was hard to read the expression on a dog's face, but the urbane chuckle that rolled out of that massive barrel chest sounded amused. Hunt something long enough and it becomes a game, and Kit had been on the old werewolf's trail for a long, long time. Since before he joined the Biters.

"I've heard that," Gabriel said. "But your wolf's head isn't here to slide the silver home, is he? So it's your choice, cardinal. We'll kill each other one day, but it doesn't have to be tonight."

"If you think you can win, why offer?"

Gabriel grinned, a wet gape of red mouth and white fangs. "I might win, but you'll hurt me. I'm too busy to be laid up, and I'd end up with a dead second-in-command after he tried to kill me. You?"

"Did you hurt him?"

Gabriel didn't need to ask who Madoc meant. "I was going to kill him," he said. "I haven't. Take that and walk. Or don't."

After a moment, Madoc lifted the sword from Gabriel's throat. There was a bare line shaved down to the skin just above his jugular.

"I'll just tell Kit you were here," he said. An ordinary wolf he could take out, but Gabriel had a reputation and it wasn't Madoc's job to fight him. And he'd receive no thanks if he stole that from Kit.

"Go on," Gabriel encouraged as he slowly let go of Madoc's hand. The possibility of betrayal kept them slow and careful as they stepped back from each other. "It'll amuse me to think he's scorching his ass off here while I'm in a Cali vineyard."

Madoc smiled thinly. "What, are you moonlighting as a watchdog now?"

The silver and black snarled and lurched forward with a garbled "fuck you." Gabriel scruffed him and—almost casually—tossed the six feet of heavy muscled monster toward the smashed window.

"Tell Bennett he won't get a pass again," Gabriel said. "I'm not a sentimental man. And give Agent Kitaen my regards. I'm sorry I missed him in Casper."

He spun on one heavy paw and dropped onto all fours as he ran for the window and into the dark. Old habits made Madoc take a step after him, but howls broke out like music in the night. Gabriel had more backup.

Madoc picked up the silver wolf's dropped shotgun and broke it open. The homemade shells dropped out and hit the ground. He tossed it aside and glanced around the room. Someone whimpered on the floor, and there were people who could still breathe, but no one looked like they were about to get up.

Good.

He ditched the shotgun and stalked over to Took. Whatever he'd been about to say dried up in his throat as Took tipped back his head to peer up at him out of bloody eyes.

"Madoc," he rasped as he curled his mouth in a crooked smile. "I knew you'd come."

Love sucked, Madoc thought dimly as he dropped onto his knees. All that anger and justified frustration—Took knew better than to walk into a trap—drained away, and all he was left with was the desire to fix this. Fix everything.

"Really?" Madoc rasped as he wiped blood from Took's cheek. He grazed a finger over the raw hollow pierced just under his cheekbone. "Because it's not like you left a note."

Took laughed, the sound rough in his throat, and grabbed Madoc's shoulder to push himself to his feet. He wobbled, winced, and grabbed his side as the smell of his blood filled the air.

"We need to go back to Charleston," he said. "You were right. Someone did set me up, just not who you thought or for the same reason."

Madoc unfolded gracefully and wedged his shoulder under Took's arm. "So I wasn't right at all?" he said.

"Not about much," Took said with a laugh as they staggered out of the bar. "If it helps, I fucking missed it."

The truck was still parked outside. Madoc half expected it to have four flat tires, but apparently Gabriel's offer had been genuine. The vehicle looked unmolested. Madoc didn't trust how long the truce would hold. Gabriel might not have cared much about his dead, but once whoever was out there learned that the cardinal had killed them all, that might change.

He shoved Took into the passenger seat and then boosted himself over the hood to get the driver's side. The keys were in the ignition. Madoc revved the engine, the growl of it in the dark a challenge answered by wolves that sounded closer than they'd been, and spun it around to head for the dirt track back to what passed for a main road.

Halfway there, the headlights caught yellow eyes at the side of the road. Gabriel stood in the shadow of the trees and watched them approach. He dropped his long muzzle in some sort of acknowledgment as they passed him, but those acid-yellow eyes weren't focused on Madoc.

A dozen questions occurred to Madoc. He weighed them all and then deliberately discarded them. Immortality was best navigated when you knew what answers you could live without. Took had come to VINE with secrets—a con man's sharp mind and the stomach for a kill—and if Madoc had ever chased the answers, he'd have had to do something about it.

Or should, he supposed. Since whatever the answer *was* about what connected Gabriel and Took, Madoc knew he wouldn't act on it.

Silence made the facade of his loyalty to the Accord, to the deeper ties of the boyar, easier to keep up. He wouldn't be easier to kill, and there would be a price to pay one day, but if the Senate found out he had something to live for—to want—outside of duty and death, they might decide to empty their pockets.

"I'd tell you the truth," Took offered from the passenger seat, "if you asked."

Madoc shot him a look. "You know me that well?"

"Better than my own father," Took said dryly as he rubbed his hand through his hair and blood streaked through it like wax.

"Yet you really thought I'd ever hurt you?" Madoc asked as he spun the truck hard around the turn at the end of the road. It left a dark track of rubber etched onto the sun-bleached gray. That would make it easier for The Salt guards to find it.

He didn't get an answer from Took. Maybe, he thought sourly as he called Tac to report the werewolves, Took knew he'd rather not know.

THE PREFAB hut did triple duty as the air field's office, a crash pad for the pilots, and a place to stash contraband for the staff at The Salt. Madoc dangled a Ziploc bag with a bloody, neatly clipped blonde ponytail in it and wondered who'd paid to get it here. Not that they'd get it now. He tossed it onto the small, stained desk with the rest of the morbid keepsakes and supposedly magical bones and tatters he'd found under the fold-out bed. A few of them pricked against his fingers with the cold sting that he felt sometimes on the other side of the world, but most were just rags and dead parts.

"So, is one of our Salted undead a fool with their money," he asked as he fastidiously wiped his hands. "Or do they just want to compromise one of the guards?"

The sound of the shower in the small water closet flicked off. Madoc listened as Took dragged his clothes back on and cursed softly under his breath as he coughed out a strangled curse.

"Could be both," Took said after a second. "Not all of them are up there with the boyars. The hair was probably for Ellis McKinley, and he was stupid enough to think that his victims couldn't testify against him because he raised them afterward."

The silver itched under Madoc's fingertips, a little pain that he'd felt often enough that it was a pleasure, and then he shrugged off the leather jacket. He hung it over the back of a chair and stripped off the thin undershirt.

"Time for another purge anyhow," Madoc said. It wasn't unexpected. The Salt was a sour duty, physically harsh and emotionally worse. The presence of a single boyar had a weight to it, a gravity that pulled at your soul instead of your flesh. There were ten of them imprisoned here, salt-mad and bloated with plots. It was enough to turn anyone's head far enough that they'd say something, promise something, they couldn't take back. "It's almost due anyhow."

Took grunted his agreement as he shouldered the cubicle door open and stepped out in a cloud of calla-lily-scented steam. He was clean and his shirt was damp from a quick scrub in the sink, but he moved as though it hurt, and the wounds on his face and jaw were still raw.

"Tac will be torn," Took said absently as he hitched his trousers up over his hips. "He wants out, but he takes pride in doing a good—"

He stumbled to a halt over his own tongue as he looked up and caught sight of Madoc. Whatever sting lingered on Madoc's ego was soothed a little by the flash of hunger and appreciation that passed over Took's face. He looked… caught.

"When did you last feed?" Madoc asked.

Took blinked in confusion and then rubbed his hand over the back of his neck. "I… yesterday."

"From whom?"

Took was a good liar. He met your eyes, he kept the answers simple, he didn't stumble or justify.

"Some man," he said. "In a club. I didn't get his name."

Madoc walked over to him and reached up to tug his collar out of the way. The bruises had faded, but the scar was still pink and tender against Took's skin. He rubbed his thumb over the raw heart of it and watched as Took shuddered in reaction.

"This would have healed," Madoc said. "Are you starving yourself? Because in the end, you'll just lose control and kill someone. I'd rather not have to clean that up."

Took licked his lips but didn't lean away from Madoc's touch. "I feed twice a day. That's what the doctors recommended. I'm in control."

Of course, Madoc realized with the sour taste of guilt. Whoever had made Took hadn't taught him how to be an Anakim, had probably not intended for him to even remember he was a person, and the one person who should have stepped in had let Took push him away. All Took had left was VINE's doctors and their "theories," the Senate's best efforts to castrate the Anakim until they were just humans with bad teeth.

"What did they give you?" he asked. "Injections? Pills?"

Took looked flustered for the first time as he looked away. "They provide everything I need," he said. "I'm fine."

"Maybe if you were a lawyer or an accountant," Madoc said. A vampire took more than nutrients from blood, and while he knew a few Anakim who'd tried the no-bite diet, he didn't know anyone who'd stuck to it. "You'll get yourself killed. Or me."

Even with Took's eyes still averted, Madoc could tell he hadn't convinced him. It was in the stubborn set of his jaw and tightness of his throat.

"I don't want to hurt anyone," Took said. His voice was thick with the memory of nightmares. Just because he couldn't—wouldn't—remember that missing year didn't mean that it was gone. Madoc knew that. In a long life, there were a lot of old wounds you tried to forget. Some of them were just anchored too deep. "He wanted me to do it, but I wouldn't. It was the one thing he couldn't make me do."

There was something in Took's voice that was more than stubbornness. It felt brittle, dangerous, like the sort of thing you couldn't put back together again if it broke.

Something in Madoc instinctively shied away from that resolve. Sometimes sanity lay in the line you'd drawn in the sand, even if no one else could see it. Took would have to find his compromise with that on his own, but for now, they didn't have time to wait for Took to patch himself back together. If Waring's silence had given Annabelle and the dhampir children some protection, it had expired, and Took was the only one who had any ideas about what lay back in Charleston. He needed to be in one piece in order to walk them through his theory.

"You can't hurt me," Madoc pointed out. He smirked as Took finally flicked a wary glance back at him. "I'd like to see you try."

"I think I already did," Took murmured quietly as he skimmed his hands up Madoc's lean hips to his waist. The brush of callused fingertips sent a tremor of pleasure through Madoc's skin. It faded too quickly. "That's not what I wanted."

Madoc shushed him with a kiss. He lipped at the soft curve of Took's mouth until he coaxed it open and he could chase the tart sweetness of old blood over Took's tongue. It should have tasted weaker, watered down with supplements and the vampiric equivalent of anemia, but it hit the back of Madoc's throat like good whiskey.

"You didn't ask me to love you," Madoc said as he pulled back. Because, fuck it, he wanted to say it just once. "You don't owe me anything."

Took didn't flinch at the admission. That was something.

"I do," he disagreed. "You didn't do it. I know that now."

Madoc grazed a kiss along Took's jaw. It was glazed with a starburst of little scars, like threads under his lips. "Because you know I love you and I'd never hurt you?" It was a promise as much as anything else—a pledge.

"Well, yeah, and because you were in New York," Took said.

For some reason that didn't sting. It was such a typically *him* response that it just made Madoc chuckle against Took's throat.

"Heartwarming," he drawled as he worked his way down to the still pulse point in Took's throat. He bit down roughly on the thin skin, careful not to graze the old wound with his fangs, and felt Took clutch desperately at him.

Hunger clenched in Madoc's groin, a hot drag of lust at his balls and cock, but he tried to ignore it. The justification for this was that it was what Took needed, not just what Madoc wanted.

"I always *wanted* to trust you," Took said, his voice stiff with the discomfort of honesty. "There was no reason to, though, and that scared me. It made me second-guess myself, because my mind's not what it was. I can't trust it like I used to."

That sounded almost rote, like something he'd learned at someone else's knee. It pricked at something in Madoc's brain. There was a familiar cant to the words, but he couldn't put his finger on it just yet. He flagged it for later attention.

"The minute you looked at this case, you knew there was something wrong," Madoc pointed out. "Without you, Waring would be dead and Nora Aron would still be in her box. You're still a smart bastard and a bit of a dick about it. Not that much has changed."

"And you say you love me?" Took joked awkwardly.

"Yes," Madoc said simply. He did. Everyone knew it. Even Took knew it, for all he didn't trust it. He tilted Took's chin down and kissed him again, words murmured between his lips. "Prickly, smartass, suspicious...."

"Ruined?"

Madoc bit him. This time he didn't bother to guard his fangs. Took yelped at the sharp little pain and then leaned into it, one hand cupped around the back of Madoc's skull. His mouth slanted hungrily over Madoc's, slick with blood and edged with wickedly sharp, still-new fangs. The scrapes they left on Madoc's lips, along the edges of his tongue, made Took gasp and lick hungrily at the small wounds. It was sweet foreplay, but a dribble of blood wasn't enough to mend him.

"Did I hurt you?" Madoc asked as he grabbed a handful of Took's hair, knuckles pressed against the hard bones of his skull, and pulled his head back.

Passion glazed Took's eyes, his pupils swollen and rimmed with blue as he licked black-stained lips.

"No," he admitted slowly. "But I don't... I've never...."

Virginity hadn't impressed Madoc that much for a long time. It was just something that someone hadn't gotten around to yet. You might as well be excited that someone hadn't eaten a steak before. But the idea of being Took's first Kiss was different. The mixture of nerves and lust as Took looked at his throat, his tongue pressed absently against the point of his fang as he thought about it, caught in Madoc's balls and twisted into a hard knot of lust.

"If you do it wrong," Madoc said as he guided Took's head down to his throat, "I'll tell you."

Took licked his throat and then kissed the wet spot, lips soft and cool as the desert air. "This is sex, right?" he asked as he gripped the curve of Madoc's ass in both hands and pulled him closer. The hard jut of his erection pushed against Madoc's hip, eager under his slouched trousers. "Or am I just... off?"

It was a light question, but there was a hint of real fear under it, the dark undercurrent of "something wrong with me" that bubbled up in him every now and again.

Madoc nuzzled his temple as he considered how to answer the question. He stroked his thumb down to the soft dimple of skin under Took's ear.

"If you never wanted to bite me again, I'd still fuck you," he said. "If you never wanted to fuck me again, this would be really awkward."

He worked his hand down between their bodies and into Took's trousers. His fingers shackled the hard rise of Took's cock, hard flesh wrapped in cool satin, and squeezed. Took groaned and bit down.

It did hurt. Took didn't put enough pressure behind the bite—his fangs tore the skin instead of pierced it—and he chewed around the wound. It didn't matter. Pleasure crawled hot through his veins. Some Anakim claimed it was a pulse of their old life, a reminder from Enoch that they'd once been human. Madoc had always run cool, even when he breathed, so it was a sweet rush of silken lust. And it was Took.

Took mumbled an apology as he nuzzled against Madoc's neck. He lapped at the blood that spilled down Madoc's throat and pressed closer as he sucked hungrily on the wound. Madoc groaned thick approval in the back of his throat as he tipped his head back pliantly, his fingers buried in Took's dense, sandy-blond hair. It curled damply around his fingers.

He tugged on Took's cock in time with the ragged, thirsty pressure against his throat. Each time he twisted his fist around the wet, tender head, Took moaned something hungry and half-strangled against his throat.

Under his pants, Madoc's cock was so hard it ached. The throb of frustration clenched heavily in his balls and spread down his tense thigh muscles and up into his stomach. The ache of it settled behind the familiar sting of the thorn hooked through his navel until he could hardly feel the throb of the old brand.

Took unlatched from Madoc's throat and lifted his head. His lips were black with blood, and the raw hole in his cheek had already faded to a puckered scar.

"So," Took said as he licked the blood off his lips. He leaned to brush a kiss over Madoc's lips. The taste of his own blood came back, spiced with the curse of another vampire's Kiss. The sharpness of it, pine and snow and the ozone of a storm, caught on Madoc's tongue like mulled wine. It almost distracted him from the sly curve of Took's mouth against his. "You want to try and bend me over this bed? Because I'm not sure it can take it."

Madoc wanted to hesitate, to protest nobly that it wasn't necessary, that he'd wall his feelings up and play the platonic friend... once, that is, he let go of Took's dick. It was the sort of thing he supposed a good man would do.

But he wasn't a good man, so he didn't. Instead he pushed Took down on the narrow cot, his lean body sprawled over the thin mattress and old sheets and his long legs dangled over the bottom of it. His feet were braced against the floor, and his trousers were already slung low around his hips.

A twinge of duty reminded Madoc that they didn't have time for this, but he paid it off with a promise of quick and dirty. He unbuckled his belt and shoved his trousers down to his thighs. His cock rose eagerly toward his stomach, already thick and swollen with blood. He gave it a quick stroke with one hand as he looked down at Took.

He looked well fucked already, his eyes heavy with satiation and his lower lip dimpled where his fangs were still extended. Blood stained his lips, and his cock was swollen as he dragged his own hand down the length of it. It would be heavy in Madoc's mouth, broad enough that his fangs would scrape the sides and spill blood before he spilled his seed. Or that bloody mouth would be wrapped around Madoc's cock, the scrape of razor-sharp fangs a dangerous bit of foreplay.

Lust dried Madoc's mouth out as he swallowed the knot of hunger wedged in his throat. There were a lot of things he wanted to do to Took, or with him, but quick and dirty. He wanted to be done before the pilot came to hammer on the door. As cardinal, he could have killed anyone who caught him in a compromising position, but Agent Madoc would just have to deal with the fact that someone had seen him pull out of Took's ass so he could drag his trousers up.

Although the idea it would get back to West was not... without appeal.

"Turn over," Madoc said.

Took gave his cock one last stroke, his fingers slick with come, and rolled over. His ass was lean and tight with muscle, a faded tattoo tucked into the crease of his thigh. He tucked one knee under him to raise his hips up off the bed.

"Not yet," Madoc said as he pressed his hand down into the small of Took's back.

He bit down on his tongue until the skin split, and chewed on the wound to fill his mouth with blood. Under his hand, Took squirmed on the bed to rub his cock against the rough cotton bedding. Madoc pulled the tight, still tanned cheeks apart with both hands, and Took swore under his breath as he clenched his hands in the sheets. The backs of Took's thighs clenched as Madoc squeezed the taut globes of his ass in his fingers.

"Please," Took groaned as he twisted on the bed. His trousers were still caught around his thighs, so he couldn't spread them far, but he tried. "Madoc, God, please?"

There had been times Madoc had kept a lover on the sweet edge of orgasm until they begged him to come. He'd been there himself, and pride had kept the word caught behind his teeth until his lover had given in and fucked him anyhow.

No one had ever been desperate enough for him to beg before he even started. Madoc was surprised at the jolt of lust it delivered down his spine to his ass. He did as he was asked and pressed a bloody kiss to Took's asshole. He licked his way around the tight ring of muscle and then pushed his tongue inside, the passage slicked with spit and blood.

Took swore raggedly at Madoc as he writhed under him, caught between the rough scrape of cotton and wool against his tender cock or the slick tongue at work inside his ass.

"Fuck," he suddenly choked out. "It's… is it meant to be… I don't know. Hot?"

Madoc smirked as he leaned back. He skimmed one last kiss over the now slippery, still-tight hole before he crawled up onto the bed. "There's a reason humans find us addictive," he said as he sprawled over Took's back, his painfully hard cock pressed against the crease of Took's ass. Each restless twitch of Took's lean hips flicked back along Madoc's tender nerves to clench in the sweet spot between his balls and his ass. He pressed a kiss to the nape of Took's neck and breathed in the scent of him. "After this, whatever we are, I won't let you go again. You don't have to be my lover, or even my friend, but I won't just let you crawl away again."

Took reached back and grabbed Madoc's neck to pull him down for a kiss. "That's not your call," he said between their lips. "Now are you going to fuck me or not?"

Bastard.

Madoc chewed the kiss onto Took's lips as he reached down to grab his cock. He guided the head of it to Took's slick hole and pushed. The muscle stretched around him, still tight, and the glaze of his own blood was a chaser of afterthought pleasure down his cock. Took's ass tightened around him, and the long play of muscle from his hips to his shoulders clenched as he pushed into him.

"Shit," Took rasped out. He bit his lower lip and pressed his face into the fold of his arm. "I think your cock is bigger than mine too."

The snort of laughter escaped Madoc. "You hadn't noticed before?" he asked as he grabbed Took's hip, fingers hooked around the jut of bone. He thrust his hips forward in slow, measured strokes, his cock buried deeper each time. "You spent enough time with it in your mouth."

Took pushed back against him and lifted his hips off the bed to meet Madoc's downward thrust.

"Shut up," he grumbled. "It's just… been a while."

Madoc finally buried himself inside Took. The tight squeeze of muscle around his cock made his hips ache to thrust, but he held still as he lowered himself down so he sprawled along the tight length of Took's back.

"It was a few days ago," he said as he worked his hand under Took's hip to the hard jut of his cock. "If it was that forgettable, maybe I have to try harder."

Took choked on whatever he'd been going to say as Madoc squeezed the base of his cock hard. His ass tightened around Madoc's cock, and he pushed back against him. Madoc let him squirm for a second, pleasure tight as a bruise in his balls, and then shoved him back down onto the bed. His cock slid deeper inside, and Took rasped out something that might have been meant to be "fuck" but never got that far.

Madoc tightened his grip on Took's cock as he pulled back, the air chill around the base of his cock before he thrust back in. As he slid home, it drove Took's hips down into the bed, his cock wrung between Madoc's fist and the hard mattress. The cot rattled and groaned under them as they fucked, a broken spring hard under Madoc's knee as he braced himself for a better angle.

It worked. His cock nudged against the smooth bump of Took's prostate with each slow thrust. Took made a strangled sound and then again as Madoc chewed bloodlessly along his neck. He came between Madoc's fingers with a wet spill of sticky fluid, and Madoc pulled out. He twisted his sticky hand down the length of his cock in two quick, impatient jerks and came over Took's back and hip. Come dripped down to smear over the faded tattoo under Took's balls.

He rolled off and sprawled out on the bed, trousers still caught around his thighs. There were a lot of things he should do, but instead he lay and wondered what to say.

"I was afraid you'd done it," Took said. "I don't think I really believed it."

"Sophistry," Madoc pointed out. He still took Took's hand and wove their fingers together. It was a small memory to stash away, but he liked it. Sometimes, when he had to be the cardinal and let the smoke have him, small memories were all you had to anchor who you wanted to be. "It doesn't matter."

Took frowned as though he didn't believe that, but before he could say anything, a fist hammered at the door.

"We're ready to go," the pilot yelled through the door. "If you want to leave tonight, we need to go now."

Chapter Nineteen

QUICK LOOKED unconvinced.

"You've built a whole lot of castle on, what, some offhand thing a crazy, survivalist wolf said?" he said as he paused the game on his phone and set it down on the desk. "Are you sure it's not going to just fall down?"

Took weighed that for a second. "No," he admitted. "But it's true. I always take point. The only reason I didn't in Appleberg is because I thought Gatlin had wasted my time. Besides, if I am wrong, then you'll be the only one who knows."

Light flicked off the lens of Quick's glasses as he sat up. He didn't need them to see anymore, and he'd replaced his old Coke-bottle lenses with plain glass ones. It was just habit to have them on, something to straighten or peer off. Or, when he wanted to buy some time, to take off and polish.

"Shouldn't you be in there with Waring?" he asked. "Pretty sure Madoc wouldn't want SSA Crane in there on his own with our witness."

"Waring sat through the best that VINE had to offer," Took pointed out as he pulled a chair out and flopped down. He felt more alive than he had since he died, Madoc's blood like an infusion of coffee into Took's veins. The scars on his wrists were still there, bulky under the long sleeves of his T-shirt, but they didn't itch or ache when he turned his hands. The door creaked open behind him and he glanced around. Lawrence hesitated in the doorway, and despite Took's best intentions, he felt himself bristle. He squashed the resentment and gestured for her to come the rest of the way in as he went on. "West couldn't interrogate a man who already confessed. They'll be fine for an hour."

Lawrence carefully closed the door behind her and leaned back on it. "I thought you and SSA Crane were friends," she said.

"We were," Took said, then caught himself. This case might not have the fallout that West had wanted, but that didn't mean they'd be at odds, any more than their relationship's failure in the wake of Took's kidnapping had made them enemies. It was just life. Sometimes things didn't work out, but it was West who supported Took when he thought Madoc had been the one who turned him. That meant that Took owed him something. He corrected himself. "Are. It doesn't make him a good interrogator."

Quick kicked the chair next to Took out for Lawrence and reached for his keyboard. "It doesn't mean I'm going to take an hour to get this done either," he said. "I lifted everything the local Proverbial church had on their servers, while being preached at for a cup of underwhelming soup, but you have to give me some parameters to look for. I don't suppose anyone has just dropped a confession in there."

Lawrence glanced from one to the other. "I missed the start of this," she said. "Is this to do with the werewolves that you met? Madoc says he believes that one of them really was Gabriel, the head of the Hounds."

"He didn't introduce himself to me," Took said dryly as he shied away from the topic. He didn't think Lawrence was as good as him, but she wasn't stupid either. It was her job to catch liars and people with secrets, and Took was both. "And sort of. I think that the missionaries didn't just take the scriptures over to the poor, benighted humans of Europe. I think they brought something back."

"Probably clap," Quick interjected. He raised his fingers in the air and wriggled them expectantly. "Parameters, Took."

Took hesitated as he rubbed his hand over his jaw. He could hear the chatter of the VINE offices behind him, the carefully pitched murmur of office small talk, the clatter of keys, and the stutter-hum of the printer. None of the agents in there had any idea how bad he was about to make their lives.

If he was right.

"How many missions were the Arons involved in?" Took asked after a moment's thought.

There was a pause as Quick darted his fingers over the keyboard. "Many," he said lightly after a moment. "They led one every two years as a couple when they were first married. Then, once they had kids, one of them would go every other year. That's only our late and lamented Arons. Before that, their father was deeply involved in the Proverbial Church as well. In fact, he was the Deacon of a church we know and love in Appleberg, before he moved to Charleston."

"How many of the children on those missions died?"

"None,"

"What?" Lawrence blurted out the interruption.

"Check that again," Took said. Any death on a Mission would be recorded by the Church. It was a way to show respect for the dead, to remember their sacrifice. The Franklin boy who'd died should be marked down there and, morbid as it was, if he was the only martyr on the Arons' missions, they'd have been considered failures. "You must have missed something."

Quick snorted his opinion of that but tapped at the keys. His smug expression hung around for a minute and then faded as he scanned the screen.

"Now that doesn't make sense," he muttered. "If you look at the official documents, flight registers, carnets, and the rest, the same amount of people left the country as came back. But when you go into the different family registers, they lost three or four people each trip."

Lawrence leaned forward. "Even for a Proverbial mission, that's a lot of dead children. Sacrifice is one thing, slaughter is another."

"At least one of them was just left behind," Took pointed out. "Maybe to make room."

"For whom?" Lawrence asked with a frown. "Do you think they smuggled dissidents out of the Empire?"

"When it started, maybe," Took said. He made himself admit that it wasn't a bad theory. Jealous as he was to see Lawrence take his place, she wasn't bad at it. "How many of the families who lost children had ties of some sort to Appleberg?"

Quick raised his eyebrows. "Are you going to share your theory?" he asked. "Or wait for the rest of us to catch up?"

It wasn't a theory yet, just a hunch and a lot of ideas that didn't quite make sense of everything that had happened. It was like a jigsaw puzzle. He had all the pieces. He just needed to get the outline, and the rest would fall into place.

"I'm giving Lawrence the chance to show her chops," he said. Next to him, Lawrence flinched at the challenge and straightened up attentively in her chair. Even Quick glanced up from the computer to give Took a reproachful look for that one. He wasn't wrong. Took ignored it and pushed on. "Appleberg?"

"I'd forgotten what a dick you could be," Quick muttered as he hunched back down to work. This time it took a bit longer. "If we include the Arons, eight of the families either lived in the area, attended the church at some time, or their children attended the Proverbial summer camp that is located just outside of town. Although that closed a few years ago."

"Why?"

"No reason listed," Quick said with a shrug. "Bad touches probably."

The Arons had worked at the summer camp, Took remembered, during the years they didn't go away on missions. Annabelle Franklin had gone there. The photo of her in the salmon-pink camp T-shirt flicked into his mind. Even a month in the outdoors hadn't given her any color in her cheeks.

"Do you have a picture of the Aron children?" Took asked. He swiveled around in his chair and pointed to the screen mounted on the wall. Quick snorted at the change in subject, but after a moment, the pictures of two boys and a girl appeared on the screen. Before her years in the ground, Nora Aron had been a brown-haired little girl with see-through gray eyes and pallid skin. Her brothers were just as pale, with blond hair and brown respectively, but the same strange, almost translucent, eyes. "What about Annabelle Franklin?"

Keys clicked and then Annabelle joined the grid, a few years older and a little more faded but with the same eyes.

"Son of a bitch," Lawrence murmured. "All of them?"

"We'll see," Took said. He turned to look at Quick. "I want to see pictures of the kids from every single family that went on one of the Aron's missions. Start with the ones that have ties to Appleberg."

Quick hadn't caught on yet. He glanced curiously from the screen to Took and Lawrence but finally shrugged. "It'll take me a minute," he said. "They aren't in our files, so I'll need to trawl social media."

It turned out that Quick was wrong, at least partially. Most of the Mission children he pulled off their parents' Facebook pages or from sheets of posed selfies, children with curly hair and tans at the beach or in profile at their birthday parties. The others he didn't need to trawl social media for. They popped up from the missing persons database. Nine missing children from Appleberg, the three missing Aron kids—two Aron kids now, Took supposed—and six they hadn't even known about.

The children on the missing reports had all disappeared in the same three-month period, after Waring had gone to jail, and they all had the same pallor, and the same washed-out, almost colorless eyes behind glasses they probably didn't need.

Took stared at Nora's picture. If she woke up her eyes would be gray, the same as Madoc's. He wondered what color Madoc's had been back when he was still alive—maybe the same gray as Annabelle Franklin's or the sepia brown of Brian Larkin.

There had been no reason for anyone to see it before. Dhampir children in the US were too rare for anyone to just jump to the conclusion that a pallid child was one of them. Especially when it was a pallid child from a staunch Proverbial clan. Besides, none of the Anakim had any reason to fear their children going missing then. They had all disappeared before Waring's murders started, before the Aron family died. Once you saw them all together, though, the effect was amplified, unmistakable, until even Quick couldn't miss it.

"Holy fucking hell," he muttered. His hands were still for once as they settled on the keys. "They are all dhampirs. Shit is about to hit the fan."

THAT TURNED out to be an understatement.

The Director of VINE, a harder, more polished version of her daughter, was in front of a computer monitor in Philly. Her clipped questions were aimed at how VINE had missed something like this right under their nose. The fact that her daughter was involved didn't seem to make her want to cut them any slack.

"Not for the first time in connection to this case, I am disappointed," she said icily. Took, relegated to the back of the room after he'd given his testimony, gave a reluctantly sympathetic glance to Lawrence. She looked like she hadn't heard it. "Not only did you miss the connection to the Arons, you apparently just *overlooked* a dozen other missing children since we arrested Waring. We already had a shit show to navigate with the public after you discovered the kidnapped dhampir might be alive after all. Now this. Should I just expect mistakes and dhampir children every time you turn over a rock now?"

West cleared his throat. "The Biters' lack of overview has always been a problem—"

He never could read a room, Took thought wryly as Lawrence turned her cold glare onto him. This wasn't the sort of disaster that could be used to score political points. Not yet, at least.

"Apparently one that you should be well versed in, SSA Crane," Lawrence said pointedly. "Since a child-trafficking ring has apparently been run out of your city for the entire duration of your time in charge there."

While West tried to splutter his way out of responsibility for that on the two other screens, Charleston's Anakim and human representatives in the Senate bickered over each other as to what the priority was next.

"If Waring is innocent," Isaac Garcia, still human and breathing at sixty-four, said as he leaned in to peer through the screen, "we need to issue a statement that clears his name, and an apology, as soon as possible. As it is, this could completely alter the balance of power in the district. Liam Waring could become a real threat, not just a pain in our—"

"Ridiculous," Robin Dale, his Anakim counterpart, snapped as he jabbed his finger at the web camera. "This whole problem with the Proverbials and their dhampirs might have no connection to the Waring case. For all we know, Waring still murdered those families and kidnapped their children."

"But we don't know that," Garcia fired back. "He never confessed, remember? The conviction was carried on a wave of outrage and grief for those children. Or, for all we know, those dead families were somehow involved in this too. The murders only started after the Aron family was killed."

West, visibly sweating despite his best efforts to be calm, raised his hands. "Obviously what we all agree on is that we don't know enough. That's why we haven't decided what we're going to do yet," he said. "If we—"

He was shouted down by the mayor, who wanted assurances that the Proverbial churches and their missionaries would be "left out" of any statements. "It would be irresponsible to publicize their involvement and demonize whole congregations who had no idea."

The district attorney countered with an indignant plea for justice. "If they ignored the evidence of what went on, then they're just as guilty."

Only Chief of Police Graven had held his tongue so far. He stood at the end of the table with his arms crossed across his chest and watched Madoc through hooded eyes.

"VINE has started to work on the logistics of the situation," West said. "There are obviously a lot of moving parts to consider, and we cannot risk acting too quickly."

Another round of agreement and disagreement—the static of Isaac's electronic indignation hard on Took's ears—kicked off. Graven finally broke his silence. The rough growl of his voice compelled attention without being raised.

"This pantomime is wasting time," he said. "Why don't you just tell us what we're going to do, cardinal."

Madoc raised his eyebrows and started to say something diplomatic. Before he could get more than the "I'm just an agent—" out, Dale interrupted him.

"Save the false modesty and the fake deference for another time." Dale had been caught in his twenties for the last two hundred years. He added sharply, "The Biters do what needs to be done. That's what they're for. So what needs to be done?"

This time Madoc didn't bother to hedge. He pushed himself off the wall and stepped forward. West held his ground at the head of the table as he straightened his back and spread his knees, as though he thought Madoc would just pull him bodily out of the chair.

He shouldn't have worried. Madoc didn't need the chair to claim the attention of everyone in the room, physically or electronically. The focus shifted naturally to him as he started to speak. Took felt an odd tickle of smugness as he watched everyone's eyes shift to Madoc. He'd always enjoyed watching Madoc work a room, but now he felt a little bit more... possessive.

"We still don't know what this group wants with these children," Madoc said as he braced his knuckles on the table.

"Cult," the mayor interjected. "I have seen no evidence that the leaders of the Proverbial Church have had any involvement in this terrible situation."

Madoc gave him that point with a tilt of his head and a midexplanation correction. "This *cult* wants. The mayor is right, the abduction of dhampir children is far from the public doctrine of the Proverbials' mission. Whatever aim the cult has, however, they want these children." His attention flicked to the Anakim faces in the room, physically or not, and he smiled thinly. "Some of us are old enough to remember what excuses were made in the past when they stole our children. To save their souls. To raise them to kill their own. I remember the platitudes my own family used as they tried to starve the Devil out of me, beat it out. Whatever their motivation, however, they have gone to great lengths over the years to bring them here, to raise them and we can use that to draw them out."

It was West's turn to interrupt as he shifted in his chair. "I still say the best option is to press Waring for this information. Once he spills his guts about what he did or didn't do, we can decide how best to proceed then."

He always favored caution. It had been West who told Took that he didn't have enough—any—evidence against Madoc, that he couldn't afford to make any accusations until he had something concrete to back him up.

It had seemed like good advice at the time, but now Took wondered if it wouldn't have been better to just rip the Band-Aid off back then. Madoc would still have been hurt by the accusation, but Took wouldn't have wasted two years trying to resolve whether he could trust the Biters or not.

Of course, his dark little voice of paranoia murmured to him, that wouldn't have suited West's purposes.

It wasn't a lie—West had been upfront about his ambitions to clear some of the old blood from VINE's upper echelons—but it wasn't relevant either. Maybe Took had just gotten so used to suspicion that he needed to slot in someone he didn't trust.

Took leaned forward and cleared his throat to catch the attention of the assembled dignitaries.

He saw the flicker of morbid interest in a few eyes, the recognition and dark fascination about exactly *what* had happened to him, but for once, it didn't make his brain claw at the inside of his skull to get out of there. Maybe the psych panel would bounce him from the team at the next eval, but for now, he was an active agent and he was still the best at what he did. They could pocket their prurient curiosity until he was done.

"Waring is willing to help," he said. "But the price for him is pain."

"It'll harden him," Graven said dourly.

Took cocked an eyebrow at that. The bits and pieces he remembered of his torture hadn't particularly improved his life.

"Maybe," he said. "The problem is that each time he speaks, the magic backlash knocks him out for hours. By the time he tells us anything useful, he'll be cognitively impaired or dead. And we might be too late to find any of these children."

Graven scowled but nodded. "So what do we do?"

"We get one actionable piece of information from Waring," Madoc took back the meeting. He gave the assembled dignitaries a dry smile. "Then we act on it."

Dale snorted and curled his lip enough to show the fine white point of a fang. "That's not a plan. That's a declaration you don't trust us."

"You?" Madoc inclined his head in a faintly courtly nod. "Perhaps, but who do you trust? We know this… cult… had someone in the Charleston fire department, and they were willing to burn down an entire neighborhood to cover their tracks. It's more than likely there's also sleeper agents in the police force and possibly even in VINE itself."

The DA glanced between Graven and the mayor as he weighed where the backlash from that would land. "What makes you so sure?" he asked.

"It's what I'd do," Madoc said. He glanced at Dale, and something in his expression made the Senate representative carefully fold his lips back over his fangs. "It's what I've done before."

It was the director who picked a side first. She rapped her finger hard against the table. "I trust my people," she said harshly. "But I trust them to accept that there are children's lives on the line here too. Madoc can tell us what we need to know, but I will expect a full report afterward."

It was only the mayor and West who objected in the end, and they were both outranked by the yes votes from the Senate reps. In the end they had to bend their heads and agree.

"You understand how this works, Agent Madoc," the director said as she leaned forward and fixed him with her remaining bright green eye. A wing of hair hung over the side of her face and hid the socket, although she'd made no effort to disguise the raw, red scar on her jaw. "If you get these children back, then we'll be happy to claim responsibility. If you don't, then anything dubious you do was done without our knowledge."

Madoc smiled at her.

"That's how it's always worked, Director Lawrence."

She snorted and glanced past Madoc's shoulder to her daughter. "This could end your career. If you aren't willing to take part in this, nobody will make you."

Lawrence crossed her arms. "I'm a Biter," she said. "I'd think less of me."

A faint smile touched Director Lawrence's mouth. "Good girl," she said. Then she glanced at Madoc and arched her eyebrow. "Although I think you've stolen my daughter, Agent Madoc. This assignment was just supposed to season her in the field, not make her yours for life."

Madoc shrugged. "I have a knack for finding talent."

Director Lawrence glanced over the assembled Biters and sighed. "That will be a shame if you mess this up."

She killed the vid-link and the screen flickered to black.

"Do we have a plan?" Quick asked. "Because my backup plan to this career path is crime, so…."

Madoc just smirked as he strode out of the briefing room. As the rest of them followed, Took wondered if that was how people felt when he chased a theory. Maybe, but as he glanced down Madoc's back from shoulders to lean hips, he doubted they got such a nice view when they followed him.

WARING LOOKED tired. He was slumped over the table, his head on his arms, and he looked up with a sigh when the door opened. Heather Waring crossed the room at a run and tackled him into a hug. Her slim arms wrapped around him, bitten nails caught in his shirt, and she buried her face in his shoulder.

"Oh, Dom. My baby. My baby," she sobbed into his shoulder as she tried to rock him as though he were still a baby. "I told them they were wrong about you. I told them you were a good boy."

After a stiff moment, Dom awkwardly hugged her back. When the magic didn't backlash into him, he sighed out two years of tension and slumped into his mother's embrace.

"He still has to help us," Took said as he slipped into the seat on the opposite side of the table. After a second, Waring looked up and gave him a bleak look, as though Took had finally worked out a trick that Waring couldn't resist. It hadn't worked the first time VINE tried it on him—Took had watched the videos—but two years under The Salt was a long time to be alone. "If he doesn't, then all we have is a theory that we can't prove. People will protest and your husband will rouse opposition in the Senate and maybe even stir up some old hostilities. At the end of the day, though, he'll still be executed out there, and no protests will bring him back."

Waring glared at him. He was lucky that he didn't know the truth. There were a dozen sorcerers in the Senate worth their keep, plenty of street-corner oracles who traded an hour's blindness for a five-second peep into the future, and warlocks with hex bags that, nine times out of ten, just rotted on the string. A true sorcerer, though? They'd wrap him in iron and send him to the New Scholomance to either learn his craft or serve as magic's tithe.

From what Took had heard over the years, a clean death at Tac's knife in The Salt might be a better choice. But it wasn't one that he could offer. They needed Waring.

"We can't tell your father about this yet," Took said as he glanced toward the black glass wall where Madoc waited. "But we thought it would help if your mother was here with you?"

For a second, Waring buried his face back in his mother's shoulder, but then he pushed her away. He gently stroked her cheek, tears wet on his fingers, and then shook his head firmly as he turned away.

Took raised a hand to get the guards to open the door.

"No," Heather protested. "He's my son. I won't leave."

"He has the right to decide who's here," Took said. "I'm sorry."

Heather balked as she clutched her son's arm and shook it to try to make him look at her. "You need me here, Dom. Please," she said. When that didn't work, she looked at Took. "He's just a child. He can't make these decisions."

"He's an adult now," Took corrected her. He glanced at the door. "It's his choice."

One of the guards abandoned their post by the door and came in to escort her out. She resisted at first, head twisted to look over her shoulder as if that might be the last chance she got to see her son. But then gave in and let them march her out.

Waring waited until the door closed and then finally looked up. The expression on his narrow face was unfriendly but expectant.

"I'm going to tell you what I think I know," Took said as he set a manila folder on the desk. "Unless you correct me, I'm going to assume I'm right. Don't correct me unless I get something important wrong."

Waring hunched his shoulders and chewed on the inside of his cheeks.

"Whatever protection they had," Took pointed out, "disappeared when you spoke in The Salt. It will be a year before you can recast your spell. Do they have that long?"

They both knew the answer was no. After a second, Waring looked up and Took assumed that was agreement.

"Annabelle Franklin was your friend," Took said as he slid the photo over the table. "You met because you were both interested in alchemy, but when that didn't work as reliably as you wanted, you started to explore real magic."

That was supposition, but Waring had to have started to study magic at some point. That gap in the timeline was as good as any.

"At some point you or she worked out there was something off about her family—more than their piety and happiness to spend a son on the Proverbial's mission back in Europe. Your family was less proactive, but they don't think the Senate is right either. So something that was bad enough you thought you had to intervene, something that didn't just affect Annabelle, but her friends."

Took dealt the missing-person leaflets out onto the table. Annabelle Franklin, the three Aron siblings, the Ford twins with their matched casts, Kerry Davison, Brendan Colt, and Paul Imran. Waring looked at the faces the same way he had his mother's, like someone in a desert who'd just seen water.

"This is what you did first," Took said. Now that he'd seen the faces, the ghost images he'd picked up from Waring's mind filled themselves in. The only Aron daughter they'd been able to get out pressed up against the window of the car as she cried for her sister. Annabelle was in the front seat, her face a terrifying mix of guilt and resolve. "You got the children away. Most of them were easy. Children do disappear, and no one involved could really kick up too much of a fuss. The Davisons could hardly tell the police that the connection between their daughter's disappearance and that of Brendan Colt was that they were both dhampirs and their families belonged to a cult that had kidnapped them from Europe."

Despite all his practice, Waring couldn't stall the flash of surprise that flicked over his face. Took wasn't sure if that was because he was right or if Waring hadn't known that detail. He wanted to know, for the sake of completion, but that could wait.

"It went wrong at the Arons," he said.

A bitter smile tucked the corners of Waring's mouth at what must have seemed like an awful understatement to him. "They were ready for you," Took said. "And Hunters know about magic, know where to buy it from the alley witches and how to disrupt it too."

He'd spent enough hours in the river near their house as a kid, feet bruised and hands shriveled, as he caught toads for his mother to thread onto thorns. It was surprisingly easy to defang a sorcerer if you had prior warning. They might fight each other with storms and starlight, but a human with a dead, mutilated toad and a knife could end one easily enough.

"After that…." Took paused as he took in the freaked-out expression on Waring's face. It was ridiculous that a sorcerer who could hop bodies like a cuckoo hopped nests would be disturbed by just thinking things through. Madoc was the only person who'd always found it reliably entertaining as a party trick. "Well, I know you hid Annabelle and the others. Then you turned up bloody handed at the end of a trail of murders that nearly bisected the country."

Waring licked his lips but hesitated to say anything. He didn't consider his own innocence important enough to break his silence. Took supposed he could see why Lawrence had read that as guilt. But he had some extra information.

He took out a photo of one of the dhampirs that Waring had been accused of murdering and laid it on the table. Matthew Kennedy had the same stamp as the cult's stolen children—eyes like green glass and skin like pearls—but he carried himself as though that made him exceptional, not a freak. He'd been eighteen, older than Waring but still a child as far as the Anakim were concerned.

The first time Took had seen him was in that filthy trap house, hung up to bleed like a deer carcass. Guilt scratched at the back of his throat that he hadn't realized the monster was just a boy in a box that Took couldn't see. It was just self-indulgence. He couldn't help Matthew anymore, no matter how much he beat himself up, but maybe he could make up for it a bit by rescuing the others.

"I know the cult got him," Took said as he tapped the image. "The Proverbial missionaries had kept them stocked with… new blood… for years. But ten dhampirs? Even in Europe that many vanished children would raise questions and the Empire ask those sharply. So they had to hunt closer to home, right?"

Waring barely nodded, but the magic jolted through him anyhow, and his lips and fingertips singed. He shuddered, and pinched his lips tightly, and tucked his chin down into his chest.

"You wanted to help," Took said sympathetically. "You tried to, but whoever it was in Appleberg that was behind this had better information, better connections, right? They got there first, and by the time you caught up, the family was dead and the dhampir children were gone. That's how you got caught red-handed in the mess these people had left behind."

He didn't phrase it as a question. That might give Waring… wriggle room… in his bargain with magic.

Waring opened his mouth cautiously, afraid of the backlash, and tested his voice with a ragged "I…" When nothing crackled under his skin, he exhaled slowly and tried again, his voice broken and rusty. "I tried to stop it. I wanted to warn someone, tell my dad or—"

Sparks flickered in the pit of his mouth, and the smell of singed spit filled the room. He shut up, and Took finished for him.

"You didn't know who to trust," he said. "And you couldn't afford to trust the wrong person, because then the spell would be broken and the cult could find Annabelle and the others. You'd die rather than let that happen, right?"

Waring stared at him with a flash of fear in his eyes but braced his hands flat against the table and waited. Some people would guess he'd fallen in love with a dhampir, but Took thought the boy had just picked up honor somewhere. Or both.

This time Took spread out a map of Appleberg on the table. Annabelle and Waring were resourceful and smart, but they were still kids. Where else would they go than somewhere they knew?

"Prove it," Took challenged him. "They're here, aren't they? And if they're this close, then someone will see them, maybe even someone who just wants to help. But will they trust the right people?"

Waring took a ragged breath and jabbed his finger down on the map. His blistered fingertip flattened against the fenced-in space outside of Appleberg where Annabelle Franklin had spent so many summers—the summer camp that the Proverbial Church had just stopped using for no reason that year.

This time the magic lashed like a whip. It scorched through Waring and made his veins stark and black against his skin as the blood burned. Then it bounced back into Took. Heat lashed through his veins and rattled around inside him like a pinball of electricity. He flinched backward and crashed into the wall. Bright streamers of power arced between him and Waring, as though the magic itself was pissed at Took for interfering. It pushed into his head, pressed against his ears as though they were going to pop, and he felt the staples that held his mind together stretch and rip. Something black and harsh snarled from the darkness he kept down there.

"No," he rasped out, and the cold flushed through him. It filled him from ears to fingertips, until there was no room left for the crackle of sorcery. Then, with one last whip kiss of pain, it left him.

For a second, Took hung in the static comfort of that cold anger. It felt like nothing—numb and still.

Then Madoc stepped out of the shadows and dropped to his knee next to him. His hand on the back of Took's neck was icy, but it flickered the memory of warmth through Took's bones—a kiss on his knuckles, the look in his eyes when he tilted Took's face up for a kiss.

Offended by the saccharine sentimentality of it all, the cold anger slunk back to where it lived.

"Are you all right?" Madoc asked as he hooked an arm around Took's shoulders.

"Fine," Took said. He let Madoc haul him back to his feet. "You know it's maybe twelve feet from the observatory to the door? It was a bit dramatic to take the shadows."

Madoc brushed a kiss over his cheek and murmured, "Maybe I'm trying to impress you." He propped Took against the wall and turned to the guards. "Get Waring into a Viper. If he wants credit for this, I want confirmation and an escort. Get Sheriff Anderson and whatever deputies he can pull off cow-tipping duty in case we need them."

On the floor, singed and scarred, Waring struggled to turn a groan into words. The wounds on his hands had split open and bled through his bandages like stigmata. As he tried to speak, the magic still in his blood jolted and spasmed through him.

Took crouched down and pressed his hand to the boy's shoulder.

"We know what we're doing," he said. After a second, he glanced at Madoc's back and made a decision that he probably should have made a while ago. "You can trust him."

Chapter Twenty

THE VIPER bounced along the rutted country road toward Appleberg. Madoc slouched in the passenger seat, leather uncomfortably hot against his skin, even though it would have been worse if he still sweated, and divided his attention between the road ahead and the rearview mirror. In the back seat a still barely half-conscious Dom Waring sat next to his mother, her arm wrapped tightly around his shoulder. She gripped his bicep as she looked around nervously.

"You know what happened," she blurted out as she caught Madoc's eyes on her. "Why does he have to go out to this place? Can't you just let him go, let me take him home? All he did was try to help people. *Your* people."

"So he says," Madoc countered. "If he wants that to stand up before the Senate? He needs more than a sob story and a sweet face to convince them he's innocent."

Heather glared at him and went back to rubbing gel into her son's burned hands. It wouldn't help. The blisters were under the skin, not on top, but she persisted. Perhaps it was a mother's instinct, not that Madoc would know anything about that. His grandmother would have been more likely to stick his hand back in the fire to teach him not to get burned than offer him a salve.

"Should we have brought her?" Lawrence asked as she veered around the thin, black ribbon of a snake in the road. "If things go wrong, she could be in danger."

"Then don't let anything go wrong," Madoc told her. The sun had started to come up. Madoc grimaced as a ray bounced off the front of the car and caught his eyes. He fished his sunglasses out, slipped them on, and glanced in the mirror again. "Don't worry, Mrs. Waring. If your son told us the truth, then this will give him his life back."

Heather reached for her son's hand and clutched it. Her knuckles showed tight and white through her skin as she squeezed down. Waring barely stirred, even though it must have ached down to his charred bones.

"You say that like it's meant to matter," she said bitterly. "You're the ones who put him under Salt in the first place. I told you that he was innocent, that my son would never do that, but nobody would listen. How am I supposed to trust you now?"

Madoc studied her face, rendered in lilac tones through the purple lens.

"You don't have to," he said. "Just trust your son."

She winced and turned back to her son, one hand raised to touch his scarred cheek. "I did," she said. "I do. That's not the point."

Lawrence lifted her foot off the pedal and the car slowed down. She glanced in the rearview mirror.

"What do you mean?" she asked sharply. "Mrs. Waring?"

Madoc grabbed the wheel and wrenched it to the left. The Viper's tires squealed as the heavy SUV veered sharply across the road and the heavy truck that accelerated out of the trees only clipped their rear bumper.

In the back seat, Heather screamed in shock as she wrapped her body around Dom's to protect him. Lawrence bounced off the door and grabbed at the dashboard to steady herself.

"What the hell?" she blurted out in shock.

The Viper tipped over the shoulder of the road and crashed into a tree. The hood crumpled and the windshield cracked across in three jagged lines. A branch broke jaggedly off the tree and crashed down onto the car.

Lawrence wheezed as she slumped against her seat belt. One hand fumbled at the clip on her gun as she tried to pull herself together. When she pushed herself upright, there was a bloody split through her eyebrow. She staunched the blood with her sleeve.

"I'm sorry," Heather said. Her voice was wet and frightened as she fumbled at the catch on her seat belt. "I am, but he's *my* son, and I have to put him first. Those other parents would do the same."

Lawrence twisted around and grabbed at her arm. "What did you do?" she demanded.

"What I had to," Heather said as she pulled away, bloody runnels left in her skin from Lawrence's nails. She tumbled out of the car onto the concrete and scrambled to her feet, both arms raised over her head. The heavy truck had slowed to a stop in the road and the men inside clambered out. Through the broken glass, Madoc caught fractured glimpses of camo gear and automatic weaponry, tattooed arms and hard-worn faces. Heather limped toward them, one shoe forgotten in the car. "He's in the car. Don't hurt him. Please."

"Bitch," Lawrence hissed as she dragged her gun free. "What do we do?"

Madoc's door was wedged against a rock. Rather than fight with it, he twisted and kicked out the front window with one heavy-soled boot. It shattered into a thousand diamond-shaped pieces and burst out over the front of the car.

"Exchange insurance information?" he said wryly as he boosted himself out through where the glass had been. "We've been looking for these gentlemen for a long time. We should go and say hello."

Lawrence cursed him. She shouldered her door open and climbed out, too much of her weight supported against the Viper's door to bode well for a fight.

"Look at that," one of the men jeered. He looked over his shoulder at his friends and jabbed the muzzle of his gun in Madoc's direction. "It's none other than the fucking cardinal himself. I'm gonna put his fangs on earrings for my wife."

Madoc plucked his broken sunglasses off his nose and pitched them aside into the road. The dawn made his eyes sting, the world around him washed-out, as though he'd looked directly into a light, but it was bearable. Most things were.

"Maybe you should keep them for yourself," Madoc said. "You seem to be short a few."

The man flushed, a quick, easy swab of red over his cheekbones, and glowered at Madoc. "Ain't gonna be a wetmouth, ain't gonna need to wet teeth," he blustered. "When I get to Heaven, God's going to know I got there on purpose."

One of the other men, dressed in jeans and a sweat-stained gas-station T-shirt, snorted. He wore a slim metal stake in a holster on his thigh and carried himself like he knew what he was doing.

"Shut up, Thomas," he said as he reached up to clip Thomas around the back of the head. "Your soul is between you and God. This is temporal business."

Madoc chuckled as he shifted his feet on the road to anchor himself. "I don't think he knows what that means."

Heather grabbed at Thomas's arm. "My son," she said anxiously. "You'll be careful, won't you? My son's in the car."

"Your son near ruined us all," Truckstop snapped. "You're just lucky we need him for now. It's the only reason I'm going to let him see another sunset. Get her the fuck out of our way."

There was one woman in the group, a lean young woman with fresh burn marks on her neck. She'd swapped a deputy's uniform for black leather and old denim, but Madoc recognized the deputy that Took had saved from the explosion. She grabbed Heather's elbow and dragged the older woman back to the truck. When Heather protested once too often, the blonde slapped her impatiently. The crack of a hard callused hand over Heather's mouth shut her up.

"What do you think this is going to get you?" Madoc asked. Mindful of where they were in his peripheral vision, he shifted position as the hunters started to spread out around him. "VINE knows about you now. The chief of police back in Charleston? He's wanted an excuse to incorporate your town, and now he's got it. Whatever you had here, it's gone now."

Truckstop hitched his gun against his shoulder. "You don't get it," he said. "You think this is about us? It's about Leveling the Accord, it's about restoring what *should* have been the natural order. Maybe we're done here, but you think we're the only ones? Once we get those kids back, we'll send them away to new homes, to places where they can grow up right with God. First, though, we'll get rid of you. One less monster for them to kill."

He pulled the trigger. The gun jarred back against his shoulder and the bullets stitched across the road toward Madoc, a trail of splintered pocks in their wake. He stepped into the shadows were time ran slowly, the spray of bullets like spilled metallic honey, and just sidestepped it before he dropped back into the world. The butt of a gun caught him across the jaw and slammed him backward. He flew through the air and came down hard on the road. It caught him across his shoulders and back and knocked the metaphorical wind out of him.

Habit dragged him back to his feet just in time to take a boot to the gut. It connected hard enough that he felt the bones in his pelvis grind against each other. This time he kept his feet, but only just, and managed to avoid the slash of a serrated knife that would have gutted him.

Too fast. Too strong.

Madoc caught sight of the muzzle of Truckstop's gun out of the corner of his eye as it tracked him. He caught the knife under his arm as the man swung at him again and Madoc spun him around so he caught the whip of bullets across his back. It perforated him from hip bone to nipple, blood bright and syrupy where it soaked through his skintight, bleached-out camo shirt.

The man yanked free and staggered backward, but he stayed on his feet. He grinned at the expression on Madoc's face.

"Not as easy as you thought," he spat out as he yanked his shirt up. His stomach was already half-healed, the bullet holes sealed into soft, pocked scars. "Not once we even out the playing field. The game's changed, wetmouth."

It wasn't, and it had.

Madoc shook his head to dislodge the high-pitched tone that hummed in his ear. He weighed up his opponents—six armed assailants who were close to his strength and speed. Those were not good odds. The out-of-uniform deputy and Thomas lunged at him. One aimed high and one low. He twisted out of the way of Thomas's unsophisticated roundhouse and cracked his knee into the deputy's temple as she tried to twist her weight around his legs to take him down. She rattled out a surprised yelp but managed to python herself around his legs like hobbles.

A gun cracked and Thomas yelped in surprise as blood sprayed out of his shoulder. It would heal, but the joint was pulverized. That took a bit more time for the body to jigsaw back together. It didn't always get it right the first time either. Madoc had broken Pall's knee four times before it healed into something that would bear weight.

Madoc glanced past the stunned Thomas's pulped shoulder to nod acknowledgment to Lawrence. She ignored him, tongue caught between her teeth as she tried to get a clear bead on Truckstop.

Not quite six to one, then. It didn't improve the odds that much, but it was better than nothing.

Madoc let the deputy trip him. He rolled as he hit the ground and grabbed the first foot that swung at his head. A quick, heel-of-the-hand punch to the joint the man had his weight on snapped it out of true. The man went down hard, mouth agape with shock and pain, and Madoc slit his throat down to the bone with the knife on his belt. Then he twisted, one sharp clean pop and jerk, and tossed the head away. It rolled over the uneven ground, bounced off Truckstop's foot, and ended up under the wheel. Glassy blue eyes stared blankly at the tableau.

"Do you really think humans were ever our biggest issue?" Madoc mocked Truckstop as he kicked the deputy off, the impact of his heel against the point of her jaw enough to crack it into an awkward, broken angle. "Don't flatter yourselves. I've fought more of my own kind than any Hunters."

Not that they were human, or not completely, Madoc supposed. They weren't vampires, and their blood didn't have the skunked smell of a werewolf, but nothing human clicked their broken jaw back together like the deputy just had.

For a second, he considered sorcery, but six sorcerers willing to work together? A human with an Anakim's right hook was more believable. Besides, he doubted Thomas could spell sorcerer, never mind be one.

Like a Goat. Took had told him that's what Gabriel said about these faux Hounds, fake Hunters. *But not rotted.* Stronger than any Goat that Madoc had put down, but that would make sense if he was right.

"Madoc!" Lawrence's voice cut through the muggy, mosquito-noisy air along the road. She sounded terrified, and Truckshop grinned when he heard her. Madoc kept one wary eye on his opponents as he shifted to have her in his periphery. She held up the radio, and it crackled with the staticky sound of Quick's scream. "They have the other team, at the campground. They knew."

Truckstop looked pleased with himself as he slung his gun up over his shoulder. "Like I told you," he said, "games change. We're playing by our rules now. You want your people back alive? Get on your knees."

Lawrence stayed hunched behind the door of the car, radio in one hand and gun on the other. "Sir? What do we do?"

She wanted a heroic, last minute save, the sort of thing that the old stories about Cardinal Madoc were ripe with, the sort of story this was meant to have been.

The threats were to-the-point and unimaginative, scored across plain sheets of paper and signed as though it were something to be proud of.

"How did you get these?" Madoc asked as he flicked through them.

"If they threatened him, then they threatened her," Took didn't answer him. "Except she hasn't told us, so that means she's probably theirs. We can't trust her, but—"

"We can use her," Madoc finished for him.

Now it looked like they'd been used.

"Sir?" Lawrence tried again. "Madoc?"

The truth was Madoc couldn't lose Took again, not like this. Death was one thing, but trapped and tortured? No, Madoc couldn't live with that thought. So he did something for Truckstop that he hadn't done since the first night they landed on this continent.

The Bathory's cardinal, once the most feared man in half of the US, knelt down on the concrete and laced his hands behind his head. For the first time in living memory, Madoc just gave up.

BLOOD OOZED stickily from the raw sockets in Madoc's gums. Truckstop had held the pliers as he worked all the teeth he wanted free. His wife would have a full set of tacky ivory jewelry before the month was out. It wouldn't last, but it wasn't pleasant.

His arms were twisted behind him and broken over a silver bar that slotted under his arms and was secured with silver wire. His shoulders dislocated and upper arms broken, he'd been thoroughly worked over with fist, boot, and submachine gun butt. Most had delivered the beating with a businesslike thoroughness until he stopped healing so quickly. A few had gloated as they tried to punt his testicles back inside him, but he had killed their friend, so he supposed he couldn't blame them.

The wheels hit a bump and pain scraped along Madoc's abused bones. Next to him Lawrence sat in tense resentment while Heather Waring sobbed noisily over her silent son. A sharp turn rolled Madoc against the side of the truck, his arms twisted even more awkwardly than before.

He passed the trip with a short list of who could have done this. It was a very short list.

At last the truck stopped. The engine grumbled on, overclocked and overused, as they dragged Madoc and the others out of the back. A rough hand on his collar hauled him to his feet and marched him toward a low-slung wood building that proclaimed itself the clubhouse with a carved sign over the door.

Six steps up onto the veranda and then they threw him through the door. With Madoc's hands behind him, it was impossible to catch his balance or preserve his dignity. He hit the ground and rolled, half gagged on his own bloody drool.

It was Lawrence who caught his arms and pulled him into a sitting position. She dodged a backhand to the head and hunched over him protectively as the other hunters filed into the room.

One of the men, bony and unremarkable in his camo, saw the pale, grubby kids huddled against the wall. Despite everything, he had the gall to sound relieved, a father reunited with his daughter. "Kerry! Thank God."

He slung his shotgun over his shoulder and crossed the room to pull her into a hug. That she tried to flinch away from him didn't seem to matter as he petted her hair and told her how he'd missed her.

"Leave her alone," Annabelle Franklin, her face familiar at this point, protested as she lunged forward. "She doesn't belong to you."

It was Took who pulled her back and muttered something in her ear. He gave Madoc a quick, guilty look but stayed where he was until the one-sided reunion was over and the men had dragged in Waring and his hysterical mother. Annabelle tried to run over to him, but one of the guards grabbed her arm and slammed her back into the wall. No sentimental reunions for her, then.

Once everyone was inside, Took staggered over the room to Madoc. Sympathy made him wince as he saw the hobble bar stretched over his back. Instinct made him reach for it and rip his fingers open on the barbed wire ties, but one of guards grabbed a pale kid and dragged him out of line.

"Hands off," he snapped.

Took glared but did as he was told.

"I missed something," Took admitted as he sank down next to Madoc. He brushed his hand carefully over Madoc's battered cheek. "I don't even know what. Who."

Madoc tilted his face into Took's hand. "We all did."

"Where's Pally?" Lawrence asked sharply. "Quick?"

Took shuddered. He nodded out the door into the bright morning light. "They shot Pally in the head," he said, "and dumped him into a well."

"That—" Lawrence blurted. She caught herself before all the words got out. That wouldn't be enough to kill Pally. He was an old vampire, nearly as old as Tepes himself, and it would take fire to keep him down.

But it would be enough to incapacitate him until nightfall, and that would be too late for them. She swallowed hard. "Quick?"

"Waste not, want not," Took said as he looked over his shoulder. "They need to build the kids up again. I'm next. They're going to keep us like cows, milk us until we run dry, and then throw us in the well."

There was a touch of panic under his voice at the thought of being a captive again. Madoc turned his head and pressed a bloody kiss against Took's palm. "No," he promised.

Lawrence grimaced at them both and pulled away. She started to scramble to her feet, but a bullet punched into the ground next to her and made her drop reluctantly back onto her knees.

"How did they even do this?" she demanded in frustration. "I saw Madoc fight these bastards on the road. Even if they are stronger, he could have beat them if he hadn't lain down and given up. The three of you should have made short work of them. Pally alone—"

Took grimaced. "We nearly did, but—"

"Like I told him," Sheriff Anderson interrupted as he walked into the room, one hand wrapped around the thin arm of a scruffy little girl. From her age and the faded red in her hair, it was Augusta Aron. There was blood on his shirt and lips, a gory tint that he licked eagerly and absently at. "We need the children, but we don't need all the children. All it took was a demonstration, and your friends saw the error of their ways."

He pointed with his gun toward a gory halo of blood and hair painted onto the wall. Something was crumpled at the bottom of the wall, roughly covered by the jackets and shirts of the other children, but Madoc tried not to look at that.

"Brave man," Madoc said. "To kill children."

"He was a sacrifice," Anderson said. He shoved the little girl into another guard's hands and wiped with sudden fastidiousness at the blood on his uniform shirt. "We've all sacrificed, cardinal. Every Proverbial family that lost a child. Every parent who took one of these undead cuckoos into the nest to raise. Generations of sacrifice."

"Why?" Took asked.

Anderson glowered him. "I wasn't talking to you, wetmouth," he spat as he took a quick step across the floor. There was contempt in his voice, but he couldn't hide the flash of envious satisfaction as he pistol whipped Took to the ground. "This was a conversation between equals."

Was it? Madoc swallowed the gritty blood in his mouth and stared at Anderson. Dhampir darkened in the sun and faded in the dark. If they'd locked Madoc up long enough before they killed him, that first time, he'd have been as pale as the little ghost child under guard back in Charleston. He'd never seen one of them so dark they were weathered. Of course, he'd never seen one of them grow old.

"Did they steal you from Europe too?" he asked.

"Rescued," Anderson corrected him as he turned to look at him. "My parents saved me, raised me in the Church, beat the devil out of me."

"Made a Hunter out of you," Madoc said.

Anderson smiled like that was a compliment to his parents' childrearing skills.

That had happened in the old days. Dhampir were perfect Hunters if you raised them right—strong, dangerous, and most Anakim had an instinctive reluctance to hurt them. VINE never imagined it would be a problem over here. Dhampir were always rare—Anakim reproduced with their bite ten times as often as with childbirth, at least—but even more so in America. It had taken two hundred years for the first dhampir to be born on this continent. Either the long trip over the salt sea had rendered them generationally infertile or it was something in the air of their unfriendly new home. Either way, no one had been likely to lose track of one of their rare children.

It hadn't occurred to anyone that Hunters would import them from Europe.

"That isn't what you're doing with these kids, though," Took said as he pushed himself up onto his elbows. Blood poured from the split in his forehead. "Matthew was practically an adult when you kidnapped him to replace the children Waring rescued—"

"Stole," Anderson corrected flatly as he avoided looking at Took.

Madoc spat out half a tooth—maybe Thomas could make his wife a ring out of it—and looked Anderson over. He remembered the church pew under his ass when he was a child, the preacher's finger jabbed his way as the mean old bastard held him up as an example of sin, the children who wouldn't play with him, his lover who never really thought he had a soul and had turned on him all too easily. It had nearly ruined him.

What would that be like for a whole, long life of drymouthed "sacrifice"?

"How much did they hate you?" Madoc asked.

Anderson stared at him for a second and then grimaced and took a step back. "I raised myself above them," he said. "I took secret pride in how strong I was, how much they needed me. They knew that. That's when I realized that I had another sacrifice to make."

"He killed his son," Annabelle blurted from where she hunched against the wall. "Fed his grandson nightshade and bloodmeal from vampires, cut his wrists and bled him into buckets that they all drank from. So they'd be strong and fast. Like him. Like us. Over and over again until Garrett couldn't, didn't wanna, come back."

Anderson turned and pointed his gun at her. "We purified him. His soul was finally clean and it went to heaven."

The threat of the gun didn't have any effect on Annabelle. She spat at him, a wet gobbet of defiance that caught on his sleeve. "You raised us like cattle, told us you loved us, and ground our blood in your tea. Called it alchemy. If God hates us so much, why do you all want to be like us?"

Anderson swung the gun to point at the boy next to Annabelle. He rested his finger on the trigger and hissed, "Shut up."

This time the threat worked.

His deputy stepped forward, her eyes bright with admiration that came close to worship as she looked at the sheriff. "We'll change everything. The vampires won't be able to flout their strength, their long lives, over us anymore. We will be equals, and then you'll all learn your place."

Crouched on the floor next to her son, Heather piped up. "And we can leave now?" she said. "We have nothing to do with this. My husband would support you. Our family has always had Hunter sympathies. We've donated to the cause."

Anderson stared at her. "Money. Words. Sacrifice is blood and bone, Mrs. Waring. Maybe once you understand that, you'll be glad to give your son to the cause. Bring him. Waring and the vampire. If she objects, send her down with the vampire in the well."

WARING GAGGED and choked as Anderson poured a cup of blood down his throat. Black crusted the sides of his mouth and around his nostrils. He'd retched once already and Anderson had held his mouth shut until he swallowed the bile back down again.

"Dhampir blood is free of the curse," Anderson said as he dipped the cup back into the bucket at his feet. He drank from it himself this time. "We're damned for the sin of our birth, but we cannot share that with others."

Strung up over a galvanized tub, his arms slashed open from wrist to armpit, Madoc choked on a laugh at how badly wrong Anderson had that. Dhampir blood wasn't as addictive as a draft of vampire ichor, but the curse would still undermine the will of a human who drank it. They just rotted on the inside instead of the outside.

"All you need to do is hide this place again," Anderson said as he pinched Waring's chin in his fingers. "Annabelle told us you were the sorcerer. We know what you did. Now do it again. Hide us from VINE and everyone else that wants to find us."

Waring gaped at him, half drunk on old blood and dizzy with it. He couldn't explain to Anderson how that wouldn't work.

"Tell him," Madoc said. He craned his neck to catch Waring's eye. "Tell him what a fool he is. Just like you told Took."

Waring shuddered and closed his eyes.

"How did he get Annabelle to talk, do you think?" Madoc asked.

Waring opened his eyes and stared into Anderson's. His mouth twisted in a grim smile as he spat out, "I can't."

Magic bent him like a bow as it arced out of him. Each time he broke his pact, it was worse, the smell of scorched marrow sickly meaty in the air, but Madoc didn't have time for sympathy. As Anderson sprung back from the sting of magic and his deputy ran to his side, Madoc twisted up to grab the rope they'd strung him from. A hook was caught through his heels, slippery with blood, and rather than waste time, Madoc just tore it free.

He screamed at the raw flash of pain and dropped in a tangle of limbs into the tepid bath of his own blood. It sloshed over him, stuck to his clothes and hair as he struggled up onto his knees.

"No!" Anderson yelled in frustration as he snapped his gun up. "You can't stop me!"

He pulled the trigger at the same time that Madoc reached out and pulled himself through the shadows—all of himself, even the quarts not currently in his body. His blood, handed up like nonaddictive sacrament to the guards, yanked them all through into the cold, gray other.

Waring, glutted on Madoc as he was, tripped across for a second. He looked oddly bright in the shadows, as though someone had outlined him in silver, and almost relieved. Then his magic snapped him back to the punishment he'd bargained for.

Anderson stumbled as the blood in his veins—his own long-stolen heritage and Madoc's fresh injection—pulled at him. He grabbed at a wall to steady himself and fell through it. His people staggered and blustered as they yelled at him for an explanation.

The clamor made something move in the forest, with a clatter of dry-wood limbs and the sketchy outline of something darker than the shadows under the trees. Nearby, a giant, its warped bones naked expect for tendons and its bony, antlered skull studded with a hundred different eyes, turned slowly, weightlessly toward them.

"Watch me," Madoc told him coldly as he braced himself against the tug toward the sea. "I told you not to cross me, Sheriff."

Anderson staggered to his feet and lurched toward Madoc, his hand extended desperately. The cross on his arm blistered and warped as something took exception to the ink.

"I know things," he blurted out as he groped at Madoc's arm with his fingertips. "Secrets. Like your toy, the blond wetmouth. I know who took him. I know why. We all talk, you see, us alchemists. We tell each other things."

He managed to get hold of Madoc's wrist to anchor himself. A laugh twisted his mouth as he thought that was a win.

"He's more of a monster than me," Anderson rasped. "They shouldn't have turned him. They shouldn't have been able to turn him. It's—"

Madoc snapped Anderson's neck in a single sharp motion. The plan had been to leave him here to suffer, but Madoc wasn't the only one who passed through this space. Since he didn't want to leave the job half done, he twisted again until the skin ripped and he could lob the head, the face still set in an expression of surprise, toward the forest.

The deputy seemed to realize the gravity of her situation as she started to scream—a ragged, endless howl that clawed out of her. The antlered beast in the sky answered her.

Madoc left them there.

He let his bones and the meat of him drag him back into the world. Took caught him as he fell and pulled him close, his mouth soft as he pressed a frantic kiss to Madoc's temple and made promises he probably didn't mean. Madoc let himself slump into Took's embrace. He doubted this was how he'd die, but it wouldn't be the worst way to go.

Epilogue

THE ANAKIM couple cooed over Augusta Aron as she clumsily offered her hand. There had been offers from across the country to foster the rescued children, many desperate enough that they'd had to make sure the children had guards. A few of the older children had balked at the idea, but they needed to find out what it was to be Anakim and to get their strength back. Some of them wanted to find out if their parents back home had ever wanted to find them again.

Until Nora woke up or died, she stayed in VINE custody with Took's cat tucked under her chin as it took five breaths for every one she inhaled. Annabelle, though, was the only one who'd outright refused. As a stopgap compromise, she'd moved in with Lawrence, who'd grown up more Anakim than human. Now Annabelle hovered next to Took behind the glass as she watched the two men offer Augusta Aron their dog's lead to hold.

"They have *pets*?" she muttered under her breath.

"I have a cat," Took said. Although it might be *had*, since Snack seemed to have relocated her affections. "Quick has an iguana. Even the Anakim get lonely."

Annabelle shrugged. "It doesn't seem right," she said. "You're not supposed to be like… people."

"Are you?" Took asked.

She glanced at him and then down at her hands. The translucency had faded back to ivory, and she'd even gained a few freckles.

"I don't know," she said. "Nobody ever thought I was, not really, until Dom. And being my friend nearly destroyed him."

"Maybe you should trust him then," Took said. The advice he wished he'd taken earlier. "He seems a better judge of character than anyone else in your life before now."

The children's families, the only families they'd ever known, at least, had all been arrested. Before they took her away, Annabelle's adoptive mother had spat in her face and said it was her fault that her brother—or the boy she always thought was her brother—died. That was the first wave of arrests. They would go on for a while. So far they'd found a few of the other children the cult had taken—both the ones kidnapped from Europe and those that Waring would have died for—but not enough.

"Maybe," Annabelle admitted as they turned away from the window. "Will you want to talk to me about it again? What we did, the alchemy?"

"People will," Took said. "Not today."

She nodded and stuck her hand out. "Thank you," she said. "I was taught to think vamp…. Anakim… were monsters, but you treated us all fair."

He solemnly shook her hand, delivered her back to Lawrence, and then took a car back to VINE. Now that the dhampir children were settled, there was some business he needed to take care of.

It was full dark by the time he got there, but SSA Crane's receptionist waved him through without question. He'd been a frequent visitor over the last few years. West was still at work at his desk, bent over files, with only a small desk lamp for light. After so many years working with Anakim, he acted like a need for light was a weakness.

"Did you tell Anderson we were on the way?" he asked as he closed the door behind him.

West looked up, his half smile of greeting wilted as his brain caught up with Took's question. He spluttered out an indignant denial.

"That's… how can you even ask me that question?" West demanded. "I've stuck by you through thick and thin, supported you, listened to your paranoid suspicions about Agent Madoc."

"That's not an answer."

"No," West snapped. He made an impatient gesture with one hand and sat back in his chair to compose himself. "No. I see what this is. Now that you're back on good terms with Madoc, you need someone else to blame for everything. Is that it?"

Took reached into his jacket and pulled out a DVD. He put it down gently on the table and tapped the plastic case with his finger.

"You visited me in the hospital after Madoc rescued me."

West licked his lips. "I…. We were lovers, Took, remember. That meant something to me, even if it was just a distraction from Madoc for you."

That might have worked a month ago, not now that Took had taken the time to think things through. He was always better when he could hide behind a theory instead of having to fumble with emotions.

"It was the first time that I was alone," Took said. "The first time Madoc or one of the Biters wasn't with me. I remember, because I woke up afraid, as though someone had come in the night and whispered suspicion in my ear. It probably worked better than you thought it would, I was suggestible and there was already so much about my mind I couldn't trust."

West stared at him. "Ridiculous."

Took shook his head. "I was wrong about you. I never rated you as a profiler, but you played me like a fiddle for years. Asked just the right questions to make me convince myself, sowed just the right seeds and lied to me about what my psych report said."

That took a second. "I didn't think you were ready," he said. "The psychiatrists didn't know about your paranoia, your irrational fears—"

"They do now." Took tapped his finger against the DVD case again. "I'm going to tell Madoc about this. If I was you, I'd think of something useful to tell him when he finds you."

He turned to leave, but West stopped him on the way out the door.

"There's no proof," he said. "Not of anything."

Took studied West's face in the glass. "I don't think that matters," he said. "Madoc loves me. He'll believe me."

"I LOVE you," Took said as he handed Madoc an envelope and dropped down into the chair on the other side of the desk. "I should have trusted you. No matter what. I want to make that up to you."

Madoc stared at him over the desk for a second.

"You love me?"

"Yeah," Took said. "I do, and I know that what I did—what I thought—is hard to forgive, to get past, but I want to."

Madoc tilted his head. There was something darkly sensual in the slow once-over he gave Took. It made Took shift in the chair with a slow, familiar cramp of lust. "How?"

"That." Took pointed with his chin at the envelope. "It's the only secret I have left. The only one I remember, anyhow. So now you have it."

Madoc turned the envelope between his fingers. "So if you trust me—finally, now—with this, I have to forgive you. It'd be churlish of me not to?"

"I… not *have* to," Took stammered. "I just wanted to… I know I can trust you. Whatever you want to do with that, I know it's the right thing."

Madoc flipped the envelope open and slid out the old, heavy photo. It was one of the only things that Took still had from back then, from the first time he'd shed his life. He'd been nine or ten and Gabriel had him up on his shoulders. They looked happy. Maybe that was why his mother had taken the picture and kept it long enough to give to Took before he left.

"That's my father. His name's…."

"Gabriel," Madoc said as he propped the photo against his lamp. He smiled thinly at Took's shocked expression. "I'm not the profiler you are, but I have done this for a long time. When you thought the Hounds might be involved in this, you kept it a secret. That means you had a connection to them, and he let you live. Family."

Took inhaled. "Okay. What are you going to—"

Madoc leaned over the desk, grabbed Took's shirt, and dragged him into a sharp, sweet kiss. Blood mingled in their mouths as their tongues tangled.

"I love you," Madoc said as he leaned back enough to get words out. "I don't need an apology. All I need is you."

"I should have trusted you," Took admitted as he crawled up onto the table.

"You should," Madoc agreed. He leaned back in his chair and let Took chase his mouth. "And I will point that out in the future, but I still love you. You don't have to jump through hoops for that."

"I would," Took admitted as he brushed kisses over Madoc's lips and down his throat. He scraped his fangs over the pale, cool skin and left red marks that faded slowly. "At least one."

Madoc pulled him into his lap. "Okay," he said as he pulled Took's head back and gently bit his throat. His fangs pricked the skin, dimpled it, but didn't sink in. Madoc grazed his tongue over the tender spot as he said, "Say it again."

"I love you," Took said. He tensed himself for the sweet slice of pain as Madoc bit down, against the jolt of pleasure as it spread out from there, but instead Madoc leaned back.

"I have waited a long time to hear you say that," he said as he studied Took's face. "Took."

"Really?"

"If you want," Madoc said. "It's a stupid name, but if it's yours...?"

Took hesitated. Part of him wanted to be Luke Bennett again, but that still felt dangerous. "Took," he said. "For now."

This time Madoc didn't hesitate as he bit down on Took's neck. He lapped tenderly at the wound as he hitched Took back up onto the table and leaned over him.

"Luke. Took. Gabriel's son," Madoc promised against Took's skin. "You're still mine."

TA MOORE is a Northern Irish writer of romantic suspense, urban fantasy, and contemporary romance novels. A childhood in a rural seaside town fostered a suspicious nature, a love of mystery, and a streak of black humor a mile wide. As her grandmother always said, "She'd laugh at a bad thing, that one," mind you, that was the pot calling the kettle black. TA studied history, Irish mythology, and English at University, mostly because she has always loved a good story. She has worked as a journalist, a finance manager, and in the arts sectors before she finally gave in to a lifelong desire to write.

Coffee, Doc Marten boots, and good friends are the essential things in life. Spiders, mayo, and heels are to be avoided.

Website: www.nevertobetold.co.uk
Facebook: www.facebook.com/TA.Moores
Twitter: @tammy_moore

BONE
TO PICK

TA MOORE

Digging Up Bones: Book One

Cloister Witte is a man with a dark past and a cute dog. He's happy to talk about the dog all day, but after growing up in the shadow of a missing brother, a deadbeat dad, and a criminal stepfather, he'd rather leave the past back in Montana. These days he's a K-9 officer in the San Diego County Sheriff's Department and pays a tithe to his ghosts by doing what no one was able to do for his brother—find the missing and bring them home.

He's good at solving difficult mysteries. The dog is even better.

This time the missing person is a ten-year-old boy who walked into the woods in the middle of the night and didn't come back. With the antagonistic help of distractingly handsome FBI agent Javi Merlo, it quickly becomes clear that Drew Hartley didn't run away. He was taken, and the evidence implies he's not the kidnapper's first victim. As the search intensifies, old grudges and tragedies are pulled into the light of day. But with each clue they uncover, it looks less and less likely that Drew will be found alive.

www.dreamspinnerpress.com

TAKE THE EDGE OFF

TA MOORE

You don't end up an ex-car thief and ex-con because you're good at resisting temptation… and Cal Tate's rich new boss is very tempting.

Cal has always been the bad boy who lovers don't bring home to Mom, but now he'd like someone other than a debt collector waiting for him. He has a legit job as a driver with his brother's company, and he's got a doctor on the hook, but he still can't help crawling into bed with Joseph Bailey.

Joe has never met anyone as easy in their own skin as his new driver—or as ridiculously beautiful. He's in London to downsize the family business… and to investigate the abusive emails that imply a dark secret around his mother's death. But unpicking the lies he's been told makes Joe realize he isn't sure who he is without them.

When his life falls apart, the only person he can be himself with is Cal. But with the escalating threats from his anonymous stalker, Joe doesn't know if there's any chance for a happy future for him and Cal.

www.dreamspinnerpress.com

TA MOORE

DOG DAYS

A Wolf Winter Novel

The world ends not with a bang, but with a downpour. Tornadoes spin through the heart of London, New York cooks in a heat wave that melts tarmac, and Russia freezes under an ever-thickening layer of permafrost. People rally at first—organizing aid drops and evacuating populations—but the weather is only getting worse.

In Durham, mild-mannered academic Danny Fennick has battened down to sit out the storm. He grew up in the Scottish Highlands, so he's seen harsh winters before. Besides, he has an advantage. He's a werewolf. Or, to be precise, a weredog. Less impressive, but still useful.

Except the other werewolves don't believe this is any ordinary winter, and they're coming down over the Wall to mark their new territory. Including Danny's ex, Jack—the Crown Prince Pup of the Numitor's pack—and the prince's brother, who wants to kill him.

A wolf winter isn't white. It's red as blood.

www.dreamspinnerpress.com

TA MOORE

STONE THE CROWS

Sequel to Dog Days
A Wolf Winter Novel

When the Winter arrives, the Wolves will come down over the walls and eat little boys in their beds.

Doctor Nicholas Blake might still be afraid of the dark, but the monsters his grandmother tormented him with as a child aren't real.

Or so he thought…until the sea freezes, the country grinds to a halt under the snow, and he finds a half-dead man bleeding out while a dead woman watches. Now his nightmares impinge on his waking life, and the only one who knows what's going on is his unexpected patient.

For Gregor it's simple. The treacherous prophets mutilated him and stole his brother Jack, and he's going to kill them for it. Without his wolf, it might be difficult, but he'll be damned if anyone else gets to kill Jack—even if he has to enlist the help of his distractingly attractive, but very human, doctor.

Except maybe the prophets want something worse than death, and maybe Nick is less human than Gregor believes. As the dead gather and the old stories come true, the two men will need each other if they're going to rescue Jack and stop the prophets' plan to loose something more terrible than the wolf winter.

www.dreamspinnerpress.com